P9-DHD-872

D0015222

what happened to *goodbye*

ALSO BY
Sarah Dessen

❋ — ❋ — ❋

That Summer

Someone Like You

Keeping the Moon

Dreamland

This Lullaby

The Truth about Forever

Just Listen

Lock and Key

Along for the Ride

WITHDRAWN

what happened to goodbye

Sarah Dessen

Viking

An Imprint of Penguin Group (USA) Inc.

Fitchburg Public Library
5530 Lacy Road
Fitchburg, WI 53711

Viking

Published by Penguin Group

Penguin Group (USA) Inc., 345 Hudson Street, New York, New York 10014, U.S.A.

Penguin Group (Canada), 90 Eglinton Avenue East, Suite 700, Toronto, Ontario, Canada M4P 2Y3
(a division of Pearson Penguin Canada Inc.)

Penguin Books Ltd, 80 Strand, London WC2R 0RL, England

Penguin Ireland, 25 St Stephen's Green, Dublin 2, Ireland (a division of Penguin Books Ltd)

Penguin Group (Australia), 250 Camberwell Road, Camberwell, Victoria 3124, Australia
(a division of Pearson Australia Group Pty Ltd)

Penguin Books India Pvt Ltd, 11 Community Centre, Panchsheel Park, New Delhi – 110 017, India

Penguin Group (NZ), 67 Apollo Drive, Rosedale, Auckland 0632, New Zealand
(a division of Pearson New Zealand Ltd.)

Penguin Books (South Africa) (Pty) Ltd, 24 Sturdee Avenue, Rosebank,
Johannesburg 2196, South Africa

Penguin Books Ltd, Registered Offices: 80 Strand, London WC2R 0RL, England

First published in 2011 by Viking, a member of Penguin Group (USA) Inc.

3   5   7   9   10   8   6   4   2

Copyright © Sarah Dessen, 2011

All rights reserved

Excerpt from "Families Cheating at Board Games" reprinted by gracious permission of
Ben Lee and West Bay Music Publishing.

LIBRARY OF CONGRESS CATALOGING-IN-PUBLICATION DATA

Dessen, Sarah.

What happened to goodbye / by Sarah Dessen.—1st ed.

p. cm.

Summary: Following her parents' bitter divorce as she and her father move from town to town,
seventeen-year-old Mclean reinvents herself at each school she attends until she
is no longer sure she knows who she is or where she belongs.

ISBN 978-0-670-01294-7 (hardcover)

[1. Divorce—Fiction. 2. Identity—Fiction. 3. High schools—Fiction.
4. Schools—Fiction.] I. Title.

PZ7.D455Wha 2011   [Fic]—dc22   2010041041

Printed in U.S.A.   Set in ITC Century   Book design by Nancy Brennan

Without limiting the rights under copyright reserved above, no part of this publication may be re-
produced, stored in or introduced into a retrieval system, or transmitted, in any form or by any
means (electronic, mechanical, photocopying, recording or otherwise), without the prior written
permission of both the copyright owner and the above publisher of this book. The scanning, up-
loading, and distribution of this book via the Internet or via any other means without the permission of the publisher is illegal and punishable by law. Please purchase only authorized electronic
editions, and do not participate in or encourage electronic piracy of copyrighted materials. Your
support of the author's rights is appreciated.

For Gretchen Alva, with love and admiration

– –

* — * — *

Break away from
what you've known
You are not alone
We can build
a brand new home
You are not alone

—Ben Lee, "Families Cheating at Board Games"

* — * — *

what happened to *goodbye*

One

❉ ✿ ❉

The table was sticky, there was a cloudy smudge on my water glass, and we'd been seated for ten minutes with no sign of a waitress. Still, I knew what my dad would say. By this point, it was part of the routine.

"Well, I gotta tell you. I see potential here."

He was looking around as he said this, taking in the décor. Luna Blu was described on the menu as "Contemporary Italian and old-fashioned good!" but from what I could tell from the few minutes we'd been there, the latter claim was questionable. First, it was 12:30 on a weekday, and we were one of only two tables in the place. Second, I'd just noticed a good quarter inch of dust on the plastic plant that was beside our table. But my dad had to be an optimist. It was his job.

Now, I looked across at him as he studied the menu, his brow furrowed. He needed glasses but had stopped wearing them after losing three pairs in a row, so now he just squinted a lot. On anyone else, this might have looked strange, but on my dad, it just added to his charm.

"They have calamari *and* guac," he said, reaching up to

push his hair back from his eyes. "This is a first. Guess we have to order both."

"Yum," I said, as a waitress sporting lambskin boots and a miniskirt walked past, not even giving us a glance.

My dad followed her with his eyes, then shifted his gaze to me. I could tell he was wondering, as he always did when we made our various escapes, if I was upset with him. I wasn't. Sure, it was always jarring, up and leaving everything again. But it all came down to how you looked at it. Think earth-shattering, life-ruining change, and you're done. But cast it as a do-over, a chance to reinvent and begin again, and it's all good. We were in Lakeview. It was early January. I could be anyone from here.

There was a bang, and we both looked over to the bar, where a girl with long black hair, her arms covered with tat-toos, had apparently just dropped a big cardboard box on the floor. She exhaled, clearly annoyed, and then fell to her knees, picking up paper cups as they rolled around her. Halfway through collecting them, she glanced up and saw us.

"Oh, no," she said. "You guys been waiting long?"

My dad put down his menu. "Not that long."

She gave him a look that made it clear she doubted this, then got to her feet, peering down the restaurant. "Tracey!" she called. Then she pointed at us. "You have a table. Could you please, maybe, go greet them and offer them drinks?"

I heard clomping noises, and a moment later, the wait in the boots turned the corner and came into view. She looked like she was about to deliver bad news as she pulled out her order pad. "Welcome to Luna Blu," she recited, her voice flat. "Can I get you a beverage."

"How's the calamari?" my dad asked her.

She just looked at him as if this might be a trick question. Then, finally, she said, "It's all right."

My dad smiled. "Wonderful. We'll take an order of that, and the guacamole. Oh, and a small house salad, as well."

"We only have vinaigrette today," Tracey told him.

"Perfect," my dad said. "That's exactly what we want."

She looked over her pad at him, her expression skeptical. Then she sighed and stuck her pen behind her ear and left. I was about to call after her, hoping for a Coke, when my dad's phone suddenly buzzed and jumped on the table, clanging against his fork and knife. He picked it up, squinted at the screen, put it down again, ignoring the message as he had all the others that had come since we'd left Westcott that morning. When he looked at me again, I made it a point to smile.

"I've got a good feeling about this place," I told him. "Serious potential."

He looked at me for a moment, then reached over, squeezing my shoulder. "You know what?" he said. "You are one awesome girl."

His phone buzzed again, but this time neither of us looked at it. And back in Westcott, another awesome girl sat texting or calling, wondering why on earth her boyfriend, the one who was so charming but just couldn't commit, wasn't returning her calls or messages. Maybe he was in the shower. Or forgot his phone again. Or maybe he was sitting in a restaurant in a town hundreds of miles away with his daughter, about to start their lives all over again.

A few minutes later, Tracey returned with the guacamole and salad, plunking them down between us on the table. "Calamari will be another minute," she informed us. "You guys need anything else right now?"

My dad looked across at me, and despite myself, I felt a twinge of fatigue, thinking of doing this all again. But I'd made my decision two years ago. To stay or go, to be one thing or many others. Say what you would about my dad, but life with him was never dull.

"No," he said now to Tracey, although he kept his eyes on me. Not squinting a bit, full and blue, just like my own. "We're doing just fine."

× × ×

Whenever my dad and I moved to a new town, the first thing we always did was go directly to the restaurant he'd been brought in to take over, and order a meal. We got the same appetizers each time: guacamole if it was a Mexican place, calamari for the Italian joints, and a simple green salad, regardless. My dad believed these to be the most basic of dishes, what anyplace worth its salt should do and do well, and as such they provided the baseline, the jumping-off point for whatever came next. Over time, they'd also become a gauge of how long I should expect us to be in the place we'd landed. Decent guac and somewhat crisp lettuce, I knew not to get too attached. Super rubbery squid, though, or greens edged with slimy black, and it was worth going out for a sport in school, or maybe even joining a club or two, as we'd be staying awhile.

After we ate, we'd pay our bill—tipping well, but not extravagantly—before we went to find our rental place. Once we'd unhitched the U-Haul, my dad would go back to the restaurant to officially introduce himself, and I'd get to work making us at home.

EAT INC, the restaurant conglomerate company my dad worked for as a consultant, always found our houses for us. In Westcott, the strip of a beach town in Florida we'd just left, they'd rented us a sweet bungalow a block from the water, all decorated in pinks and greens. There were plastic flamingos everywhere: on the lawn, in the bathroom, strung up in tiny lights across the mantel. Cheesy, but in an endearing way. Before that, in Petree, a suburb just outside Atlanta, we'd had a converted loft in a high-rise inhabited mostly by bachelors and businessmen. Everything was teak and dark, the furniture modern with sharp edges, and it was always quiet and very cold. Maybe this had been so noticeable to me because of our first place, in Montford Falls, a split-level on a cul-de-sac populated entirely by families. There were bikes on every lawn and little decorative flags flying from most porches: fat Santas for Christmas, ruby hearts for Valentine's, raindrops and rainbows in spring. The cabal of moms—all in yoga pants, pushing strollers as they power walked to meet the school bus in the mornings and afternoons—studied us unabashedly from the moment we arrived. They watched my dad come and go at his weird hours and cast me sympathetic looks as I brought in our groceries and mail. I'd known already, very well, that I was no longer part of what was considered a traditional family unit. But their stares confirmed it, just in case I'd missed the memo.

Everything was so different, that first move, that I didn't feel I had to be different as well. So the only thing I'd changed was my name, gently but firmly correcting my homeroom teacher on my first day of school. "Eliza," I told him. He glanced down at his roll sheet, then crossed out what was there and wrote this in. It was so easy. Just like that, in the hurried moments between announcements, I wrapped up and put away sixteen years of my life and was born again, all before first period even began.

I wasn't sure exactly what my dad thought of this. The first time someone called for Eliza, a few days later, he looked confused, even as I reached for the phone and he handed it over. But he never said anything. I knew he understood, in his own way. We'd both left the same town and same circumstances. He had to stay who he was, but I didn't doubt for a second that he would have changed if it had been an option.

As Eliza, I wasn't that different from who I'd been before. I'd inherited what my mother called her "corn-fed" looks—tall, strawberry blonde, and blue-eyed—so I looked like the other popular girls at school. Add in the fact that I had nothing to lose, which gave me confidence, and I fell in easily with the jocks and rah-rahs, collecting friends quickly. It helped that everyone in Montford Falls had known each other forever: being new blood, even if you looked familiar, made you exotic, different. I liked this feeling so much that, when we moved to

Petree, our next place, I took it further, calling myself Lizbet and taking up with the drama mamas and dancers. I wore cut-off tights, black turtlenecks, and bright red lipstick, my hair pulled back into the tightest bun possible as I counted calories, took up cigarettes, and made everything Into A Production. It was different, for sure, but also exhausting. Which was probably why in Westcott, our most recent stop, I'd been more than happy to be Beth, student-council secretary and all-around joiner. I wrote for the school paper, served on yearbook, and tutored underachieving middle school kids. In my spare time, I organized car washes and bake sales to raise funds for the literary magazine, the debate team, the children in Honduras the Spanish club was hoping to build a rec center for. I was that girl, the one Everyone Knew, my face all over the yearbook. Which would make it that much more noticeable when I vanished from the next one.

The strangest thing about all of this was that, before, in my old life, I hadn't been any of these things: not a student leader or an actress or an athlete. There, I was just average, normal, unremarkable. Just Mclean.

That was my real name, my given name. Also the name of the all-time winningest basketball coach of Defriese University, my parents' alma mater and my dad's favorite team of all time. To say he was a fan of Defriese basketball was an understatement, akin to saying the sun was simply a star. He lived and breathed DB—as he and his fellow obsessives called it—and had since his own days of growing up just five miles outside campus. He went to Defriese basketball camp in the summer, knew stats for every team and player by heart, and wore a Defriese jersey in just about every school picture from kindergarten to senior year. The actual playing time on the team he eventually got over the course of two years of riding the bench as an alternate were the best fourteen minutes of his life, hands down.

Except, of course, he always added hurriedly, my birth. That was great, too. So great that there was really no question that I'd be named after Mclean Rich, his onetime coach and the man he most admired and respected. My mother, knowing resistance to this choice was futile, agreed only on the condition that I get a normal middle name—Elizabeth—which provided alternate options, should I decide I wanted them. I hadn't really ever expected that to be the case. But you can never predict everything.

Three years ago my parents, college sweethearts, were happily married and raising me, their only child. We lived in Tyler, the college town of which Defriese U was the epicenter, where we had a restaurant, Mariposa Grill. My dad was the head chef, my mom handled the business end and front of house, and I grew up sitting in the cramped office, coloring on invoices, or perched on a prep table in the kitchen, watching the line guys throw things into the fryer. We held DB season tickets in the nosebleed section, where my dad and I sat screaming our lungs out as the players scrambled around, antlike, way down below. I knew Defriese team stats the way other girls stored knowledge of Disney princesses: past and present players, shooting average of starters and second stringers, how many Ws Mclean Rich needed to make all time winningest. The day he did, my dad and I hugged each other, toasting with beer (him) and ginger ale (me) like proud family.

When Mclean Rich retired, we mourned, then worried over the candidates for his replacement, studying their careers and offensive strategies. We agreed that Peter Hamilton, who was young and enthusiastic with a great record, was the best choice, and attended his welcome pep rally with the highest of hopes. Hopes that seemed entirely warranted, in fact, when Peter Hamilton himself dropped into Mariposa one night and liked the food so much he wanted to use our private party room for a team banquet. My dad was in total DB heaven, with two of his greatest passions—basketball and the restaurant—finally aligned. It was great. Then my mom fell in love with Peter Hamilton, which was not.

It would have been bad enough if she'd left my dad for anyone. But to me and my dad, DB fanatics that we were, Peter Hamilton was a god. But idols fall, and sometimes they land right on you and leave you flattened. They destroy your family, shame you in the eyes of the town you love, and ruin the sport of basketball for you forever.

Even all this time later, it still seemed impossible that she'd done it, the very act and fact still capable of unexpectedly knocking the wind out of me at random moments. In the first few shaky, strange weeks after my parents sat me down and told me they were separating, I kept combing back through the last year, trying to figure out how this could have happened. I mean, yes, the restaurant was struggling, and I knew there had been tension between them about that. And

I could vouch for the fact that my mom was always saying my dad didn't spend enough time with us, which he pointed out would be much easier once we were living in a cardboard box on the side of the road. But all families had those kinds of arguments, didn't they? It didn't mean it was okay to run off with another man. Especially the coach of your husband and daughter's favorite team.

The one person who had the answers to these questions, though, wasn't talking. At least, not as much as I wanted her to. Maybe I should have expected this, as my mom had never been the touchy-feely, super-confessional type. But the few times when I tried to broach the million-dollar question— why?—in the shaky early days of the separation and the still-not-quite-stable ones that followed, she just wouldn't tell me what I wanted to hear. Instead, her party line was one sentence: "What happens in a marriage is between the two people within it. Your father and I both love you very much. That will never change." The first few times, this was said to me with sadness. Then, it took on a hint of annoyance. When her tone became sharp, I stopped asking questions.

HAMILTON HOMEWRECKER! screamed the sports blogs. I'LL TAKE YOUR WIFE, PLEASE. Funny how the headlines could be so cute, when the truth was downright ugly. And how weird, for me, that this thing that had always been part of my life— where my very name had come from—was now, literally, part of my *life*. It was like loving a movie, knowing every frame, and then suddenly finding yourself right inside of it. But it's not a romance or a comedy anymore, just your worst freaking nightmare.

Of course everyone was talking. The neighbors, the sports-writers, the kids at my school. They were probably still talk-ing, three years and twin little Hamiltons later, but thankfully, I was not around to hear it. I'd left them there, with Mclean, when my dad and I hitched a U-Haul to our old Land Rover and headed to Montford Falls. And Petree. And Westcott. And now, here:

× × ×

It was the first thing I saw when we pulled in the driveway of our new rental house. Not the crisp white paint, the cheerful green trim, or the wide welcoming porch. I didn't even notice, initially, the houses on either side, similar in size and style, one with a carefully manicured lawn, the walk lined with neat shrubs, the other with cars parked in the yard, empty red plas-tic cups scattered around them. Instead, there was just this, sitting at the very end of the drive, waiting to welcome us per-sonally.

We pulled right up to it, neither of us saying anything. Then my dad cut the engine, and we both leaned forward, looking up through the windshield as it loomed above us.

A basketball goal. Of course. Sometimes life is just hi-larious.

For a moment, we both just stared. Then my dad dropped his hand from the ignition. "Let's get unpacked," he said, and pushed his door open. I did the same, following him back to the U-Haul. But I swear it was like I could feel it watching me as I pulled out my suitcase and carried it up the steps.

The house was cute, small but really cozy, and had clearly been renovated recently. The kitchen appliances looked new, and there were no tack or nail marks on the walls. My dad headed back outside, still unloading, while I gave myself a quick tour, getting my bearings. Cable already installed, and wireless: that was good. I had my own bathroom: even better. And from the looks of it, we were an easy walking distance from downtown, which meant less transportation hassle than the last place. I was actually feeling good about things, basketball reminders aside, at least until I stepped out onto the back porch and found someone stretched out there on a stack of patio furniture cushions.

I literally shrieked, the sound high-pitched and so girly I probably would have been embarrassed if I wasn't so startled. The person on the cushions was equally surprised, though, at least judging by the way he jumped, turning around to look at me as I scrambled back through the open door behind me, grabbing for the knob so I could shut it between us. As I flipped the dead bolt, my heart still pounding, I was able to put together that it was a guy in jeans and long hair, wearing a faded flannel shirt, beat-up Adidas on his feet. He'd been reading a book, something thick, when I interrupted him.

Now, as I watched, he sat up, putting it down beside him. He brushed back his hair, messy and black and kind of curly, then picked up a jacket he'd had balled up under his head, shaking it out. It was faded corduroy, with some kind of insignia on the front, and I stood there watching as he slipped it on, calm as you please, before getting to his feet and picking up whatever he'd been reading, which I now saw was a textbook of some kind. Then he pushed his hair back with one hand

and turned, looking right at me through the glass of the door between us. *Sorry,* he mouthed. Sorry.

"Mclean," my dad yelled from the foyer, his voice echoing down the empty hall. "I've got your laptop. You want me to put it in your room?"

I just stood there, frozen, staring at the guy. His eyes were bright blue, his face winter pale but red-cheeked. I was still trying to decide if I should scream for help when he smiled at me and gave me a weird little salute, touching his fingers to his temple. Then he turned and pushed out the screen door into the yard. He ambled across the deck, under the basketball goal, and over to the fence of the house next door, which he jumped with what, to me, was a surprising amount of grace. As he walked up the side steps, the kitchen door opened. The last thing I saw was him squaring his shoulders, like he was bracing for something, before disappearing inside.

"Mclean?" my dad called again. He was coming closer now, his footsteps echoing. When he saw me, he held up my laptop case. "Know where you want this?"

I looked back at the house next door that the guy had just gone into, wondering what his story was. You didn't hang out in what you thought was an empty house when you lived right next door unless you didn't feel like being at home. And it was his home, that much was clear. You could just tell when a person belonged somewhere. That is something you can't fake, no matter how hard you try.

"Thanks," I said to my dad, turning to face him. "Just put it anywhere."

Two

❀ ❀ ❀

When your dad is a chef, people always assume that at home he does all the cooking. This was not the case in our family. In fact, after spending hours in a restaurant kitchen either preparing food or overseeing others as they did so, the last thing my dad wanted to do when he finally got to leave was turn on the stove.

Because of this, my mom was always left to her own devices, which were decidedly not gourmet. If my dad could make a perfect white sauce, my mom preached the gospel of Cream Of: Cream of Chicken soup over chicken breasts, Cream of Broccoli soup over baked potatoes, Cream of Mushroom over, well, anything. If she was feeling really fancy, she'd sprinkle some crumpled potato chips on top of whatever she'd thrown together and call it a garnish. We ate canned vegetables, Parmesan from a shaker, and frozen chicken breasts, thawed in the microwave. And it was fine. On the rare nights my dad was home and could be coerced to cook, it was always on the grill. There, he'd flip salmon steaks or thick T-bones between layups on our battered basketball goal, the backboard of which was papered with Defriese stickers so completely you could hardly see any white at all. Inside, my mom would open a bagged salad, toss on some boxed croutons, and top it off with bottled dressing. The contrast might have seemed weird. But somehow, it worked.

When my parents' marriage first imploded, I was in a total state of shock. Maybe it was naïve, but I'd always thought they had the Great American Love Story. She was from a wealthy southern family that bred beauty queens, he the late, only child of an autoworker and a third-grade teacher. They could not have been more different. My mom was a debutante who literally went to charm school; my dad wiped his mouth with his sleeve and did not own a suit. It worked until my mom decided she didn't want it to anymore. And just like that, everything changed.

When she left my dad for Peter, I honestly could not believe it was happening, even as I witnessed the debris—snickers in the hallways at school, her moving out, the sudden, heavy fatigue in my dad's features—all around me. I was in such a daze that I didn't even think to object when it was decided for me that I'd spend the weekdays with my mom at Casa Hamilton and the weekends at our old house with my dad. I just sleepwalked along with it, like everything else.

Peter Hamilton lived in The Range, an exclusive gated community by a lake. You had to pass through a guardhouse to get in, and there was a separate entrance for landscapers and repairmen, so the residents could be protected from the sight of the lower classes. All the houses were enormous. The foyer of Peter's place was so big that whatever you said there rose up, up, up toward the high ceiling overhead, leaving you speechless. There was a game room with a Defriese pinball machine (a welcome gift from the booster club) and a pool with the Defriese insignia painted on the bottom of the deep end (compliments of the contractor, a huge DB fan). It always struck me, without fail, that the one person who would have truly appreciated these things was the only one who would never get to: my dad. I couldn't even tell him about them, as doing so seemed like yet another insult.

As far as cooking went, Peter Hamilton didn't. Neither did my mom. Instead, they had a housekeeper, Miss Jane, who was pretty much always on hand to prepare whatever you wanted, and even what you didn't. There was a healthy, pretty snack waiting for me every day after school, a balanced dinner—meat, vegetable, starch, bread—on the table promptly at six on nongame days. But I missed the Cream Ofs and the potato chips, the same way I missed everything about my old life. I just wanted it back. It wasn't until my mom told me she was pregnant with the twins, though, that I understood that this was never going to happen. Like a bucket of water over the head, the news of their impending arrival snapped me out of my daze.

My mother didn't tell me about this when she split with my dad, but if I did the math—and oh, how I hated having to do the math—it became clear that she not only knew about it, but it was the reason she finally came clean. All I knew was that there was so much news coming at me at such a fast clip (such as: we're separating, you'll be moving to another house for half the week, oh, and the restaurant's closing) that I didn't think anything else could shock me. I was wrong. Suddenly, I had not only a new stepfather and a new house, but a new family, as well. It wasn't enough to wipe out the one I loved: she was replacing it, too.

My parents had separated in April. That summer, when I knew I had half siblings on the way, my dad decided he would sell Mariposa and take a consulting job. The owner of EAT INC, an old teammate of his from college, had been trying to hire him forever, and now what they were offering seemed like just what he needed. A change of direction, a change of place. A change, period. So he said yes, planned to start in fall, and promised me that he'd come back whenever he could to visit me, and fly me out during the summers and vacation. It didn't occur to him for a second that I'd want to come along, just as it didn't occur to my mom that I wouldn't move in full-time with her and Peter. But I was tired of them—of her—making my decisions for me. She could have her bright and shiny new life, with a new husband and new kids, but she didn't get to have me, too. I decided I was going with my dad.

It was not without drama. Lawyers were called, meetings were held. My dad's departure was held up first weeks, then months, as I spent hours sitting at a conference table in one office or another while my mom, red-eyed and pregnant, shot me looks of betrayal that were so ironic they were almost funny. Almost. My dad was quiet, as her lawyer and his had me clarify again that this was my choice, not his urging. The court secretary, flushed, acted like she didn't spend the entire time looking at Peter Hamilton, who sat next to my mom, holding her hand with a grave expression I recognized from double overtimes with only seconds left to play and no time-outs left. After about four months of wrangling, it was decided that—surprise!—I could actually make this decision for myself. My mother was livid, because of course she knew nothing about doing what you wanted, and only what you wanted, other people's feelings be damned.

Our relationship since I'd left had been tepid at best. Under the custody arrangement, I was required to visit in summers and for holidays, both of which I did with about as much enthusiasm as anyone would do something court ordered. Each time, the same thing immediately became clear: my mom just wanted a clean, fresh start. She had no interest in discussing our previous lives or the part she may or may not have played in the fact that they no longer existed. No, I was supposed to just fold myself in seamlessly with her new life, and never look back. It was one thing to reinvent myself by choice. When forced, though, I resisted.

In the two years or so we'd been on the road, I did miss my mom. When I was really homesick in those first lonely, bumpy days at a new place, I wasn't lonely for my old house or friends, or anything else specific, as much as just the comfort she represented. It was the little things, like her smell, the way she always hugged too tight, how she looked just enough like me to make me feel safe with a single glance. Then, though, I'd remember it wasn't her that I was really yearning for as much as a mirage, who I'd *thought* she was. The person who cared enough about our family to never want to split us all into pieces. Who loved the beach so much that she thought nothing of packing up for a spur-of-the-moment road trip east, regardless of weather, season, or if we could really even afford to stay at the Poseidon, the dumpy ocean-view motel we preferred. Who sat at the end of the bar at Mariposa, glasses perched on her nose, reviewing receipts in the lazy hours between lunch and dinner service, who sewed together cloth squares in front of the fire, using all the bits and pieces of our old clothes to make quilts that were like sleeping under memories. It wasn't just me that was gone. She was, too.

When I thought of my mom most, though, was not on the first day of a new school, or a holiday we weren't together for, or even when I caught a glimpse of her—fleeting—when the TV cameras flashed to her at a Defriese game before I could change the channel. Instead, weirdly enough, it was when I was cooking dinner. Standing in a strange kitchen, browning meat in a pan. Adding a chopped green pepper to a jar of store-bought sauce. Opening a can of soup, some chicken, and a bag of potato chips at dusk, hoping to make something from nothing.

x   x   x

Whenever my dad came in to take over a new restaurant, there was always one person who pretty much personified resistance. Someone who took each criticism personally, fought every change, and could be counted upon to lead the bitch-and-moan brigade. At Luna Blu, that person was Opal.

She was the current manager, the tall girl with the tattoos who'd finally gotten us a waitress. When I came in the next day for an early dinner, she was dressed like an old-style pinup girl: dark hair pulled up and back, bright red lipstick, jeans, and a fuzzy pink sweater with pearl buttons. She was pleasant as she got me a Coke, smiling and gracious as she put in my order. Once I was settled with my food and they sat down to talk, though, it was clear my dad had his work cut out for him.

"It's a bad idea," she was saying to him now from the other end of the bar. "People will revolt. They expect the rosemary rolls."

"The *regular* customers expect them," my dad replied. "But you don't have that many regulars. And the fact of the matter is, they're not a cost-effective or practical thing to be offering to people as a complimentary appetizer. What you want is more people ordering more drinks and food, not a few filling up on free stuff."

"But they serve a purpose," Opal said, her voice slightly sharp. "Once people have a taste of the rolls, it makes them hungrier, and they order more than they would otherwise."

"So those people I saw sitting up here last night, drinking discount beer and eating rolls and nothing else," my dad replied, "they're the exception."

"There were only, like, two people at the bar last night!"

My dad pointed at her. "Exactly."

Opal just looked at him, her face flushing red. The truth was, no one looked kindly on their bosses bringing in a hired gun to tell them what they were doing wasn't working. It didn't matter if the place was losing money or had the worst reputation/food/bathrooms in town, and any and all improvements would only benefit them. People always complained at the beginning, and usually the senior staff members did it the loudest, which was why EAT INC often fired them before we even showed up. For whatever reason, this was different and therefore difficult.

"Okay," she said now, her tone even, controlled, "so suppose we do away with the rolls, then. What will we offer people instead? Pretzels? Peanuts? Maybe they can throw the shells on the floor to add more of that ambiance you're so sure we're lacking?"

"Nope." My dad smiled. "I'm thinking pickles, actually."

Opal just looked at him. "Pickles," she repeated.

I watched as he picked up the menu in front of him. It was the same one I'd found on our kitchen table that morning, covered in notes and cross-outs in black Sharpie pen, so ravaged it looked like one of my term papers from when I'd taken AP English with Mr. Reid-Barbour, the hardest teacher in my last school. Based on just a glance, things didn't look promising for most of the entrées and all of the desserts.

Now, he slid it between them on the bar, and Opal's eyes widened. She looked so dismayed I couldn't even watch, instead going back to wrestling with the Sudoku puzzle in the paper someone had left behind on the bar. "Oh my God," she said, her voice low. "You're going to change everything, aren't you?"

"No," my dad said.

"You've eliminated all our meat dishes!" A gasp. "And the appetizers! There's, like, nothing left."

"Ah, but there is," my dad said, his voice calm. "There are the pickles."

Opal leaned closer, squinting at the menu. "Nobody orders the pickles."

"Which is unfortunate," my dad said, "because they're very good. Unique. And incredibly cost-effective. The perfect giveaway starter."

"You want to give people fried pickles when they come in the door?" Opal demanded. "We're an Italian place!"

"Which brings me to my next question," my dad said, flipping the menu over. "If that's really the case, why are you serving guacamole, tacos, and fajitas? Or pickles, for that matter?"

She narrowed her eyes at him. "I'm sure you already know that the previous owners of this place ran a very successful Mexican restaurant. When the new management came in and changed the menu, it only made sense to keep some of the more popular dishes."

"I do know that," my dad said. "But the average POTS does not."

"POTS?"

"Person Off the Street. Your generic customer, the person walking by, looking for a place to try for dinner." He cleared his throat. "My point is, this restaurant is in an identity crisis. You don't know what you are, and my job is to help you figure it out."

Opal just looked at him. "By changing everything," she said.

"Not everything," he replied, flipping the menu over. "Remember: pickles."

It wasn't pretty. In fact, by the time they were done and my dad finally came to join me, he looked exhausted, and it wasn't like this was his first time doing this. As for Opal, she disappeared into the kitchen, letting the doors bang loudly behind her. A moment later, something clattered loudly to the floor, followed by an expletive.

"So," my dad said, pulling out the bar stool beside mine and sliding on. "That went well."

I smiled, then pushed my plate closer to him so he could help himself to the chips and salsa I hadn't eaten. "She likes the rolls, I guess."

"It's not really about the rolls." He picked up a chip, sniffed it, then put it back down. "She's just running a muddle."

I raised my eyebrows, surprised. Since the whole Peter Hamilton thing, my dad's love of Defriese basketball had waned almost to nothing, which was understandable. But he'd been a fan for so long, the legend and lingo of the team such a big part of his life, that certain habits were impossible to break. Like invoking Mclean Rich's most famous offensive move—which consisted of distracting a team with one pass or play so they wouldn't notice a bigger one happening at the same time—when he thought someone was trying to work it on him. He didn't notice or chose not to acknowledge this slip, though, so I let it pass without comment as well.

"She'll come around," I said instead. "You know that first meeting is always the hardest."

"True." I watched him run a hand through his hair, letting it flop back over his forehead. He'd always worn it long and somewhat shaggy, which made him look even younger than he was, although the divorce had added a few lines around his eyes. Still, he had the kind of ramshackle good looks that had pretty much guaranteed a new girlfriend, if not wannabe stepmother, in each place we'd landed so far.

"So," I said. "Ready for the latest update?"

He sat back, taking a breath. Then he slapped his hands together and shook them out—his version of a reset—before saying, "Absolutely. Hit me."

I pulled my list out of my pocket, unfolding it on the bar between us. "Okay," I began. "All the utilities are up and running, except the cable's still not getting half the channels, but that should be fixed by tomorrow. Recycling is on Thursday, garbage pickup is Tuesday. I can register at the school on Monday morning, just need to bring my transcripts and come early."

"And where is that?"

"About six miles away. But there's a city bus stop about a block over from us."

"Cool," he said. "What about supplies?"

"I found a Park Mart and stocked up this morning. The toaster in the kitchen is busted, so I got a new one. Oh, and I got an extra key made."

"Met any neighbors yet?"

I thought of the boy I'd found on the porch as I picked up my Coke, taking a sip. It wasn't exactly a meeting, though, so I shook my head. "But I'm guessing on the right is a family, professors. On the left, students. I could hear bass thumping all last night."

"Me, too," he said, rubbing his face again. "Not that I was sleeping anyway."

I glanced at the marked-up menu, which was on his other side. "So. Pickles, huh?"

"You had them yesterday," he said. "They were good, right?"

"Better than these tacos. They all fell apart the minute I picked them up."

He reached over, taking my fork and helping himself to a bite from my plate. He chewed, his face impassive, before replacing it and saying, "Meat isn't drained enough. That's half the battle on a good taco. Plus, there's too much cilantro in that salsa."

"But they still have a loyal following," I reminded him.

He shook his head. "Well, I guess they'll be joining up with the bread people."

"Vive la révolution," I said, just to make him laugh. It worked, kind of.

There was another bang from the kitchen, this one followed by a long series of clattering. He sighed, pushing back from the bar. "Time to meet my kitchen staff," he said, sounding less than enthusiastic. "You going to be okay on your own tonight?"

"Oh, yeah," I said. "I've got a ton of unpacking to do."

"Well, call or come back if you get lonely. I'll try to get out of here at a decent hour."

I nodded, closing my eyes as he kissed my cheek then ruffled my hair as he passed behind me. Watching him go, noting his slow gait and how stiff he seemed in his shoulders, I felt that same pang of protectiveness that had become like second nature since the divorce. There was probably a term for it, some brand of codependence, a daughter acting too much like a wife, once said wife takes off. But what was I supposed to do? We had each other. That was all.

My dad could take care of himself. I knew that, the same

way I knew there were so many things about his life I couldn't fix, no matter how hard I tried. It was probably why I worked so hard to handle the things I did. Getting us settled, taking care of details, keeping the chaos we'd chosen as neat as possible. I couldn't mend his broken heart or give him back the love of his team. But getting a new toaster, making sure we had enough soap and paper towels, and agreeing about the pickles? That, I could handle.

This was especially true now that I didn't know if I'd have a chance to do it again. I was in the second semester of my senior year, my college applications—which had been a challenge, to say the least, with my patchwork transcript—already submitted. In the fall, like the last two, I knew I'd probably be somewhere else, and again, I didn't know where. What I was sure of, though, was that I would be going it alone. The thought made me sad enough to want to do everything I could now for my dad, as if I could bank it away for my eventual absence.

I paid my check—that was another one of my dad's rules, no freebies—then got up and headed outside for the short walk back to the house. It was a crisp day, early January, with that kind of quickly waning afternoon light that always makes it feel like the dark snuck up on you. I'd cut down the alley just to the left of Luna Blu, which I was pretty sure was a shortcut to our street, when I came upon Opal. She was sitting on a milk crate by the side door of the restaurant, her back to me, talking to a guy in jeans and an apron, who was smoking a cigarette.

"I mean, it takes serious nerve to just come in here and call yourself an expert on any and all things," she was saying. "Oh, and you can just *tell* he's used to women falling all over him and agreeing to everything he says, even when it's stupid bordering on offensive. The man is clearly in love with himself. I mean, did you see that hair? What kind of grown adult can't get a simple age-appropriate haircut?"

The guy with the cigarette, who was tall and skinny with a seriously protruding Adam's apple, let out a guffaw, nodding at me as I approached. Opal turned, laughing, too. Then her eyes widened, and she jumped to her feet. "Hi," she said too quickly. "Um, I didn't realize . . . How was your meal? Good?"

I nodded, silent, then slid my hands farther into my pockets as I walked between them. About two beats later, I heard footsteps behind me, running to catch up.

"Wait," Opal called out. Then, "Please?"

I stopped, turning to face her. Up close, I realized she was older than I'd first realized, probably in her early thirties rather than twenties. Her cheeks were flushed, either from the cold or being embarrassed, as she said, "Look. I was just blowing off steam, okay? It's not personal."

"It's fine," I told her. "It has nothing to do with me."

She looked at me for a moment, then folded her arms over her chest. "It's just . . ." she said, then stopped, taking a breath. "It's kind of jarring, to suddenly be under scrutiny like this. I know it's not an excuse. But I'd appreciate it if you wouldn't . . . you know . . ."

"I wouldn't," I told her.

Opal nodded slowly. "Thanks."

I turned and started walking again, ducking my head

against the cold. I'd only taken a couple of steps when I heard her say, "Hey, I didn't catch your name earlier. What was it again?"

I never picked the moment. It always chose me. I just knew, somehow, what would work at the exact instant that I needed it to.

"I'm Liz," I said, turning back to her.

I liked the sound of it. Simple, three letters.

"Liz," she repeated, sealing the deal. "It's nice to meet you."

×   ×   ×

Back at the house, I unpacked my suitcase, finished putting away the groceries, and moved our couch four places in the living room before deciding it looked best in the very spot my dad and I had unceremoniously dropped it the day before when we brought it in from the U-Haul. Just to be sure, though, I plopped down on it with a glass of milk and booted up my laptop.

My home page was still set to my last Ume.com home page, the one for Beth Sweet. At the top was a picture of me, taken on the beach, our bungalow a pink-and-green blur behind me. There was my list of activities (yearbook, volunteering, student council) and interests (travel, reading, hanging with my friends). Said friends were just below, all one hundred and forty-two of them, face after tiny face I would, most likely, never see again. I scrolled down to my comment section, scanning the handful of new ones there:

Girl, we miss you already! The last board meeting sucked without you.

Beth, I heard from Misty you moved. Awful short notice, hope you are ok. Call me!

What happened to goodbye?

I leaned a little closer to the screen, reading these four words again, and once more. Then, against my better judgment, I clicked on the face beside them, bringing up Michael's page.

There he was, sitting on the seawall, in his wet suit, his hair wet and wicking up in the back. He was looking to the right, at the ocean, not the camera, and seeing him I felt that same little nervous tug in my stomach. We'd only known each other a couple of months, since meeting on the beach one morning when I was taking a walk and he was out catching early swells. I spent 6:45 to 7:15 with him for weeks, working up to . . . well, nothing, as it turned out.

But he was right. I hadn't said goodbye. It had been easier, like always, to just disappear, sparing myself the messy details of another farewell. Now, my fingers hovered over my track pad, moving the cursor down to his comment section before I stopped myself. What was the point? Anything I said now would only be an afterthought.

In truth, since my parents' split, I hadn't had much faith in relationships and even less of an inclination to start any lasting ones of my own. At home, I'd had several friends I'd known since grade school, girls I'd played Rainbow Soccer with and stuck close to in middle school. I'd had a couple of boyfriends, and gotten my heart broken more than once. I was a normal girl in a normal town, until the divorce happened.

Then, suddenly, I wasn't just one of the group anymore: no one else had a coach for a stepdad, a scandal at home, and new siblings on the way as an aftermath. It was all so public and awful, and while my friends tried to be there for me, it was too difficult to explain what was going on. So I pulled back from everything and everyone I'd known. It hadn't been until we got to Petree that I realized I'd been changing even before we started moving, that my reinvention began when I was still in the most familiar of places. Once the setting was totally new, though, I finally could be, as well.

Since we'd been moving, I'd gotten smart about dealing with people. I knew I wouldn't be staying forever, so I kept my feelings at the temporary stage, too. Which meant making friends easily, but never taking sides, and picking guys I knew wouldn't last for the long haul, or any haul at all, for that matter. My best relationships, in fact, usually started when I knew we were about to move to a new place. Then, I could just go all in and totally relax, knowing that whatever happened, I could cut and run. It was why I'd started hanging out with Michael, a boy who was older, out of school, and with whom I could never have had any sort of future. That way, when I didn't, it was no surprise.

I clicked back to Beth Sweet's page, then signed out. BE THE U IN UME! the subsequent page read. SIGN UP FOR YOUR NEW ACCOUNT NOW! I was just typing my e-mail address and Liz Sweet when my computer made a cheerful beeping noise and my webcam activated itself.

Crap, I thought, quickly putting down my laptop on the coffee table and darting into the kitchen. HiThere!, the video-chat application, had come preloaded on my computer, and no matter what I did I couldn't seem to disable it. Which shouldn't have been an issue, really, as none of my friends used it anyway. Unfortunately, someone else did.

"Mclean?" A pause, some static. "Honey? Are you there?"

I leaned against the fridge, closing my eyes as my mother's voice, pleading, drifted through our empty house. This was her last resort, after I'd ignored her messages and e-mails, the one way she still, somehow, was always able to track me down.

"Well," she said now, and I knew that if I looked at my screen, I'd see her there, craning her neck, looking around for my face in yet another room she didn't recognize. "I guess you're not home. I just had a free moment, wanted to say hello. I miss you, honey. And I was thinking about your applications, if you'd heard anything, and how if you end up here at Defriese, we can—"

This thought was interrupted by a sudden shriek, followed by another. Then, babbling and what sounded like a struggle before she spoke again.

"Okay, you can sit in my lap, but be careful of the computer. Connor! What did I just say?" More muffled noises. "Madison, honey, look in the camera. Look there! See? Can you say hi to Mclean? Say, hi, Mclean! Hi, big—Connor! Give me that pencil. Honestly, both of you, just—"

I pushed off the fridge, then out the kitchen door onto the deck. Outside, the air was cold, the sky clear, and I just stood there, looking at that basketball goal, her voice finally muffled behind me.

From where I was standing, I had a partial view of the

dining room of the house next door, where a woman with short, frizzy hair, wearing a plaid sweater and glasses, was sitting at the head of the table. There was an empty plate in front of her, the fork and knife crossed neatly across its center. To her left was a man I assumed to be her husband, tall and skinny, also with glasses, drinking a glass of milk. Their faces were serious, both of them focused on whoever was sitting at the other end. All I could see, though, was a shadow.

I went back inside, pausing in the kitchen to listen. There was only silence and the fridge whirring, but I still approached my laptop with caution, creeping around to the front and peeking over to make sure there was only the screen saver in view before I sat down again. As I expected, there was a HiThere! message bubble, bouncing cheerfully from side to side as it waited for me.

Wanted to say hello, sorry we missed you! We will be home all night, call and tell us about your new place. I love you. Mom

My mother was like Teflon, I swear to God. I could tell her a million times I didn't want to talk to her right now and needed some space, but it made no difference to her whatsoever. As far as she was concerned, I wasn't furious, choosing to avoid her. I was just busy.

I shut my laptop, having lost any momentum I had to tackle a new Ume.com account. Then I sat back, looking at the ceiling. A beat later, bass began thumping again from the other side of the house.

I stood up, then walked down the hallway and into my room. From my bed, I had a perfect view over the hedge to the small, white house on our right. There were still several cars parked in the yard, and now I watched as an SUV pulled in beside them, bumping up on the curb and almost sideswiping the mailbox. A moment later, the tailgate opened and a beefy-looking guy in a peacoat hopped out from behind the wheel. He whistled through his fingers—a skill I'd always admired—and went around to the back of the car, pulling at something as another couple of guys spilled out from the house's front door to join him. A moment later, they were carrying a keg up the front steps. When they came through the door, someone cheered from inside. Once the door shut behind them, the bass got even louder.

I looked up the street in the direction of Luna Blu, wondering if I should take my dad up on his offer and go hang out there. But it was cold, and I was tired, and it wasn't like I really knew anyone there either. So instead, I went back to the kitchen.

In the other neighbor's house, the couple had moved from the table into the kitchen, where the woman in plaid was now standing by the sink while her husband ran the water and piled in a couple of plates. As she spoke, she kept glancing at the back door, shaking her head, and after a moment he reached over a dripping hand, squeezing her shoulder. She leaned into him, her head against his chest, and they stood there together as he kept scrubbing.

It was a study in contrasts, to be sure. Like a choice I could make, one story or another: the rowdy college kids, their evening just beginning, the middle-aged couple whose night was coming to an end. I went back to the couch, where I stretched out, this time making sure to turn my laptop away from me first. I stared up at the ceiling for a little while, feeling that bass vibrating softly beneath me. *Thump. Thump. Drip. Drip.* It was kind of soothing, these sounds of lives being lived all around me, for better or for worse. And there I was, in the middle of them all, newly reborn and still waiting for mine to begin.

× × ×

I awoke with a start at the sound of a crash.

I sat up, blinking, not knowing where I was at first. This was common in the initial days at new houses, so I didn't panic as much as I once had. Still, it took a minute to get my bearings and calm my pounding heart before I felt ready to get off the couch and go investigate.

It did not take long to find the source of the noise. On the edge of our front porch, a flowerpot was broken into pieces, dirt spilling out in all directions. The likely culprit, a heavyset guy in a U T-shirt and some Mardi Gras beads, was stumbling back in the direction of the party next door, while a group of people on the porch there applauded, laughing.

"Uh-oh!" a skinny guy in a parka yelled at him, pointing in my direction. "Watch out, Grass. You're busted!"

The big guy turned sloppily, and looked at me. "Sorry!" he called out cheerfully. "You're cool, though, right?"

I wasn't sure exactly what this meant, other than I was probably going to be needing a broom and a trash bag. Before

I could answer, though, a redheaded girl in a puffy jacket walked out into the side yard between our two houses, holding a beer. She popped the cap, then handed it to him and whispered something in his ear. A moment later, he was coming back my way, holding it out like a peace offering.

"For you," he said, doing a weird almost curtsy and practically falling down in the process. Someone hooted from behind him. "My lady."

More laughter. I reached out, taking the can, but didn't respond.

"See?" he said, pointing at me. "I knew it. Cool."

So I was cool. Apparently. I watched him make his way back to his friends, pushing through the pack and going back inside. I was about to pour the beer into the bushes and go look for that trash bag when I thought of the house on the other side, with the sad, older couple, and reconsidered. My names always chose me, and what followed were always the details of the girl who would have that name, whoever she was. Beth or Lizbet or Eliza wouldn't ever have considered joining a party of strangers. But Liz Sweet might be just that kind of girl. So I ducked back inside, grabbed my jacket, and went to find out.

× × ×

"Jackson High?" The blonde at the keg rolled her eyes, sighing dramatically. "You poor thing. You'll *hate* it."

"It's a prison," added her boyfriend, who was in a black T-shirt and trench coat, sporting a hoop hanging from both nostrils. "Like the Gulag, but with bells."

"Really," I said, taking a tiny sip of my beer.

"Totally." The girl, who was small and curvy, wearing the meteorologically incongruous outfit of slip dress, sheepskin boots, and heavy parka, adjusted her ample cleavage. "The only way to survive is with a deep sense of irony and good friends. Without either of those, you're screwed."

I nodded, not saying anything. We were in the kitchen of the white house, where I'd ended up after making my way through the crowds packed on the porch and in the living room. Judging by the décor—U Basketball stickers covering the fridge, stolen street signs on the walls—the residents were college students, although many in the assembled crowd were my age. In the kitchen, there wasn't much except the keg, which had crumpled cups all around it, and a beat-up table and chairs. The only other décor was a row of paper grocery bags, overflowing with beer cartons and pizza boxes, and a cardboard cutout of a bodybuilder holding an energy drink. Someone had drawn a beard on his face, big nipples on his chest, and something I didn't even want to look too closely at on his nether regions. Nice.

"If I were you," the blonde advised as another group of people came in from the side door, bringing a burst of cold and noise with them, "I'd *beg* my parents to enroll me in the Fountain School."

"The Fountain School?" I said.

"It's, like, this totally free-form alternative charter school," the guy in the trench explained. "You can take meditation for gym. And all the teachers are old hippies. No bells there, man. They play a flute to recommend you switch classes."

I didn't know what to say to this.

"I loved the Fountain School," the blonde sighed, taking a swig off her beer.

"You went there?" I asked her.

"We met there," the guy said, sliding his arm around her waist. She snuggled into him, pulling her parka closer around her skimpy dress. "But then there was this, like, total Big Brother–style shakedown and she got kicked out."

"All that talk about respecting others and their choices," the girl said, "and they have the nerve to search my purse for drugs. I mean, what is that?"

"You did pass out in the Trust Circle," the guy pointed out.

"The *Trust* Circle," she said. "Where's the trust in that?"

I glanced around, thinking it might be time to look for other conversation options. The only other people in the kitchen, though, were two guys taking tequila shots and a girl leaning against the fridge having a weepy, drunk conversation on her cell phone. Unless I wanted to go outside, I was stuck.

The door banged open again behind me, and I felt another burst of cold air. A moment later, the girl in the puffy jacket who'd been responsible for me getting my beer was stepping up beside me, pulling a bottled water out of her pocket, and twisting the top off.

"Hey, Riley," the girl in the slip dress said to her. She cocked a thumb at me. "She's new. Starts Jackson on Monday."

Riley was thin with blue eyes, her hair pulled back into a ponytail at the base of her neck, and she had silver rings on almost every finger. She smiled at me sympathetically and said,

"It's not as bad as they've told you, I promise."

"Don't listen to her, she's a misguided optimist," the guy said. To her he added, "Hey, you seen Dave yet?"

She shook her head. "He was having a big sit-down with his parents tonight. I'm thinking they maybe didn't let him out after."

"*Another* sit-down?" the blonde said. "Those people sure can meet, can't they?"

Riley shrugged, taking a sip of her water. Her lipstick, a bright pink, left a perfect half-moon on the bottleneck. "I think he was hoping they'd decided to loosen up a bit," she said. "I mean, it's been two months. The fact that he's not here, though, doesn't bode well."

"His parents are so overprotective," the blonde explained to me. "It's crazy."

"Like the Gulag," her boyfriend added. "But at home."

"Seriously. The kid is on the straight and narrow his entire life, and then one night, he's just unlucky enough to get busted with a beer at a party." The blonde did a combo cleavage adjustment–eye roll, a move it was clear she'd perfected. "It was one beer! Even the court just gave him community service. But in their eyes, he might as well have killed someone's grandma or something."

"Hard-core," her boyfriend agreed.

I watched as Riley took another sip, then consulted her watch. As she did so, I noticed she had a tattoo on her inner left wrist, a simple black outline of a circle the size of a dime. "Okay," she said. "It's nine forty. We leave here at ten thirty at the latest in order to make curfew. No exceptions, no disappearing. *Capisce*?"

"You are such a mom," the blonde complained. Riley just looked at her. *"Capisce,"* she said finally.

"Ten thirty," the guy said, then saluted her. "Got it."

Riley gave me a smile, then walked back into the living room, picking her way over to the sofa. There, a dark-haired guy in an army jacket was gesturing wildly, telling a story to a couple of girls gripping plastic cups, who looked to be hanging on his every word. I watched her as she sat down on his other side, tucking a piece of hair behind her ear, and listened as well.

When I turned back to Gulag guy and Trust Issues, I found them suddenly—and passionately—making out, his hands sliding under her jacket. I glanced at the girl at the fridge, still weeping, and decided to head outside for some air.

On the side porch, people were smoking and shifting around in an effort to stay warm. It was a cold, crisp night, the stars so bright they seemed close enough to touch. Without even thinking about it, I started looking. *One*, I thought as I found Cassiopeia. Two was Orion. Three, the Big Dipper. Some people step over cracks, knock on wood, or toss salt over their shoulders. I never let myself look up at the night sky without finding at least three constellations. It just made me feel safer, more centered. Like no matter where I was, I could find something I recognized.

It was my mom who had taught me about the stars. She'd been an astronomy minor in college—one of the many surprises about her, actually—and my dad had bought her a tele-scope for their five-year wedding anniversary. She kept it on the small deck outside their bedroom, and on clear nights we'd huddle around it together, her finding the constellations and then pointing them out to me. "One," she'd say, and point to the Little Dipper. "Two," I'd say, and find one of my own. Then we'd both look hard, hard as we could, for another. Whoever found and named it first was the winner. Because of this, whenever I saw the night sky, no matter where I was, I was reminded of my mom. I wondered sometimes if when she looked up, she thought of me, as well.

Whoa, I thought as I felt a lump rise in my throat. Where did *that* come from? I'd only had about four sips of beer, but clearly, that was enough to threaten entirely too much nostalgia. I was just setting my can down when I saw the blue lights.

"*Cops!*" a voice yelled from behind me, and suddenly, everyone under the age of twenty-one was in motion. People from inside came bursting out the door, while those on the deck jumped the rails or pounded down the steps, taking off across the lawn into the darkness. I saw a couple of people dart across my porch and around the other side to the drive-way, while still others took off down the street, their purses and jackets flapping behind them. One skinny girl with braids, wearing earmuffs, was not so lucky, getting corralled by an officer who was coming up the walk. I watched as he led her by the arm to his car, depositing her in the backseat. There, she slumped against the opposite window, putting her head in her hands.

"You!" A bright light flashed across me, then slid back right into my eyes, making everything invisible beyond it. "Stay right there!"

My heart started pounding, my face suddenly flushed despite the cold. As the light grew brighter, closer, shaking slightly with every step the cop took toward me, I had to make a choice. Mclean, Eliza, Lizbet, and Beth all would have remained still, following orders. But not Liz Sweet. She bolted.

Without even thinking, I ran down the deck stairs, hit the grass, and started across the muddy, frozen backyard. The light and the cop followed me, catching an arm here, a foot there. When I reached the thick row of bushes that marked the beginning of my own yard, he yelled at me to freeze or else. Instead, I plunged through them headfirst, crashing out the other side.

I landed on the grass, then immediately sprang to my feet to keep running. "Hey!" the cop bellowed, as the bushes began to rustle, the flashlight dancing above them. "If you know what's good for you, you'll stop right where you are. Now!"

I knew I should do just that: he was close behind me, and I'd never make it to my house before the light hit me again. But in my panic, I scrambled forward anyway, even as I heard him coming through. I took one running step, and another, then suddenly felt a hand close around my left arm and yank me sideways. Before I even knew what was happening, I'd tumbled over a low wall on my left and was falling again. This time, though, I landed not on something, but someone.

"Umph," whoever it was said, as together, we toppled down

what felt like a flight of stairs, although it was suddenly too dark to say for sure. A second later, I heard footsteps, scrambling, and then there were two bangs, like doors slamming shut. Wherever I'd landed, the bottom was flat and everything smelled like dirt. Plus it was dark. Really dark.

"What the—" I said, but that was all I managed before I was shushed.

"One sec," a voice said. "Just let him get by."

A beat later, I heard it: a *thump-thump-thump* noise, slowly growing louder, from overhead. As it grew closer, a yellow light appeared. When I looked up, I could see it, spilling through the cracks between what was, in fact, two shut doors above us. "Damn it," I heard someone say, over a few huffs and puffs. Suddenly, the doors rattled, rising up slowly, before being dropped back down with a thud. Then the light was retreating, back the way it came.

In the silence that followed, I just sat there, trying to catch up with everything that had just happened. Sleep, crashing flowerpot, beer sips, Gulag, blue lights, and now . . . what? It occurred to me I should probably be nervous, as I was not only underground, but also not alone. And yet, for some reason, there was an odd calmness around me, a sort of familiarity, even in the midst of all this strangeness. It was the weirdest feeling. I'd never experienced anything like it.

"I'm going to turn on a light," the voice said. "Don't freak."

Of all the things to say to someone you've just pulled down into some dark place with you, this was probably the worst. And yet, a second later, when there was a soft click and a flashlight popped on, I was not at all surprised to see my neighbor, the porch crasher, sitting beside me in jeans and a thick plaid shirt, a knit cap pulled down tight over his long hair. We were at the bottom of a short flight of stairs that led up, up to a set of doors, latched with a hook-and-eye closure.

"Hi," he said, all casual, like we were meeting under the most normal of circumstances. "I'm Dave."

× × ×

In the last few years, as I'd been traveling with my dad, I'd had my share of new experiences. Different schools, various kinds of cultures, all new friends. But within five minutes, it became clear that never in my life had I ever met anyone like Dave Wade.

"Sorry if I startled you," he said as I sat there, open-mouthed, staring at him. "But I figured it's better to be surprised than busted."

I couldn't respond at first, too distracted by my surroundings. We were in what appeared to be a basement, a small space with wooden plank walls and a dirt floor. A single, worn lawn chair took up most of the square footage: a stack of books was beside it, another flashlight propped on top.

"What is this place?" I said.

"Storm cellar," he replied, as if this was of *course* the first question you'd ask after someone pulled you underground. "For tornadoes and such."

"This is yours?"

He shook his head, reaching to put the flashlight on the ground between us. As he did so, a moth fluttered past, casting weird shadows. "It's part of the house behind mine. Nobody's lived here for years."

"How'd you know about it?"

"I found it when I was younger. You know, exploring."

"Exploring," I repeated.

He shrugged. "I was a weird kid."

This, I believed. And yet, again, I was struck by the fact that not once during this entire incident had I been scared. At least not by him, even before I knew who he was. "So you just hang out here?"

"Sometimes." He got up, brushing himself off, and sat down in the chair, which creaked. "When I'm not crashing on your back porch."

"Yeah," I said as he sat back, crossing his legs. "What, do you not *like* being at home or something?"

He looked at me for a second, as if weighing his response. "Or something," he said.

I nodded. The digging and going underground might have been kind of weird. But this, I understood.

"Look," he said, "I didn't mean to freak you out. I was just coming out and saw the lights, then heard you coming. Actually, grabbing you was kind of an impulse move."

I looked up at the doors again. "You have good instincts."

"I guess. You know what's weird, though? I just put that hook and eye in last week. Lucky thing." He squinted up at it, then turned back to me. "The bottom line is, you don't want to get arrested for drinking under age. It's not fun. I know from experience."

"How do you know I haven't been already?" I asked.

He studied me, all seriousness. "You don't look like the type."

"Neither do you," I pointed out.

"This is true." He thought for a moment. "I rescind my earlier statement. You could very well be a delinquent, just like me."

I looked below me again, taking in the small, tidy space. "This doesn't really look like a den for delinquents."

"No?" I shook my head. "What were you thinking? Junior League?"

I made a face, then nodded at the stack of books: in the thrown light, I could barely make out one of the spines, which said something about abstract geometry and physics. "That's pretty heavy reading material."

"Don't go by that," he said. "I just needed something to prop the flashlight on."

From above us, I heard a sudden burst of music. The cops, apparently, were gone, and the party was starting up again with whatever legal stragglers remained. Dave got up, climbing the stairs, and popped the hook, then slowly pushed open one of the doors overhead and stuck his head out. Watching from below, it occurred to me he looked younger somehow: I could easily picture him as an eight- or nine-year-old, digging tunnels in this same backyard.

"Coast is clear," he reported, letting the door drop fully open, hitting the ground with a thud. "You should be able to get home now."

"I'd hope so," I said. "Since it's only, like—"

"—fourteen feet, seven point two inches, to your back deck," he finished for me. I raised my eyebrows, and he sighed. "I told you. Weird kid."

"Just kid?"

Now, he smiled. "Watch your step."

He climbed up the stairs out onto the grass, then turned the light back on me as I followed him out, offering his hand as I neared the top. I took it, again feeling not strange at all, his fingers closing around mine, supporting me as I stepped up into the world again.

"Your friends were at the party," I said. "They were looking for you."

"Yeah. It's already been kind of a long night, though."

"No kidding." I slid my hands in my pockets. "Well . . . thanks for the rescue."

"It was nothing," he replied.

"You kind of saved my ass," I pointed out.

"Just being neighborly."

I smiled, then turned to cross those fourteen feet, seven point two inches back to my house. I'd only taken a couple of steps when he said, "Hey. If I saved your ass, you should tell me your name."

I'd been in this place many times in the last two years, not to mention once already today. The name I'd chosen, the girl I'd decided to be here, was poised on the tip of my tongue. But in that place, at that moment, something happened. Like that quick trip below the surface had changed not only the trajectory of my life here, but maybe me, as well.

"Mclean," I said.

He nodded. "Nice to meet you."

"You, too."

I could hear the music from the party, that same bass thumping, as I crossed to the deck. As I pulled open my side door, I glanced back, just in time to see him climbing back down the stairs, the flashlight's glow rising up around him.

I went into my house, kicking off my shoes and padding down the hallway to the bathroom. When I turned on the light, the brightness startled me, as did the faint dusting of dirt that covered my face. Like I, too, had been tunneling, digging, and had only just now come up for air.

Three

✳ ❀ ✳

Jackson High was not the Gulag. It was also no Fountain School. Instead, it was pretty much just like all the other public high schools I'd attended: big, anonymous, and smelling of antiseptic. After filling out the typical mountain of paperwork and having a rushed meeting with a clearly overworked guidance counselor, I was handed a schedule and pointed toward my homeroom.

"Okay, people, quiet down," the teacher, a very tall guy in his early twenties wearing leather sneakers and a dress shirt was saying as I approached the door. "Typically, we've got twenty minutes' worth of stuff to do in five minutes. So help me out, all right?"

No one appeared to be listening, although there was a barely discernable reduction in volume as people made their way to a half circle of tables and desks, some pulling out chairs, others hopping up on tables or plopping on the floor below. A cell phone was ringing; someone in the back had a hacking cough. By the door, there was a TV showing two students, a blonde girl and a guy with short dreads, sitting at a makeshift news desk, with a sign behind them that said JACKSON FLASH! The teacher was still talking.

". . . Today is the last day to hand in your yearbook orders," he was saying, reading off various pieces of paper that were on the desk in front of him as a few more people straggled in. "There will be a table in the courtyard during all three lunches. Also, doors will open early for the basketball game tonight, so the earlier you get there, the better seat you'll get. And where's Mclean?"

I jumped, hearing this, then raised my hand. "Here," I said, although it came out sounding entirely too much like a question.

"Welcome to Jackson High," he said, as everyone, en masse, turned to look at me. On the TV screen, the student reporters were signing off, waving as the picture went black. "Any questions, feel free to ask me or anyone here. We are a friendly bunch!"

"Actually," I said, reflexively going to correct him, "it's . . ."

"Moving on," he continued, not hearing me, "I've been instructed to tell you again that you are not to touch the wet paint outside the cafeteria. Most people would know this without being told, but apparently some of you are not like most people. So: keep your dirty mitts off the wet paint. Thank you."

The bell sounded, drowning out the various responses to this message. The teacher sighed, looking down at the papers he obviously hadn't gotten to, then shuffled them into a stack as everyone got up again.

"Make it a good day!" he shouted halfheartedly, as people

started spilling into the hallway. I hung back, standing to the side of his desk until he glanced up and saw me. "Yes? What can I do for you?"

"I just," I began, as a pack of girls in cheerleader uniforms filed in, gabbing, "I wanted to say my name isn't—"

"Wendy!" he called out suddenly. His eyes narrowed. "Didn't we just have a conversation about dressing appropriately for school?"

"Mr. Roberts," a girl groaned from behind me, "get off my case, okay? I'm having a bad day."

"Probably because it's January and you're half naked. Go change," he replied. He looked back at me, but only for a second before his attention was again diverted by a crash in the back of the room. "Hey!" he said. "Roderick, I told you not to lean on that shelf! Honestly . . ."

Clearly, it was useless to try to do this now, so I stepped out into the hallway, looking down at my schedule as Wendy— a big girl in what I had to admit was a very short skirt for *any* season—huffed out behind me. I retraced my steps to the guidance office, figuring I'd try to tackle the rest of the building from there. Once I found it, I hung a right toward what I hoped was Wing B, passing a group of people gathered in front of the main office.

". . . sure you understand our position," an older man with curly hair, wearing a dress shirt and jacket, his back to me, was saying. "Our son's schooling has been a top priority ever since we realized his potential as a small child. Which is why we had him at Kiffney-Brown. The opportunities there—"

"—were exceptional," a short, thin woman finished for

him. "And, as you're aware, it was when he transferred here that all these problems began."

"Of course," the woman opposite them, in a pantsuit and sensible haircut that screamed administrator, even without the laminated ID hanging around her neck, replied. "But we believe he can get everything he needs, both academically and socially, here at Jackson. I think that by working together, all of us, we can help him to do just that."

The man nodded. His wife, clutching her purse with a weary expression and looking less convinced, glanced at me as I passed. She looked familiar, but I couldn't place her, at least not at first. So I kept walking, taking a left and consulting my schedule again.

I was scanning doorways and room numbers when I saw Riley. She was sitting on a bench, leaning slightly forward and craning her neck to look out in the hall, a backpack parked beside her. I knew her instantly, from the rings on her fingers and the same puffy jacket, now tied around her waist. She didn't look at me as I passed, too intent on watching the group in the hallway.

My math class was supposedly in room 215, but all I could find were 214, 216, and a bathroom that was out of order. Finally, I figured out what I needed was on the next corridor down, so I doubled back. I was just approaching Riley again when she jumped to her feet, grabbed her bag, and darted out into the main hallway ahead of me. The group was farther down now, by the stairs. The only person in the hallway was a guy with short hair wearing a white button-down oxford and khakis.

"What did they say?" Riley said as she ran up to him.

He glanced at the group, then back at her. "They'll agree to let me stay if I keep up my U courses. And about a hundred other attached strings."

"But you can stay," she said, clarifying.

"Looks that way, yeah."

She reached up, throwing her arms around his neck and giving him a hug. He smiled down at her, then glanced over at the group by the office. "Hey, shouldn't you be in class?"

"It's fine," Riley said, flipping her hand. "I have drama, they won't even notice I'm gone."

"Don't waste an absence on this," he said. "It's not worth it."

"I just wanted to make sure they weren't going to pull you out. I was freaking."

"Everything's fine," he said. "Don't freak."

Don't freak. It was only when I heard this that it hit me. I looked at the guy again: short hair, clean-cut. Your generic High School Boy. Except he wasn't. He was Dave Wade, neighbor and storm-cellar dweller. The clothes might have been different, the hair short, but I knew his face. It was the one thing that no matter what, you could never really change.

Riley stepped back from him. "Okay. But I'll see you at lunch, right?"

"David?" His mom was standing by the office door, holding it open. Just beyond, I could see his dad and the administrator disappearing down a hallway. "We're ready to go in now."

Dave nodded at her, then looked back at Riley. "Duty calls," he said, and gave her a rueful smile before walking away. She watched him go, biting her lip, before turning around and starting down the stairs. A moment later, the door banged, and I saw her jogging up the walk that led to the adjacent building, her bag bouncing against her back.

I looked at my schedule again, took a breath, then walked over to the other hallway and scanned the doors until I found 215. I wasn't exactly looking forward to interrupting just as the teacher got things under way, much less having to take a seat with all those eyes on me. But it was better than a lot of other options, especially the ones Dave had spared me from the other night. I was lucky to be here. So I reached for the knob, took a breath, and went inside.

× × ×

Two periods later, I braved the cafeteria, taking a chance on a chicken burrito that didn't look entirely inedible. I brought it outside, along with a wad of napkins and a bottled water, then settled myself on the wall that ran along the main building. Farther down, a group of guys with handhelds played games in tandem; on my other side, a very tall, broad-shouldered guy and a pretty blonde girl were sharing an iPod and a pair of earbuds, arguing—albeit good-naturedly—about what was playing as they listened.

I pulled out my phone, turned it on, then clicked open a new text message and typed in my dad's number. MADE IT TO LUNCH, I wrote. YOU?

I hit SEND, then scanned the courtyard before me, taking in the array of typical groups and cliques. The stoners kicked around a Hacky Sack, the drama girls talked too loudly, and those who cared about the world sat at various tables lined up along the walk, collecting money and selling baked goods for various causes. I was unrolling the foil on my burrito, wondering where exactly Liz Sweet belonged among them, when I saw the blonde, busty girl I'd met at the party on Friday night. She was cutting across the grass, wearing tight jeans, high boots, and a cropped, red leather jacket that was clearly more for show than warmth. She looked irritated as she passed by, heading for a group of picnic tables on the edge of the parking lot. After taking a seat at one she crossed her legs, pulled out a cell phone, and looked up at the sky as she put it to her ear.

My phone beeped and I picked it up, scanning the screen.

JUST BARELY, my dad had replied. THE NATIVES ARE VERY RESTLESS.

My dad expected to encounter resistance when he first came into a restaurant, but apparently Luna Blu was an extreme case. There were several "lifers," as he called them, people who had worked there for years for the original owners, an older couple who'd moved to Florida the year before. They'd thought they could manage things long-distance, but their balance sheet quickly proved otherwise, and they decided to sell to EAT INC in order to enjoy their golden years. According to what my dad had told me the day before at breakfast, Luna Blu had been running for the last year or so on little else but the goodwill of its longtime regulars, and even they weren't showing up the way they used to. There was no point in trying to tell that to the natives—employees—however. Like so many before them, they didn't care that my dad was only the messenger. They still wanted to shoot him.

I took a tentative bite of my burrito. By the time I'd opened my water, taken a sip, and braved another taste, I saw Riley was approaching the blonde at the table. I watched as she dropped her backpack on the ground, then slid onto the bench beside her, leaning her head against the blonde's shoulder. After a moment, her friend reached up, giving her a couple of pats on the back.

"Hi!"

I jumped, spilling some beans across my shirt, then looked up. A girl in a bright green sweater, khakis, and white sneakers, a matching green headband in her hair, was smiling down at me. "Hi," I said, noticeably less enthusiastically.

"You're new, right?" she asked.

"Um," I said, glancing back at Riley and her friend. "Yeah. I guess I am."

"Great!" She stuck out her hand. "I'm Deb. With the student hospitality committee? It's my job to welcome you to Jackson and make sure you're finding your way around okay."

Hospitality committee? This was a first. "Wow," I said. "Thanks."

"No problem!" Deb reached down, brushing off the wall beside me with one hand, then sat down next to me, placing her purse—a large, quilted number, also green—beside her. "I was new last year," she explained. "And this is such a big school, and so hard to navigate, I really felt there was a need for some kind of program to help people get comfortable here. So I started Jackson Ambassadors. Oh, wait, I forgot your welcome gift!"

"Oh," I said, "you don't have to—"

But already, she was unzipping her green bag and pulling out a small paper one, tied with a blue-and-yellow ribbon, from within it. There was a sticker on the front that said JACKSON TIGER SPIRIT! also blue and yellow. And shiny. She handed it to me, clearly proud, and I felt like I had no choice but to take it.

"In there," she said, "you'll find a pencil, a pen, and the schedules for all the winter sports. Oh, and a list of numbers you might need, like guidance and the main office and the library."

"Wow," I said again. Across the courtyard, Riley and her friend were now sharing a bag of pretzels, passing them back and forth.

"Plus," Deb continued, "some *great* giveaways from local merchants. There's a coupon for a free drink at Frazier Bakery, and if you buy any muffin at Jump Java, you can get another for half off!"

Sitting there, I realized that one of two things could happen from here. Either I would hate Deb, or we'd be best friends and Liz Sweet would end up just like her. "That's really nice," I said as she beamed at me, clearly proud. "I appreciate it."

"Oh, it's no problem," she said. "I'm just trying to make people feel a little more at home than I did."

"You had a tough time?"

For a moment, and only a moment, her smile became slightly less perky. "I guess so," she said. Then she brightened. "But things are great now, seriously. I really like it here."

"Well," I said, "I've moved around a lot. So, hopefully it won't be so bad."

"Oh, I'm sure it won't be," she said. "But if you have any problems, my card's in there as well. Don't hesitate to call or e-mail, okay? I mean that."

I nodded. "Thanks, Deb."

"Thank you!" She smiled at me, then put a hand to her mouth. "Oh, goodness, I'm so rude! I didn't even get your name. Or did—"

"Mclean!"

I blinked, sure I hadn't heard this right. But then it came again. Yes, someone was calling me. By my real name.

I turned my head. There, at the picnic table, was the blonde girl, now standing, her hands cupped over her mouth. Yelling. At me.

"Mclean!" she said, then waved. "Hey! We're over here!"

"Oh," Deb said, glancing at her, then back at me. "Well. Looks like you've already made some friends."

I looked back at the table, where Riley was watching me as well, the bag of pretzels in one hand. "I guess so," I said.

"Well," Deb said, "maybe you don't need the packet at all. But I just thought . . ."

"No," I told her, suddenly feeling bad for some reason. "I'm glad to have it. Really."

She smiled at me. "Good. It's nice to meet you, Mclean."

"You, too."

She stood, then turned on one pert sneaker and started down the walkway, reaching up to adjust her headband as she went. I glanced at the blonde. *Come on*, she mouthed, waving at me again. So this was my moment, I thought, picking me again, although not exactly the way I'd expected. Still, I got to my feet, tossing my burrito in a nearby trash can, and headed across the courtyard to see what would happen next. I was almost there when I looked back in the direction Deb had gone, finding her a moment later by the bus parking lot. She was sitting under a tree, her green purse beside her, sipping a soda. Alone.

× × ×

The blonde's name was Heather. How she knew mine was not yet clear.

"I had to save you," she explained as I approached their table. "That girl Deb is a spazzer freak. I considered it an act of charity to call you over here."

I looked back at Deb, sitting under the tree. "She didn't seem so bad."

"Are you *kidding*?" Heather said, incredulous. "She sat next to me in bio last year. Spent the entire semester trying to recruit me to her various groups, all of which she is the sole member of. It was like sharing a Bunsen burner with a cult member."

"What's in the bag?" Riley asked, nodding at the welcome packet, which I was still holding.

"A hospitality gift," I said. "From the student ambassadors."

"Ambassa*dor*," Heather corrected me, adjusting her ample cleavage. "Hello? She's the only one!"

I wasn't sure what I was doing here, now that I'd been saved from Deb. Before I found out, though, there was one more issue to clear up.

"How did you know my name?" I asked Heather.

She'd been checking her phone, and now looked up at me, squinting in the sunlight. "You told me at that party, before it got busted."

"No," I said. "I didn't."

She and Riley exchanged a look. Now I was acting like a cult member. Heather said, "Then I guess Dave must have mentioned it."

"Dave?"

"Dave Wade? Your neighbor? You did meet him on Saturday, didn't you?" she asked. "He's not exactly forgettable."

"He's not as weird as he seems," Riley said to me.

"He's weirder," Heather added. When Riley shot her a look, she said, "What? The boy hangs out in the basement of an abandoned house. That's not normal."

"It's a storm shelter. It's not like he built it, or something."

"Do you even *hear* what you're saying?" Heather sighed loudly. "Look, you know I love Dave. But he is kind of a freak."

"Isn't everybody?" Riley said, picking out another pretzel.

"No." Heather adjusted her bosom again. "I, for instance, am completely normal in every way."

Riley snorted, eating another pretzel, and they were both quiet for a moment. Now, I thought. Now is when I introduce myself as Liz Sweet, clear this whole thing up. Then I'd just have to do it again in homeroom tomorrow and I'd be all set, just where I needed to be for all this to work the way I wanted it to. But for some reason, standing there, I couldn't. Because despite my best efforts otherwise, Mclean already had a story here. She was the girl who'd discovered Dave on the back porch, then taken refuge in his hideout. The girl at the party, the girl Deb welcomed in her own spazzy freaker style. She was not the same Mclean I'd been for the first fourteen years of my life. But she was Mclean. And not even a new name could change that, now.

Heather looked at Riley. "So, speaking of Eggbert, what's the story? Did his parents yank him out of here for good, or what?"

Riley shook her head. "I saw him after homeroom. He said they were letting him stay, but he had tons of hoops to jump through. They've been meeting about it with Mrs. Moriarity all morning."

"God, that sounds miserable," Heather groaned. To me she added, "Mrs. Moriarity is the principal. She *hates* me."

"She does not," Riley said.

"Actually, she does. Ever since that whole, you know . . . incident when I backed into the guardhouse. Remember?"

Riley thought for a second. "Oh, right, that was bad," she said. Then she looked at me and added, "She's a *horrible* driver. She never looks when she merges."

"Why should I always have to do the looking?" Heather asked. "Why can't other people look out for *me*?"

"The guardhouse is an object. It's defenseless."

"Tell that to my bumper. I'm still paying off the money I owe my dad for the damn body shop."

Riley rolled her eyes. "I thought we were talking about Dave."

"Right. Dave." Heather turned to me. "My point is, he's, like, an administrator's wet dream. Boy genius who skipped, like, all of junior high and was taking college courses, then came to this hellhole by *choice*. Which is something I'll never understand."

"He wanted to be normal," Riley said quietly, picking out another pretzel. Then, glancing at me, she explained, "Dave had never been in public school. He was actually going to go to college early, because he's so smart and got moved up so much. But then he decided he wanted to, you know, live like a regular teenager. So he got this after-school job making smoothies at Frazier Bakery, where my boyfriend at the time was working."

"Nicolas," Heather said. She sighed. "Man, that boy could blend. You should have seen his biceps."

Riley ignored this, continuing, "Dave and I had actually known each other when we were kids, but we'd fallen out of touch. Once he was working with Nic, though, we picked right back up where we'd left off and started hanging out."

"At which point he fell totally in love with her," Heather told her. Riley shook her head. "What? It's the truth. I mean, he's supposedly over it now, but there was a time—"

"He's like a brother to me," Riley said. "I could never think of him that way."

"Also, she only dates dirtbags," Heather told me.

Riley sighed. "True. It's a sickness."

Heather gave her a sympathetic look before reaching over, patting her back the same way I'd watched her do earlier from a distance. Then she looked at me. "So, you going to sit down or what? You're making me nervous, just standing there."

I glanced back at Deb, alone under her tree, and then the random groups, as intricately divided as genuses in the animal kingdom, spread out between us. "Sure," I said, stuffing my welcome bag into my backpack. "Why not."

× × ×

After school, I took a bus to Luna Blu, then cut down the alley to the kitchen entrance. I found my dad in the cramped office—a converted supply closet, by the looks of it—sitting at a desk. There were papers spread out all around him, and he had his phone to his ear.

"Hey, Chuckles. It's Gus," he was saying. "So, look, it's not as bad as you feared. That said, though, it's far from good."

Charles Dover was the owner of EAT INC. A former DB and NBA player, he was over six seven and built like a Mack truck, the last person anyone would ever want to call a name like Chuckles. My dad, though, had been one of his best friends since his own glory days riding the Defriese bench. Now Chuckles was a TV commentator and a multimillionaire. He traveled around the country a lot for the network, and he loved to eat, which is how he'd ended up owning a company that bought up and rehabbed restaurants before selling them off to new owners. Mariposa had been his favorite restaurant whenever he was in town for Defriese games, and now that he'd lured my dad away from there, he worked him hard. But he also paid well and took very good care of us.

I dropped my backpack on the floor of the office, not wanting to disturb them, then headed out into the restaurant proper. It was empty except for Opal, who was standing by the front door, surrounded by a stack of cardboard boxes. The UPS man, who was parked outside, was in the process of wheeling in even more.

"Are you sure there hasn't been some kind of mistake?" she asked him as he put another one by the hostess stand. "This is a lot more than I was expecting."

He glanced at a clipboard that was balanced on the top

box. "Thirty out of thirty cartons," he said, then handed it to her. "All here and accounted for."

Opal signed the sheet and gave it back to him. She was in a cotton long-sleeved shirt printed with cowboys and horses, a black miniskirt, and bright red boots that came up past her knees. I hadn't figured out yet if her look was punk or retro. Maybe petro.

"You know," she said to the UPS guy, "it's pathetic what a person has to do to secure ample parking in this town. *Pathetic*."

"Can't fight city hall," he replied, ripping off a sheet and handing it to her. "Hey, you got any more of those fried pickles lying around? Those I got here the other day were wicked good."

Opal sighed. "*Et tu*, Jonathan?" she said sadly. "I thought you loved our rolls!"

He shrugged. "They were good, for sure. But those pickles? Crispy and crunchy, and, you know, pickly? Damn! They're just beyond."

"Beyond," Opal repeated, her voice flat. "Fine. Go back and ask Leo to throw a few in for you."

"Thanks, doll."

He walked past me, nodding, and I nodded back. Opal put her hands on her hips, surveying the boxes, then added over her shoulder, "And tell him to send someone out here to help me carry these upstairs, would you?"

"Will do," the delivery guy said, pushing into the kitchen, the door swinging out, then back again behind him. I watched as Opal bent down over one of the cartons, examining it, then pushed herself back to her feet, rubbing her back.

"I'll help you, if you want," I said.

She spun around, startled, her face relaxing—a bit—when she saw me. "Oh, thank you. The last thing I need is for Gus to come out here and start asking a bunch of questions. He's already out to get me as it is."

I waited a beat, for her to realize what she'd just said. One. Two. Then—

"Oh, God." Her face reddened. "I didn't mean that how it sounded. I just—"

"It's okay," I told her, walking over and picking up one of the smaller cartons. "Your boxes of secrets are safe with me."

"I wish they were boxes of secrets," she said with a sigh. "That would be infinitely less humiliating."

"Then what are they?"

She took a breath, then said, "Plastic buildings, trees, and infrastructure."

I looked down at the box. MODEL COMMUNITY VENTURES, read the return address.

"It's a long story," Opal continued, hoisting a box onto her hip. I followed her into the side dining room. "But the condensed version is that I sold my soul to the head of the town council."

"Really."

"I'm not proud." She went down a small hallway, past the bathrooms, then bumped open a doorway with her hip, revealing a narrow set of stairs. As we started up them, she said, "They were about to shut down the parking lot beside us, which would have been totally devastating, business-wise. I knew they were looking for someone to take on the project of assembling this model of the town for the centennial this summer, and that nobody wanted to do it. So I volunteered. On one condition."

"Parking?"

"You got it."

We reached the top of the stairs, entering a long room lined with tall, smudged glass windows. There were a few tables stacked along one wall, some empty garbage cans, and, inexplicably, two lawn chairs right in the middle, an upended milk crate between them. On it was a pack of cigarettes, an empty beer bottle, and a fire extinguisher.

"Wow," I said, setting down my box. "What is this place?"

"Mostly storage now," she replied. "But as you can tell, the staff have been known to use it on occasion."

"To set fires?"

"Ideally, no." She walked over, picking up the fire extinguisher and examining it. "God! I have been looking *everywhere* for this. The kitchen guys are such kleptos, I swear."

I walked over to one of the big windows, peering out. There was a narrow balcony, made of wrought iron, over which I had a perfect view of the street below. "This is nice," I said. "Too bad you can't seat people up here."

"We used to," she said, picking up the beer bottle and tossing it in a nearby trash can, followed by the cigarettes. "Way back in the day."

"Really," I said. "How long have you been here?"

"I started in high school. It was my first real job." She

picked up the milk crate, moving it to the opposite wall, then folded the chairs, one by one. "Eventually, I left for college, but even then I came back and waited tables in the summers. Once I graduated, I planned to get a full-time job with my double degree in dance and art history, but it didn't exactly work out." She looked at me, then rolled her eyes. "I know, I know. Who would have guessed it, right?"

I smiled, looking back out the window again. "At least you did what you liked."

"That has always been my defense, even when I was flat broke," she said, wiping off the milk crate with one hand. "Anyway, I was back here and unemployed when the Melmans decided they needed someone else to take over the day-to-day for them. So I agreed, but only on a temporary basis. And somehow, I'm still here."

"It's a hard business to get out of. Sometimes impossible," I replied. She looked at me. "That's what my dad says, anyway."

For a moment, she was quiet, instead just taking the folded chairs and stacking them against the wall. "You know," she said finally, "I understand he's just here to do a job, and that we needed to make some changes. I'm sure he's a good guy. But it just feels . . . like we're being invaded. Occupied."

"You say it like this is a war."

"That's kind of how it feels," she replied. She sat down on the milk crate, propping her head in her hands. "I mean, with half the menu gone, and cutting out brunch. I think maybe I should have gone with the rolls. Out with the old, in with the new, and all that."

She looked tired suddenly, sitting there saying this, and

I felt like I should say something supportive, even though we hardly knew each other. Before I could, though, there was a bang from the stairs, and the skinny cook I recognized from the alley a few days earlier appeared on the landing, carrying a box. My dad, also with one in his arms, was right behind him.

"Yo, Opal, where you want us to put these?" the cook asked.

Opal jumped to her feet. "Leo," she said, quickly walking over to take the box from my dad's arms, "I can't believe you asked Gus to do this."

"You said to get someone to help me!"

"Someone," she muttered, under her breath. "Not the boss, for God's sake."

"It's fine," my dad said easily. To me he added, "Mclean! I didn't even know you were here. How was the rest of the day?"

Opal turned, looking at me, confused, and I suddenly remembered I'd told her my name was Liz. I swallowed, then said, "Okay, I guess."

"Gus, seriously," Opal said to him. "I'm so sorry. . . . It will only take me a second to get the rest of those boxes up here, I promise." She shot Leo a dark look, but he was just standing there, fiddling with the strings of his apron.

"What?" he said as she continued to glare at him. "Oh. You mean me?"

"Yes," she replied, sounding more tired than ever. "I mean you."

He shrugged, banging back down the stairs. Opal still looked mortified, but my dad hardly seemed to notice as he walked over to stand beside me at the window, looking out at the street.

"This is a great space," he said, glancing around him. "Did it used to be dining room?"

"About ten years ago," Opal replied.

"Why'd they stop using it?"

"Mr. Melman felt people were too slow going up and down the stairs. All the food was cold once it got here, because the kitchen was so far away."

"Huh," my dad said, walking over to one of the walls and knocking on it. "In such an old building, I'm surprised there wasn't a dumbwaiter."

"There was," Opal told him. "But it never worked right. You'd put your food in and never see it again."

"Where was it?"

She walked over to the wall by the stairs, pushing aside one of the tables there. Behind it, on the wall, you could see the imprint of something square, protruding slightly. "We had it plastered over," Opal said. "Because people kept riding in it after closing. Serious liability."

"No kidding." My dad walked over, checking it out. As he did, Opal glanced at me again, and I wondered what she was thinking.

"So," my dad said, turning back to the room proper. "What's with the boxes? I didn't realize we had a big order coming in today."

"Um," Opal said, as Leo reappeared, carrying three boxes stacked precariously, one on top of another. "We didn't. This is . . . something else."

My dad looked at her. "Something else?"

"I was just telling Liz"—she glanced at me, and I felt my

dad do the same, though I didn't look at him—"that it's this model for the town council. They needed someone to run the project and a place to do it in. And they were about to shut down our parking lot, so I kind of volunteered."

She trailed off, surveying the various cartons dispiritedly as Leo added his to the collection. My dad said, "What's it a model of?"

"The town. It's for the centennial this summer," she replied. She pulled a piece of paper out of her back pocket, reading aloud from it. "'Providing both a community project and public art, this living map will allow your citizens to see your town in a whole new way.'"

"Looks like it might take up some space," my dad said.

"I know." She shoved the paper back in her pocket. "I didn't realize how big it was. I'll find another place for it, and soon. I just have to make some calls."

"Yo, Opal!" a voice yelled up the stairs. "The linen guy is here and our towel order's short. And that lady's still on hold for you."

"What lady?"

"The one Leo told you about," the voice replied.

Opal turned to Leo, who was standing the window. "Oh," he said. "You, um, have a phone call."

She said nothing, just gave him a look before heading downstairs without comment. My dad glanced at Leo, then said, "Once all the boxes are up, you've got peppers to slice. And make sure that walk-in's clean by opening. No grit anywhere, and Windex the door."

"Sure thing, boss man," Leo said less than enthusiastically.

My dad watched, his expression unreadable, as Leo ambled across the room and down the stairs. Once the door at the bottom banged shut, he said, "I can't tell if this is a restaurant or a charity foundation. I mean, that guy can't even work a spray bottle."

"He does seem a little useless," I agreed.

"It's epidemic here." He walked over to the windows again, looking out. "Unfortunately, I can't fire everyone. At least not right away."

I stood with him, watching the street below. It was a pretty spot, framed by tall trees on either side, bending toward us. "Opal seems nice."

"I don't need her to be nice," he said. "I need her to take control of her staff and implement the changes I tell her to. Instead, she argues every single point, wasting endless amounts of time."

We were quiet for another moment. Then I said, "Did you know she's worked here since she was in high school?"

"Yeah?" He didn't exactly sound interested.

I nodded. "It was her first job. She really loves this place."

"That's nice," he said. "But all the love in the world won't save a sinking ship. You have to either bail or jump overboard."

I thought of Opal, sitting on that milk crate, looking so tired. Maybe she was ready to find an island somewhere in need of a dancer or art historian, and my dad was doing her a favor by giving her a plank to walk. I wanted to believe that. It was part of the job, too.

"Look, I'm sorry for the outburst. I'm in a crap mood right now," he said, sliding a hand over my shoulder. "Hey, want to come down for the staff meal? It's the first run of the all-new menu. I could use someone there who actually likes me."

"I'm your girl," I said.

He smiled at me, and I followed him to the stairs. We were halfway down when he paused, looking back at me. "She called you Liz," he said. It wasn't a question, exactly. But I knew what he was asking.

"A misunderstanding," I told him. "I'll straighten it out."

He nodded, and led me the rest of the way to the bar and main dining room. There, the employees were gathered around for the mandatory nightly meeting and staff meal he implemented at every restaurant. I looked for Opal, finding her at the end of the bar, taking in the plates lined up all down it, a different dish on each, with a wary look on her face.

"All right, everyone. Can I have your attention, please?" my dad said.

The group grew quieter, then silent. I watched him square his shoulders and take a breath.

"Tonight," he began, his voice loud and confident, "we start the first phase of the reincarnation of Luna Blu. Our menu is smaller, our dishes less complicated, our ingredients fresher and more local. You will recognize some items. Others are brand-new. Now if you could just pick up a menu and read along with me, let's start at the top."

Opal passed out the one-page, laminated menus stacked on a nearby bar stool. As the group looked them over, there were some grunts. Some groans. One boo, although I couldn't tell where it was coming from. It wasn't going to be easy, this moment, or this night. But my dad had seen much worse. And as he continued, I slid into a booth just behind him, so he'd know I was there.

× × ×

"Disaster."

This was the one-word response I received the next morning when I found my dad already awake, scrambling eggs in the kitchen, and asked him how things had gone the night before. I'd tried to stay up and wait for him, but had fallen asleep around midnight when he still wasn't home. Now I knew why.

"First new menu run is always tough," I reminded him, pulling two plates out of the cabinet.

"This wasn't tough," he replied, stirring the eggs with a flick of his wrist. "It was ridiculous. We were in the weeds in the first hour and never recovered, with only half the tables seated. I've never seen such rampant disorganization. And the *attitude*! It's mind-boggling."

I put the plates on our small kitchen table, then got some forks and napkins and sat down. "That stinks."

"What stinks," he said, still on a roll, "is that now I have to go back there and figure out how to fix it all before service tonight."

I stayed quiet as he turned, sliding a generous portion of yellow, fluffy eggs onto the plate in front of me. But what I'd said was true: the first night of a new menu always went terribly, with staff members either imploding or exploding, the customers left unhappy or downright angry, and my dad deciding the whole effort was doomed. This sequence was almost required, part of the process. He never seemed to remember this from place to place, though, and reminding him was useless.

"The thing is," he continued, dumping some eggs on the other plate before sitting down across from me, "a restaurant is only as strong as its chef. And this place has no chef."

"What about Leo?"

"He's the kitchen manager, although God only knows who thought he was qualified for that position. The chef quit about a week ago, after Chuckles starting asking questions about some hinky stuff his financial guys found in the books. Apparently, he did not feel like providing an explanation."

"So you need to hire someone?"

"I would," he said, "but no chef worth his salt would take the job with the state of the place right now. I need to implement the new menu, streamline operations, and clean house, both literally and figuratively, before I even think about bringing anyone else in."

"That sounds easy," I said.

"Shutting the door and cutting our losses would be the easiest," he replied. "I'm thinking that might be the way to go."

"Really?"

"Yep." He sighed, then looked out the kitchen window, taking another bite. For someone who made his living out of a love of food, my dad was a fast, messy eater. He never lingered or savored, instead just wolfing down what was on his plate like someone was timing him. He was almost finished as I got up to pour myself a glass of milk, only a few bites of my own meal taken.

"Well," I said carefully, "I guess it was bound to happen sometime."

My dad swallowed, then glanced at me. "What was?"

"No potential," I replied. When he raised his eyebrows, I said, "You know. A place that really can't be fixed, even by you. A hopeless situation."

"I guess so," he replied, wiping his mouth with a napkin. "Some things can't be saved."

This was a fact we both knew well. And maybe that wouldn't be such a bad thing, I thought as I opened the fridge, letting this ship sink. Sure, it would mean another move, another change, another school. But at least I'd get to start right, not like I had here, where I was stuck with Mclean, despite my best—

"The thing is," he said suddenly, interrupting this quickly snowballing train of thought, "there *is* some good talent in the kitchen."

If I'd been paying closer attention, I probably would have heard it, the sound of the bottom getting hit. Followed by the beginning of this small rise.

"Not Leo, obviously," he continued, glancing at me. "But a couple of the line guys, and one of the prep cooks. And there are possibilities on the floor as well, if I can just weed out the gloom-and-doomers."

I slid back into my seat, putting my glass in front of me. "How did the customers like the new menu?"

"The few we had, who actually got their meals hot and complete," he said with a sigh, "were raving."

"And the pickles?"

"Went over huge. Opal was furious." He smiled, shaking his head. "But the new menu, it's good. Simple, flavorful, plays to all our strengths. The few we have anyway."

Now I was sure he was going to stay in. This, when he went from using "them" to "us"—an outsider to one within—was another sign.

His phone, parked by the sink, suddenly jumped and buzzed. He reached over, grabbing it and flipping it open. "Gus Sweet. Oh, right. I did want to talk to you. . . ."

As a voice crackled from the other line, I glanced over at our neighbors' house, just in time to see Dave Wade's mom coming out her side door. She was dressed in jeans, a white, cable-knit sweater, and sensible shoes, a tote bag over one shoulder, carrying a foil-covered pan in her hands. As she walked down the steps, she moved carefully, looking down so she wouldn't trip.

". . . Yes, that's exactly what I said," my dad was saying as she crossed the driveway and started up our steps, equally cautiously. "Why? Because I don't like the look of the order I got yesterday."

Mrs. Wade was almost to our side door. I got up to meet her, just as she leaned into the screen, covering her eyes with her free hand. When she saw me, she jumped back, startled.

"Hello," she said as I pushed the door open. "I'm Anne Dobson-Wade. I live next door? I wanted to welcome you to the neighborhood, so I made some brownies."

"Oh," I said. She extended the dish to me, and I took it. "Thank you."

"They are nut-free, gluten-free, and sugar-free, made with

all organic ingredients," she said. "I didn't know if you had any allergies."

"We don't," I replied. "But, um, thanks for the consideration."

"Of course!" She smiled at me, a bit of frizz blowing in the wind coming in behind her. "Well, as I said, we are right next door. If you need anything or have questions about the neighborhood, I hope you'll let us know. We've been here forever."

I nodded in response to this, just as Dave came out of her door, wearing a green T-shirt and jeans, and began dragging the garbage can down to the curb. His mom turned, saying something to him, but he didn't hear her over the wheels scraping the pavement, and kept walking. Then my dad started yelling.

"I don't care if you've been supplying them for a hundred years. Don't run a muddle on me. I can tell a light order when I see it." He paused, allowing the other person, who was now talking even more quickly, to say something. "Look. This isn't up for debate, okay?"

Mrs. Dobson-Wade looked at my dad, clearly alarmed at his tone. "It's a work call," I explained, as behind her, Dave came back up the driveway. When he saw me talking to his mom, he slowed his steps, then stopped entirely.

"Who am I?" my dad said was saying as Dave Wade and I, strangers but not, just stared at each other over his mother's small, bony shoulder. "I'm the new boss at Luna Blu. And you are my former produce purveyor. Goodbye."

He hung up, then slammed his phone down for emphasis on the table, the sound making me jump. Only then did he look up and see me and Dave's mom at the door.

"This is Mrs. Dobson-Wade," I said, keeping my own voice calm, as if to prove we weren't both total maniacs. "She made us some brownies."

"Oh." He wiped his hands together, then came over. "That's . . . Thank you."

"You're very welcome!" There was an awkward beat, with no one talking, before she said, "I was just telling your daughter that we've lived here for over twenty years, so if you need any information on the neighborhood, or schools, just let us know."

"I'll do that," my dad said. "Although this one's already gotten herself settled in pretty well, from what I can tell."

"You're at Jackson?" Mrs. Dobson-Wade asked me. I nodded. "It's a fine public school. But there are other options if you wanted to explore them, in the private sector. Exemplary ones, actually."

"You don't say," my dad replied.

"Our son was at one of them, Kiffney-Brown, until last year. He decided to transfer, not that we were very happy about it." She sighed, shaking her head. "You know teenagers. So difficult when they decide they have a mind of their own."

I felt my dad look at me, but this time I kept my gaze straight ahead. I wasn't about to field this one. "Well," he said finally. "I suppose . . . that is true, sometimes."

Mrs. Dobson-Wade smiled, as if he'd offered more agreement than he had. "Did I hear you say you're the new chef at Luna Blu?"

"More like the interim," my dad said.

"Oh, we love Luna Blu," she told him. "The rolls are amazing!"

My dad smiled. "Well," he said, "next time you come in, ask for me. I'll make sure you're taken care of. I'm Gus."

"Anne," she said. She glanced behind her, seeing Dave, who was just standing there still looking at me, having not come any closer. "My husband, Brian, will be along in a moment, and that's my son, David. David, this is Gus and—"

Everyone looked at me. "Mclean," I said.

Dave raised a hand in a wave, friendly, but still kept his distance. I thought of what Heather and Riley had told me: boy genius, smoothie maker, cellar dweller. Right now, I thought, he didn't look like any of the people they'd described, which was unsettling in a way that was entirely too familiar.

The side door banged again, and Mr. Wade finally came out. He was tall and reedy, with a beard, and carried a messenger bag, which he strapped across himself as he came down the stairs. In his other hand was a bike helmet covered in reflector stickers.

"Brian!" Mrs. Wade called out. "Say hello to our new neighbors."

Mr. Wade came over cheerfully, a smile on his face, and joined our little confab on the deck. Standing together, he and Anne looked like a matched set of rumpled academics in their thick glasses, he with his helmet, she with her NPR tote bag over one shoulder. "Nice to meet you," he said, shaking my hand and then my dad's. "Welcome to the burg."

"Thanks," my dad said.

"Gus is the interim chef at Luna Blu," Anne informed him.

"Oh, we love Luna Blu!" Brian said. "Those rolls! They're the perfect dinner on a cold night."

I bit my lip, making a point of not looking at my dad as we all just stood there, smiling at each other. Meanwhile, behind them, Dave gave me a look that was hard to read—almost apologetic—and walked back to the house, going inside. The sound of the door swinging shut behind him was like a whistle being blown to end a huddle. With it, we all broke.

"I've got to run to the lab," Dave's mom said, stepping back from the door. Brian smiled, following her as he put on his helmet. "Please let us know if we can be of any help as you get settled."

"We'll do that," my dad said. "Thanks again for the brownies."

They waved, we waved. Then we stood there, silent, watching them as they went down the deck stairs, back to their driveway. Under the basketball goal, they stopped, and Brian leaned down so Anne could give him a peck on the cheek. Then she went to her car, and he to his bike, which was chained to their front deck. He wheeled it down the driveway, she backed out, and at the road, he went left, she right.

"Well," my dad said after a moment. "They sure do like those rolls, huh?"

"No kidding." I lifted up the pan she'd given me, taking a hesitant whiff. "Can brownies actually be sugar-, gluten-, and nut-free and still be good?"

"Let's find out," he said, lifting the Saran Wrap covering

it. He reached in, took one, and stuck the entire thing in his mouth, devouring it. After chewing for what seemed like a long time, he finally swallowed. "Nope."

Point taken. I put the pan down. "Everything okay on the produce front? It sounded kind of intense."

"That guy is an idiot," my dad grumbled, getting up to slide his breakfast plate into the sink. "Not to mention a thief. Maybe now I'll get some decent vegetables. Shoot, that reminds me, I set up a meeting at the farmers' market in ten minutes. You going to be okay here?"

"Yeah," I said. "Absolutely."

As he picked up his phone and left the room, I looked back at Dave's house. His parents seemed nice enough, hardly the strict Gulag types Heather had described. But then again, as Riley had said, no one was really normal, and you couldn't tell a thing from the outside anyway. One thing, however, was clear: there was no escaping Mclean now. I was her, I was here, and it looked like we'd be sticking around. Nothing left to do but bail, and rise.

Four

✳ ❀ ✳

"Hello?"

"It's me," my mother said. "Don't hang up."

I *knew* it had been a bad idea to answer without looking at the caller ID. Normally, I was vigilant about such things, but in the crush of the pre-homeroom main hallway, I'd let down my guard.

"Mom, I can't talk right now," I said, as someone with a huge backpack bumped me sideways from behind.

"You always say that, no matter what time I call," she replied. "Surely you can spare a moment or two."

"I'm at school," I said. "My next class starts in five minutes."

"Then give me four." I rolled my eyes, annoyed, and as if she could see this, she added, "Please, Mclean. I miss you."

And there it was, the tiniest twinge, like that tickle in your throat right before the tears begin. It was amazing to me that she could always find my tender spot, the one I was never even able to pinpoint myself. It was like she'd had it built into me somehow, the way scientists in sci-fi movies always put a secret button to deactivate the robot if it goes crazy and turns on them. Because you just never know.

"Mom," I said, ducking out of the main hall and down a side alcove, where I was pretty sure my locker was supposed to be, "I told you. I just need a little time."

"It's been two weeks!" she protested. "How long are you planning to stay upset with me?"

"I'm not planning anything. I just . . ." I sighed, so sick of trying to explain why I needed space from her. It was constantly under negotiation, her trying to yank me closer, me straining to pull back. Even with hundreds of miles between us I still felt under her thumb. "I need a break."

"From me," she said, clarifying.

"From all this. I'm in a new place, and new school. . . ."

"Only because you want to be," she reminded me. "If it was up to me, you'd still be here, enjoying all the perks of your senior year with the friends you've known forever."

"Yes," I said, "but it's not up to you."

She exhaled loudly, the sound like a wave breaking into my ear. This was the bottom line, the main issue, the thing we always came back to, no matter how much circling we did before or after. My mother wanted control over me and I wouldn't give it to her. It made her crazy, so she in turn made me crazy. And repeat.

It reminded me of when I was little, and my grandparents had a cat named Louis Armstrong. My parents were too busy with the restaurant to deal with pets, and as a result I was crazy for any animal I could get my hands on. Louis, however, was old and mean and had absolutely no interest in children, diving under the couch the minute he heard me coming. Undaunted, I'd sit on the carpet under the side table and try to get him to emerge: calling his name, offering treats, once even reaching under and attempting to pull him out, only to receive full-arm scratches in return.

After that, I pretty much gave up, electing to spending my time at my grandparents' watching TV on their old set, which got only three channels. Then, one day, the weirdest thing happened. I was sitting there, watching some cloudy, old movie while the adults talked in the next room, and I felt something brush against my leg. Looking down, I was shocked to see Louis Armstrong, elusive no more, passing by and giving me a little flick of his tail. Sure, it wasn't the all-out adoration I'd craved. But it was something. And I never would have gotten it—or the slow build to almost-affection that followed in the next few months—if I hadn't just left him alone.

I had tried to explain this to my mother. I'd even referred to the cat. But she just didn't get it, or chose not to. Forget cats and couches. I was her daughter, I belonged to her. I was supposed to cooperate.

This latest standoff, only a couple of weeks old, had a familiar impetus. She'd called a day or two before we'd left Westcott, as I was busy packing things up. I made the mistake of telling her this, and she went ballistic.

"Again?" she demanded. "What is your father thinking? How can he possibly think this is good for you?"

"Mom, it's a consulting job," I told her for the umpteenth time. "The work doesn't come to you. You go to the work."

"*He* goes to the work," she replied. "You should be here, in the same school, until you graduate. It's ludicrous that we're allowing you do to otherwise."

"It's my choice," I said, repeating what I considered my mantra.

"You're a teenager," she told me. "I'm sorry, Mclean, but by definition, you don't know how to make the right choices!"

"But if I stayed with you," I said, trying to keep my voice level, "*that* would be the right choice?"

"Yes!" Then, realizing my point, she exhaled, annoyed. "Honey, anyone would tell you that living in a stable home with two responsible parents and a well-established support system is infinitely better than—"

"Mom," I said. She kept talking, so I repeated, louder, "*Mom.*"

Finally, silence. Then she said, "I just don't understand why you want to hurt me like this."

It's not about you, I thought, but then she was crying, which always took the fight out of me.

If we'd just left it at that, it probably would have blown over. Instead, though, she'd gone back to her lawyer, who in turn called my dad making all kinds of subtle threats about "filing paperwork" and "revisiting our current agreement in light of recent events." In the end, nothing happened, but the whole thing made me decide to cut her off until I felt calm enough to talk. And I didn't, not yet.

This entire issue, our issue, had been further exacerbated for the last few months by my college applications. When I'd just started junior year, she'd sent me a package in Petree via FedEx containing a stack of books with chapters with titles like "Hot Ink: How to Write a Power Essay"; "The Wow Factor: Reaching Admissions Officers"; "Play Your Strengths: Presenting Yourself in the Best Possible Light." It wasn't until I called to thank her—we were on decent terms at the time—that I began to understand her sudden, passionate interest in my collegiate future.

"Well, I figured you could use it," she said. I could hear one of the twins near the receiver, fussing. "Defriese early admission is coming up fast."

"Early admission?" I said.

"I've been doing some reading, and I really think it's the way to go," she continued. "That way your application is in their pool for the longest possible time, even if you don't get in the first group accepted."

"Um," I said, shutting the book slowly, "actually, I haven't really decided where I want to apply yet."

"Oh, I know you haven't made any final choices. But of course Defriese will be on the list." She shifted whatever baby she was holding, the crying fading out. "You could live at home, even, and not have to deal with the dorms."

I froze, there in my Petree kitchen, looking at the stainless-steel fridge. "Mom," I said slowly. "I don't think I want to do that."

"Well, how can you know?" she asked, her voice rising. "It's only the beginning of your junior year."

"Then why are you sending me these books?"

"Because I wanted to help you!" She sniffled. "And I don't see why you wouldn't want to come back here and live with me and Peter and the kids."

"I'm not making my college decision based on what you want, Mom," I said slowly.

"Of course not!" she said. Now she was crying. "When do you ever care what I want?"

In the end, I stuck the books under my bed and tried to forget about the entire thing. When the actual time came to think about school, though, I dug them back out and scanned the tips, which were actually pretty helpful. In the end, I did apply to Defriese, although not early admission, and only as a peace offering. I had no intention of going, unless I got in nowhere else. The last resort of last resorts.

"Mom," I said now as I peered down the row of nearby lockers, finally locating number 1899. "I really need to get ready for first period."

"It's only been two minutes."

I didn't say anything. What can you say to that?

"What I mean," she said, quickly regrouping, "is that I haven't even had a chance to talk to you about the beach. That's the whole reason I called. I have really exciting news!"

"What?"

She sighed. Yet again, I was not saying my lines with enough punch. "Well," she began, ignoring my lack of enthusiasm, "we just got word that the remodel has passed all its inspections. The decorator has the painters in as we speak. And you know what that means."

I waited.

"You can finally come down with us!" Clearly, this was the Big Finish. "I mean, I know how much you love the beach, and we have such great memories of going there together. I can't believe Peter and I have had this house for two years and you've never even seen it! We're planning to go check it out next weekend, and then try to get down as often as we can. Now, I've been looking at your school calendar, and I noticed—"

"Mom," I said, cutting her off mid-breath. "I really have to go to class."

Silence. Then, "Fine. But will you *promise* to call me later? I really want to talk to you about this."

No, I thought. Out loud I said, "I'll do my best. I've got to go now."

"I love you!" she said, scrambling to get in these last three words while she could. "It's going to be fabulous! Just like—"

Click.

I reached up, grabbing the handle of my locker too hard and yanking it. It flew open with a blur of pink, barely missing clocking me in the face. When I grabbed the door, steadying it, I saw there was a mirror still attached inside, bright raspberry colored and decorated with pink feathers. The word *SEXXY* was written across the bottom of the frame. I was staring at my face in it, speechless, when Riley popped up behind me.

"Already decorating?" she said, eyeing the feathers.

"It's not mine," I told her, lacking the energy after my mother to explain further.

"Sure it isn't." She smiled, her face friendly as I opened my bag, stowing a couple of textbooks on one of the empty shelves. "Hey, I need to ask you something."

I had to admit I was surprised. We'd met just twice, and the second time only because of Heather's intervention, or act of charity, whatever you wanted to call it. I shut the locker, feathers blurring past again, and started walking toward my homeroom. "Okay."

Riley tucked a piece of hair behind her ear—I noticed her tattoo again, that simple circle—then fell into step beside me. The halls were still packed with people and noise, all that energy of a day that hasn't quite started yet.

"It's about Dave," Riley said as we sidestepped two girls carrying guitar cases. "Was he on the bus this morning?"

"The bus?"

"To school," she said. "You guys take the same one, right?"

"I take the city bus," I told her.

"Oh, right. Okay."

This seemed like it should be the end of our conversation: question asked, question answered. But she still kept walking with me, even though my Spanish class was the only one on the dead-end hallway we were on. "I did see him, though. His mom brought over some brownies."

"Oh, boy." She raised her eyebrows. "Let me guess: no nuts, no gluten, no sugar, and no taste."

"Pretty much," I replied. "How'd you know?"

She shrugged. "Experience. Dave's house is not the place you want to go looking for a snack. Unless you've got a real yen for wheat germ and veggie jerky."

"Veggie jerky?"

"Dried vegetables," she explained.

I raised my eyebrows.

"Yep. It tastes just like it sounds."

"Poor Dave," I said.

"I think that's why he likes working at Frazier Bakery so much," she told me as a guy wearing headphones bumped me from the side. "The sugar and chemicals abound there, and he's got a lifetime of making up to do."

We were at my classroom now. Inside the open door, I could hear Señor Mitchell greeting people in his cheerful immersion-or-else Spanish. "His parents seemed nice, actually. I was kind of surprised."

"Surprised?" she said. "Why?"

"I don't know." I shifted my bag to my other shoulder. "You and Heather made them sound super-strict."

"Oh, right," she said, nodding. "Well, the truth is, Dave's changed a lot since he transferred here. I think it's a good thing, because he's, like, a real person now. But it freaks his folks out. I think they liked it better when he was just like them, completely under their control."

"Yeah. I get that." I was thinking of my mother as I said this, the pleading, desperate tone of her final words before I'd hung up on her. Stop trying, I wanted to tell her, and make her understand. Stop forcing it and I just might come to you. I just might. "But you can't help it if you change, I guess. It just happens."

"Yeah, it does." She smiled. "Hey, I'll see you later, okay?"

I nodded, and she turned around, stuffing her hands in her

jacket pockets and starting back down the hallway. I thought of her sitting on that bench a few days earlier, leaning forward to listen as Dave stood with his parents and the administrators. I couldn't even imagine anymore what that would be like, to have so much—or anything at all—invested in a friendship. It was hard enough just taking care of myself.

The bell rang, and Señor Mitchell turned, seeing me. "*Hola*, Mclean!" he said, beckoning me toward him, like we hadn't just met, and only the day before. Odd how it was so easy for a stranger to assume such familiarity. Especially when those who were supposed to know you best often didn't, not at all.

× × ×

My phone, zipped away in my backpack, buzzed twice during Spanish. When I scrolled through the screen on my way to second period, I saw only one name, two times: HAMILTON, PETER. I stuffed it back in, deeper this time, picturing my mother watching the clock as she wondered how, exactly, I defined *later*. Minutes? Hours? Maybe she was calling to ask me. I wouldn't be surprised.

I couldn't believe she was bringing up the beach again. Ever since Peter had bought her that house for a wedding gift—because houses *are* standard gifts, right?—she'd been pushing me to come there for a visit. Before now, it was always too difficult, involving at least one flight and possibly two, far enough away from everything that I could argue my way out of any invitation. Now, though, not only was I only four hours from Colby, the town where the house was, but also right smack on the route that took them there. Lucky me.

I had nothing against the beach. In fact, there was a time

when I loved it more than just about anything. Because my dad was always at the restaurant, real family vacations were a rarity: it was like disaster could sense every time he ventured outside of city limits, and struck accordingly. But my mom had grown up at the coast, in South Carolina, and she loved nothing more than to take off on impulse and just drive east until she saw the ocean. It didn't matter if it was the hottest day in July or the dead of February. I'd come home from school, or wake up on a Saturday morning, and she'd have that look on her face.

"Road trip?" she'd ask, but she knew I wouldn't say no. The car would already be packed with our pillows, a cooler, warm clothes in winter, beach chairs in summer. We never wanted to spend the money for the nice hotels, even off-season, which was how we'd found the Poseidon, a ramshackle, 1960s-era motel in North Reddemane, a tiny town just down from Colby. The pool was lined with cracks, the rooms smelled *just* enough like mildew to notice, and everything from the taped-up bell at the front desk to the bedspreads had seen a million visitors and much better days. But the views were incredible, the screen doors of each room opening pretty much right into the sand, and it was walking distance to the other two businesses in town, which happened to sell everything we needed. After we stayed there once, we never went anywhere else.

We spent our days either walking on the beach or sunbathing, with breaks for food at Shrimpboats, which, as the only restaurant in North Reddemane, served breakfast, lunch, and dinner. Beside Shrimpboats, there was Gert's Surfshop, a clapboard shack and gas station that sold bait, cheap souvenirs, and basic groceries. My mom and I, however, were partial to the handmade rope bracelets, decorated with seashells and weird-shaped beads, with *GS* written in Sharpie marker on the backside. We had no idea who made them, only that they were always on display by the front register and we seemed to be the only ones who ever purchased them, something we did on every trip down. My mom called them Gerts, and there was a time when my wrist never sported fewer than two or three of them, in various stages of wear and tear.

This was my mother as I liked to remember her, hair in a sloppy ponytail, wearing cheap sunglasses and smelling of sunscreen and salt. She read terrible romance novels during the day (her guiltiest of pleasures), and at night, sat with me on the rickety chairs outside our room and pointed out constellations. We ate fried shrimp, watched bad TV, and took long walks, whether it was bitter cold or the perfect summer day. At the end of the weekend, we'd drive back as late as we could, arriving home to find the house pretty much just as we'd left it, my dad having been there only to sleep, shower, and grab a bite to eat now and then. I don't remember him ever being with us at the Poseidon, and that was okay. It was our thing.

Now, though, like everything else was since the divorce, the beach would be different. And the truth was, those weekends, spontaneous and shabby, were some of the best times I'd had with my mom before everything fell apart. I had enough that was separated into distinct Before and Afters: my home, my name, even the way I looked. I didn't want all my memories remade, redone, remodeled, like her fancy beach house. I liked them as they were.

My mom, though, clearly had other ideas: by lunch, I had four messages. I got a cheap and soggy grilled cheese and went out to the wall, taking a bite before playing them back.

"Honey, it's me. Just wondering when you might have a break between classes. I really want to talk to you about the house! Call me back."

Beep.

"Mclean, it's me. I'm going to take the kids to the grocery store, so when you call try me on my cell. If I don't pick up, it just means I'm in that dead spot just before town, so leave a message, and I'll call you back just as soon as I get it. Can't wait to make plans! I love you!"

Beep.

"Mclean? Um, hi. This is Opal, from the restaurant? I'm here with your dad. . . . He's had a little accident." A pause, at the worst possible time. I heard an intercom, some buzzing. "He's okay, but we're at the hospital, and he says his insurance card is at the house, and you'd know where it was. Can you call me back at this number when you get this?"

Beep.

"Hi, honey, me again. I'm back from the grocery, saw you didn't call yet, so when you do, just try the home—"

I fumbled with the phone, hitting the END button once, twice, trying to clear the screen so I could call out. My heart was suddenly racing, those words filling my head: *accident, hospital*. And behind them, harder to see: *okay. Okay. Okay.*

My phone took forever to dial, each beep seeming like an eternity as I looked around the full courtyard in front of me, seeing nothing. Finally, an answer.

"Hello?"

"Opal," I said. "It's Mclean. I just got your message, is my dad okay? What happened? When did he—"

"Whoa, whoa," she said. "Take a breath. Mclean? It's all right. He's just fine. Here."

Now I could hear that I was breathing hard, almost panting. The sound, primal, filled the phone for the next few seconds and then, like a dream, my dad was suddenly there.

"I told her not to call you," he said. He sounded bored, like he was waiting in line at the post office. "I knew you'd totally freak."

"I am not freaking," I told him, although we both knew I was. I took a breath as instructed, then said, "What happened?"

"Just a little knife slip."

"Really?" I was surprised.

"Not mine," he said, sounding offended. "It was one of the prep guys. I was teaching a little fillet class . . . things got out of hand."

My heart was finally starting to beat normally again as I said, "How out of hand?"

"Just a few stitches," he replied. "And a puncture of sorts."

"I'm surprised you even went to the hospital," I said, which was the truth. My dad's hands were covered with scars from various accidents and burns, and usually, unless he'd hit a vein or something, he'd wait until after work to deal with it, if he did anything at all.

"It was not my idea," he grumbled. "Trust me."

"You have to go to the hospital when you cut open your hand!" I heard Opal say in the background. "It is company policy. Not to mention common sense."

"Anyway," my dad said, ignoring this, "the upshot is that I need my insurance card. Which I think is at the house . . ."

"It is," I said. "I'll get it."

"But you're in school. I'll just send Leo."

I thought of Leo, big and gangly, banging around in the file box where I kept our important papers. "No," I said. "I'd better do it. Look, I'll be there soon."

"Wait," he said just as I was about to hang up. "Don't you need a ride?"

That, I hadn't thought about. I was about to tell him this when I happened to look across the courtyard to a single bench by the entrance to the gym. There a girl sat, a green floral purse beside her, wearing a green raincoat with matching green earmuffs, sipping a Diet Coke through a straw.

"I think I'm covered," I told him, getting to my feet and picking up my bag. "I'll be there soon."

×　×　×

"This one time," Deb said as she edged her small, tidy car into the right-turn lane, "my mother spilled an entire cup of boiling water on her stomach. You know, like the kind you get at a coffee shop, to make tea with, superhot? We had to take her to the emergency room."

I nodded, forcing a smile. "Really."

"But she was fine!" she added quickly, glancing at me. "Totally fine. Didn't even scar, although we were both sure she would."

"Wow," I said.

"I know!" She shook her head, slowly accelerating as signs for the hospital began to appear. "Modern medicine. It's amazing."

I peered ahead, taking in the big red EMERGENCY with an arrow beneath as it appeared. Despite my dad's assurances, I was strangely nervous, my stomach tight ever since we'd hung up. Maybe Deb had picked up on this, and it was why she'd pretty much talked nonstop since I'd approached her and asked for a ride. I'd barely had time to explain the situation before she had launched into a dozen stories to illustrate the point that Things Happened, But People Were Okay in the End.

"It's just a knife cut," I said for about the tenth time. I wasn't sure if this reassurance was for me or her. "He gets them all the time. It's part of the job."

"I can't believe your dad is a chef!" she said, easing into the turn lane. "That is so exciting. I hear Luna Blu is amazing."

"You've never been there?"

She shook her head. "We don't eat out much."

"Oh." I wasn't sure what to say to that. "Well, I'll have to take you sometime. To thank you for the ride."

"Really?" She seemed so surprised I had a twinge of pity, although I wasn't sure why. "God, that would be so great. But you totally don't have to. I'm just happy I could help out."

As we headed up the road to the emergency room entrance, I saw a couple of doctors pass by, both in scrubs. Off to the left, a man in a wheelchair with an oxygen mask was sitting in the sunshine. None of this helped my nervousness, so I distracted myself by saying, "Yeah, but it must get kind of old, right? Being a student ambassador, and everyone always asking for something."

Deb leaned farther over the steering wheel, peering at the parking options. She was so precise and responsible, in her perfect green headband, her neat car with a memo pad stuck to the dash, a pen clipped to its side. She seemed older than she was, older than she should be. "Not really," she said, turning into a nearby lot.

"No?"

She shook her head. "You're actually the first person who's asked me for anything."

"I am?" I didn't mean to sound so surprised, and could tell immediately by her reaction—a slight flush, a nervous swallow—that it didn't do much for her confidence. Quickly, I added, "I mean, I'm glad. Makes me memorable, I guess."

Deb cut the engine, then turned to look at me. Her expression was clearly grateful, happy. What must it be like to be so genuine, so fragile, your entire world of thoughts so easy to read on your face? I couldn't even imagine. "Well, that's nice to hear! I hadn't even thought about it that way!"

There was a sudden blast of siren from behind us, and an ambulance came racing up to the emergency room entrance. *He's fine,* I told myself, but even so my heart jumped.

"Come on," Deb said, pushing open her door and reaching

into the backseat for her purse. "You'll feel better once you see him."

As we walked across the lot, she reached into her bag, taking out a pack of gum and offering it to me. I shook my head, and she put it back, not taking a piece herself. I wondered if she even chewed gum, or just carried it as a courtesy. I was pretty sure I knew the answer.

Earlier, when we'd stopped by my house, it was no surprise that she'd been polite and complimentary. "What a lovely place," she said, standing in our sparsely furnished living room. "That quilt is gorgeous."

I looked over at the sofa. Tossed over one arm was one of my mom's quilts, made way back when she'd first taken up the hobby. The truth was, she was really good at it, and could do all kinds of intricate patterns. At our old house, we'd had tons of them, both as décor and to use when it was chilly. When we left I'd boxed most of them up with the rest of our stuff in storage, only to have my mom give me a new one as I stood in Peter's driveway saying goodbye.

"I've been working on it nonstop," she said as she pressed it into my hands. Her eyes were red: she'd been crying all morning.

I took it, looking down at the neatly stitched squares. The fabric was pink and yellow and blue and varied: denim, corduroy, cotton. "This is really nice."

"It's baby clothes," she told me. "So you have something to remember me by."

I'd taken it, and thanked her. Then I'd put it in a box in the U-Haul, where it had basically stayed until I brought some stuff back to her house during one summer break and left it in my closet. I knew I should have kept it, but like so much else with my mom it just felt so loaded. Like under it, I'd suffocate.

"Thanks," I'd said to Deb, back at the house. "We just moved in, so things are still kind of all over the place."

"I'd love to live here," she said. "This is such a great neighborhood."

"Is it?" I asked, digging around in the file box for my dad's insurance card.

"Oh, sure. It's in the historical district." She walked over to the doorway, examining the molding. "My mom and I looked at a house for sale on this street a couple of weeks ago."

"Really? Are you thinking about moving?"

"Oh, no," she said. She was quiet for a moment. Then she said, "We just . . . Sometimes for fun, on the weekends, we go to open houses and pretend we're buying. We decide where we'd put everything, and what we'd do to the yard. . . ." She trailed off, looking embarrassed. "I know it sounds silly."

"Not really." I found the card inside a book of stamps, and slid it into my pocket. "I do stuff like that, too, sometimes."

"You do? Like what?"

Now I was stuck. I swallowed, then said, "You know. Like, when I start a new school I always kind of change myself a little bit. Pretend I'm someone different than I was in the last place."

She just looked at me, and I wondered what on earth it was about her that made me be so honest. Like she was sick with truth, and really contagious. "Really," she said finally. "I bet that's hard, though."

"Hard?" I said, walking back to the door and pushing it open for her.

She walked out, adjusting her purse over her shoulder as I locked the door. "I mean, just having to change each time. It's like starting over. I'd kind of, I don't know. . . ."

I glanced over at Dave Wade's, thinking of Riley and her asking about him. There were no cars in the driveway, no signs of life. Wherever he was, he wasn't at home.

". . . miss who I was before," Deb finished. "Or something."

Then I'd said nothing: I didn't know how to respond to this. Instead, I just followed her to the car, and we'd come here. Now, though, as we walked up to the emergency room sliding doors, I glanced at her again, envying her confidence, even in the face of what I knew others thought about her. Maybe it was easier for some than others, though, changing. I hardly knew her at all, but I already couldn't imagine her being any other Deb than this one.

Inside the hospital, we were hit with that immediate hospital mix of disinfectant and uneasiness. I gave my dad's name to a squat man behind a glass window, who typed a few things on his computer before sliding a piece of paper across to me that read A1196. The four digits made me think back to that morning, searching for my locker, when my biggest concern had been getting my mom off the phone and out of my hair.

"I think it's this way," Deb said, her voice calmer than I felt as she led us down a hall, taking a right. Somehow, she just seemed to *know* when I needed her to take the lead, like my fear was that palpable.

There were not rooms but cubicles with curtains, some

open, some closed. As we passed by, I tried not to look but still caught glimpses: a man lying in a bed in his undershirt, hand over his eyes, a woman in a hospital gown, mouth open, asleep.

"A1194," Deb was saying. "A1195 . . . Here! This is it."

The curtain was closed, and for a moment we stood there as I wondered how you were supposed to knock or even know you had the right place. Then, though, I heard something.

"Seriously. You have got to let the roll thing go. It's done."

There was a loud sigh. "Okay, I understand the pickles have been well accepted, but that doesn't mean . . ."

I eased the curtain open, and there they were: my dad, seated on the bed, his hand and wrist wrapped in bandages and gauze, and Opal in a nearby chair, legs crossed, looking irritated.

"There she is," my dad said. He smiled at me, which was about the most reassuring thing I'd seen, well, ever. "How's it going?"

"Forget about me," I replied, walking over to him. "How are you?"

"Completely fine," he said easily, patting the bed beside him. I sat down, and as he slid his good arm over my shoulders, I felt a lump rise in my throat. Which was ridiculous, as it was obvious this was true, he was okay. "It's just a flesh wound."

I smiled, swallowing, and glanced at Opal. She was watching me, her face kind, so kind I had to look away. "This is Deb," I said, nodding to where she stood at the curtain's opening, purse over her shoulder. "She gave me . . . She's my friend."

Hearing this, Deb smiled, clearly pleased. Then she took a step forward, sticking out her hand. "Hi," she said. "It's so nice to meet you! I'm very sorry about your accident. Mclean was so worried!"

My dad raised his eyebrows, glancing at me, and I felt myself flush.

"That's probably because it was me that called," Opal said. "I'm not exactly known for my poise in emergencies."

"This was not an emergency," my dad said, squeezing my shoulder again. I let myself lean into him, breathing in his familiar smell—aftershave, laundry detergent, a hint of grill smoke. "If it had been up to me, I would have just wrapped it and kept cutting."

"Oh, no!" Deb said, aghast. "You have to get medical attention when you cut yourself. I mean, what about staph infections?"

"See?" Opal pointed at Deb, vindicated. "Staph infections!"

"Knock knock," came a voice from outside the curtain. A moment later, a plump nurse with red hair, wearing a smock decorated with hearts, came in. She looked at my dad, then down at the chart in her hand. "Well, Mr. Sweet. Just need your card and a little paperwork and you'll be rid of us."

"Wonderful," my dad said, taking the clipboard as she offered it to him.

"Oh, now, don't say that! You'll hurt my feelings!" the nurse said, her voice too loud as she smiled widely at him. Across the room, Opal raised her eyebrows. I, however, was not surprised in the least. I had long ago grown used to the effect my father had on females. Maybe it was his longish hair, or those blue eyes, or the way he dressed or carried himself, but it seemed like wherever we went, women were drawn to him like magnets. And the less he reciprocated, the more they did it. It was so weird.

I handed the nurse my dad's card, then steadied the clipboard as he uncapped a pen with his good hand, scanning the papers in front of him. As he signed, I glanced at the nurse, who beamed at me. "Aren't you sweet, taking care of your daddy. Is your mom out of town?"

She'd clearly already noticed no ring, but was just double-checking: this was also a trick I'd seen before, performed by waitresses and hotel clerks, even one of my teachers. So obvious.

"Excuse me," Opal said suddenly, before I could come up with a response, "but we'll need to be sure that these charges are sent to our company. Can you help me with that, or do I need to talk to someone else?"

The nurse glanced at her, as if just now noticing she was there, even though Opal—in faded jeans, red cowboy boots, and a bright orange sweater—was hard to miss. "I can direct you to the proper department for handling that," she said coolly.

"Thanks so much," Opal replied, equally polite.

Deb, just inside the curtain, looked at Opal, then the nurse, then back at Opal again. But my dad was oblivious as always as he handed back the clipboard, hopping down off the bed. "All right," he said. "Let's blow this taco stand."

"Mr. Sweet!" the nurse said. "We still have a few more forms to fill out. You'll need to—"

"What I need," my dad replied, grabbing his coat from where it was lying across the pillow, "is to get back to my kitchen before the whole place collapses. Like Opal said, forward the bill to EAT INC. You've got the info, right?"

Opal nodded, pulling a card out of the bag at her feet. "Sure do."

"Perfect. Then pass it on, and let's go." Opal handed the card to the nurse, who looked less than enthused to be taking it. Again, my dad didn't notice as he shrugged on his coat, then looked at me. "You need to go back to school, correct?"

I glanced at my watch. "By the time I get there, it'll practically be time for final bell."

He sighed, clearly not happy about this. "Home, then. We'll drop you on the way back to the restaurant."

"Oh, I can drive her," Deb offered. When my dad glanced at her, she smiled, as if she might need his approval to actually do this. "I mean, it's no problem at all."

"Great. Let's go," he said, pushing the curtain aside. He was out and down the hallway before any of us even got close to following.

Everyone looked at me, but I just shrugged. This was my dad as dictator, the side of his personality that came out during the busiest rushes and whenever we were moving. He wasn't always a bossy person, but under certain circumstances he behaved like a general on the battlefield, whether he had willing troops or not.

The nurse tore off a couple of sheets of paper, handing one to Opal, who took it and headed out the way my dad had gone. The other she handed to me, along with my dad's card, seeming to take quite a while to complete the exchange.

"If your dad has any problems with that wound," she said as she finally let go of it, "my direct line is on the release notes. I'm Sandy."

"Right," I said. I could feel Deb's shock from behind me, like heat coming off of her. Sure enough, when I turned she was staring, openmouthed. "Thanks."

I walked out into the hallway, and she rushed out behind me, still aghast. "Oh my God!" she hissed as we passed by the man in the undershirt, who was now sitting up, a doctor leaning over him. "That was so inappropriate!"

"It happens," I replied, spotting my dad and Opal just outside the front entrance. "Mclean?" he called out, impatient. "Let's go."

Deb immediately picked up her pace, following orders like a good soldier. As I fell in behind her, I glanced down at the discharge papers, with Sandy's loopy script spelling out her name and number in red pen. It seemed like a correction, something marked right that was wrong, and I folded it over, stuffing it deep in my pocket as I stepped through the doors to leave this place, too, behind me.

Five

❃ ✾ ❃

The noise was oddly familiar, but at first I couldn't place it.

Thump. Thump. Thump. Clank.

I opened my eyes, blinked, and then looked at the slope in the ceiling, following it to the edge of the molding where it hit the window. Beyond that, there was only clear glass, some sky, and the dilapidated roof of the house where Dave had taken over the cellar. It was so big, though, that I wasn't sure it was a residence at all. More likely, I'd decided, it was a business, long shuttered: the windows were boarded up, weeds growing up all around it. I'd seen a FOR SALE sign that looked equally ancient on its other side when I was walking to the bus stop. Now, though, from this weird angle, I noticed something else: a few letters painted on the roof, once red, now faded to the lightest of pinks. I couldn't make them all out, but the first looked like it might be an *S*.

Thump. Thump. Swish.

I sat up, glancing out the window beside me. My dad's truck was already gone. It was only 9:00 a.m. after a blistering Friday rush he'd worked pretty much one-handed, but the farmers' market was on Saturday mornings, and he always liked to get there early to have the best pickings of what was on offer.

Thump. Thump. Laughter. And then a crash.

I felt the house shake slightly, and then everything was still again. I sat there for a moment, waiting for what, I had no idea, before finally sliding my feet onto the floor and grabbing my jeans from the nearby chair, where I'd tossed them late the night before. Outside, it was quiet now, my footsteps all I could hear as I made my way down the hallway.

As I first stepped into the kitchen, I thought I was still asleep and dreaming when I saw the basketball rolling toward me. Behind it, the door to the deck was open, cold air blowing in, and I just stood there and watched as the ball came closer, then closer still, slowing with each turn. *So weird,* I thought. I was sure I'd been awake, seen the truck gone, but—

"Whoops! Sorry about that."

I jumped, startled, then looked up to see a guy standing on the porch, just past the open doorway. He was about my age, with short, tight dreads springing up from his head in all directions, wearing jeans and a red long-sleeved T-shirt. His face was familiar, but I was still too asleep to figure out why.

I looked at the ball, then back at him. "What—"

"My comrade has a bit of an overenthusiastic throw," he said as he stepped inside, grabbing it from my feet. As he looked up at me, smiling apologetically, my memory sputtered up a flash of him on a TV screen, holding some papers. That was it: he was from the morning announcements at school.

"Which wouldn't be so bad, except his aim kind of sucks."

"Oh," I said. "Right. I just . . . I didn't know what was going on."

"Won't happen again," he assured me. Then he turned, lifting the ball with both hands over his head, and pitching it toward the driveway. "Incoming!"

There was a *thunk*, followed by a series of bounces, each one sounding more distant. A moment later, someone said, "What kind of a throw was that?"

"Dude, you didn't even try to catch it."

"Because it wasn't anywhere near me," his friend replied. "Were you *aiming* for the street?"

The guy glanced at me, then laughed, like I was in on this joke. "Sorry again," he said, and then he was jogging across the deck, out of sight.

I was standing there, still trying to process all this in my half-awake state, when I felt my phone buzz in my back pocket. *So that's where it was,* I thought, remembering how I'd been searching my room for it just before bed the night before. I pulled it out, glancing at the screen. As soon as I saw my mother's number, I realized that in the chaos of the previous day, I'd never called her back. Whoops.

I took a breath, then hit the TALK button. "Hi, Mom," I said. "I—"

"Mclean!" Bad sign: she was already shrieking. "I have been worried sick about you! You were supposed to call me back twenty-four hours ago. You *promised*! Now, I understand that we are currently having some issues—"

"Mom," I said.

"—but we're never going to be able to work through them if you don't respect me enough to—"

"*Mom,*" I repeated. "I'm sorry."

These two words, like a brick wall, stopped her. In my mind, I could just see all the other things that had been poised on her tongue, piling up like cars on the freeway. *Crash. Crash. Crash.*

"Well," she said finally. "Okay. I mean, I'm still upset. But thank you for saying that."

I glanced outside, the phone still at my ear, just in time to see the guy who'd chased down the ball take a shot at the goal. It went up and wide, banging off a nearby tree before bouncing back to the driveway, where Dave Wade, in jeans and an unzipped blue rain jacket, scooped it up in his arms. He shook his head at something his friend was saying, then took a jump shot. I was watching his face, not the backboard, as it clanged off the rim. He didn't look surprised.

"I do have to tell you, though," my mother said now, over the still-tentative silence between us, "I was very hurt you never called me. I don't think you realize, Mclean, how hard it is to always be reaching out to you, and to continually be rebuffed."

Dave's friend went up for a layup, stumbled, and sent the ball into the backyard. "I didn't mean to not call," I told my mom, watching as he jogged after it. "But Dad got hurt, and I had leave school to go to the hospital."

"*What?*" she gasped. "Oh my God! What happened? Is he all right? Are you all right?"

I sighed, holding the phone away from my ear. "He's fine," I told her. "Just needed some stitches."

"Then why did you have to go to the hospital?"

"He didn't know where his insurance card was," I replied. "So . . ."

Before I could finish this thought, though, I heard her exhale, a long, hissing noise like a tire losing air, and I pictured whatever truce we might have had deflating right along with it.

"You had to leave school because your father misplaced his card?" I knew better than to answer this, as it was not an actual question. "Honestly! You are not his mother, you're his daughter. He should be keeping up with *your* documents, not the other way around."

"It was fine, okay?" I replied. "Everything's fine."

She sniffled, then was quiet for a second before saying, "I was *so* excited yesterday about having you come down to the beach with us. As soon as I heard the house was ready, all I could think of was you."

"Mom," I said.

"But then even *that* has to be so complicated," she continued. "I mean, you didn't even want to hear about it, and that used to be something you loved so much. It makes me incredibly sad that instead of having a normal life—"

"Mom."

"—your father is dragging you from one place to another, and you're having to take care of him. Honestly, I can't for the life of me understand why you don't . . ."

There was another *bang* from behind me and I spun around just as the door was knocked open, the basketball again soaring through it. It hit the linoleum and bounced, right at me, and as I grabbed it, the phone between my ear and shoulder, I was suddenly infuriated. My mother was still talking—God, she was *always talking*—as I stomped to the open door and out onto the deck.

"Sorry!" Dave's friend yelled when he saw me. "That was my—"

But I wasn't listening as, instead, I took every bit of the anger and stress of the last few minutes and days put it behind the ball, throwing it overhead at the basket as hard as I could. It went flying, hitting the backboard and banging through the netless hoop at full speed before shooting back out and nailing Dave Wade squarely on the forehead. And just like that, he was down.

"Oh, shit," I said as he crumpled to the pavement. "Mom, I have to go."

I tossed my phone on a deck chair, then ran down the steps to the driveway. Dave was lying in the driveway, stunned, while his friend stood a few feet away staring at me, wide-eyed. The ball had rolled into the street, stopping by a garbage can.

"Holy crap," the friend said. "What kind of shot was *that*?"

"Are you okay?" I asked Dave, dropping to my knees beside him. "I'm so sorry. I was just—"

Dave was blinking, looking up at the sky. "Wow," he said slowly, then slid his gaze over to meet mine. "You are *much* better than us at this game."

I wasn't sure how to respond to this. I opened my mouth to try, or at least to apologize, but nothing came. Instead, we just stared at each other, and I thought of a few nights earlier, sitting on those hard wooden stairs, the sky above us. Strange meetings, above and below ground, like crazy collisions, re-fracting then attracting again.

"Dude, that was incredible," his friend said, shaking me loose from this trance. "You went down like a mighty oak, felled in the forest!"

I sat back on my heels as Dave pushed himself slowly up on his elbows. Then he shook his head hard, like they do in car-toons when they're trying to unscramble their brains. It would have been funny, maybe, if I hadn't been the one responsible for the damage in the first place. "I really didn't mean to—" I finally managed.

"It's okay." He did another head shake, then got to his feet. "No permanent damage."

"*That's* a relief," said his friend, who had gone to chase down the ball and now returned, bouncing it in front of him. "I know he's not much to look at, but this boy's brain is like a national treasure."

Dave just looked at him, his expression flat. To me, he said, "I'm fine."

"And I'm Ellis," his friend said, sticking out his hand. I shook it slowly. "Now that we're acquainted, you have *got* to teach me how to do that shot. Seriously."

"No," I said, sounding sharper than I meant to. They both looked surprised. "I mean . . . I don't really know how to do it."

"Dave's medulla oblongata begs to differ," Ellis replied, pressing the ball into my hands. "Come on. Please?"

I felt my face flush. I didn't want to. In fact, I couldn't

believe I'd even thrown the ball in the first place, much less that it had gone in. It was a testament to my dad's teaching—administered basically since I could walk, at parks and our home court—that I could not touch a basketball for years and still make his signature shot.

While my dad loved basketball, and lived it and breathed it for most of his young life, he was not the best player: a bit on the short side, with a passable jump shot and a decent layup. But he was fast and passionate, which usually got him playing time, even if it wasn't much. To his teammates and friends, though, he was more known for the various custom shots that he developed and honed during practice downtime and in neighborhood pickup games. There were dozens of them: the Slip 'n' Slide (a sort of backward spin move), the Ascot (a neck-level fakeout, then sudden burst to the basket), the Cole Slaw (you kind of had to see it to understand). But of them all, the Boomerang was the most famous. It was more of an assault than a shot, and required an overhand throw, practiced aim, and more than a bit of luck. Clearly, I'd had two of the three.

Now as I stood there with these two guys, both watching me expectantly, I suddenly heard the rattle of my dad's truck. When I looked up, he was downshifting, turning into the driveway. It wasn't until he was approaching and I saw his face, surprised, that I realized I was still holding the basketball. He pulled up, looked at it, then at me, and cut the engine.

"Look," I said to Ellis. "I . . . I can't. Sorry."

He looked at me, quizzical, as I knew this apology sounded entirely too heartfelt under the circumstances. Then again, it wasn't really for him. Or even for Dave, who deserved it, considering the hit he'd taken. Instead, even as the words came I knew they were really for my dad, whose eyes I could feel on me as I handed off the ball, and walked off the court and back inside. Game over.

× × ×

"Okay, try this one. Four-letter word, has an a in it. Clue is country in Micronesia."

I heard chopping, then water running. "Guam."

A pause. "Hey. That fits!"

"Yeah?"

I watched from the doorway of the Luna Blu kitchen as Tracey, Opal's worst waitress, hopped up onto a prep table, crossing her legs. Across from her, at an identical table, a slim blond guy wearing an apron was chopping tomatoes, a huge red, pulpy pile in front of him.

"All right," she said now, peering down at the folded newspaper in her hands. "How about this? Shakespeare character born via C-section."

The guy kept chopping, using the knife to push another pile into the ones on the table. "Well—"

"Wait!" Tracey whipped out the pen front behind her ear, clicking it open. "I know this one! It's Caesar. I'll just . . ." She frowned. "It doesn't work, though."

The guy rinsed the knife, then wiped it with a bar towel. "Try Macduff."

She squinted down at the page for a second. "Holy crap. You're right again! You're entirely too smart to be a prep cook. Where'd you go to college, again?"

"Dropped out," the guy replied. Then he looked up, seeing me. "Hey. Can I help you?"

"Better straighten up," Tracey told him, although, I noticed, she herself did not get off the prep table or put down her paper. "That's the boss's daughter."

The guy wiped his hands, then walked over. "Hey. It's Mclean, right? I'm Jason. Nice to meet you."

"We call him the professor, though," Tracey called out, folding her puzzle up. "Because he knows *everything.*"

"Hardly," Jason said. To me he added, "You looking for your dad?"

I nodded. "I was supposed to meet him here, but he's not in the office or out on the floor anywhere."

"I think he's upstairs," he replied, pointing at the ceiling above us. "With Opal's, um, community project."

Tracey snorted. She was short but built like a bull, with broad shoulders and muscled arms, and wearing the same sheepskin boots I'd seen her in my first day, this time with a denim dress. "Her gang of juvenile delinquents, he means."

"Now, now," Jason said, walking over and picking up his knife again. "We can't judge."

"*I* can," Tracey replied. "Did you see them, lined up outside earlier? All smoking and surly with about a thousand piercings among them? God. You could just smell the teen angst, it was so thick."

Hearing this, I realized it did explain the crowd of people—mostly kids my age, a few older, a few younger—I'd seen clumped around the front doors of Luna Blu on my way in. It was a Monday afternoon before opening, but clearly they weren't there for food: there was a sense of obligation to their gathering, something forced, not chosen. And Tracey was right, there had been a lot of smoke.

"Hit me with another one," Jason said now, nodding at Tracey's paper.

She peered down at it, running her finger along the page. "Okay, how about . . . eight-letter word for fuel, last letter is an *e*. I put down gasoline, but it's messing up everything around it."

"Kerosene," Jason said, starting on the tomatoes again.

"Holy crap, that's right, too!" Tracey shook her head, impressed. "You're wasted here. You should be, like, teaching or something."

He shrugged, saying nothing, and I took this pause as my exit, thanking them as I headed out of the kitchen and down the hallway. In the restaurant, a girl with yellow-blonde hair and a nose ring was wiping down the bar, while a couple of other waits chatted as they rolled silverware at a table by the window. I headed into the side room, to the stairs that Opal had led me up the day all her boxes had arrived. I'd just started up them when I heard my dad's voice. Glancing above me, I spotted him and Opal halfway up, talking.

". . . all for helping the community. But this is ridiculous. We can't be running a rehab program above the restaurant," he was saying.

"I know," Opal replied. She sounded tired. "That's exactly what I told Lindsay when I went to her office this morning."

"Lindsay?"

"Lindsay Baker," Opal said. "She's the councilwoman

who's in charge of this whole thing. But she insisted that they're renovating their offices and the community center is totally booked up. There's no place that can handle an ongoing project like this."

"So what you're saying," my dad said, "is that there is not a single room in the entire town for this to happen other than ours."

"No," Opal replied uneasily. "But that is what *she* said."

My dad sighed. Above them, in the attic room, I could hear thumping, footsteps, and voices. "And why did you volunteer for this again?"

"Parking! I did it for parking," Opal told him. "But when I brought that up today, she totally ran a muddle on me about it. She started in about community responsibility and civic pride and I—"

"Wait, wait," my dad said. "What did you just say?"

I'd heard it, too. It wasn't something we could ignore, either of us.

Opal blinked at him. "Community responsibility?"

"Before that."

She thought back. Above them, in the large room, I heard more thumping. "Oh, running a muddle," she said finally. "Sorry. It's just this basketball term. It means when you—"

"I know what it means," my dad said. "I'm just . . . surprised to hear it coming from you."

"Why?"

Now it was my dad who had to pause. "Well," he said after a moment, "I just didn't realize you were, um, into the game."

"Oh, God. My dad was a *hard-core* DB fan," she told him.

"He's an alum, and so are all my brothers. Basically, I had to go there or I'd shame the entire family."

"Really."

Opal nodded. "Although he's not been happy with the new coach. I don't keep up with it that much, but apparently there was some kind of scandal. Something to do with his personal life, or—"

"Anyway," my dad said, cutting her off. I felt my face flush. "Let's get back to the crisis at hand. What are our options here?"

"Well," Opal said slowly, "I think for the time being the best we can hope for is that the councilwoman takes pity on us and finds another room. Which might happen. But . . . not today."

"Right," my dad said. "Today, we have a roomful of criminals to deal with."

"They're not criminals," Opal told him. "They just owe community service."

"Isn't that the same thing?"

"Well, not—"

There was a loud *thud* from above them, followed by some guffaws. Opal glanced up the stairs. "I think I'd better get up there. I'm supposed to be supervising."

My dad looked, too, then sighed, shaking his head. "What did you say that councilwoman's name was?"

"Baker. Lindsay Baker."

"Okay," my dad said, turning to go down the stairs, "I'll give her a call, see if I can move things along."

"Oh," Opal said quickly, "I . . . I don't think that's a good idea."

"Why not?"

Opal swallowed. "Well," she began, as another thump sounded from the room, "it's just that she's kind of . . ."

My dad waited.

". . . a force," she finished. "As in, to be reckoned with. She has a tendency to kind of, um, overwhelm people."

"I think I can handle her," my dad said as I moved off the bottom step, out of sight, to wait for him in the dining room. "You just deal with the criminals."

"They're not criminals," Opal called out. "They're—"

My dad shut the door on this, apparently not interested in alternative definitions. When he spotted me, he gave a weary smile. "Hey there," he said. "How was your day?"

"Uneventful," I said as we walked around to the bar side. "You?"

"Just the usual chaos. You hungry?"

I thought back to the soggy turkey sandwich I'd had for lunch, ages ago. "Yeah."

"Good. Come back to the kitchen with me and I'll fix you something."

I was about to reply when, turning the corner, we suddenly came face-to-face with a tall guy in an army jacket, wearing a backward-facing baseball hat. There was a huge black-ink tattoo of an eagle covering his neck. He looked at my dad, then at me, and said, "Hey, where's the probation thing? I need my sheet signed."

My dad sighed, then nodded behind us. "Up the stairs. Shut the door behind you."

The guy grunted, then walked past us, slouching his

hands into his pockets. At the table by the window, the two waits rolling silverware tittered. My dad shot them a look, and they quickly quieted, just as his phone rang. He pulled it out of his pocket, then glanced at the screen, his brow furrowing.

"Chuckles," he said to me, flipping it open. "Hello? Yeah, I did. The ice-machine repair guy was just here. Well . . . do you want the bad news, or the bad news?"

By the sound of it, it would be a few minutes, so I wandered back into the dining room. The door to the stairs was open, despite what the tattooed guy had been told. When I went to shut it, I heard Opal talking and started toward her voice instead.

"What this really is," she was saying, "is an opportunity for you, as citizens of this town, to get to know the center of it in a way you never would otherwise. Street by street, corner by corner. House by house. It's like you're mapping your own world. So that's cool, right?"

There was no answer to this, other than a cough and some shuffling. Once on the landing, I could see Opal, facing a group of about twenty or so teens and near-teens, all of whom looked about as excited as if they were attending a root canal. Opal herself, wearing a black dress and her cowboy boots, her hair piled up on her head, was flushed, clearly nervous.

"And the great thing is," she continued, talking a bit too fast, "with this many people, doing even a couple of hours a week, we should make really good progress. I mean, according to the directions." She waved a stapled packet of paper she was holding in one hand. "It's pretty basic, by the looks of it.

Once we get the base down and put it together, it's just a matter of matching the pieces to the numbers."

Crickets. And silence.

"So, um," she said, "I'm really glad so many folks showed up. I mean, I know some of you didn't have a choice. But if you stick with this, I think you'll find that we'll have a good time and do something worthwhile for the community."

Nothing. I watched Opal's shoulders sink as she sighed, then said, "Well, I guess that's all we have time for today. We'll plan to be back here on Wednesday at four. So if you want me to sign your time sheets . . ."

Suddenly, the entire room was in motion, everyone coming to life with a flurry of movement. Within seconds, Opal was mobbed by out-thrust hands and fluttering pieces of paper.

"Okay, okay," she said, "one at a time, I'll get to everyone. . . ."

I stepped around the mob, walking into the room, which had been cleared out and swept, the boxes now lined up against one wall. A few large ones were labeled with big black numbers; the rest had letters, all jumbled up and out of order. I thought of Tracey's crossword, all those words fitting and not fitting, as I scanned them, another puzzle unsolved.

By now, we'd been in town for three full weeks. It was the longest I'd been Mclean—or at least called myself that—in two years, and I still wasn't quite used to it. Even hearing Jason say it, moments earlier, had been jarring. It probably said something that my own name sounded weirder to me than the ones I'd chosen to take on over these last few years. But the truth was, I still wasn't sure who this Mclean was, here. I kept waiting for her to turn up, falling into place as easily as Eliza and Lizbet and Beth before her, but so far it hadn't happened. Instead, I still felt unformed, like a cake half baked with edges crisp, but still mushy in the middle.

Part of this was because in the last three towns, I'd quickly decided on a set persona: perky rah-rah girl, black-clad drama queen, student government joiner. Faking all of these things was easy, because I could plan them out, selecting the friends and activities that best suited whomever I'd decided to be. At Jackson, though, it was not so cut and dry. I didn't pick Mclean's friends. Somehow, they kept picking me.

That day at lunch, I'd come out to the courtyard, planning to take a place along the wall. I wanted to look over my Western Civ notes because there'd been subtle hints at the possibility of a pop quiz, and I hated surprises. I'd just gotten settled and started reading when a shadow fell across my notebook. A gum-popping shadow.

"Got a minute?" Heather said when I looked up at her. She was wearing her fake-fur coat and jeans, a big, red wool knit cap pulled over her blonde hair. Before I could answer, she said, "Good. Come on."

She turned, clearly confident that I'd follow this command, and started over to the picnic table I now knew was her and Riley's daily lunch spot. Sure enough, as I watched her go—not having moved an inch—I saw Riley on one side, sipping a Coke and twisting her hair with one hand. Across from her was Dave Wade. It was the first time I'd seen him since I'd decked him with the ball, which probably explained why I felt a sudden rush of embarrassment.

"Hello?" Heather said from about five feet away. She sounded impatient, as if I had actually agreed to something. "Are you coming or what?"

I just looked at her, not sure how to respond to this. Finally, I said, "I have a pop quiz this afternoon."

"Come *on*," she said, and before I could stop her, she'd come back, grabbed my hand, and was pulling me to my feet. I barely had a chance to reach for my bag before I was being dragged over to the table, where she deposited me, my notebook still open, on the bench beside Dave Wade. As he glanced up, I had a flash of him hitting the pavement again, and my face flushed, deeper this time.

"You know Mclean, right?" Heather said, plopping down across from me, beside Riley.

"We've met," he said, keeping his eyes on me. As I shifted beside him, trying to organize my notes in my lap, I realized that really, this was the most mundane encounter we'd had: no secrets kept, police chasing, or flying basketballs. Yet, anyway.

"She's graciously agreed to be our tiebreaker," Heather told him.

"Oh, God." Riley rubbed a hand over her face, and I realized her eyes were kind of red. She'd been crying. "Just when I didn't think this could get any more embarrassing."

"We're all friends here," Heather told her. "And besides, so far you've gotten completely conflicting advice. There's mine, which is actually, you know, what you should do. And then there's his"—she cocked a finger at Dave, who raised his eyebrows—"which is not."

"Would you believe," Dave said to me, "that this is her actually trying to be unbiased?"

"Okay, here's the situation," Heather said, ignoring him. "Riley's been seeing this guy, and she just found out he cheated on her. He says he's sorry. Does she hear him out or kick him out?"

I looked at Riley, who was now directing her full attention to picking at a spot on the table. "Um," I said. "Well—"

"I said she should give him the boot. Like, literally and figuratively," Heather explained. "But Eggbert over here is telling her to be all codependent."

"Whoa, whoa, whoa," Dave said, holding up his hand. "Actually, what I said was she should get his reasons for doing what he did, and then proceed from there."

"He cheated on her," Heather said flatly. Riley flinched, picking harder. "What reason could possibly make that okay?"

"People do make mistakes," Dave pointed out.

"Look," Riley said, waving a hand between them, "I appreciate this town hall approach to my problem. But I can handle this, okay?"

"You said that last time, though," Heather pointed out.

Now Dave looked surprised. "Last time? Wait, he's done this before?"

Riley looked up at him. "Well . . . yeah. There was this other thing, a couple of months ago."

"You didn't tell me about that," he said.

"You were. . . ." Riley glanced at me. "Busy. At the time."

"Oh," Dave said.

"He got arrested," Heather explained to me. Now Dave flinched. "What? It was one beer. I got busted for that in *middle* school, it's so basic."

"Heather." Riley's voice was a bit sharp. "Remember when you said I should tell you when you're crossing the lines of what's conversationally appropriate?"

"Yeah."

Instead of replying, Riley fixed her with a flat, hard stare. I could almost feel the weather changing around us, it was so severe. "Fine," Heather said after a moment, picking up her phone. "Make your own choice. It's your funeral."

We all just sat there for a second, nobody talking, and I looked longingly over at the spot on the wall, where I'd been able to sit alone and worry about something small and easy like the whole of western civilization. I was just working up a way to get back over there when Dave said, "So. Mclean. How's the entry been?"

"Entry?" I repeated.

"To this," he said, gesturing with a flip of his hand at the courtyard. As he did so, I noticed for the first time the tattoo on his wrist. It was a black circle, in the same spot and the same shape as Riley's. Interesting. "Our fine educational establishment."

"Um," I said, "it's been . . . fine, I guess."

"Glad to hear it," he said.

"Of course it helps," Heather said, tugging her hat down

over her ears, "that she fell in with the right crowd."

"And who would that be?" Dave asked.

She made a face at him. "You know, there are actually people who would *love* to have the chance to hang out with me."

"Oh, right. How is Rob these days?" he said.

"He's history, not that it's any of your business." To me she said, "He can say what he wants, but he knows the truth. Me and Riley, we're the best thing that ever happened to this boy."

"Cut out the first two words of that sentence and I'll agree with you," Dave said. Heather rolled her eyes, but Riley looked up, giving him a wan smile.

"Oh, for God's sake," Heather said. "I wish you two would just go out, fail miserably as a couple, and get it over with."

"Well," said Dave, sitting back, "it's nice to know we'd have your blessing."

Just then, I felt someone on my left. I glanced up, just in time to see Deb, her purse tucked tightly to her side, passing beside me. As our eyes met, her face brightened with recognition; when she saw I wasn't alone, though, she bit her lip and kept moving.

I don't know what possessed me to put in motion what happened next. It was impulse or instinct, the best or worst thing under the circumstances. Regardless, before I knew it, it was done.

"Hey," I called out. "Deb!"

Beneath the table, Heather kicked my shin, but I ignored her. As for Deb, she was clearly so unused to being casually addressed at school that she visibly jumped at this, the sound of her own name, then whirled around to look at me, surprised, her mouth a tiny O shape. She was wearing jeans, a pink cardigan sweater, and a navy jacket. The ribbon in her hair matched her lip gloss, which matched her quilted purse.

"Yes?" she asked.

"Um," I said, realizing I had no plan past this first greeting. "How's it going?"

Deb looked at me, then at the rest of the group at the table, as if weighing whether this was a trick or not. "Fine," she said slowly. Then, in only an incrementally more friendly tone, she added, "How are you?"

"Do you want to sit with us?" I asked her. I felt both Riley and Heather look at me, but I kept my eyes on Deb, who looked so surprised—shocked, even—that you would have thought I'd asked her to lend me a kidney. "I mean," I continued, and now Dave was looking at me, too, "there's, um, room here. If you do."

Deb, no fool, looked at Heather, who was staring at me, an incredulous look on her face. Forget borrowing a kidney: by her face, you'd think I'd offered to eat one. "Well," she said slowly, pulling her purse a little closer to her side, "I—"

"She's right," Dave said suddenly, scooting a bit down from me to create a bigger space between us. "The more, the merrier. Have a seat."

Riley narrowed her eyes, twisting the top off her water again. Meanwhile, Deb was looking at me, so I tried to convey with one look both reassurance and confidence. Somehow, though, it worked, because she came over—slowly—and slid onto the bench beside me, parking her purse in her lap and folding her hands over the top of it.

This time, I did have to say something. I'd pulled Deb into this, so the least I could do was try to make her feel welcome. But my mind just went blank, then blanker still as I began trying desperately to come up with any conversation starter. I was just about to say something about the weather—the weather!—when she politely cleared her throat.

"I like your tattoo," she said to Dave, nodding at the circle on his wrist. "Does it have special meaning?"

I knew I was not the only one surprised that this was the topic she chose to broach: Heather and Riley were staring at her, as well. But Deb was giving Dave her full attention as he glanced down at his wrist, then said, "Yeah, actually. It, um, represents someone I was very close with, once."

Hearing this, Riley closed her eyes, and I thought again about the matching circle on her own wrist. You didn't just get a tattoo with someone for nothing.

"What about you?" Heather asked Deb suddenly. "Do you have any tattoos?"

"No, I don't."

"Really?" Heather said, raising her eyebrows. "I'm so surprised."

"Heather," I said.

"I would actually love to have one," Deb continued, glancing at me. "But I haven't found anything I feel passionate enough about yet." To Dave, who was watching her with an attentive expression, she added, "I think it's important that it really have meaning to you if it's going to be a part of you forever."

Heather's eyes widened, and I felt like kicking her in the shin but restrained myself. Dave said, "That's very true, actually."

Deb smiled as if he'd paid her a compliment. "Yours looks kind of tribal to me, with the thick lines and the black."

"You know about tribal tattoos?" Dave asked her.

"A little," Deb replied. "Although personally, the Japanese designs are my favorites. The fish, and the foo dogs. The artwork is so imperial and classic."

"Are you *kidding* me with this?" Heather interjected, incredulous. "How do *you* know about tattoos?"

"My mom had a friend who had his own shop," Deb said, either unaware of or just ignoring her tone. "I used to stay there after school until she was done at work."

"You," Heather said, her voice flat, "hung out at a tattoo shop."

"It was a while back." Deb smoothed her hands over her purse. "Very interesting, though. I learned a lot."

Dave, on Deb's other side, suddenly caught my eye and I was surprised to see him smile at me, like we were the only two in on a joke. Even more unexpectedly, I felt myself smile back.

"So, Deb," I said. "Hypothetical situation. Your boyfriend cheats on you. Do you grant him another chance, or end things?"

Heather rolled her eyes. Riley, though, was watching us.

"Well," Deb said after a moment. "Honestly, I'd need more details before I could say."

"Like what?" Dave asked her.

She thought for a moment. "Length of the relationship, first. I mean, if it's really early days, it doesn't bode well. Better to move on."

"Good point," Riley said quietly. Heather looked at her, raising her eyebrows.

"Also," Deb continued, "I'd have to consider the circumstances. Was it a fling, with someone he hardly knew, or a person he actually cared about? The first could be explained as a misstep . . . but if real emotions are involved, it's a lot more complicated."

"True," I said.

"Finally, a lot would depend on his behavior. I mean, did he confess, or did I find out some other way? Is he actually sorry, or just mad he got caught?" She sighed. "Really, though? The bottom line I always ask myself is: if I look at everything I've had with this person, good and bad, am I better or worse off without them? If the answer is better . . . well, then, that's the answer."

We all just sat there, looking at her. No one said anything, and then the bell rang. "Well," Riley said, blinking a few times. "That was . . . very informative. Thank you."

"Sure," Deb said, friendly as ever.

Riley and Heather both got to their feet, picking up their bags and trash, while on our side, Deb and I did the same. Only Dave stayed where he was, taking his time screwing the cap onto his water bottle. When he finally got to his feet, he looked at me.

"You never answered," he said as Deb unzipped her purse, looking for something inside.

"What?"

"The question. Stay or go. You never answered."

I looked over at Riley, who was pulling on her backpack, smiling at something Heather had just said as she did so. "I'm not good with advice," I said.

"Ah, come on," he said. "That's a cop-out. And this is a hypothetical."

Everyone was starting toward the main entrance now, Heather and Riley ahead, with me, Dave, and Deb bringing up the rear. I shrugged, then said, "I don't like complications. If something's not working . . . you gotta move on."

Dave nodded slowly, considering this. I thought he might push further, or maybe counter, but instead, he turned to Deb. "It was very nice talking to you."

"And you, as well!" Deb said. "Thanks for the invitation."

"That was me, actually," I said.

Dave laughed, glancing at me, and I felt myself smile again. "See you around, Mclean."

I nodded, and then he turned, falling in beside Riley and sliding his hands into his pockets.

People were moving all around us, en route to different buildings, as Deb and I just stood there together. Finally, she said, "He's very nice."

"He's something," I replied.

She considered this, zipping her purse shut. Then she said, "Well, everyone is."

Everyone is something, I thought now as I stood upstairs at Luna Blu, looking across all those boxes. For some reason, this had stuck with me, simple and yet not, ever since she'd said it. It was like a puzzle, as well, two vague words with one clear one between them.

Looking closer, I saw now that one of the boxes had been opened, some packing materials loose on the floor around it. Inside, it contained stacks of plastic sheets of house and building parts. There were pieces with cutouts of doors and windows, and others printed to look like brick and wooden facades. Fronts and backs of small houses, block-like stores, and longer buildings with rows of windows that had to be offices or schools. There were dozens of sheets in the box, with the parts for a couple of structures on each one. So many pieces.

"I know what you're thinking," I heard Opal call out from behind me. When I turned, I saw she was signing the last of the sheets, for a heavyset guy who'd been leaning against the wall. When she was done, he took it without a thank-you, then trudged off to the stairs.

"And what is that?" I asked.

She stuck her pen behind her ear, then came over to stand beside me. "That this is an impossible amount of work, an undoable task that will, mostly likely, never be completed in a million years."

I didn't say anything, because she was kind of right.

"Or maybe," she continued, reaching down into the box to pull out one sheet printed with brick house parts, "that's just what *I'm* thinking."

"At least you have a lot of help," I told her.

She gave me a flat look. "I have a lot of *people*. Not the same thing."

I watched her for a second as she turned the piece in her hand, studying it. From downstairs, I could hear the sounds of the restaurant getting ready to open: chairs scraping as they were pushed aside to be swept under, the voices of the staff laughing and chatting, the clinking of glasses being stacked behind the bar. It was as familiar to me as a song I'd been hearing my whole life, covered by various people but the basic tune the same.

"I mean," she continued, "can you even imagine how hard it's going to be to put together all these tiny houses, and then find the right places for them, not to mention each tree and streetlight and fire hydrant?"

"Well—"

"I mean, there are hundreds of these things. And they all have, like, a hundred pieces. And it's supposed to be done by June? How in the world is *that* going to happen?"

I wasn't sure if this was a rhetorical question. But she had stopped talking, so I said, "Well, it's like you just told them. You start with the base, and work your way up. It's basic engineering."

"Basic engineering," she repeated. Then she looked at me. "Did I really make it sound that simple?"

"You sure did."

"Huh. I'm a better liar than I thought."

"Hey, Opal!" a voice called up the stairs. "You up there?"

"It depends," she replied over her shoulder. "What do you need?"

"Copier's on the fritz again and we only have two special sheets printed."

She sighed, looking up at the ceiling. "Did you try the paper-clip trick?"

Silence. Then, "The what?"

"Did you put a paper clip under the toner cartridge . . ." She trailed off, clearly having decided this was too complicated to convey from a distance. "I'll be right there."

"Okay," the voice replied. "Oh, and Gus wants to talk to you, too. Oh, and also the towel guy's here and says he needs cash, not a check—"

"I'll be right there," she said again, louder this time.

"Ten four," the voice replied. "Over and out."

Opal reached up, massaging her temples, the pen behind her ear jumping up and down as she did so. "Basic engineering," she said. "I hope you're right."

"Me, too," I said. "Because that's a lot of boxes."

"Tell me about it." She smiled, then squared her shoulders, dropping her hands, and started over to the stairway. "Hit the lights on the way out, will you?"

"Sure thing."

I heard her head down, her footsteps fading, and then turned to follow her. As I did, though, I saw, sitting on the table by the wall, the directions she'd been holding as she'd given her speech earlier. I picked them up, impressed by their heft: rather than a few stapled sheets, as I'd thought, they were like a booklet, sizable and thick. I flipped past the first pages, the table of contents and introduction, the company's contact info, to page eight, where the actual directions began. STEP ONE, it read at the top, with about four paragraphs of tiny type beneath it, complete with diagrams labeled with letters and numbers. *Whoa,* I thought, and flipped forward a bit, only to see more of the same. Then, though, remembering what I'd just said to Opal, I turned back, finding STEP ONE again. FIND FOUR CORNERS (A, B, C, D) OF BASE, it read, and ARRANGE ON STABLE SURFACE AS PICTURED.

Downstairs, a phone was ringing, and someone was yelling they needed lemons. I walked over to the box with the uppercase A on it, ripping it open, then dug around for a few moments before I found the top left corner labeled A (BASE). I carried it across the room and put it down on the floor, as pictured. Like a blinking cursor on an empty page, it was just the first thing. The beginning of the beginning. But at least it was done.

× × ×

After an early dinner at the bar with my dad—broken up by two phone calls and a kitchen crisis—I headed out of Luna Blu, cutting down the alley toward home. It was almost dark as I turned onto our street and crossed it to my house, the only one with no lights on. I was digging around in my bag for my keys when I heard a car pull up behind me. I barely glanced at it and the two people inside, then went back to hunting. When I finally found them a minute later, I looked back and realized it was Dave and Riley.

She was behind the wheel, with him in the passenger seat, and in the light from his front porch I could just make out their faces. Riley was sitting back, her eyes focused upward, while Dave said something, gesturing with one hand. After a moment, she nodded.

Inside, the house was kind of cold, so I turned up the heat, then dropped my bag on the couch and went into the kitchen, turning on lights along the way. I got a glass of water, kicked off my shoes, and sat down on the couch with my laptop. It had just finished starting up, icons lining up along the bottom of the screen when I heard it: the happy *ping* noise of HiThere! announcing a call. Apparently, my mother was done with the silent treatment.

A few days earlier, when I'd finally called her back after hanging up on her yet *again*—this time because I'd flattened Dave with the Boomerang—she didn't pick up. Peter did.

"Your mother can't talk right now," he said. His voice was stiff, protective. "She's upset and needs some space."

My first thought, hearing this, was to laugh out loud. Now *she* wanted space? And of course, I was supposed to just honor that, instantly, even though she had never once been willing to do the same for me. I wanted to tell Peter this, try to explain my side, but I knew there was no point. "Okay," I said instead. "I understand."

Two days passed, then three, and my voice mail stayed empty, my caller ID limited to my dad's number and Luna Blu's only. No HiThere! bubbles, no cheery good morning/good night texts, not even an e-mail. It was not the longest we'd gone without talking, but was certainly the first time the lack of contact was her doing, not mine. And the truth was, it was kind of weird. All this time I'd thought the only thing I wanted was for my mom to just leave me alone. Then she did.

Now though, apparently, she was ready to talk. Or fight. Or something. So I clicked the little bouncing bubble, and my screen opened up to show . . . Peter. To say I was surprised was a serious understatement.

"Mclean?" He had to be in his office: there was a big Defriese logo on the wall, a wood console visible behind him, lined with framed pictures of very tall people, him looking short beside them in comparison. "Can you see me okay?"

"Um," I said, suddenly feeling nervous. For all his impact on my life, I didn't know my stepfather that well. We were far from chat-buddy status. "Yeah. Hi."

"Hi." He cleared his throat, leaning in a bit closer. "Sorry if I surprised you. I didn't have your number, but found this contact info on your mom's laptop. I wanted to talk to you about something."

"Okay," I said.

I was used to seeing Peter from a distance—across a table, down a hallway, on the TV. Up close, he looked older, and kind of tired. He had on a dress shirt, the collar loosened, and no tie. A diet soda can sat by his elbow. "Look, I know you and your mother haven't been getting along that well lately, and I'm not trying to get in the middle of anything. But . . ."

There was always a but. Whether you were family, or faux family. Always.

". . . I really care about your mother, and she really cares about you. She's very sad right now and I want to make her happy. I'm asking for a little help in accomplishing that."

I swallowed, then felt self-conscious when I realized he could actually see I was nervous. "I don't know what you want me to do."

"Well, I'll tell you." He leaned back a bit. "We've got a game down there this weekend, playing the U. Katherine and the twins are coming down with me, and I know she'd really like to see you."

It was always jarring when he called her by her full name. Until they'd married, she was Katie Sweet. Now she was Katherine Hamilton. They sounded like totally different people, not that I was anyone to talk.

"She was planning on inviting you earlier this week," he was saying now, "but then, apparently, you all had some differences. Or something."

I nodded. Or something. "I thought she was too upset to talk to me."

"She's hurt, Mclean," he replied. "I'm not asking you to come here, or even go to the beach. That's between you and her. But I am hoping you'll consider letting us meet you halfway."

He made it sound so reasonable, I knew to refuse would make me look like a brat. "Does she know you're calling me?" I asked.

"This is all my idea," he replied. "Which means that if you agree, I plan to take full credit."

It took me a minute to realize he was being funny. Huh. So Peter Hamilton had a sense of humor. Who knew? "She might not want to see me, you know. It sounded like she was pretty mad."

"She wants to see you," he assured me. "Just show up at Will Call at one on Saturday. I'll handle the details. All right?"

"Okay."

"Thanks, Mclean. I owe you one."

That was an understatement. But I bit this back, instead just nodding as he said he'd see me that weekend. We both reached forward to end the call at the same time, and, noticing the other, both paused, not wanting to be first. Finally, after an awkward beat, I took the initiative and clicked the HANG UP button. Just like that, poof, he was gone from the screen. Goodbye.

× × ×

A half hour later, I remembered the next day was garbage pickup, so I shrugged on my jacket and headed out to roll the can down to the curb. I had just turned to go back up the driveway when I saw Riley's car still parked just down from my house. Her lights were off, and I could see her behind the wheel, wiping at her face with a tissue. I walked a little closer, and moment later, she looked over and saw me.

"I'm not stalking you, I promise," she said through her open window. Then she looked down at the tissue, folding it carefully. "I just . . . wasn't ready to go home yet."

"I know the feeling," I said. "You okay?"

She nodded. "Just the typical dirtbag drama. It's so embarrassing. I am not flaky like this about anything else in my life, I swear. . . ." She stopped, then cleared her throat. "I'm fine."

On the main road, past the stop sign ahead, a bus passed by, engine chugging. I turned to go back to my house, figuring we didn't really know each other well enough for me to offer any more than I already had.

"He likes you, you know," she called out to me suddenly.

I stopped, looked back at her. "What?"

"Dave." She cleared her throat. "He likes you. He won't admit it to me yet, but he does."

"He doesn't even know me," I said.

"Are you saying he *wouldn't* like you if he did?" She raised her eyebrows. "Answer carefully. This is my best friend we're talking about here, and he's a really nice guy."

"I'm not saying anything," I told her. She was still looking at me, so I added, "I'm not sure he's my type."

"Don't tell me," she said. "You're a dirtbag girl, too?"

"Not exactly. I'm more . . ." I trailed off, for some weird reason thinking of Peter's face, blinking off my computer screen. "A girl who's not looking for anything right now. Even with a really nice guy."

She put her hands on the wheel, stretching back, and as she did I saw that circle tattoo on her wrist again, identical to Dave's. There had to be quite the story there, not that I was going to ask about it now. "I get it. And I appreciate you being honest, at any rate."

I nodded, then slid my hands into my pockets. "Good night, Riley."

"Good night," she replied. "And Mclean?"

"Yeah?"

"Thanks."

I wasn't sure what the gratitude was for: coming to check on her, what I'd said, or maybe, actually, what I didn't say. I chose not to ask. Instead, I just walked back to my driveway, letting her leave on her own terms, in her own time, without an audience. When you can't save yourself or your heart, it helps to be able to save face.

Six

✤ ✿ ✤

The day of the DeFriese game, my dad and I were supposed to have breakfast together, just the two of us. It had been so crazy between school and the restaurant for the last week that we'd hardly seen each other, communicating mostly through hurried conversations, as one of us was coming or going, and scribbled notes on the kitchen table. This was normal, especially for the first month or so we were in a new place. A restaurant was like a demanding girlfriend, requiring every bit of his attention, and I'd gotten used to riding out his absences until things settled down. Still, I was looking forward to some face time. So when my phone beeped an hour before we were supposed to meet, my heart sank.

AHBL, his message said. SO SORRY.

AHBL was a family code that stood for All Hell Breaking Loose. It was what my dad had often told my mom over the phone when he called from their restaurant, Mariposa, to say he wouldn't make dinner, or the movie he was supposed to meet us at in ten minutes, or any number of my school conferences or recitals. Basically, his standard reason for not being with us for, well, anything. My dad believed that panic was contagious, especially in a restaurant setting. All it took was one person losing it—over being in the weeds, totally backed up on orders, burning an entrée already late, or a wait list that would have to be seated way past closing—to set everyone else off in a domino effect. Because of this, calling my mom to say the sky was falling, even when it was, was not an option. Enter these simple four letters, AHBL, to convey the urgency without the hysteria.

As a shorthand, it had long ago made the jump from the restaurant setting to everyday use. It was what I thought the night I walked into our old kitchen and found both my parents home during the restaurant rush, sitting and waiting for me, their expressions grim. What I doodled on a yellow legal pad in any number of lawyer's conference rooms as the tug-of-war over my custody raged on around me. And what I always thought in that too-long pause between when I shared something with my mother I knew she wouldn't like and the moment she freaked out about it.

Even though it had been three days since my HiThere! chat with Peter, I still hadn't told my dad about seeing my mom that weekend. It was just too weird and awkward on so many levels that I decided to push it out of my mind until I absolutely had no choice but to deal with it. Which was not easy, as all around me the town was gearing up for the game. I'd forgotten what it was like to live in a basketball-crazed place. Just about everyone I saw had on a U sweatshirt or T-shirt, the local stations were covering every detail of the lead-up to tip-off like it was a national news event, and light blue U flags flew from porches and whizzed past on car antennas. The only place the game wasn't discussed was at our house, where my dad and I had avoided the subject like a live land mine. Until now, when my phone beeped again.

LATE LUNCH? my dad had written. NOT HERE, PROMISE.

I bit my lip, my fingers poised to respond. What I had to say, though, seemed entirely too delicate to convey via keypad. So after a shower and some breakfast, I walked up to Luna Blu to tell him in person.

I'd just stepped off the curb to cross the street when I heard a door shut. When I glanced back, there was Dave Wade, in jeans and a flannel shirt, sliding his keys into his pocket as he started down the street just a few feet behind me. I thought of what Riley had said, that he might like me, and suddenly felt self-conscious. Today was complicated enough, and it was not even noon yet. I nodded at him and kept walking.

When I crossed the street, though, he did the same. And when I turned down the Luna Blu alley, he did that, too. I slowed my pace as I got closer to the kitchen entrance, waiting for him to pass me and continue on to the street. He didn't. In fact, within moments he was right behind me, having slowed down as well.

Finally, I turned around. "Are you following me?"

He raised his eyebrows. "What?"

"You just walked, like, two feet behind me the entire way here."

"Yes," he agreed, "but I'm not following you."

I just looked at him. "What would you call it, then?"

"Coincidence," he proclaimed. "We're just headed in the same direction."

"Where are you going?"

"Here," he said, pointing at the kitchen door.

"No, you're not."

"I'm not?"

Suddenly, the door swung open, and there was Opal, wearing jeans, shiny black shoes, and a white sweater, a coffee cup in one hand. "Please tell me," she said to Dave, skipping any greeting, "that you are here for the community project."

"Yep," he replied. Then he shot me a look that could only be described as smug. "I am."

"Oh, thank God." Opal pushed the door open farther and he stepped through. Then she said to me, "You saw all the people here the other day. I had tons! And now, today, when the local paper and freaking Lindsay Baker are coming in twenty minutes, no one. Not a single person!"

She was still holding the door, so I stepped inside behind Dave, who was standing there awaiting instruction. Opal let the door bang shut, then hurried around him and started down the hallway to the restaurant, still talking.

"Plus the walk-in conked out at some point last night, so we lost half our meat and all of the fish. On the day of the De-friese game! The repairman can't get here until this afternoon and he'll charge double overtime, and all the suppliers are totally out of everything because everyone else ordered so big for game day."

That explained my dad's text, at least. Sure enough, as

we passed the main door to the kitchen, I could see him in the walk-in, poking at something with a screwdriver. Jason the prep cook was standing behind him with a toolbox, like a nurse handing off instruments during surgery. It was not the time to interrupt—you never wanted to bug anyone when they were doing hardware repair on old kitchen equipment—so I continued following Opal and Dave through the restaurant and to the stairs that led to the attic.

"The last thing I was worried about," Opal was saying now as she started up the stairs, "was not having enough delinquents for this freaking photo op." She stopped, suddenly, both walking and talking, and turned back to look at Dave. "Oh. Sorry about that. I didn't mean to call you—"

"It's okay," he told her. "Kind of comes with the community-service requirement."

She smiled, relieved, and turned back around. "Seriously, though. I had such a turnout on Wednesday, and now today nobody shows up? I don't get it."

"Did you sign their sheets?" Dave asked her.

Opal paused. "Yeah, I did."

"Oh."

She looked back again. "Why?"

"Well," he said, "it's just that I've heard that once some people get a signature, it's easy to just copy it. The court office is usually too busy to do more than double-check the name matches."

Opal looked appalled. "But that's so wrong!"

Dave shrugged. "They *are* delinquents."

"So, wait." She narrowed her eyes at him. "Does that mean

you're just here for one day and a signature, then?"

"No," he said. Then he glanced at me, like I was going to vouch for him, before saying, "I'm not a true delinquent. Just did something stupid."

"Haven't we all," Opal said, sighing.

"Opal?" someone yelled up the stairs. "There's a reporter at the front door asking for you."

"Oh, crap," she said, taking a panicked look around the attic space. Behind her, I saw the boxes had all been opened, and someone had constructed the rest of the model's base around the one piece I'd put down. Everything looked ready to begin, except for the fact that we had only one delinquent. Or sort-of delinquent. "She's early. What am I going to do? It's supposed to look like I have a whole crew here!"

"Two isn't a crew?" Dave asked.

"I'm not part of this," I said. "I just came to see my dad."

"Oh yes, but, Mclean," Opal said, desperate, "you can just pretend, right? For a few minutes? I will owe you big."

"Pretend to be a delinquent?" I said, clarifying.

"You can do it," Dave advised me. "Just don't smile, and try to look like you're considering stealing something."

I actually had to fight not to smile at this. "It's that easy?"

"I hope so," Opal said, "because I'm about to recruit everyone I can get my hands on. Can you guys please start taking some stuff out and just, you know, make it look like it's in progress?"

"Sure," Dave said.

"Bless you," she replied, setting her coffee cup down on a nearby table with a clank. Then she was bolting down the stairs, announcing, "I need anyone here under thirty upstairs, stat! No questions! Now, now!"

Dave watched her go, then looked at me. "So," he said. "What exactly are we doing here?"

"It's a model," I told him, walking over to the A box and pushing the flaps all the way open. "Of the town. Opal got roped into organizing the assembly of it for the city council."

"And that's Opal," he said, nodding at the stairs, where, distantly, we could still hear her voice, ordering all hands on deck.

"Yep."

He walked over to the model, bending over it, then reached for the directions, which were lying to the side, flipping them open. "Look at that," he said, turning a page. "Our houses are actually on here."

"Really," I said, unloading a few shrink-wrapped stacks of plastic pieces from the box.

"In your yard," he said, turning another page, "we should put someone lying prone in the driveway, felled by a basketball."

"Only if we put a weeping girl in a car in front of yours," I replied.

He glanced at me. "Oh, right. Riley said she saw you last night."

"I feel bad for her," I said, pulling out more stacks. "With the cheating and all. She seems like a nice girl."

"She is." He flipped another page. "She just has really lousy taste in guys."

"You two seem really close," I said.

He nodded. "There was a time when she was literally my only friend. Except for Gerv the Perv."

I raised my eyebrows as downstairs, a door slammed. "Gerv the what?"

"Just this kid I used to hang out with at my old school." When he glanced up and saw me still watching him, he added, "I told you I was weird. So were my friends."

"Friend."

"Friend," he repeated. Then he sighed. "When you're four-teen and mostly taking college courses, it's not like you have much in common with everyone else in your classes. Except for the other weird, smart kid."

"Which was Gerv," I said, clarifying.

"Gervais," he corrected me. "Yeah. Riley coined his nick-name because he was always staring at her chest."

"Classy."

"I only hang with the best," he said cheerfully.

I sat down, taking one of the shrink-wrapped stacks of plastic pieces and ripping it open. "So you and Riley . . . you weren't ever a couple?"

"Nope," he said, taking his own stack and plopping down a couple of feet from me. "Apparently, I'm not up to her low standards."

"You have the same tattoo, though," I pointed out. "That's a pretty serious thing to do with someone."

He flipped over his wrist, exposing the circle there with the thick outline. "Ah, right. But it's not a couple thing. More of a friend thing. Or a childhood thing. Or," he said, ripping open the plastic bundle in his lap, "a wart thing."

"Excuse me?"

"Long story," he said, shaking out the pieces. "Okay, so where do we start, you think?"

"No idea," I said, spreading out all my pieces on the floor around me. I'd been thinking I'd take a stab at it without the directions, but as soon as I looked at it closely I knew that wasn't happening. There were many tabs and pieces, each labeled, making up a crazy quilt of letters and numbers. "This looks seriously impossible."

"Nah," he said. Then, as I watched, he collected four flat segments from his own pile, clicked them together, then added a couple of curved ones. Finally, he picked out a thicker, shorter one and pressed it into the bottom with the palm of his hand. One, two, three, and he had a house. Just like that.

"Okay, so that," I told him, "was impressive."

"One of the bonuses of being a delinquent," he replied. "Good spatial skills."

"Really?"

"No," he said. I felt my face flush, feeling like an idiot. But he just picked up the house, glancing at the bottom of it, then carried it over to the base. "I was just really into model making when I was a kid."

"Like trains?" I asked, picking up a piece from beside me. It had an *A* and a 7 on it and I had no idea what to do with it. None.

"Model trains?" he replied. "Are you trying to insult me or something?"

I looked at him, wondering if he was serious. "What's wrong with model trains?"

"Nothing, technically," he said, squatting down by one edge of the base. "I, however, did war models. Battlefields, tanks, soldiers. Aircraft carriers. That kind of thing."

"Oh," I said. "Well, that's totally different."

He looked over at me, his expression flat, then placed the model on a spot on the base, pressing it down with the heel of his hand. When it clicked, he stood, taking a step back.

"So," he said after a moment. I could hear someone— or several someones actually, by the chaotic thumping— climbing the stairs up toward us. "What do you think?"

I walked over beside him. Together, we looked down at the tiny house, the sole thing on this vast, flat surface. Like the only person living on the moon. It could be either lonely or peaceful, depending on how you looked at it.

"It's a start," I said.

×   ×   ×

Twenty minutes later, between Dave, me, and the handful of Luna Blu employees impersonating delinquents who'd joined us, the model was looking pretty good. After a few minutes of chaos and complaining all around, we'd settled into a system. Dave and the prep cook Jason—who, it turned out, knew each other from attending some academic camp years earlier— assembled the pieces, and the rest of us matched them to the proper spot where they belonged. So far, we'd managed to get about ten different structures on the upper left-hand corner of the base: a handful of houses, a couple of buildings, and a fire station.

"You know, I think I used to live in this neighborhood," Tracey said to me as we secured a long, square building where the diagram indicated. "This is a grocery store, right?"

I glanced down at the building as I pressed it in, waiting for the click I now knew meant it was secured. "I don't know. It doesn't say what it is."

"None of them do," Leo, the cook, called out from beside one of the boxes where, as far as I could tell, he'd done little other than pop bubble wrap while the rest of us worked. "Which seems kind of stupid to me. How can it be a map if you can't tell where you are by looking at it?"

"Leo," Jason said, looking up at him as he fit a roof onto another house, "that is so profound."

"Oh, for God's sake, it is not," Tracey snapped, getting to her feet and crossing the room. As I followed her, she added, "Jason is convinced that Leo is some kind of genius, masquerading as a moron."

"Like an idiot savant?" Dave asked, concentrating on putting together an office building.

"You got the idiot part right," Tracey replied. She sighed, then peered over Jason's shoulder, watching as he assembled something. "Where does that go? Right by the one we just put on?"

He glanced at the directions, which were opened up on the floor beside him. "Yep, think so."

"I knew it!" She clapped her hands. "I did live over there. Because that's my old bank and that grocery store next to it is the one I got banned from that time."

"You got banned from a grocery store?" I asked.

"Oh, I've been banned from everywhere," she replied easily, flipping her hand.

"What she means," Leo informed us, "is that she was known around town for writing bad checks."

"They weren't bad," Tracey said, taking the building from Jason as he handed it to her. "I just didn't have any money."

"I think that's the same thing," Jason said, not unkindly.

Tracey bent over the model base. "So if that's where I shopped, and that was my bank, then my apartment was . . ." She ran a finger down the center of a small strip of road, right to the edge. ". . . apparently nonexistent. I was off the map, I guess."

"Here be dragons," Leo said, popping another row of wrap.

We all looked at him. Tracey said, "Jesus, Leo, are you high right now? Because you know what Gus said, if he catches you one more time—"

"What?" Leo said. "No, I'm not high. Why would you think that?"

"You're talking about dragons," she pointed out.

"I said 'Here be dragons,'" he said. When he realized we were all still looking at him, he added, "It is an expression they used to use, you know, back in the day. When they made maps, for the parts that hadn't been discovered yet. The area they didn't know. 'Here be dragons.'"

Jason shook his head, smiling, and popped a roof onto another building. "Man," he said, "that is seriously deep."

"Will you stop with that shit?" Tracey said. "He's not a genius! He's functioning on, like, half his brain cells on any given day."

"At least he's got half," Dave told her.

"Such the optimist," I said as I passed behind him. He

looked up at me and grinned, and again, I felt this strange urge to smile back. And I was not someone who smiled a lot. Especially lately.

"Hello, hello!" I heard Opal, sounding entirely too cheery, call out as she came up the stairs. "Everyone ready for the paparazzi?"

Tracey rolled her eyes. Then, under her breath she said, "She always gets so stupid when she's nervous."

Jason shushed her, which she ignored, then tossed her the house he was holding. As she and I bent down over the model again, Opal emerged, a woman in jeans and clogs behind her. A curly-headed guy with a camera around his neck, who looked half asleep, brought up the rear.

"So, here you see a group of our local youth volunteers, working away," Opal said. "We're only at the very start of the project, but I think you can still get a really good idea of what the end result will look like. Basically, it's a representation of the downtown area. . . ."

The reporter had pulled out a pad and was making notes on it as the photographer moved around the model, popping off his lens cap. He squatted down right beside Dave, who was putting a roof on a house, and snapped a couple of frames.

"I'd love to talk to a couple of the kids," the reporter said, flipping to a fresh page on the pad. "Why they're here, what about this project interested them . . ."

"Oh, of course!" Opal said. "Yes! Well, let's see . . ." We all watched her make a show of scanning the room as if there were, in fact, multiple options, before looking squarely at Dave. "Maybe, um . . ."

"Dave," I said under my breath.

"Dave," she continued, "could, um, speak to that point?"

The reporter nodded, then moved closer to where he was sitting, her pen at the ready. "So, Dave," she said. "How'd you get involved in this?"

Oh, dear, I thought. But Dave played along, saying, "I was looking for a good volunteer opportunity. I'm in a place right now where I just felt I needed to give back to the community."

"Really," the reporter said.

"Really?" Tracey said to me.

"Community-service requirement," I told her, my voice low.

She nodded knowingly. "Been there."

"Anyway," Opal said, her voice still entirely too high, "I think we're all really excited about having this chance to show our town in a way we haven't seen it before—"

"Small and plastic?" Tracey asked.

"—and," Opal shot her a look, "provide an interactive, lasting representation that can be enjoyed by generations to come."

The camera was clicking as the photographer moved around us, getting shots of me and Tracey, then Jason, then Dave again.

"Hello? Anybody home?"

I saw Opal, who was standing by the stairs, visibly flinch at this sound. Her face flushed as she turned, calling over her shoulder. "Lindsay, hello," she said. "We're up here."

There was the sound of footsteps—footsteps in heels—coming closer, and a woman emerged. She was tall and thin, with china-doll features and blonde hair falling in a perfect bob right to her shoulders, and was wearing a black suit and high heels. She smiled at us, her teeth incredibly straight and white, then strode across the floor like a beauty queen working the runway. Confidence just wafted off of her, like a strong scent.

"Check it out," Tracey whispered as I struggled to breathe. "Opal's nemesis."

"What?" I said.

"Since high school," she replied. "They competed over everything."

"Maureen," the councilwoman said, extending a hand to the reporter, who shrank back a bit before accepting it. "It's so great to see you again! I was just commenting to the mayor about your piece on the waste-treatment center options. Very thought-provoking, although I do wonder where you got some of your statistics."

"Oh," the reporter said, sounding nervous. "Well, um, thanks."

"And thanks, also," Opal jumped in, "for coming by! I think it's so good for our volunteers to see how this project is really about the entire community, all the way up to our representatives."

"Of course! I was thrilled to be asked. How *are* you, Opal?" The councilwoman reached out, giving her a quick, one-shoulder-pat-and-done hug, which Opal reciprocated in an identical fashion. "The restaurant looks great. I heard you've actually been kind of busy lately!"

Opal forced a smile, her lips pressed together. "We have. Thanks."

The councilwoman turned, scanning all of us working on the model with narrowed eyes. From off to the left, I heard Leo pop another bubble. It was the only sound until she said, "So . . . is this your entire group?"

"Oh, no," Opal said quickly. "We just had, some, um, scheduling issues today. But we wanted to go ahead and get started anyway."

"Great!" The councilwoman took a slow stroll around the entire model, her heels clicking. The reporter took a few shots of her, then turned back to Dave, who was the only one still working. "Well, it's hard to tell from the outside, of course. But I'm sure you're making a good start."

Opal winced, then said, "We are! We're thinking it will actually move pretty quickly once we get all our people in place."

"And when do you plan to have it completed?" the reporter asked, flipping another page on her pad.

"May," the councilwoman told her.

"What?" Opal said. "May? I . . . I thought the centennial was in June."

"It is. But the town celebration begins May sixth, and we're going to put this in the main post office to kick it all off," the councilwoman replied. She looked at Opal. "Oh my God! I told you that, right? I was *sure* I did."

We all watched Opal swallow. "Um," she said. "Actually—"

"Where the hell is everybody?" my dad's voice boomed from the bottom of the stairs. Now it was my turn to flinch, just out of reflex. "Are we not opening for lunch on game day in less than an hour?"

"Gus!" Opal said, or rather kind of shrieked. Beside me,

Tracey closed her eyes. "We're all up here with the council-woman, showing her the model."

"The what?"

"The model," she repeated. Then she cleared her throat, her face pink, and said to the councilwoman, "That's Gus. He's—"

These words, however, were drowned out by the sound of my dad stomping up the stairs. *Fee-fi-fo-fum*, I thought, and then he appeared on the landing, face red, expression an-noyed. "Leo!" he said. "Didn't I tell you fifteen minutes ago I needed all the vegetables prepped ASAP? We're opening the doors and half the side work isn't done. Who the hell is sup-posed to be setting up in the dining room?"

"That would be me," Tracey said cheerfully. He glared at her, and she directed her attention back to the model, quick.

"I thought these were youth volunteers?" the council-woman said to Opal.

"Gus," Opal said, her voice rushed, "this is Councilwoman Baker. Remember, I told you that she was helping us with the parking. . . ."

My dad glanced at the councilwoman, then back at us. "Ja-son, get down there and finish the vegetable prep. Leo, I need the pots boiling and the carts stocked for service, now. And Tracey, if that dining room isn't set up in fifteen and spotless, you'll have more than enough time to volunteer for any proj-ect, I promise you."

"Hey!" Tracey protested. "How come I'm the only one you're threatening to fire?"

"Go!" my dad barked, and she did, tossing down the house

she was holding and going to the stairs faster than I'd ever seen her move. Leo and Jason followed, in equally rapid time, leaving just me and Dave. I picked up the house, walking back over to the model, while he focused on assembling another building, his head ducked down.

Opal gave a helpless look to the councilwoman. "It's game day," she said, trying to explain. "Our cooler broke, and . . ."

The councilwoman ignored her, instead breaking out that big smile again as she walked over to my dad. "I'm Lindsay Baker," she said, holding out her hand. "You're Gus Sweet?"

My dad, distracted, shook her hand. "Yeah, that's me."

"I believe you left me a message yesterday," she replied. "Something about having no room for this project?"

"Actually, I said it was a complete and total nuisance and I wanted it gone," he replied. Then he looked at me and said, "What are you doing here?"

"Just needed to talk to you about something," I said. "You were fixing the cooler, though, so I didn't want to interrupt."

"Smart girl." He sighed, then ran his hand through his hair. "I gotta get back down there. Come down in five or so?"

I nodded. As he turned for the stairs, the councilwoman said, "Mr. Sweet?"

My dad paused, looked back. "Yeah?"

She was still smiling at him, totally unfazed that he was barely giving her the time of day. It was obvious she was the kind of woman who was used to getting attention not just from men but from women, children, even animals. I knew the type. I'd been raised by one who came from a family of the same. "Concerning the model, I'd love to talk to you about it further.

At a more convenient time, of course. Maybe we can set up a meeting at my office later this week?"

Opal looked at her, then at my dad. "That would be great," she said quickly. "We would love that."

My dad, however, just grunted, then went downstairs without comment. A few moments later, we heard him start yelling again. But Councilwoman Baker, hardly bothered, was looking at the space where he'd been standing with an intrigued expression, like someone had told her a good riddle and she was enjoying figuring out the answer. Uh-oh.

"Look, Lindsay, I really appreciate you coming by," Opal said to her. "If you want to just tell me a good time to get together, I'll make sure we can—"

"Oh, dear, I've really got to run," the councilwoman said, glancing at her watch. "But I'll come back in a week or so. By then you'll have more volunteers and a bit of progress, don't you think?"

Opal swallowed again. "Um . . . of course. Yes."

"The truth is, for now, this project has to stay here," she continued, heels clacking. She was coming right toward me, and I felt this urge to jump out of the way, which was crazy. This woman was nothing to me. "It's a good space and you *did* offer it, if I remember correctly. Maybe you can communicate that to Gus? I don't think he realized it when he called me."

The reporter let loose with a nervous cough while her photographer, for some reason, chose this moment to snap a shot of Opal. I pictured it in my mind, with the caption below: SCREWED.

"Oh, it's going to really look like something when I come

back, I just know it," the councilwoman continued. Then she stopped, right in front of me, and stuck out her hand. "We haven't met, I don't think. I'm Lindsay Baker."

To say I was surprised to be addressed was an understatement. It wasn't just me either: behind her, Dave looked up, raising his eyebrows. "Mclean Sweet," I said.

"Do me a favor." Her hand, closed around mine, her grip strong, once I extended it. "Tell your dad I said it was really nice to meet him. Okay?"

I nodded, and she smiled. God, her teeth were bright. It was like she traveled with her own black light or something.

"Maureen?" she said over her shoulder. The reporter jumped. "Walk with me. I want to give you some of my thoughts on that article. Bye, Opal! See you at spin class!" And then she was moving as if she knew even without turning around that the reporter would fall in behind her. Which she did, scurrying past me, the photographer loping in her wake.

We all watched them go, none of us saying anything until we heard the door at the bottom of the stairs swing shut. Then Opal exhaled, collapsing against a nearby table. "Oh my God," she said. "Is it just me, or does anyone else feel like they just had a stroke?"

"She is kind of intense," I agreed, walking over to the directions Jason had left behind and picking them up.

"Kind of intense? Did you even *see* that?" she demanded. "The way she comes in and rolls over everyone and everything? God. It's exactly the way she was in high school. And she's so *nice*, at least to your face. All the better to hide her dark, evil soul."

Dave looked up at her, eyes wide. "Wow."

"I know!" Opal buried her head in her hands. "She makes me nuts. Plus, she's, like, incredibly good at spinning. I don't even know how I got into this! All I wanted was parking."

We both just looked at her. Downstairs, my dad was yelling again.

"Well," I said, after she'd been in this position, like an ostrich, for a good fifteen seconds, "parking *is* important."

"It's like, I know what I want to say to her," Opal said, dropping her hand. "I plan to be professional and prepared. But when the actual moment comes . . . it's not so simple. You know what I mean?"

Just then, the door banged open again downstairs. "Mclean?" my dad called up. "You needed to talk to me?"

Hearing this, I felt my own heart jump, remembering the real reason I was there. I looked at Opal, then answered both her question and my dad's with the same answer. "Yeah," I said. "I do."

× × ×

Ever since the divorce, and my ensuing epiphany that I did in fact have a choice and an opinion concerning it, I'd justified every bit of my anger toward my mom simply because of how she'd wrecked my dad. Cheating on a man with someone he greatly admired, in the public forum, and then leaving him for said person while his own life crumbles into pieces? Even now, just thinking about it never failed to get me mad all over again.

I couldn't keep people from talking about my mom and Peter Hamilton on the street or at Mariposa, couldn't go back in time and change what she'd done. But I could run interference with the morning paper, carefully taking out the sports section and chucking it into the recycling before he woke up in the morning. I could refuse to talk to my mom on the phone in his presence, and never put up any of the framed pictures of her and Peter and the twins she kept giving me for my room at home and then rooms, plural, everywhere since. I could talk about the past, our past, as little as possible, avoiding the entire subject of my first fifteen years in conversation whenever I could. He wasn't looking back, so I did my best not to either.

But occasionally, this was not an option. Like, say, today, when in two hours I'd be sitting right behind the coach of the number-three-ranked college basketball team, on national TV. After two years of keeping everything possibly hurtful away from him, I was about to hand him a grenade. It was no wonder that as I walked over to meet him at a table by the window ten minutes later, I literally felt sick.

"So," he said, once I sat down. Across the restaurant, Opal was at the bar, washing glasses and talking to Tracey, who was dusting the plant I'd noticed was so dirty on our first visit here, what seemed like ages ago. "What's the verdict on lunch? I can probably get away for a full hour. We can really go crazy."

I smiled, feeling even worse. The truth was, the last place my dad needed to be on a busy game day was anywhere but the kitchen here, and we both knew it. But he felt bad about canceling on me, and was trying to compensate. That made two of us.

"Um," I said, glancing over at Opal, who was wiping down the bar, the cloth in her hand making smooth, big circles across its surface. "Actually . . . I sort of have plans this afternoon."

"Oh," he said. "Well, maybe we'll shoot for breakfast tomorrow or—"

"With Mom," I blurted out. It wasn't pretty, these two words just falling from my mouth and landing like dead weight between us. Then, since I was already in it, I added, "She's coming down with Peter for the game and wants to see me."

"Oh," my dad said, and it was amazing to me how this, the same word he'd just spoken, one syllable, two letters, could sound so totally different. "Right. Of course."

Over at the bar, Opal was restocking glasses, the sounds of happy clinking drifting over to us. Everyone was bustling around, the energy building. They were opening in ten minutes.

"I'm sorry," I said. "I don't want to. But things have been pretty strained since the move, and Peter asked me to do this. I just didn't think I could blow it off."

"Mclean," he said.

"I mean, I *could* blow it off," I continued, "of course, but they're probably already on the way here and will freak out, and I know you don't need that. . . ."

"Mclean," he repeated, stopping me from going further, although I had no idea what I was planning to say. Something equally lame, I was sure. "You're *supposed* to want to see your mom."

"I know. But—"

"So you don't have to apologize to me for that," he continued. "Ever. Right?"

"I feel so bad, though," I told him.

"Why?"

He was watching me, really wanting to know. *Oh, God,* I thought, swallowing hard. This was exactly the conversation I did not want to have. "What she did," I said, starting shakily. "To you. It was really, really awful. And it feels disloyal to act like it wasn't."

It was horrible, talking about this. Worse than horrible. I felt like I was chewing thumbtacks, with each word another spoonful forced in. No wonder I'd taken such pains to avoid it.

There was a *clang* from the kitchen, followed by someone letting loose with a string of curses. But my dad kept his eyes on me, for once not distracted. "What happened between me and your mother," he said slowly, taking his time, "was just that: between us. Our relationships with you are separate things entirely. Being with your mom isn't an insult to me, or vice versa. You know that, don't you?"

I nodded, looking down at the table. Of course I knew this: it was, after all, my mother's party line, as well. But in the real world, you couldn't really just split a family down the middle, mom on one side, dad the other, with the child divided equally between. It was like when you ripped a piece of paper into two: no matter how you tried, the seams never fit exactly right again. It was what you couldn't see, those tiniest of pieces, that were lost in the severing, and their absence kept everything from being complete.

"I just hate that it's like this," I said softly. I looked up at him. "I don't want to hurt you."

"You're not," he said. "You *couldn't.* Okay?"

I nodded, and he reached over, taking my hand and squeezing it. And this simple connection, reminding me of the one between us, made me feel better than any words he'd said so far.

"Gus?" I turned, seeing Jason standing in the kitchen doorway. "Fish guy's on the phone about that rush order."

"I'll call him back," my dad said.

"He says he's about to leave for the day," Jason told him. "Do you want me to—"

"Go," I said, patting his hand. "Take the call, it's fine. We're fine."

He cocked his head to the side, studying my face. "You sure?"

"Yeah," I told him. "I have to get home anyway and get ready for . . . you know."

"The game," he said, speaking the word for me.

"Right."

He pushed out his chair, getting up. "Well," he said, "it should be a good one. I have a feeling you might have decent seats."

"I'd better," I replied. "If I'm not on the actual bench, I'm leaving."

"Of course," he said. "How are you supposed to talk smack to the refs from anywhere else?"

"Forget the refs," I replied. "I'm planning on telling Peter what I think about his offense."

He gave me a rueful smile. It was weird to be talking about basketball again after such a long time away from it. Like we were speaking a language we'd once been fluent in, but we now had to struggle with verbs and tenses.

"Have fun," he said to me. "I mean it."

"You, too," I told him. He smiled again, then started back toward the kitchen. Jason, who was waiting, pushed the door open, and my dad walked through, taking the phone as he handed it off to him. I thought again of how I'd seen them at the cooler earlier, working in tandem, the ongoing intricate dance of making this place somehow come together and perform. Through the open door, I could see the kitchen staff loading carts and chopping and cleaning, a blur of movement around my dad as he stood in the center, the phone at his ear. Always the calmest one in the chaos, even when all hell was breaking loose.

× × ×

I was halfway out the door, headed home, when I realized I'd left my jacket upstairs. I doubled back, up the alley and through the kitchen door. As I passed my dad's office, I saw him sitting at his desk, still on the phone. Opal was standing behind him, using the copy machine that was crammed in the corner. It was whirring, lit up, spitting out pages she took as they emerged, one by one.

"Sure," my dad was saying. "A staff review doesn't have to be a bad thing. I'm just saying that the situation here doesn't necessarily lend itself to HR formulas."

The copy machine started making a clicking noise, which grew steadily louder. Opal pushed a couple of buttons. Nothing happened, other than the noise changing from clicking to grinding.

"Oh, I'm sure," my dad continued, glancing back at her, "it will be enlightening."

Opal tried another button, sighed, then stepped back, surveying the machine as the grinding grew louder. Behind her, my dad was watching as she furrowed her brow, then balled up her fist, whacking the machine hard in its center. *BANG! BANG!* My dad raised his eyebrows. The machine sputtered, then began whirring again, and another copy slid out into Opal's hands. She smiled, pleased with herself, and I was surprised to see my dad smile, too. Then he turned back around.

Upstairs, Opal's volunteer force of one—Dave—remained, sitting cross-legged by the model, working with a piece in the vicinity of Tracey's old apartment. I watched him from the landing for a moment as he bent over it, his face serious as he concentrated on getting it attached in the right spot. I'd thought I was being stealthy until he said, without looking up, "I know my artistry is fascinating, but really, feel free to jump in at any time."

"I wish I could," I said. "But I have to go to the game."

"The Defriese game?" he asked, looking over at me. I nodded. "Seriously?"

"Yep."

"Wait. Do you not *want* to go or something?"

"Not really."

He stared at me openly as I walked over to get my jacket. "You know, there are people who would sell their souls for a ticket to that game."

"Would you?"

"I'd consider it." He sighed, shaking his head. "God, I just don't get you non-basketball people. It's like you're from another planet."

"I'm not non-basketball," I said. "I just—"

"Would rather work on this model than get to be there in person for probably the best game of the freaking year." He held up his hand. "Just don't even try to explain yourself. You might as well be speaking Romulan right now."

"Speaking what?"

He rolled his eyes. "Forget it."

I picked up my jacket, digging out my phone from my pocket. I had one missed call, and a text from my mom on the screen. LOOKING FORWARD TO SEEING YOU, it said. Formal, polite. WILL BE WAITING AT WILL CALL.

I felt a sudden bolt of nervousness, realizing this was actually happening. I'd be with my mom, and Peter, at the game in less than two hours. And despite my dad's confidence that this was a good thing, it suddenly felt like anything but. Which was why I panicked, and did the last thing I ever would have expected.

"Do you . . . Do you want to come?" I asked Dave.

"To the game?" he asked. I nodded. "What, do you have an extra ticket?"

"Not exactly," I said. "But I think I can get you in."

Seven

✽ ❀ ✽

I saw my mother before she saw me. And even though we were already late, and I could see her anxiously scanning the crowd, I took one last moment to study her, unaware, before she spotted my face and everything changed.

My mom had always been pretty. I look a lot like she did at my age, with the same blonde hair, blue eyes, and a frame both tall and thin enough to have slightly knobby knees and elbows. Unlike me, though, my mom had never wavered from her chosen path in high school, hitting all the marks that were expected of her as a popular southern girl: cheer team captain, homecoming queen, debutante. She dated the son of a congressman all the way from sophomore year to graduation—wearing a promise ring on a gold chain around her neck—volunteered in service league, and sang in the church choir every Sunday. In her high-school yearbook, she appears on page after page: group shots, candids, club photos. That girl in your class you can't help but feel like you knew well, even if she never learned *your* name.

College, however, was not as easy for her. During her second week as a freshman at Defriese, Mr. Promise Ring dumped her over the phone, claiming their long-distance relationship just wasn't working. She was devastated, and spent the next month holed up in her dorm room crying, leaving only to go to class and eat. It was at the cafeteria, red-eyed and pushing a tray down the food line, that she met my dad, who was doing work-study there to subsidize his tuition. He'd noticed her, of course, and always made a point of giving her a bit extra of mac and cheese or Salisbury steak, whatever he was doling out. One day he asked her if she was okay, and she burst into tears. He handed her a napkin; she took it and wiped her eyes. They were married five years later.

I loved this story, and as a kid I insisted on hearing it over and over again. I could see my dad in his hairnet (my mom called it cute), hear the hum of the bad Muzak the cafeteria always played, feel the steam from the broccoli cuts drifting up between them. I adored every image, every detail, as much as I loved the fact that my parents were so different and yet perfect for each other. Rich, popular girl meets working-class scholarship kid, who steals her heart and whisks her away to the ramshackle charm and chaos of the restaurant world. It was the best kind of love story . . . until there was an ending to it.

With my dad, my mom was different. Growing up, she'd had years of manicures and blow-outs, heels with everything, dressing not just for dinner but for breakfast and lunches as well. But when I was a kid, she was Katie Sweet, who wore jeans and clogs, her hair pulled back in a ponytail, her only regular makeup a slick of clear lip gloss. At the restaurant, she could just as easily be found up to her elbows in Clorox water, scrubbing the walk-in, as at her desk in the office, where she tracked every dime that came in and out. Occasionally, when she went to charity events or weddings, I'd see flashes of the person I'd seen in her yearbooks or old photo albums— makeup, hair, diamonds—but it was like she was wearing a costume, playing dress-up. In her real life, she wore rain boots, had dirt under her nails, and squelched around in the garden in the mud, picking aphids off the tomato plants one by one.

Now, though, my mom looked exactly like Katherine Hamilton, high-profile coach's wife. She wore her hair long and layered, got blonde highlights every other month, and sported TV-ready outfits that were selected by a personal shopper at Esther Prine, the upscale department store. To-day, she had a black skirt, shiny boots, and leather jacket over a crisp white shirt. She looked gorgeous, even though she didn't resemble my mom, or Katie Sweet, one bit. But then she said my name.

"Mclean?"

Despite everything, I felt my heart jump at the sound of her voice. Some things are primal, unshakable. I'd long ago realized my mother had a pull over me, and me her. All the angry words in the world couldn't change that, even when sometimes I wanted them to.

"Hi," I said as she came toward me, arms already out-stretched, and pulled me into a hug.

"Thank you for meeting me," she said. "It means so much. You have no idea."

I nodded as she held me tightly and entirely too long,

which was nothing new, but it felt more awkward than usual because we had an audience. "Um, Mom," I finally said over her shoulder, "this is Dave."

She released me, although she still slid one hand down to take mine as if she was afraid I'd bolt off otherwise. "Oh, hello!" she said, looking at me, then back at him. "It's nice to meet you!"

"You, too," Dave said. Then he glanced around at the crowd of fans streaming past us to the Will Call window and through the main doors of the arena, nodding at the multiple people trying to buy tickets, to no avail. "Look," he said to me, under his breath. "Like I said, I really appreciate this invite. But I don't think you understand—"

"Just relax," I said again. He'd spent most of the walk explaining to me that because I just moved here, I didn't understand how hard it was to get tickets to a game like this. You couldn't just buy them. There was no way he'd get in. I knew I could have explained the entire situation, but I just couldn't bring myself to do so. I was stressed enough about seeing my mom; rehashing the divorce, in detail, would not help matters.

"Did you find your way okay?" my mom asked me now, squeezing my hand. "This place is a madhouse."

"Yeah," I said. "Dave's been here before."

"Which is why I've been trying to tell Mclean that," Dave said, glancing at someone to our left holding a sign that said NEED TWO PLEASE!!!!!!, "you really can't just get in at the last minute."

My mom looked at Dave, then back at me. "I'm sorry?"

I swallowed, then took a breath. "Dave's just a bit concerned about whether we can actually get him in."

"In?" my mom repeated.

"To the game."

She looked confused. "I don't think it should be a problem," she said, glancing around. "Let me just see what the situation is."

"It's not going to happen," Dave told her. "But it's fine, really. You guys just—"

"Robert?" my mom called, waving at a tall, broad-shouldered guy in a suit, who was standing nearby. He had several laminated passes around his neck and a walkie-talkie in one hand, and when he came over she said, "I think we're ready to go in."

"Great," he replied, nodding. "Right this way."

He started walking and my mom, still holding my hand, followed. When I glanced back at Dave, he looked confused. "Wait," he said. "What's—"

"I'll explain later," I said.

Robert led us past the main doors, where masses of people were waiting in line, around the arena to a side door. He showed one of his passes to a woman there in a uniform and she opened it up, waving us through.

"Would you like to go to the suite or straight to your seats?" Robert asked my mom.

"Oh, I don't know," she said, looking at me. "What do you think, Mclean? We've got about twenty minutes before tip-off."

"I'm fine to go sit down," I said.

"Perfect." She squeezed my hand again. "The twins are

already down there with their sitters. They'll be so excited to see you!"

Out of the corner of my eye, I saw Dave shoot me another surprised glance, but I kept my gaze straight ahead as we crossed the corridor, then started down into the arena itself. It was already more than half full, with the pep band playing and the video screens ablaze with a cartoon of a dancing Eagle, the U's mascot, and instantly the noise surrounded us, filling my ears. I thought of my dad, all the games I'd gone to see as a kid with him, the two of us in our upper-upper-level seats, screaming our lungs out.

I felt a tap on my shoulder, and turned around to see Dave looking around him, incredulous. We were still going down the stairs, closer and closer to the court. "Is there something you're not telling me?" he asked.

"Um, sort of," I replied as we passed a row of reporters and cameramen.

"Sort of?" he said.

"Here she is!" my mom said as we reached the third row of seats, which were marked by a RESERVED sign. She held up my hand as proof, waving it at the twins, who were sitting on the laps of two college-aged girls, one with red hair and a row of rings in her ear, the other a tall brunette. "Look, Maddie and Connor! It's your big sister!"

The twins, chubby and wearing matching Defriese T-shirts, both brightened at the sight of my mom, ignoring me altogether. Not that I blamed them. Despite my mom's attempts to behave otherwise, they had no idea who I was.

"This is Virginia and Krysta," my mom continued, gesturing

to the sitters, who smiled hellos as we moved past them down the row of seats. "This is my daughter, Mclean, and her friend David."

"Dave," I said.

"Oh, sorry!" My mom turned slightly, putting the hand not still clutching mine on Dave's shoulder. He was just standing there, half in the aisle, half out, looking down at the court with a flabbergasted expression on his face. "Dave. This is Dave. Here, let's sit down."

My mom sat down next to Krysta, reached for Maddie, who was sputtering a bit, and settled her in her lap. I took the seat beside her, then waited for Dave, who looked stunned as he moved down the aisle, easing himself into the seat next to mine.

"Isn't this fun?" my mom said, bouncing Maddie. She leaned into my shoulder, pressing against me. "It's so wonderful to all be together."

"Ladies and gentlemen," a voice boomed over the speaker system. The crowd around us cheered, the sound like a wave passing from top to bottom, then up again. "Please welcome your University Eagles!"

Dave was still just looking around, eyes wide, as the team began to run out from a tunnel to our right. The band was playing, the floor beneath us shaking from everyone stomping around and above us. Despite my mixed feelings, I had that same rush that had been ingrained in me since childhood, the love of the game. Like the connection I had with my mom, despite everything, it was undeniable.

"Okay," Dave said, or rather yelled, in my ear as the crowd

thundered around us, applauding and cheering, "who *are* you, exactly?"

It wasn't the first time I didn't know how to answer this. In fact, I'd taken pains over the last few years to have a different response every time. Eliza, Lizbet, Beth . . . so many girls. In this huge crowd, with my mom on one side and this boy I hardly knew on the other, I was all and none of them. Luckily, before I had to say anything, everyone around us jumped to their feet, cheering as the players ran in front of us. I knew anything I said would be drowned out. And maybe it was because no one could hear that I answered anyway. "I don't know," I said. I don't know.

× × ×

Defriese lost, 79–68, not that I was really able to pay attention. I was too busy running my own defense.

"So," my mom said, squeezing my hand. "Tell me about *Dave.*"

It was after the game, and we were in the private back room of a local restaurant where she and Peter had made a reservation for dinner. It was called Boeuf, and was a big, incredibly dark place with heavy velvet drapes and a roaring, stone fireplace. The walls were lined with various implements of destruction: shiny scythes, swords of varying sizes, even what looked like a small battering ram. It made me uneasy, as if we might find ourselves under attack at any moment and have to seize the décor to defend ourselves.

"We're neighbors," I told my mom as the waiter slid thick, leather-bound menus in front of us. Dave, who had been invited to come along, had gone to the restroom; Peter was on his cell phone, fielding calls. The twins were at the other end of the table, strapped into matching high chairs and giggling as their sitters fed them, not that I could really see them that well. It was so dark, it was like the restaurant wasn't going for ambiance as much as blackout conditions.

"*Just* neighbors?" she asked.

Her continued emphasis of particular words was beyond annoying, but I bit my tongue. I'd decided early on in the first half, when she still hadn't let go of my hand and kept peppering me with questions about everything from school to my friends, rapid-fire style, to just endure as best I could. The only other option was to snap at her, and considering we were two rows behind Peter and his assistant coaches and thus squarely on the live TV feed, any tension would be broadcast to sports fans across the country. All of this had already been public enough. It would not kill me to keep up a calm face for two hours. I hoped.

I might have forgotten about the TV thing if not for the fact that Dave's phone was buzzing about every ten seconds as his friends spotted him on the screen. Not that he noticed, as he was completely absorbed in the game, which he was watching with his mouth half open, still in awe about his incredible vantage point.

As he watched, his eyes still glued to the action, I glanced down at his phone's screen. WHAT THE HELL! said the first message listed, from Ellis, followed by DUDE! and a few others in the same vein from names I didn't recognize. Then, with another buzz, one more came in. YOU CHARMER. It was from Riley.

"Your phone is ringing," I pointed out to him.

He glanced at me, then at it, before quickly turning back to the court. "It can wait," he said. "I can't believe you're not watching this."

"I'm watching it," I said. "It's a good game."

"It's an amazing game from, like, the best freaking vantage point *ever*," he corrected me. "I can't believe you're basketball royalty and were so secretive about it."

"I'm not basketball royalty," I said. "And what is that, exactly?"

"Peter Hamilton is your stepfather."

"Stepfather," I repeated, a bit louder than I probably should have. I cleared my throat. "Stepfather," I said again.

This got his attention. He looked at me, then down at my mom and the twins. "Right," he said slowly. Then he gave me a look that made me feel sort of weird, vulnerable. Like I'd said more than I had. "Well, thanks for the invite. Seriously."

"You're welcome." He was still looking at me, though, so I pointed at the court. "Hello? I can't believe you're not watching this."

Dave smiled, then turned back to the game, just as his phone buzzed again. This time, I didn't look at it, instead focusing on the players running past in a blur, the ball whizzing between them.

Now, at Boeuf, I told myself to be patient. I showed up with a boy—of course my mother would make assumptions. "Just neighbors," I told her. "He lives next door."

"He seems very nice," she said. "Smart, too."

"He only said, like, two words to you," I pointed out, just as one of the twins let loose with a holler, protesting something.

"What?" she said, leaning in closer and cupping her ear.

"Nothing."

Dave was now returning to the table, where he promptly crashed into the back of my chair, knocking me sideways. "Sorry," he said as he groped for his chair and sat down. "It's just so freaking dark in here. I walked into another room and joined some other table."

"Whoops."

"Tell me about it. I don't think they could see me, though." He picked up the menu, and my mom, watching him, smiled at me as if I had in fact admitted something to her in his absence. To her he said, "Thanks again for the ticket. The game was incredible."

"I'm so glad you enjoyed it," she replied. She looked at Peter, who was still talking, his phone pressed to his ear, then said to me, "He should be done with all this press in a second. Then you can tell us everything that's going on with you."

"Not much to tell," I said as I flipped through page after page of wines by the bottle, trying to get to the food options. I could hear my dad in my head, critiquing this as well. Spend enough time with a restaurant troubleshooter and you start thinking like one yourself. "Just school, mostly."

"And your father is well?" she asked, her voice cheerful, polite.

I nodded, equally civil. "He's fine."

My mom smiled at Dave, for some reason, then took a sip of her wine. "So what else? You must be doing something besides going to school."

A silence fell across us, during which all we could hear was Peter, talking about a strong offense. I could feel my mom watching me, waiting for something else she could seize and keep. But I had nothing else to share, no more to say. I felt like I'd already given her my time, and my friend. It was enough.

As I thought this, though, Dave cleared his throat, then said, "Well, there's the model we're working on."

My mom blinked, then looked at me. "A model?" she said. "Of what?"

I thought about kicking Dave, but wasn't sure I could see him well enough to make contact. Instead, I just glared in his general direction, not that he noticed. "It's of the downtown and surrounding areas," he told my mom, as the waiter glided past, filling our water glasses. "For the centennial. They're doing it above Luna Blu."

I felt my mom glance at me. I said, "Dad's restaurant."

"Really," my mom said. She was still looking at me, as if expecting me to pick this up and run with it. When I didn't, she said, "That sounds interesting. How did you get involved in it?"

I was pretty sure this comment was directed at me, but I didn't respond. So Dave, after helping himself to a roll and a pat of butter, said, "Well, to be honest, in my case it was kind of required."

"Required," my mom repeated.

"Community service," he told her. "I got into some trouble a couple of months back. So I owe hours to the, you know . . . community."

I felt my mom kind of start at this. "Oh," she said, glancing at Peter, who was still on the phone. "Well."

"He got busted drinking at a party," I told her.

"It was stupid," Dave admitted. "When the cops showed up, everyone else ran. But they said to stay where I was, and I tend to follow directions. Ironic, right?"

"Um, yes," my mom said, looking at me again. "I guess it is."

"Truthfully," he said, clearing his throat, "the volunteering hasn't been bad at all. As it turns out, my parents are a lot stricter than the courts. They've basically had me on lockdown ever since the whole thing happened."

"Well, I'm sure it was very alarming for them," my mom said. "Parenting is so difficult sometimes."

"So is being someone's kid," I said.

Everyone looked at me, and then my mom reached for her water glass, keeping her eyes straight ahead as she took a sip. So typical. Dave was openly confessing to an arrest and yet *I* was the bad one here.

"Anyway," he said now, glancing at me, "I did the first half of my hours at the animal shelter, cleaning cages. But then with budget cuts, they started closing earlier in the afternoons. So that's how I ended up working on the model with Mclean."

"The model," Peter said, joining the conversation as the waiter brought his wine, taking entirely too long to remove the empty glass and adjust the napkin beneath it. "Model of what?"

On my right, Dave was about to answer, and on my mother's side, Peter was waiting. But between them, she had that look on her face, like I was the worst daughter in the world, and I could just feel all this history swirling, swirling as I tried to remember what it had been like before. When we were just us, and things were simpler. I couldn't, though. All I knew was that she was hurt again, and it was my fault. So I did what I always did. I faked it.

"It's a model of the town," I said suddenly, the words coming without me even thinking first. "I actually wasn't supposed to be part of the whole thing. But Opal, this woman who works at the restaurant? She really needed the help, so I pitched in the other day."

"Oh," my mom said. "Well, it sounds like it might be a worthwhile way to spend your time."

"It's a huge project, though," I continued. "Tons of pieces. I don't know how she's ever going to get it done by the deadline, which is May."

"It's important to have a goal," Peter said. "Even an unreasonable one can be good for motivation."

This, in a nutshell, was my stepfather. If the coaching thing ever ended for him, I was sure there was a group in need of confidence building somewhere that would be eager for his services.

"Well, in that case," Dave said, "my goal is to graduate without any further misdemeanors."

"Aim high," I said.

"You know it."

He smiled, and I smiled back, feeling my mother watching me. I must have seemed like such a stranger to her, I realized, when she saw me like this. In a town she didn't know, with people she'd never met, and both of us wading through this limbo world between what we'd been and what we might be. Like seeing her from a distance earlier, this thought made me unexpectedly sad. But when I turned to her, she'd already looked away and was saying something to one of the sitters.

"That was a tough game," I told Peter instead. "You guys played hard."

"Not hard enough," he said. Then, lowering his voice, he added, "Thanks for coming. It's really made her happy."

"What's that?" my mom said, turning back to us.

"I was just telling Mclean about how happy we are to have the beach house finally done," he replied smoothly. "And that she needs to come visit sometime. Colby is great this time of year."

"I don't know Colby that well," I said. "We always went to North Reddemane."

"Oh, there's nothing decent in North Reddemane any-more," Peter told me. "Just a few businesses on their last legs and a bunch of teardowns."

I thought of the Poseidon, with its mildew scent and faded bedspreads, and looked at my mom, wondering if she even re-membered it. But she was just smiling at him, oblivious. "It used to be nice," I said.

"Things change," Peter said, opening his menu with his free hand. He leaned in closer, peering down at it. "Good God," he said. "I can't even see this. Why aren't there any lights on in here?"

None of us replied, instead just studying our own menus in the tiny bit of brightness thrown by the candle in the center of the table. If someone had been walking by and glanced in, I wondered what they'd think of us. How they might consider this group of people, possibly related but probably not, fumbling together through the darkness.

× × ×

"Wow," Dave said. "*That* was loud."

I turned to look at him as the taillights of Peter's SUV moved away from us. "What was?"

"That sigh you just let out," he said. "Seriously. It was almost deafening."

"Oh," I said. The lights were going over the slight bump now, disappearing down to the main road. The turn signal was already on. In a few minutes, they'd be on the highway. "Sorry."

"Don't be," he said. "I just noticed. You all right?"

I'd been overthinking my actions and carefully crafting my responses for hours now. Honestly, I had no more energy for it. So instead of answering, I just sat down right where we were, on the curb between our two houses, and pulled my knees to my chest. Dave plopped down beside me, and we just sat there for a minute, listening to the music thumping behind my neighbors' closed front door.

"I don't get along with my mom," I told him after a moment. "At all. I think . . . I think I even hate her sometimes."

He considered this. Then he said, "Well, that explains the tension."

"You felt that?"

"Hard to miss," he replied. He reached down, picking at his shoe, then looked up at me. "Whatever it's about, she's trying really hard. Like, *really* hard."

"Too hard."

"Maybe."

"Too hard," I said again, and this time, he was silent. I took a breath, cold, then added, "She cheated on my dad. With Peter. Left him, got pregnant, got married. It was a mess."

A car drove by, slowed, then kept going. Dave said, "That's pretty harsh."

"Yeah." I pulled my knees tighter against me. "But, see, that's the thing. You can acknowledge that, that easily. But she can't. She never has."

"Surprising," he replied. "It's kind of obvious."

"Don't you think?" I turned, facing him. "I mean, if you can understand that what she did was wrong, why can't she?"

"But," he replied, "those aren't the same, though."

I just looked at him as another car passed. "What?"

"First you said she wouldn't acknowledge what she'd done," he replied. "Right? Then you asked why she didn't understand it. Those are two different things entirely."

"They are?"

"Yeah. I mean, acknowledging is easy. Something happened or it didn't. But understanding . . . that's where things get sticky."

"That's us," I said. "Seriously sticky. For years now."

"I can relate," he said.

We sat there for a moment. He was picking at the grass, the blades squeaking between his fingers, while I just stared straight ahead. Finally, I said, "So your parents really freaked when you got arrested, huh?"

"'Freaked' is putting it mildly," he said. "It was basically a family DEFCON 5. Total breakdown."

"Seems kind of extreme."

"They thought I was out of control," he said.

"Wasn't it just one beer, at one party?"

"It was," he agreed. "But I'd never done anything like that before. Not even close. I hadn't even been to a high school party until a few weeks earlier."

"Big changes," I said.

"Exactly." He sat back, leaning on his palms. "In their minds, it's all the fault of Frazier Bakery. When I started working there, my downward spiral began."

I studied him for a second. "You aren't exactly a criminal."

"Maybe not. But you have to understand my parents," he said. "To them, an after-school job is something you only take if it enhances your educational future. You don't waste your time making Blueberry Banana Brain Freezes for minimum wage when you can be reading up on applied physics. It doesn't make sense."

"Blueberry Banana Brain Freezes?"

"It's a breakfast smoothie," he explained. "You should try one, they're seriously good. Just drink it slow. It's called that for a reason."

I smiled. "So why did you take the job?"

"It just looked like fun," he said. "I mean, I'd been assisting at my mom's lab since I was ten, doing research, writing up experiment notes. It was interesting, but it's not like I had much in common with the professors there. One day I was at FrayBake, getting my usual, and they had a help wanted sign up. I applied and they hired me. Simple as that."

"So much for the lab," I said.

"Yeah, well. There are plenty of kid geniuses around that

building. I don't think anyone but my mom missed me that much." He pulled at some more grass. "Anyway, I made some friends my own age, started doing things on the weekends other than read and study. Which was unnerving enough. But then, that summer, I told them I wanted to transfer to Jackson. They said absolutely not, pointing out all these statistics about the test scores and student-teacher ratio—"

"They countered with research?"

"They're scientists," he said as if this explained everything. "Eventually, I got them to agree to it, but only for a semester, and only because I already had more than enough credits to graduate."

"This was last year?"

He nodded.

"You could have graduated as a sophomore?"

"Actually," he replied with a cough, "I had enough credits after ninth grade."

"Holy crap," I said. "How smart *are* you?"

"Do you want to hear the rest of this or not?"

I bit my lip. "Sorry."

He shot me a fake-annoyed look, which made me snort, and then continued. "So I transferred. And then, you know, I started hanging out more with Riley and Heather, and went to a few parties, and blew off my Physics Bowl practice."

"Sounds pretty normal," I said. "Except for the Physics Bowl thing."

"For some people. Not for me." He cleared his throat. "Look, it's not like I'm proud of it. But I was almost eighteen and I'd never done anything, you know, normal. And suddenly, I was at this big school, where no one knew me. I could be whoever I wanted. And I didn't want to be the super-serious smart kid anymore."

I had a flash of all those schools I'd attended, a blur of hallways and closed doors. "I can understand that," I said.

"Yeah?"

I nodded.

"The point is, they were already not happy with me. And then I started planning this trip for after graduation, instead of going to Brain Camp, which didn't help things."

"Brain Camp?"

"This math thing I've done every summer since fifth grade," he explained. "I was supposed to be a counselor again this year. But Ellis, Riley, Heather, and I want to do this big road trip to Texas. Which is, you know, somewhat less academic."

I smiled. "Travel is educational."

"I pointed that out. They weren't buying it, though." He looked down at his hands again. "Anyway, it was my crappy luck that in the middle of all this I went to that party and got busted. Which made the trip a moot point."

The door to my neighbors' house banged, and someone came out and got into one of the cars parked in the front yard. They cranked the engine, hitting the gas a few times, the sound filling the street. When they pulled away, it felt even quieter than it had before.

"So you're not going?"

"I have a lot to prove," he said, his voice formal and stiff, clearly quoting. "Trust to earn back. If they feel I've made progress in those areas, they might reconsider it."

"Might."

"Might," he said. He smiled at me. "I've got a lot hanging on that 'might.' Probably too much."

"Riley says they were scared," I said finally. "That they thought they were losing you."

"I get that," he said. "But it's like, are there only two choices? Either I'm a delinquent in a fast downward spiral, or becoming a physicist, right on schedule? How is that possible?"

"You need a third option," I said.

"Or at least the chance to look around for one," he replied. "Which, I guess, is what I'm waiting for now. Toeing the line, doing my time, following the rules, and trying to figure out what comes next."

"Wow," I said. "You really are a disappointment."

"Yep," he agreed, stone-faced. "Although coming from a terrible daughter who is cruel to her mother, I'll take that as a compliment."

I smiled, digging my hands more deeply into my pockets. I was starting to really feel the cold now, and wondered what time it was.

"Seriously, though," Dave said after a moment, "for what it's worth, I can tell you that from the outside at least, your mom seems like she's trying. And sometimes that's all you can do."

"So you're taking her side," I said.

"I don't believe in sides." He sat back, planting his palms

on the strip of grass behind us. "People do crappy things for all kinds of reasons. You can't even begin to understand."

"It's not my job to understand," I said, my voice sounding sharper than I intended. "I didn't do anything. I was just an innocent bystander."

Dave didn't say anything, still looking up.

"I didn't do anything," I said again, surprised at the lump that suddenly rose in my throat. "I didn't deserve this."

"No," he said. "You didn't."

"I don't have to understand."

"Okay."

I swallowed over the lump, then blinked hard. It had been such a long day, and I was so, so tired. I wished I could just leave, disappear inside, but there was always something else required, a way to get from here to there.

Thinking this, I looked up at the sky, cold and clear overhead, and took a breath. *One,* I thought, finding the Big Dipper as tears pricked my eyes. *Two,* and I swallowed again, trying to calm myself as I spotted Cassiopeia. I was searching for a third when I felt myself starting to shake, desperate to find something familiar up there, somewhere. It was so cold, looking through my blurry gaze, but then, suddenly, I felt Dave slide his arm over my shoulders. He was warm and close, and at the same moment I realized this, I spotted the outline of Orion. *Three,* I thought, and then rested my head against him, closing my eyes.

Eight

✳ ❀ ✳

When I got to school Monday morning, the first person
I saw was Riley.

She was actually the only person I saw, as I was way late.
Our heat had gone out overnight, and what with calling the
rental agency to get a repairman set up, I'd missed the bus.
Then I had to wait for my dad to finish a phone conference with
Chuckles, who was in London, before he could give me a ride.
When I finally got there, fifteen minutes into second period, my
hair was still wet, fingers slightly numb. Plus, I was starving,
as all I'd eaten was half a banana in the car with my dad as he
raced through yellow lights and school zones, now late himself.

I was halfway up the stairs, on my way to my locker, when
I spotted Riley sitting on the radiator outside the guidance
office, her backpack at her feet. She was on the phone, talking quietly, her head ducked down as I passed her and turned
the corner. All I could think about was that text she'd sent
to Dave—YOU CHARMER—and, despite the fact that nothing
had really happened between me and him, I still felt kind of
weird. I'd meant what I said about Dave: he was a nice guy, but

I didn't have time for a nice guy, or any guy, really. I didn't feel like explaining this again, though, so I steered clear.

At my locker, I stowed some books, then as my stomach rumbled, began to dig around for an energy bar I was pretty sure I'd stashed in there the week before. When I finally found it, I ripped it open right there and took a bite. As I stood there chewing, I caught a glimpse of myself in that awful, feathered SEXXY mirror and decided it was time for it to go. When I reached up to rip it off, though, I found it was stuck on pretty well. I took another bite of the bar, then dug my fingers down the side of the mirror, dislodging it only the tiniest bit.

Damn, I thought, giving it another yank. Nothing. I stuffed the rest of the bar in my mouth, then used both hands, really trying to pry under the feathers on the edge. It resisted completely. I was just about to give up when, just as I was swallowing, the mirror suddenly came off. What happened next was in quick succession: the bite of energy bar caught in my throat, the mirror clattered to the floor, and the locker door, rapidly swinging shut, cracked me right across the nose.

I stumbled backward, simultaneously choking and seeing stars as I banged into the water fountain behind me. It came on cheerfully and dependably, shooting an arc of water over my elbow.

"Oh my God," I heard someone say. There were footsteps, and blurrily, as my eyes were squeezed shut in pain, I saw movement in front of me. "Are you okay?"

I coughed—relieved that I could breathe—then swallowed and stepped back from the fountain, stopping the water show. Which left only my nose, which was smarting like I'd been punched. "I think so," I said.

"That was *crazy*."

I opened my eyes slowly, to see what I was pretty sure was Riley in front of me, a concerned expression on her face. I blinked, and she came a bit more into focus.

"You should sit down," she said, taking my elbow. I bent my knees, easing myself down the wall to the floor. "That was a pretty big whack. I heard it all the way down the hallway."

"I don't know what happened," I said.

She turned, walking across the short hallway to where the SEXXY mirror was lying on the floor by my locker and picking it up. "I think you can blame this thing. I think once they're put up, they are not meant to be removed."

"Now you tell me." I reached up tentatively to my nose, but just the slightest touch made my whole face hurt.

"Here. Let me see." She squatted down in front of me, peering in close. "Oh, man. You've got quite a mark there. Look."

She held up the mirror at my eye level. Sure enough, I had a red bump on the middle of my nose, which seemed to be growing in size as I watched it. I wasn't sure if it was broken. But it was anything but SEXXY.

"Great," I said. "This is just what I needed today."

"Of course it was." She smiled, then reached down, picking up my backpack. "Come on. We should take you to the nurse, get some ice on that thing."

I pushed myself to my feet, feeling her watching me. I felt all shaky, in that weird way you do when your equilibrium, not to mention everything else, has been knocked askew. As if sensing this, Riley took my arm, holding my elbow. Her touch was light, but I could still feel her steering me as we turned into the main hall.

Down in the nurse's office, we were triaged behind a guy who was vomiting (ugh) and a tall girl with a fever and bright red cheeks. I was given a pack of frozen peas and told to wait. I picked a seat as far as I could from the other patients, then sat down, pressing it to my nose. Ahhhh.

Riley sat down beside me. "Is that helping?"

"Big-time," I told her. Around the peas, I said, "You don't have to stay. I'm sure you have something better to do."

"Not really," she replied. When I glanced at her, doubting this, she added, "I have a free period. I'm supposed to be in the math lab or the library, but no one really checks up."

"Lucky you," I said. "How'd you swing that?"

She shrugged, crossing her legs. "I have an honest face, I guess."

I reached up, tentatively touching my nose again. It was a bit more numb now, but the bump was bigger. Great. Across the room, the vomiter was looking sort of green. I put the peas back on.

"So," Riley said, as the nurse passed by, collecting the girl with the fever and taking her into the other room, "you and Dave, huh?"

I swallowed. Well, it wasn't like this was a surprise. "It wasn't really anything. We just went to the game."

"So I saw." I glanced at her. "My dad's a big U fan. Watching the games is pretty much mandatory at my house."

"My dad used to be like that, too," I told her. "But about Defriese."

"Not so much now, I bet."

I took the peas away again. Her face was sympathetic, though, not teasing. "No," I said. "Not so much."

We sat there for a moment, both of us silent. Then she said, "I'm sorry if I made you uncomfortable the other night. When we were talking outside your house."

"You didn't," I told her.

"It's just . . ." She looked down at her hands, then opened them up, spreading her fingers across her knees. "Dave kind of brings out my overprotective side. I don't want to see him get hurt, you know?"

"He told me you were, like, his only friend when he started here."

"Pretty much. He met Ellis in homeroom his first day, but we were the sum total of his inner circle. Plus, he was coming from Kiffney-Brown, which is like another planet. I mean, his best friend there was thirteen."

"You mean Gerv the Perv?"

"He told you about him, huh? God, is that kid a nightmare. I mean, he's supersmart and all, but a person can only take so many booger jokes, you know?" She rolled her eyes. "Truthfully, though, I probably wasn't the best choice either. It's because of me he started going to parties and doing all that other stuff that got him in so deep with his parents. He would have been better off with just Ellis."

"You and Ellis aren't friends?"

"We are now," she said. "But mostly because we have Dave in common. Ellis, you know, he's a good kid. Plays soccer, is involved with a bunch of school stuff. I mean, he does the freaking TV announcements. Definitely a better choice for Dave than taking up with me."

"I'm not sure about that," I said. "You seem like a pretty good friend."

"Yeah?"

I nodded, and she smiled.

"I try. Really, though, it's selfish in some ways. I have this weird thing about wanting to take care of everyone, not just Dave. It makes things complicated."

I shifted the peas. "Simple has its downsides, too."

"Meaning what?"

"I don't know," I said. "I move around a lot. So I hardly get to know anybody. It might be easier, but it's kind of lonely."

I wasn't sure why I was being so truthful. Maybe it was the crack to the head. Riley turned, looking at me. "You think you'll be staying here for a while?"

"No idea," I told her.

"Huh. Really."

She faced forward again. I said, "What?"

"It's just," she said, "you haven't done that here. Not made friends."

"I haven't?"

She looked at the green-faced guy across from us. "Mclean," she said. "I'm sitting here with you, in the nurse's office, during my free period. That means we're friends."

"But you're just being nice," I said.

"Just like you were nice to me, the other night at my car," she replied. "Plus, you took Dave to the game. You invited Deb into a social gathering which, believe me, no one has *ever* done here, to my knowledge. And you haven't smacked Heather yet, which is a much better record than most."

"That's not *that* hard," I told her.

"Yes, it is. She's my best friend and I love her, but she can be a total pain in the ass." She sat back, crossing her legs again. "Face it, Mclean. You might think you don't want any connections, but your actions say otherwise."

"Mclean Sweet?" I looked up to see the nurse, a clipboard in hand, standing in the doorway to the examining room. "Come on back. Let's take a look at that bump."

I stood up, picking up my bag. "Thanks for coming with me," I told Riley. "I appreciate it."

"I'll stay until you're done," she said.

"You don't have to."

She settled back in her chair, pulling out her phone from her pocket. "I know."

I followed the nurse into the room, taking a seat on the cot as she shut the door behind us. *What a weird day,* I thought as she rolled a stool over, gesturing for me to remove the peas. As she leaned in to inspect the damage, I looked through the glass of the door out into the room beyond. It was blurred and thick for privacy, so you couldn't really see details. Even so, I could make out the shape of a figure sitting there, a presence nearby, waiting. For me.

×   ×   ×

At lunch, walking out to the courtyard with my burrito and bottled water, I got the distinct feeling people were staring at me. Or maybe *gawking* was a better word. I knew my nose was swollen, but the attention I was getting—and had been getting since my run-in with the locker—seemed excessive. Then again, maybe a girl who looks like she's been in a bar fight is just big news on a slow Monday.

Riley and Heather were nowhere to be seen, so I walked over to Deb, who was sitting alone under her tree. She had an iPod on and her eyes were closed, listening.

"Hey," I said. When she didn't look up, I nudged her foot, and she jumped, then opened her eyes.

"Oh, Mclean!" she said, hurriedly taking out her earbuds. "It *is* true! I thought it was just a vicious, nasty rumor."

"What?"

"You and Riley," she said. When I just looked at her, she added, "Your fight? I heard she punched you, but I didn't want to believe—"

"Riley didn't *punch* me." I looked around the courtyard again. Several people were looking right back, and didn't even bother to break their gaze. "Who said that?"

"I heard it in the bathroom," she whispered. "Everyone is talking about it."

"Oh, for God's sake." I sat down, putting my lunch on the ground beside me. "Why would she punch me?"

Deb picked up her Diet Coke, taking a sip from her straw. "Jealous rage," she explained. "She saw you and Dave Wade at the game this weekend and just lost it."

"She and Dave aren't together," I told her, unwrapping my burrito. Honestly, though, I'd kind of lost my appetite.

"I know that, and you know that. But apparently, the rest of the school does not." She tucked a piece of hair behind her ear. "You know how it is. Most people think a girl and a guy can't just be friends, that there has to be something else going on. It's basic."

"I guess," I said.

"So . . ." she said slowly, studying my face. "What really happened?"

"I clocked myself with my locker door."

"Ouch."

"Tell me about it."

"Really, though," she said, taking another sip, "it doesn't look that bad at all. If it wasn't the girl-fight angle, nobody would even notice."

Time to change the subject. I nodded at the iPod, on the ground between us. "What are you listening to?"

"Just this mix I made," she said. "Music, you know, calms me down. I find it's helpful to just sort of zone out to it when I'm having a long day."

"I hear that," I said. "I could use some calming myself. Can I listen?"

"Sure," she said. "But—"

I was already reaching over, picking up her earbuds and sliding them into my ears, expecting to hear the soft, lulling tones of adult contemporary. Or maybe a peppy show tune. Instead, I got a blast of feedback, followed by a drumroll.

I recoiled, pulling out one earbud. The other one stayed in, filling my head with the sound of someone screaming incoherently over what sounded like a chain saw. "Deb," I sputtered, turning the iPod over and peering down at the screen. "What *is* this?"

"Just this band I was in at my old school," she said. "They're called Naugahyde."

I just looked at her. "You were in a band?"

She nodded. "For a little while."

The person in my ear was still going, their voice ragged and loud. "You," I said slowly, "were in *this* band?"

"Yeah. I mean, it was a small school. Not a lot of options." She adjusted her headband. "I'd been taking drum lessons forever, but I really wanted some collaborative experience. So when I saw the ad for a drummer, I applied, and got to sit in for some session work."

"Deb," I said, holding up my hand. "Hold on. Are you messing with me?"

"What?"

"You just . . ." I trailed off. "You don't exactly look like a speed-metal drummer."

"Because I'm not," she said.

"You're not."

"I mean, I don't quantify myself that way. I'm trained in all genres." She reached into her bag, taking out a pack of gum, and offered me a piece. When I declined, she stuck it back in, zipping it shut, then looked up at me. "Although I do like the faster stuff, if only because it's more fun to play."

I opened my mouth, still shocked, but no words came. Before I could form any, Dave suddenly plopped down beside me.

"Hey," he said, shrugging off his backpack. "What's going on here?"

I turned to look at him. "Deb," I said, "is a drummer."

"Holy crap!" he said.

"I know!" I said. "Isn't that crazy? I just—"

"What happened to your *face*?" he asked.

So much for it hardly being noticeable. "Riley punched me," I told him.

"She what?"

"That's the rumor," I said, picking up my water. "At least according to Deb."

"I heard it in the bathroom," Deb explained.

Dave looked at her, then at me again. "Whoa," he said, leaning in closer. "She really got a good hit in."

I just looked at him. "Do you really believe she'd do that?"

"To you?" he asked. "No. But she does have a good arm on her. That, I know from experience. What was this fight supposedly about?"

I looked at Deb, who quickly busied herself looking for something in her purse. Finally, I said, "Apparently, it was a jealous rage spurred by seeing us together at the game."

"Ah," he said, nodding. "Right. The jealous rage thing." He carefully raised a hand, touching my cheek. In my peripheral vision, I saw Deb's eyes widen. "What really happened?"

"My locker door attacked me."

"They'll do that." He dropped his hand, then smiled. "You need some ice or something?"

"Already got it at the nurse's office," I told him. "But thanks."

"It's the least I can do," he said. "Since I was the cause and everything."

I smiled. "You joke, but the rest of the school totally believes it. Just look around us."

Dave turned, scanning the courtyard. Since he'd joined us, we had even more of an audience. "Whoa," he said, looking back at me. "You're not kidding."

"People can't resist a love triangle," Deb said.

"Is that what this is?" Dave asked. He was talking to her, but looking right at me, and I felt my face flush.

"No," I said.

He shrugged. "Too bad. I've always wanted to be part of one of those."

"Oh, no you don't," Deb told him, shaking her head. "It's no picnic, let me tell you."

I snorted, which made Dave laugh. Deb just looked at us, not getting the joke. "Deb," I said, "is there anything you don't have experience with?"

"What do you mean?" she asked.

"It's just . . ." I looked at Dave for help, but of course he gave me none. "You're an expert on tattoos. A drummer. And now, you've been in a love triangle."

"Just once," she replied. Then she sighed. "But once was *more* than enough."

Dave laughed, then looked at me again, and I felt this little rush. Like a tiny flame flickering. *No,* I thought just as quickly. *I'm not staying here long. He's not my type.*

"So, Deb," Dave said. "You coming to Luna Blu this afternoon to work on our model project?"

"It's not *our* anything," I said. "I was just there that day to help Opal. It's for delinquents only."

"Not true," he corrected me. "It's a service project for anyone who has a hankering to serve their community."

"A 'hankering'?" I said.

"I love volunteering!" Deb exclaimed. "Is it really open to anyone?"

"Yep," Dave told her. "And don't listen to Mclean. She's practically spearheading the entire thing."

"It sounds like so much fun! I love group projects," Deb said.

"Then you should come by some afternoon. We work from four to six," Dave said.

"Are you speaking for me?" I asked him. "Because I won't be there."

"No?" he asked. We looked at each other for a moment. Then he said, "We'll see."

Deb looked at me, then at Dave, then back at me again, her expression a question. Before I could say anything, though, the bell rang, its sound ricocheting around the courtyard, making my ears ring. She jumped up, reaching for her bag, but still kept her eyes on Dave, intrigued, as he eased himself to his feet, then turned and looked down at me.

"You didn't have to take a punch for me, you know," he said. "I'm a lover, not a fighter."

"You're a freak is what you are," I said.

He stuck out his hand. "Come on, slugger. Walk with me. You know you want to."

And the thing was, despite everything I knew—that it was a mistake, that he was different from the others—I did. How he knew that, I had no idea. But I got up and did it anyway.

× × ×

That afternoon, when I got home, my dad's keys were in the door. When I pulled them out and pushed it open, I heard voices.

"Stop it. Seriously. This isn't funny."

"You're right." A pause. "It's pathetic."

There was some giggling. Then, "Look, if we rank every-one on the staff with the point system, and incorporate the evaluations like we discussed, then go off of that, then . . ."

". . . we'll have official numeric confirmation that we do, in fact, have the worst staff in town."

I heard a snicker, then a full-out burst of laughter. By the time I got to the kitchen doorway to see my dad and Opal at the table, a bunch of papers spread out between them, they were in hysterics.

"What are you guys doing?" I asked.

Opal picked up a napkin from the bowl on the counter, dabbing at her eyes, then opened her mouth to answer me. Before she could, though, she broke down again, waving her hand in front of her face. My dad, across from her, was sput-tering.

"Corporate," Opal said finally, or rather gasped, "wants us to decide who our weak links are."

"And the answer," my dad added, snorting, "is everyone."

They both burst out laughing again, like this was the

funniest thing in the world. Opal put her head in her hands, her shoulders shaking, while my dad sat back, trying to catch his breath.

"I don't get it," I said.

"That's because," my dad said, wheezing, "you haven't been at it for four straight hours."

"Four hours!" Opal said, slapping her hand on the table. "And we've got *nothing*. Zip, zilch, nada."

My dad tittered at this. He sounded like a little girl. I asked, "Why are you doing this here?"

"We can't do it at the restaurant," Opal said. She took a deep breath. "It's very serious business."

My dad howled at this, throwing his head back, which set her off again. I headed to the fridge for a drink, wondering if we had a gas leak or something.

"Okay, okay." Opal took a deep breath. "Seriously, this is ridiculous. I'm so slaphappy I can't see straight. We have to finish like—oh my God! Mclean, what happened to your nose?"

I shut the fridge to see them both staring at me. It was a little more noticeable in profile, I guessed. "I collided with my locker. I'm fine."

"Are you?" my dad asked as I came over, sitting down beside him. He reached to touch the bump and I flinched. "That looks pretty serious."

"It was a lot worse earlier," I told him. "The swelling's gone way down."

"It looks like someone punched you," my dad said.

"Nope. Just a clumsy chain reaction." I took a sip of my

drink. He was still watching me. "Dad. I'm fine."

Across the table, Opal smiled. "She's a tough girl, Gus. Stop fretting."

My dad made a face at her, then looked down at a stack of papers in front of him, rubbing a hand over his face. "Okay, so here's the thing. I know Chuckles pretty well," he said. "He likes formulas and numbers, everything laid out neatly on a spreadsheet. That's why he uses this evaluation system. It's totally cut and dry."

"Maybe so, but it leaves no room for the human side of things," Opal said. "Now, I'm the first to admit we don't have the most capable staff. . . ."

I glanced at the yellow legal pad that was by his elbow. On it was a list of names, each one with a number beside it. Scribblings and notes filled the margins, along with scratch-outs and smudges.

"But," she added quickly, "*but*, I think our people do add a flavor and personality to the Luna Blu experience that cannot be quantified on a piece of paper."

My dad looked at her. "Today at lunch," he said, his voice flat, "Leo sent out a chicken sandwich with yogurt on it instead of sour cream."

Opal bit her lip. "Well," she said after a moment, "in the Middle East, yogurt is a popular sandwich condiment."

"But we're not in the Middle East."

"It's a mistake!" she said, throwing up her hands. "People make them. Nobody's perfect."

"Which is a fine philosophy in a preschool," my dad replied. "But in a working, profitable restaurant, we need to aim for better."

She looked down at her hands. "So you're saying we fire Leo."

My dad pulled the legal pad closer, squinting at it. "If we go by Chuckles's formula, yes. By the numbers, he and everyone else we've got listed here in the top spots should go."

Opal groaned, pushing back from the table. "But they're not numbers. They're people. *Good* people."

"Who don't know the difference between yogurt and sour cream." She rolled her eyes, and he added, "Opal, this is my job. If something—or someone—isn't working, then we have to make changes."

"Like the rolls."

He sighed. "They were a cost suck, took up too much prep time, and gave us no return. It could be argued, in fact, that they *lost* us money."

"But I liked them," she said softly.

"I did, too."

Opal looked up at him, surprised. "You did?"

"Yeah."

"I thought you loved the pickles!"

My dad shook his head. I said, "He hates pickles. All kinds."

"But especially fried," he added. When Opal just stared at him, mouth open, he added, "It's not about my personal feelings, though. It's about what's best for the restaurant. You've got to take emotion out of it."

She considered this as I got up, putting my now-empty

glass in the sink. Then she said, "Well, I'll tell you one thing. I could never do what you do."

"Meaning what?" my dad asked.

"This," she said, pointing at the pad on the table between them. "Coming into a place and making tons of changes that piss everyone off, firing people. Not to mention putting in all this time and work into something, only to move right on to the next place when it's done."

"It's a job," he pointed out.

"I get that." She picked up a napkin, shredding the edge. "But how do you not get invested? In the place, and everyone in it?"

I turned off the water. I wanted to hear the answer.

"Well," he said after a moment, "it's not always so easy. But I had a restaurant of my own for many years. I was beyond invested, and that was hard, too. Harder, actually."

"Tell me about it," Opal said. "I've loved Luna Blu since I was a teenager. It's, like, where my heart is."

"Which is why," he told her, "you want it to be the best it can possibly be. Even if that means making some tough decisions."

We were all quiet for a moment. Then Opal folded the napkin, placing it neatly in front of her. Then she looked up at my dad and said, "I really hate it when you're right."

"I know," he told her. "I get that a lot."

She sighed, pushing off her chair and getting to her feet. "So tomorrow, when we meet with corporate, we'll give them these numbers . . ."

". . . and go from there," my dad said.

Opal gathered up her purse and keys. "I feel like I'm going to death row," she said, wrapping a scarf around her neck. "How am I supposed to look these people in the face, knowing they will most likely be unemployed next week?"

"It's not easy being the boss," my dad said.

"No kidding," she replied. "I wish I had some rolls to drown my sorrows in. Carbohydrates are great for guilt."

"Really," my dad said. "Are you *ever* going to let that go?"

She smiled, pulling her purse over one shoulder. "Nope," she said. "Bye, Mclean. Feel better."

"Thanks," I replied. And then my dad and I both watched as she walked across the living room to the front door, pushing it open. Halfway down the walk, she stopped, adjusting her scarf. She looked up at the gray sky for a moment, then squared her shoulders and started walking again.

I looked at my dad. He said, "She's really something."

"Everybody is." I wiped down the counter, then turned back, only to find him still sitting there, continuing to watch Opal as she crossed the street and started down the alley. "So what do you think? Is everyone really going to get fired?"

"No telling," my dad replied, gathering up some of the papers on the table. "Depends on myriad factors, everything from Chuckles's stock portfolio to how benevolent he's feeling. What she doesn't realize, though, is that people getting fired isn't the worst-case scenario."

"No?"

He shook his head. "The building itself is worth a lot more

than the restaurant right now. Chuckles could decide to just sell, wash his hands of the whole thing, and move on."

I looked back at Opal, barely visible now. "You think he'd do that?"

"He might. We'll find out tomorrow, I guess."

I turned back to the sink, pulling off a paper towel and drying my hands. My dad came over, kissing the top of my head as he picked up his phone, and started down the hallway.

Once the bedroom door was shut behind him, I went over to the table, glancing down at the pad with the names and numbers on it. Tracey was a four, Leo a three. Jason was a nine, whatever that meant. If only you could really use a failproof system to know who was worth keeping and who needed to be thrown away. It would make it so much easier to move through the world, picking and choosing what connections to make, or whether to make any at all.

× × ×

Later that night, I was in my room, trying to do some Western Civ homework, when I heard a knock on our kitchen door. I walked down the dark hallway to see Dave standing under the porch light. He had on jeans and a long-sleeved plaid shirt and was carrying a steaming saucepan in his hands, a pot holder around the handle.

"Chicken soup," he said when I opened the door. "Great for bar-fight injuries. Got a bowl?"

I stepped back and he came inside, walking straight to the stove and putting the pot down. "You cook?"

"I used to," he replied. "It was either that or stick to my mom's menu, and sometimes I wanted, you know, meat and dairy. But it's been a while. Hopefully, this won't kill us."

I got out two bowls and two spoons. "That's not exactly a ringing endorsement."

"Maybe, but look at it this way," he said. "You already got punched in the face today. What do you have to lose?"

"You know," I said, sitting down at the table, "I didn't really get punched."

"Yeah, I know." He started pouring soup into one of the bowls. "But I'd be lying if I said I wasn't kind of flattered that the whole school thinks you *might* have because of me."

"Well, I'm glad I can help with your self-esteem."

He stuck a spoon in one bowl, then handed it to me. "I know it's got to be humiliating for you. I figured the least I could do is make you some soup. Plus, I felt bad about earlier."

I took the soup, then looked up at him. "About what?"

He shrugged. "That stuff I said about you coming to help with the model. When you didn't show, I realized I sounded like a jerk."

"Why?" I told him.

"I said I was a lover, not a fighter." He sighed, sitting down across from me. "It doesn't get more jerky than that."

"Oh, sure it does."

He smiled. "Look, seriously, though. Because of skipping grades and hanging out with prodigies . . . my social skills aren't exactly great. Sometimes I say stupid stuff."

"You don't have to skip grades for that," I told him. "I've got a B-plus average and I do it all the time."

"B-plus?" He looked horrified. "Really?"

I made a face, then I leaned over the bowl, which was steaming. The last thing I'd really eaten was half of that soggy burrito, hours ago, and I realized suddenly I was starving. I ate a spoonful. The soup was thick, with egg noodles, chicken, and carrots, and was, in fact, just what I needed.

"Wow," I said as he sat down across from me with his own bowl. "This is great."

He ate a spoonful, then thought for a second. "It's not bad. Needs more thyme, though. Where are your spices?"

He was already getting up, heading to the cabinets, when I said, "Actually—"

"In here?" he asked, already reaching for the one closest to the stove.

"—we don't really—"

Before I could finish, though, it had already happened: he'd opened the door, exposing the empty space behind it. He paused, then reached for the next one. Also empty. As was the one adjacent. Finally, he discovered the cabinet that held our full array of housewares, which I organized the same way in every house when we moved in. A handful of spices—salt, pepper, chili powder, garlic salt—sat on the bottom shelf, with silverware in a plastic organizer beside it. On the shelf above, there were four plates, four bowls, three coffee mugs, and six glasses. And finally, up top, one frying pan, two saucepans, and a mixing bowl.

"Wait," he said, moving over to the next cabinet and opening it. Empty. "Is this . . . What's going on here? Are you, like, survivalists or something?"

"No," I said, embarrassed, although I wasn't sure why. I actually prided myself on keeping it minimal: it made moving easy. "We just don't spread out much."

He opened another cabinet, revealing the bare wall behind it. "Mclean," he said, "you have a basically empty kitchen."

"We have everything we need," I countered. He just looked at me. "Except thyme. Look, my dad works at a restaurant. We don't cook much."

"You don't even have baking pans," he said, still opening things and exposing empty spaces. "What if you need to roast or broil something?"

"I buy a foil pan," I told him. He just looked at me. "What? Do you know what a pain it is to pack glass pans? They always chip, if not break altogether."

He came back to the table, taking his seat. Behind him, a few of the cabinets were still open, like gaping mouths. "No offense," he said, "but that's just plain sad."

"Why?" I asked. "It's organized."

"It's paltry," he replied. "And totally temporary. Like you're only here for a week or something."

I ate another spoonful of soup. "Come on."

"Seriously." He looked at the cabinets again. "Is it like this all over the house? Like, if I open the drawers in your bedroom, I'll see you have only two pairs of pants?"

"You're not opening my drawers," I told him. "And no. But if you really care, we used to have more stuff. Each time we moved, though, I realized how little we were using of it. So I scaled back. And then I scaled back a little more."

He just looked at me as I stirred my bowl, moving the carrots around. "How many times have you moved?"

"Not that many," I said. He did not look convinced, so I added, "I've been living with Dad for almost two years . . . and I guess this is the fourth place. Or something."

"Four towns in two years?" he said.

"Well, of course it sounds bad when you say it like *that*," I said.

For a moment, neither of us said anything. The only sound was our spoons clinking. I really wanted to get up and shut the open cabinets, but for some reason I felt like it would be admitting something. I stayed where I was.

"What I mean is, it must be hard," he said finally, glancing up at me. "Always being the new kid."

"Not necessarily." I tucked one leg up underneath me. "There's something kind of freeing about it, actually."

"Really."

"Sure," I said. "When you move a lot, you don't have a lot of entanglements. There's not really time to get all caught up in things. It's simpler."

He thought about this for a second. "True. But if you never really make friends, you probably don't have anyone to be your two a.m. Which would kind of suck."

I just looked at him as he stirred his soup, carrots spinning in the liquid. "Your what?"

"Two a.m." He swallowed, then said, "You know. The person you can call at two a.m. and, no matter what, you can count on them. Even if they're asleep or it's cold or you need to be bailed out jail . . . they'll come for you. It's, like, the highest level of friendship."

"Oh. Right." I looked down at the table. "Well, I guess I can see the value in that."

We were quiet for a moment. Then Dave said, "At the same time, though, I can understand the whole blank-page thing. You don't have to constantly be explaining yourself."

"Exactly," I said. "Nobody knows you were ever friends with Gerv the Perv. Or part of a vicious, girl-fight-inducing love triangle."

"Or that your parents had an awful divorce." I looked at him. "Sorry. But that's kind of where you were going, right?"

It hadn't been. At least not on purpose. "My point is that all the moving has been just what me and my dad needed. It's been a good thing for both of us."

"Being temporary," he said.

"Getting a fresh start," I countered. "Or four."

Another silence fell. I could hear the fridge humming behind me. Weird how some things you're never aware of until there's nothing else to notice.

"So you think you'll move from here again, soon?" he asked finally. "When six months is up?"

"Don't know," I replied. "Sometimes we stay longer or shorter than that. It's really up to the company my dad works for. And next year . . ."

I trailed off, realizing only once I'd started this sentence that I didn't really want to get into it. But I could feel Dave watching me, waiting.

"There's college, and all that," I finished. "So this one

already kind of has an end date, regardless. At least for me."

We looked at each other for a moment. He was a smart guy, probably the smartest I'd ever met. So it didn't take long, only a beat or so, for him to get what I was saying.

"Right." He put his spoon down in his now-empty bowl. "Well, at least you'll be ready for the dorm. You've got living simply down."

I smiled, looking at the cabinets. "I do, don't I?"

"Yeah. Maybe I should take some lessons. Might come in handy when I'm packing for our road trip this summer."

"The road trip?" I asked. "Does that mean it's back on? Your parents gave the okay?"

"Not exactly. But they're warming up to the idea a bit." He pushed his bowl to the side. "Mostly because I said I'd spend the second half of the summer at Brain Camp, which is what they want me to do. It's all about compromise. But if it means I get to go to Texas with Ellis and Riley, it's all good."

"So Heather wasn't invited?"

He smiled. "Good assumption, but actually she was in until recently. She, uh, kind of wrecked her car and got her license pulled for points. Her dad's making her pay back all the debt and for a new policy before she can drive again, so all her money went to that."

"Was this the guardhouse incident?" I asked.

"It was." He sighed. "I swear, she is the worst driver. She doesn't look when she merges."

"So I hear." I looked down at my bowl, pushing a stray carrot around. "So what's in Texas?"

"Austin, mostly. Ellis's brother lives there, and he's always talking about how good the music scene is, all the cool stuff there is to do. Plus, it's far enough that we can stop a bunch of other places along the way."

"You're excited," I said.

"Well, unlike some people, I'm not exactly well traveled. And everyone likes a road trip, right?"

I nodded, thinking of my mom and me, driving to North Reddemane and the Poseidon. I knew he thought my life was weird, and the truth was, I didn't expect him to understand where I was coming from. How could he, when he'd lived in the same place his entire life, with the same people around him, his history and past always inescapable, inevitable? I wasn't saying my way was necessarily best. But neither was never having any change. And given the choice between these two options, I knew the life I was living was the better one for me. I might not have had spices, but I wasn't lugging useless, chipped glass pans around with me either. So to speak.

"David? Hello?"

I turned to see Mrs. Dobson-Wade, standing on her side porch, her door open behind her. She was craning her neck, scanning the side yard, a concerned look on her face.

Dave got up, walking to our door and sticking his head out. "Hey," he said. She jumped, startled. "I'm over here."

"Oh," she said. When she saw me, she waved, and I waved back. "Sorry to interrupt. But that documentary your father mentioned earlier is coming on, and I knew you wouldn't want to miss the beginning."

"Right," Dave said, glancing at me. "The documentary."

"It's about the lives of cells," Mrs. Wade explained to me. "A really fascinating, in-depth view. Highly acclaimed."

I nodded, not sure what to say to this. "I'll be there in a minute," Dave told her.

"All right." She smiled, then shut the door, and Dave came back to the table.

"Cells, huh?" I said as he sat back down.

"Yep." He sighed, stacking our bowls one in the other, and putting both spoons in the top one. "They make up everything and everyone, Mclean."

"I know," I said. "I'm sure it will be fascinating."

"Want to join us?" I bit my lip, trying not to smile as he stood up, pushing in his chair. "Yeah, it's not exactly my cup of tea either. But if I want to go to Austin, I have to play the game. Be a good son, and all that."

He walked over to the stove, where he picked up the sauce-pan, stuffing the pot holder in his pocket. Then, as I watched, he carefully shut all the open, empty cabinets. Just like that, my kitchen was normal again. At least, from the outside.

He was walking to the door now, the pot in hand, and I pushed out my chair, getting to my feet. "You know," I said, "the fact that I didn't come by today . . . it wasn't about anything you said. I'm just—"

"Not into entanglements," he finished for me. "I get it. Loud and clear."

We stood there for a moment, just looking at each other. *If I had more time,* I thought, but really, it wasn't about that. I just wasn't sure any relationship could work. If the perfect love story turned out not to be, what did that mean for the rest of us?

Dave looked over at his house again. "I'd better go. The cells and their lives are waiting."

"Thanks for the soup."

"No problem. Thanks for the company."

I pushed open my door, and he stepped through, glancing back once as he went down the stairs and across the driveway. I watched him go inside his kitchen, putting the saucepan in the sink. Then he started down the hallway, where the light of a TV was flickering in the distance.

I was almost back to my room, and my homework, when the phone rang. Which startled me, honestly, as I'd sort of forgotten it was there. My dad and I usually didn't bother with landlines, instead just using our cell phones, as it was easier than having to keep learning new numbers in every place. But here, for whatever reason, EAT INC had put in a house line for us. The few times it had rung, they were wrong numbers or telemarketers. If it wasn't for the fact that I was looking for a reason to procrastinate, I probably would have ignored it altogether.

"Hello?" I said, my tone stern, already in No mode.

"Is that Mclean?"

I didn't recognize the voice, which just made the fact that the caller knew who I was that much weirder. "Um," I said. "Yes. Who's this?"

"Lindsay Baker. From the town council. We met the other day at the restaurant."

Immediately, I saw her in my head: that yellow-blonde

hair, bright eyes, even brighter teeth. Even over the phone her confidence was palpable. "Oh, right. Hi."

"I'm calling because I've been trying to reach your father for a few days now on his cell and at Luna Blu, without any luck, and I was hoping to catch him at this number. Is he around?"

"No," I said. "He's at the restaurant."

"Oh." A pause. "That's strange. I just called there and they said he was at home."

"Really?" I looked at the clock: it was 7:30, prime dinner rush. "I'm not sure where he could be, then."

"Oh, well," she replied. "It was worth a shot. I'll keep trying him, but could I bother you to pass on my number and a message?"

"Sure."

I picked up a pen and uncapped it. "Just tell him," she said, "that I'd really like to get together for lunch and discuss what we talked about the other day. My treat, at his convenience. I'm at 919-555-7744. That's my cell, and I always have it with me."

LINDSAY BAKER, I wrote, with the number beneath it. *WANTS YOU FOR LUNCH*. "I'll tell him," I said.

"Perfect. Thank you, Mclean."

We hung up, and I looked back down at the message, realizing only then that it sounded like something the big bad wolf would leave. *Oh, well,* I thought, sticking it on the kitchen table. *He'll get the idea.*

I went back to my room and tried to immerse myself in the Industrial Revolution. About a half hour later, I heard a soft knock at the back door, so quiet I wondered if I'd imagined it. When I came out, no one was there. On the back deck rail, though, there was a small box, a sticky note attached to it.

I picked it up. It was a plastic container of thyme, already opened, but more than half full. *JUST IN CASE YOU DECIDE TO STICK AROUND,* the note said in messy, slanted writing. *WE HAD THREE OF THESE.*

I looked back at the Wades' dark kitchen for a moment, then turned around and went back inside, putting the thyme in the cupboard, right by the salt and pepper and the silverware. The note I took back to my room, where I stuck it on my bedside clock, front and center, so it would be the first thing I saw in the morning.

Nine

✳ ❇ ✳

The next day I woke up to a bright white glare outside my window. When I eased the shade aside and peered out, I saw it had snowed overnight. There were about four inches covering everything, and it was still coming down.

"Snow," my dad reported as I came into the kitchen. He was at the window, a mug of coffee in his hands. "Haven't seen that in a while."

"Not since Montford Falls," I said.

"If we're lucky, it'll delay Chuckles at the airport. That would at least buy us some time."

"To do what?"

He sighed, putting down his coffee cup. "Wave a magic wand. Poach the staff of the best restaurant in town. Consider other career options. That kind of thing."

I opened the pantry door, reaching inside to pull out the cereal. "Well, at least you're thinking positively."

"Always."

I was getting out the milk when I suddenly remembered the call I'd answered the night before. "Hey, did you leave the restaurant last night?"

"Only at about one to come back here," he replied. "Why?"

"That councilwoman, Lindsay Baker," I said. "When she called and left that message, she said they'd just told her you were gone."

He sighed, then reached up to rub a hand over his face. "Okay, don't judge me," he said. "But I *might* have told them to tell her I wasn't there."

"Really?" I asked.

He grimaced.

"Why?"

"Because she keeps calling wanting to discuss this model thing, and I don't have the time or energy right now."

"She did say she's been trying to reach you for a while."

He grunted, taking one last sip off his mug and setting it in the sink. "Who calls a restaurant in the middle of dinner rush, wanting to make a lunch date? It's ludicrous."

"She wants a date?"

"I don't know what she wants. I just know I don't have time to do it, whatever it is." He picked up his cell phone, glancing at the screen before shutting it and sliding it in his pocket. "I gotta get over there and get some stuff done before Chuckles shows up. You'll be okay getting to school? Think they'll cancel?"

"Doubt it," I said. "This isn't Georgia or Florida. But I'll keep you posted."

"Do that." He squeezed my shoulder as I reached into the fridge for the milk. "Have a good day."

"You, too. Good luck."

He nodded, then headed for the front door. I watched him pull on his jacket, which was neither very warm nor waterproof, before going out onto the porch. Not for the first time, I thought of the next year, and what it would be like for him to be living in another rental house, in another town, without me. Who would organize his details so he could be immersed in someone else's? I knew it wasn't my responsibility to take care of my dad, that he didn't ask for or expect it. But he'd already been left behind one time. I hated that I'd be the person to make it twice.

Just then, my phone rang. *Speak of the devil*, I thought, as HAMILTON, PETER popped up on the screen. I was moving to hit the IGNORE button when I looked at the clock. I had fifteen minutes before I had to leave for the bus. If I got this over with now, it might buy me a whole day of peace, or at least a few hours. I sucked it up and answered.

"Hi, honey!" my mom said, her voice too loud in my ear. "Good morning! Did you get any snow there?"

"A little," I said, looking out at the flakes still falling. "How about you?"

"Oh, we've already got three inches and it's still coming down hard. The twins and I have been out in it. They look so cute in their snowsuits! I e-mailed you a few pictures."

"Great," I said. Thirty seconds down, another, oh, two hundred and seventy or so to go before I could get off the phone without it seeming entirely rude.

"I just want to say again how much I enjoyed seeing you last weekend," she said. She cleared her throat. "It was just wonderful to be together. Although at the same time, it made me realize how much I've missed of your life these last couple of years. Your friends, activities . . ."

I closed my eyes. "You haven't missed that much."

"I think I have." She sniffed. "Anyway, I'm thinking that I'd really like to come visit again sometime soon. It's such a quick trip, there's no reason why we can't see each other more often. Or, you could come here. In fact, this weekend we're hosting the team and the boosters for a big barbecue here at the house. I know Peter would love it if you could be here."

Shit, I thought. This was just what I'd been worried about by agreeing to go to the game. One inch, then a foot, then a mile. The next thing I knew, we'd be back in the lawyers' offices. "I'm really busy with school right now," I said.

"Well, this would be the weekend," she replied. Push, push. "You could bring your schoolwork, do it here."

"It's not that easy. I have stuff I have to be here for."

"Well, okay." Another sniff. "Then how about next weekend? We're taking our first trip down to the beach house. We could pick you up on the way, and then—"

"I can't do next weekend either," I said. "I think I just need to stay here for a while."

Silence. Outside, the snow was still falling, so clean and white, covering everything. "Fine," she said, but her tone made it clear this was anything but. "If you don't want to see me, you don't want to see me. I can't do anything about that, now can I?"

No, I thought, *you can't.* Life would have been so much easier if I could do that, just agree with this statement, plant us both firmly on the same page, and be done with it. But it was never that simple. Instead, there was all this dodging and running, intricate steps and plays required to keep the ball in the air. "Mom," I said. "Just—"

"Leave you alone," she finished for me, her voice curt. "Never call, never e-mail, don't even try to keep in touch with my firstborn child. Is that what you want, Mclean?"

"What I want," I said slowly, trying to keep my voice level, "is the chance to have my own life."

"How could you think it's anything but that? You won't even share the smallest part of it with me unless it's under duress." Now she was actually crying. "All I want is for us to be close, like we used to be. Before your father took you away, before you changed like this."

"He didn't take me away." My voice was rising now. She'd fumbled around, poking and prodding, and now she'd found it, that one button that could not be unpushed. *I'd* changed? Please. "This was my choice. You made choices, too. Remember?"

The words were out before I could stop them, and I felt their weight both as they left me, and when they hit her ears. It had been a long, long time since we'd talked about the affair and the divorce, way back to the days of What Happens in a Marriage, that brick wall that stopped any further discussion. Now, though, I'd lobbed a grenade right over it, and all I could do was brace for the fallout.

For a long while—or what felt like a long while—she was quiet. Then, finally, "Sooner or later, Mclean, you're going to have to stop blaming me for everything."

This was the moment. Retreat and apologize, or push forward to where there was no way to return. I was tired, and I didn't have another name or girl to hide behind here. Which is probably why it was Mclean's voice that said, "You're right. But I can blame you for the divorce and for the way things are between us now. You did this. At least own it."

I felt her suck in a breath, like I'd punched her. Which, in a way, I had. All this forced niceness, dancing around a truth: now I'd broken the rules, that third wall, and let everything ugly out into the open. I'd thought about this moment for almost three years, but now that it was here, it just made me sad. Even before I heard the click of her hanging up in my ear.

I shut my phone, stuffed it in my pocket, then grabbed my backpack. Four hours away, my mother was crumbling and it was all my doing. The least I could have felt was a moment of exhilaration. But instead it was something more like fear that washed over me as I started down our walk, pulling my coat tightly around me.

Outside, the air was cold and crisp, the snow coming down hard. I turned the opposite way from the bus stop and started walking toward town, the snow making everything feel muffled and quiet around me. I walked and walked; by the time I realized how far I'd gone, there were only a couple of storefronts left before the street turned residential again. I had to turn around, find a bus stop, get to school. First, though, I needed to warm up. So I walked up to the closest place with an OPEN sign, a bakery with a picture of a muffin in the window, and went inside.

"Welcome to Frazier Bakery!" a cheerful voice called out

the second I crossed the threshold. I looked over to see two people behind the counter, bustling around, while a few people waited in line. Clearly, this was one of those chain places that was supposed to look like a mom-and-pop joint: decorated to look small and homey, mandatory personal greeting, a crackling (fake) fireplace on one wall. I got in line, grabbing a couple of napkins to wipe my nose.

I was so tired from the walk, and still reeling from what had happened with my mom, that I just stood there, shuffling forward as needed until suddenly I was face-to-face with a pretty redhead wearing a striped apron and a jaunty paper cap. "Welcome to Frazier Bakery!" she said. "What can we do to make you feel at home today?"

God, I hated all this corporate crap, even before I'd heard my dad rail against it endlessly. I looked up at the menu board, scanning it. Coffee, muffins, breakfast paninis, smoothies, bagels. I looked back at the smoothie options, suddenly remembering something.

"Blueberry Banana Brain Freeze," I told her.

"Coming right up!"

She turned, walking over to a row of blenders, and I took another look around me at this, the place where Dave's downfall began. You could hardly imagine a place less likely to corrupt someone. There were needlepoint samplers on all the walls, for God's sake. LIFE'S TROUBLES ARE OFTEN SOOTHED BY HOT, MILKY DRINKS, read one by the sugar, milk, and cream station. Another, over the recycling bins, proclaimed WASTE NOT, WANT NOT. I wondered where they'd ordered them, and if you could get anything mass-embroidered and framed. LEAVE ME

ALONE, mine would say. I'd hang in on my door, a fair warning, cutely delivered.

Once I got my smoothie, I went over and took a seat on a faux-leather chair in front of the faux-roaring fire. Dave was right: after two sips on my straw, I had a headache so bad I could barely see straight. I put my hand to my forehead, as if that would warm things up, then closed my eyes, just as the front door bell chimed.

"Welcome to Frazier Bakery!" one of the counter people yelled.

"Thank you!" a voice yelled back, and someone laughed. I was still rubbing my forehead when I heard footsteps, then, "Mclean?"

I opened my eyes, and there was Dave. Of course it was Dave. Who else would it be?

"Hi," I said.

He peered at me a little more closely. "You okay? You look like you've been—"

"It's just a brain freeze," I said, holding up the cup as evidence. "I'm fine."

I could tell he was not fully convinced, but thankfully, he didn't push the issue. "What are you doing here? I didn't know you were a Friend of Frazier."

"A what?"

"That's what we call the regulars." He waved at the redhead, who waved back. "Hold on, I'm just grabbing a Freaking Everything and a Procrastinator's Special. Be back in a sec."

I took another tentative sip of my smoothie, watching as he headed over to the counter, ducking behind it. He said something to the redhead, who laughed, then reached around her to the bakery display and grabbed a muffin before pouring himself a big cup of coffee. Then he punched a few buttons on the register, slid in a five, and took out a dollar and some change, which he deposited in the tip jar.

"Thank you!" the redhead and other guy working sang out.

"You're welcome!" Dave said. Then he started back over to me.

Good Lord, I thought as he approached. *I just don't have the energy for this today.* But it wasn't like there was anything I could do. I was in a public place, not to mention one that he knew well. It was almost funny that I'd ended up there. Almost.

"So," he said, standing over me now, muffin in hand. "You skipping out today or something?"

"No," I said. "Just . . . needed some breakfast. I'm about to go catch the bus."

"Bus?" He looked offended. "Why would you take public transport when I'm right here with my car?"

"Oh, that's okay. I'm . . . I'm fine."

"You're also late," he pointed out, nodding at the clock behind me. "Bus will make you later. There's no pride in tardiness, Mclean."

I looked around the room. "That sounds like something that should be needlepointed on one of these samplers."

"You're right!" He grinned. "Gonna have to take that up with management. Come on. I'm parked out back."

I went, following him down the hallway, past the restrooms, and out a rear entrance. As we walked, he continued to eat his muffin, leaving a trail of crumbs behind him like someone out of a fairy tale. I said, "What did you call that again?"

"What?"

"Your breakfast."

He glanced back at me. "Oh, right. The Freaking Everything and the Procrastinator's Special."

"I don't remember seeing that on the menu."

"Because it isn't," he replied, starting across the lot. "I kind of created my own lexicon here at FrayBake. Translated, that's a muffin with everything under the sun, and a coffee that guarantees multiple bathroom breaks for the next few hours. It caught on, and now all the counter people use it." He jangled his keys. "Here we are."

I watched him walk around a Volvo pockmarked with dents. On the passenger seat was one of those beaded covers I associated with taxi drivers and grandmothers. "This is your car?"

"Yep," he said proudly as we got in. "She's been in lockdown, but I finally got her sprung last night."

"Yeah? How'd you manage that?"

"I think it was the lives of cells that clinched it." He turned the key, and the engine, after a bit of coaxing, came to life. "Oh, and I also agreed to work in my mom's lab after the Austin trip, until I go to Brain Camp. But you do what you have to do for the ones you love. And I love this car."

The Volvo, as if to test this, suddenly sputtered to a stop. Dave looked down at the console, then turned the key. Nothing happened. He tried again, and the car made a sighing noise, like it was tired.

"It's okay," Dave called out over the sound of the engine making ticking noises, like a bomb. "She just needs a little love sometimes."

"I know all about that," I said. "So did Super Shitty."

This just came out, without me even really being aware of it. When Dave looked at me, though, eyebrows raised, I realized what I'd done. "Super Shitty?"

"My car," I explained. "My old car, I guess I should say. I don't know where it is now."

"Did you crash into a guardhouse, too?"

"No, just left town and didn't need it anymore." I had a flash of my beat-up Toyota Camry, she of the constantly blown alternators, hissing radiator, and odometer that had topped 200,000 miles before it even came into my possession. The last I'd seen it, it had been parked in Peter's huge garage, between his Lexus and SUV, as out of place there as I was. "She was a good car, too. Just kind of . . ."

"Shitty?"

I nodded, and he pumped the gas, then the brake. I could see a car behind us, turn signal on, waiting for the space. The person behind the wheel appeared to be cursing when the Volvo suddenly roared to life, a burst of smoke popping from the tailpipe.

"Nothing like driving in the snow," Dave said, hardly fazed as we turned out of the lot and headed down the hill to a stop sign, flakes hitting the windshield. As he slowed, the Volvo's brakes squealed in protest. He glanced over at me, then said, "Seat belt, please. Safety first."

I pulled it on, grateful he'd reminded me. My door was

rattling, and I was just hoping the seat belt would hold me in should it fly open at forty miles an hour. "So," I said, once we'd gotten going, "thanks for the thyme."

"No problem," he replied. "I just hope you weren't offended."

"Why would I be offended?"

"Well, you don't like clutter."

"It's one spice container," I pointed out.

"Yes, but it's a slippery slope. First you have thyme, then you get into rosemary and sage and basil, and the next thing you know, you have a problem."

"I'll keep that in mind." The car wheezed, and he hit the gas. The engine roared, attracting an alarmed look from a woman in a Lexus beside us.

"How long have you had this thing?"

"Little over a year," he said. "I bought her myself. Took all my savings bonds, bar mitzvah money, and what I'd made working at FrayBake."

The brakes squealed again. I said, "That much, huh?"

"What?" He glanced at me, then back at the road. "Hey, this is a great car. Sturdy, dependable. Has character. She might have a few issues, but I love her anyway."

"Warts and all," I said.

He looked over at me suddenly, surprised. "What did you say?"

"What?"

"You said 'warts and all.' Didn't you?"

"Um, yeah," I replied. "What, you don't know that expression?"

"No, I do." He eased us into the turn lane for school, then took his left hand off the steering wheel, turning it over to expose the black, tattooed circle there. "It's where this comes from, actually."

"That's supposed to be a wart?" I asked.

"Sort of," he said, downshifting. "See, when I was a kid, my mom and dad were both teaching full-time. So during the week, I stayed with this woman who kept a few kids at her house. Eva."

The snow was really picking up now, giving the wipers a workout. Just two small arcs of clarity, with everything blurry beyond.

"She had a granddaughter who was the same age as me and stayed there, too. She and I napped together, ate glue together. That was Riley."

"Really?"

"Yep. I told you, we've known each other forever. Anyway, Eva was just, like, straight-up awesome. She was really tall and broad, with a huge belly laugh. She smelled like pancakes. And she had this wart. A *huge* one, like something you'd see on a witch or something. Right here." He put his index finger in the center of the tattoo, pressing down. "We were, like, fascinated and grossed out by it at the same time. And she always made a point of letting us look at it. She wasn't embarrassed at all. Said if we loved her, we loved it, too. It was part of the package."

I thought of Riley's wrist, that same black circle. The sad look on her face when Deb pointed it out.

"She got cancer last year," he said. "Pancreatic. She died two months after the diagnosis."

"I'm sorry."

"Yeah. It pretty much sucked." We were turning into the school parking lot, going past the guardhouse. "The day after her funeral, me and Riley went and got these."

"That's a pretty amazing tribute," I said.

"Eva was pretty amazing."

I watched him as we turned down a row of cars, slowing for a group of girls in track pants and heavy coats. "I like the sentiment. But it's easier said than done, you know?"

"What is?"

I shrugged. "Accepting all the good *and* bad about someone. It's a great thing to aspire to. The hard part is actually doing it."

He found a spot and turned in, then cut the engine, which rattled gratefully to a stop. Never had a car seemed so exhausted. Then he looked at me. "You think so?"

I had a flash of my mom on the phone that morning, her wavering voice, the words I'd said. I swallowed. "I think that's why I like moving around so much. Nobody gets to know me well enough to see any of the bad stuff."

He didn't say anything for a moment. We both just sat there, listening as people passed by us. The ground was slippery, and everyone was struggling to stay upright, taking tentative steps and still busting here and there anyway.

"You say that," Dave said finally, "but I'm not sure it's actually true. I've only known you a month but I'm aware of plenty of bad stuff about you."

"Oh, really," I said. "Like what?"

"Well, you have no condiments or spices, for starters. Which is just plain weird. Also, you're vicious with a basketball."

"Those aren't exactly warts."

"Maybe not." He grinned. "But seriously, it's all relative, right?"

The bell rang then, its familiar tinny sound muffled by the snow on the roof and windows. We both got out, my door creaking loudly as I pushed it open. The ground was icy, immediately sliding a bit beneath me, and I grabbed on to the Volvo to support myself. "Whoa," I said.

"No kidding," Dave said, sliding up next to me and barely getting his balance at the last minute. "Watch your step."

I started walking carefully, and he fell in beside me, pulling his bag over his shoulder. His head was ducked down, his hair falling across his forehead, and as I glanced at him, I thought of all the times I'd found myself with boys over the last two years, and how none of them came anywhere close to being like this. Because I wasn't. I was Beth or Eliza or Lizbet, a mirage, like a piece of stage scenery that looked real from the front with nothing behind it. Here, though, despite my best efforts, I'd somehow ended up being myself again: Mclean Sweet, she of the messed-up parents and weird basketball connections, Super Shitty and a U-Haul's worth of baggage. All those clean, fresh starts had made me forget what it was like, until now, to be messy and honest and out of control. To be real.

We were almost to the curb when I felt Dave begin to slip

again beside me, his arms flailing. I tried to secure my own feet, with mixed results, as he tipped backward, then forward. "Uh-oh," he said. "Going down!"

"Hold on," I told him, sticking out my own hand to grab his. Instead of steadying him, however, this had the opposite effect, and then we were both stumbling across the ice, double the weight, double the impact if we fell.

It was the weirdest feeling. As my feet slid beneath me, my heart was lurching, pounding with that scary feeling of having no footing, no control. But then I looked over at Dave. He was laughing, his face flushed as he wavered this way, then that, pulling me along, equally clumsy behind him. Same situation, two totally different reactions.

So much had happened that morning. Yet it was this image, this moment, that I kept going back to hours later, after we'd made it safely to the walkway and gone our separate ways to classes. How it felt to have the world moving beneath me, a hand gripping mine, knowing if I fell, at least I wouldn't do it alone.

× × ×

The snow kept coming down, piling up into drifts, leading to school being cancelled a little bit before lunchtime. As I pushed out the front door with everyone else, all I could think was that I had a whole free afternoon, a ton of laundry that needed doing, and a paper to hand in the next day. But instead of taking the bus straight home like I planned, I got off two stops early, right across the street from Luna Blu.

The snow had killed the lunch rush, so the restaurant was mostly empty, which made it easier to hear my dad, Chuckles, and Opal, who were in the party-and-event room just off the bar area. I could see them all gathered at a table, coffee mugs and papers spread out all around them. My dad looked tired, Opal tense. Clearly, the magic wand hadn't materialized.

I walked through the dining room, to the door that led to the stairs. As soon as I opened it, I heard voices.

". . . totally doable," Dave was saying as he came into view. Deb, still in her coat, scarf, and mittens, was standing beside him, both of them studying the boxes of model parts. "Complicated, yes. But doable."

"All that counts is the doable part," she said, glancing around the room. When she saw me, her face brightened. "Hey! I didn't know you were coming!"

Neither did I, I thought. "I had a hankering to serve my community," I told her, just as Dave turned around to look at me as well. "What are we doing?"

"Just getting together a game plan," Deb said, pulling off her mittens. "Did you have any ideas about the best way to proceed?"

I walked over, standing beside her, feeling Dave watching me. I thought of that morning again, the solid circle on his wrist, the same one I'd been holding on to for dear life as we slid across the ice. *He's not my type,* some voice in my head said, but it had been so long, I didn't even know what that meant anymore. Or if this girl, the one I was now, even had a type at all.

"Nope," I said, glancing at him. "Let's just start and see what happens."

× × ×

Fifteen minutes later, a meeting was called.

"Okay, look." Deb's face was dead serious. "I know I just joined this project, and I don't want to offend anyone. But I'm going to be honest. I think you've been going about this all wrong."

"I'm offended," Dave told her flatly.

Her eyes widened. "Oh, no. Really? I'm so—"

"I'm also joking," he said.

"Oh, okay. Whew!" She smiled, her cheeks flushing. "Let me start by just saying that I'm so glad you invited me here. I *love* this kind of stuff. When I was a kid, I was crazy for miniatures."

"Miniatures?" I asked.

"You know, dollhouses and such. I especially loved historical stuff. Tiny re-creations of Revolutionary War cottages, Victorian orphanages. That kind of thing."

"Orphanages?" Dave said.

"Sure." She blinked. "What? Anyone can have a dollhouse. I was more creative with my play."

"Dave was, too," I told her. "He was into model trains."

"It was not trains," Dave said, annoyed. "It was war staging, and very serious."

"Oh, I *loved* war staging!" Deb told him. "That's how I ended up with all my orphans."

I just looked at both of them. "What kind of childhood did you people have?"

"The bad kind," Deb replied, simply, matter-of-factly. She slid off her jacket, folded it neatly, and put it with her purse on a nearby table. "We were always broke, Mom and Dad didn't get along. My world was messed up. So I liked being able to make other ones."

I looked at her, realizing this was the most she'd ever volunteered about her home life. "Wow," I said.

Dave shrugged. "I just liked battles."

"Who doesn't?" Deb replied, already moving on. "Anyway, I really feel, from my experience with large model and miniature structures, that the best approach in construction is the pinwheel method. And what you have going here is total chessboard."

We both just looked at her. "Right," Dave said finally. "Well, of course."

"So honestly," she continued as I shot him a look, trying not to laugh, "I think we need a total re-approach to the entire project. Are those the directions?"

"Yeah," I told her, picking up the thick manual by my feet.

"Great! Can I see?"

I handed them over, and she immediately took them to the table, spreading them out. Within seconds, she was bent over the pages, deep in thought, drumming on her lip with one finger.

"Can I tell you something?" Dave whispered to me. "I *love* Deb. She's a total freak. And I mean that in a good way."

"I know," I said. "Every day she kind of blows my mind."

It was true. Deb might have been a spazzer freak, speed-metal drummer, tattoo expert, and constructor of orphanages. What she wasn't was timid. When she took something over, she took it over.

"Think wheel," she kept saying to me as I stood over the

model, holding a house in one hand. "We start in the middle, at the hub, then work our way out from the center, around and around."

"We were just kind of putting things in as we pulled them out of the boxes," I told her.

"I know. I could tell the first moment I saw this thing." She gave me a sympathetic look. "But don't feel bad, okay? That's a beginner's mistake. If you kept it up, though, you'd end up climbing over things, houses piercing your knees, kicking fire hydrants off accidentally. It would be a serious mess. Trust me."

I did, so I followed her direction. Gone were the pick-a-piece, put-it-together, find-its-place days. Already, she'd developed her own system and fetched a red pen from her purse to adapt the directions accordingly, and by an hour in, she had us running like a machine. She gathered the pieces for each area of the pinwheel—she termed them "sectors"—which Dave then assembled, and I attached to their proper spot. Create, Assemble, Attach. Or, as Deb called it, CAA. I fully expected her to make up T-shirts or hats with this slogan by our next meeting.

"You have to admit," I said to Dave when she was across the room on her cell phone, calling the toll-free-questions line at Model Community Ventures for the second time for clarification on one of the directions, "she's good at this."

"Good?" he replied, snapping a roof on a building. "More like destined. She makes us look like a bunch of fumbling idiots."

"Speak for yourself," I said. "She said my approach was promising, for a beginner."

"Oh, don't kid yourself. She's just being nice." He picked up another piece of plastic. "When you were in the bathroom, she told me your sectors are sadly lacking."

"That is not true! My sectors are perfect."

"You call that perfect? It's total chessboard."

I made a face, then poked him, and he poked me back. He was laughing as I walked back to the model, bending down to inspect my sector. Which looked just fine. I thought.

". . . of course! No, thank you. I'm sure we'll talk again. Okay! Bye!" Deb snapped her phone shut, then sighed. "I swear, Marion is *so* nice."

"Marion?"

"The woman at Model Community Ventures who answers the help line," she said. "She's just been a godsend."

"You made friends," I said, "with the help line lady?"

"Well, I wouldn't say we're *friends*," she replied. "But she's really been great. Usually, they just put those numbers on there but nobody answers. I can't tell you how many hours I've spent on hold, waiting for someone to tell me how to glue an eave properly."

I just looked at her. From across the room, Dave snorted.

"Hey, is Gus up there?" someone called up the stairs.

I walked over to see Tracey on the landing below. "Nope. He's in a meeting in the event room with Opal."

"Still? God, what are they doing in there?"

I had a flash of the pad with all those numbers, how her

name had been awfully close to the top. "I don't know," I said.

"Well, when he finally emerges," she said, pulling a pen out from her hair and sticking it back in with her free hand, "tell him that councilwoman called *again*. I don't know how much longer I can put her off. Clearly, she's undersexed and highly motivated."

"What?"

"She's hot for your dad," she said, speaking slowly for my benefit. "And he is not getting the message. Literally. So tell him, would you?"

I nodded and she turned, walking back to the dining room, the downstairs door banging shut behind her. It wasn't like I should have been surprised. This was the pattern. We landed somewhere, got settled, and eventually he'd start dating someone. But usually, it was not until he knew he had an end date that he'd take that plunge. Sort of like someone else I knew.

"Mclean?" I heard Deb call out from behind me. "Can I have a quick discussion with you about your approach in this area here by the planetarium?"

I turned around. Dave, who was carrying a structure past, said cheerfully, "And *you* said your sectors were perfect."

I smiled at this, but as I walked over to take her critique, I was distracted. I didn't even know why. It was just a phone call, some messages. Nothing that hadn't happened before. And it wasn't like he'd called her back. Yet.

× × ×

At five o'clock, with three sectors done that had passed Deb's rigorous inspection, we decided to knock off for the night. When we came downstairs, the restaurant had just opened. It was warm and lit up, and my dad and Opal were sitting at the bar, a bottle of red wine open between them. Opal's face was flushed, and she was smiling, happier than I'd ever seen her.

"Mclean!" she said when she spotted me. "I didn't even know you were here!"

"We were working on the model," I told her.

"Really?" She shook her head. "And on your snow day, to boot. That's some serious dedication."

"We got three sectors done," Dave told her.

She look confused. "Three what?"

"Sectors." Nope, still lost. I didn't even know how to explain, so I just said, "It looks really good. Serious progress."

"That's great." She smiled again. "You guys are the best."

"It's mostly Deb," I said. Beside me, Deb blushed, clearly pleased. "Turns out she has a lot of model experience."

"Thank God somebody does," Opal replied. "Maybe now Lindsay will relax about this whole thing. Do you know she keeps calling here? It's like she's suddenly obsessed with this project."

I glanced at my Dad, who picked up his wineglass, taking a sip as he looked out the window. "Well," I said, "she should be happy next time she stops by."

"That," Opal said, pointing at me, "is what I love to hear. She's happy. I'm happy. *Everybody's* happy."

"Oh my goodness," Deb said, her eyes widening as Tracey came toward us with a heaping plate of fried pickles, placing it right in front of Opal. "Are those—"

"Fried pickles," Opal told her. "The best in town. Try one."

"Really?"

"Of course! You too, Dave. It's the least we can do for all your hard work." She pushed the plate down, and they both went over to help themselves.

"Wow," Dave said. "These are amazing."

"Aren't they?" Opal replied. "They're our signature appetizer."

Wow, indeed, I thought, looking at her as she helped herself to a pickle, popping it into her mouth. My dad was still looking out the window. "So the meeting went well?" I asked.

"Better than well," Opal said. She leaned forward, lowering her voice. "Nobody's getting fired. I mean, we presented our arguments, and he just . . . he got it. He understood. It was *amazing.*"

"That's great."

"Oh, I feel so relieved!" She sighed, shaking her head. "It's like the best I could hope for. I might actually sleep tonight. And it's all because of your dad."

She turned, squeezing his arm, and he finally turned his attention to us. "I didn't do anything," he said.

"Oh, he's just being modest," Opal told me. "He totally went to bat for our staff. If I didn't know better, I'd think he actually didn't want anyone to get fired either."

I looked at my dad. This time, he gave me a shrug. "It's over," he said. "That's all that matters."

"Is that Mclean I see?" I heard a voice boom from the back of the restaurant. I turned, and there was Chuckles, huge and hulking and striding right toward us. As usual, he had on an expensive suit, shiny shoes, and his two NBA championship rings, one on each hand. Chuckles was not a believer in casual wear.

"Hi, Charles," I said as he gathered me in a big hug, squeezing tight. He towered over me: I was about level with his abs. "How are you?"

"I'll be better once we tuck into that buffalo," he said. Dave and Deb, standing at the bar, watched him, both wide-eyed, as he reached over with his impressive arm span to pluck a pickle from the plate in front of them.

"Chuckles just invested in a bison ranch," my dad explained to me. "He brought ten pounds of steaks with him."

"Which your dad is going to cook up as only he can," Chuckles said, gesturing to Tracey, who was behind the bar, for a wineglass. "You're joining us, right?"

"Sure," I said. "But I need to go home first and change. I've got model dust all over me."

"Do it," Chuckles said, easing his huge frame onto a bar stool next to Opal as Tracey reached over with the wine bottle, filling his glass. "I'm just going to hang here with these gorgeous women until my food's ready."

My dad rolled his eyes, just as Jason stuck his head out of the kitchen. "Gus," he called. "Phone call."

"I'll see you in a half hour or so?" he said to me as he got up. I nodded, and he walked back to Jason, taking the phone from him. I watched him say hello, and a grimace come across his face. Then he turned, and walked back toward his office, the door swinging shut behind him.

"I should go, too," Deb said, zipping up her jacket. "I want to get home and whiteboard my ideas for the model while they're still fresh."

"Whiteboard?" Opal said.

"I have one in my room," she explained. "I like to be ready when inspiration strikes."

Opal looked at me, and I shrugged. Knowing Deb like I did, this made total sense to me. She slid on her earmuffs, then pulled her quilted purse over her shoulder. "I'll see you guys."

"Drive safe," I told her, and she nodded, ducking her head as she stepped out into the snow and walked away. Even her footprints were neat and tidy.

"These pickles are really good," Chuckles said to Opal as I gathered up my own stuff from the bar. "But what happened to those rolls you used to give out here?"

"The rolls?"

He nodded.

"Actually, we, um, decided to do away with them."

"Huh," Chuckles said. "That's too bad. They were really something, from what I remember."

"Have another pickle," she said, pushing the plate closer to him. "Believe me. Pretty soon those rolls will be a distant memory."

I glanced at her as she lifted her wineglass again to her mouth, and she smiled at me. My dad had been right. Thirty days, give or take, and she'd come around.

Dave and I said our goodbyes, then walked down the corridor to the back entrance. We were just passing the kitchen door when we saw Jason, rummaging around on a shelf for some pans. "Be careful out there," he said. "It's still really coming down."

"Will do," I said.

"Hey," Dave said to him, as he stood up, the pan in hand. "Did I see your name on the Brain Camp Listserv the other day?"

"I don't know," Jason said. "If it's there, it's not my doing. I haven't been in touch with them in ages."

"You went to Brain Camp, too?" I said.

"He didn't just go there," Dave told me. "He's, like, a Brain Camp legend. They pretty much genuflect to his IQ scores."

"Not true," Jason said.

"Order up!" I heard Tracey call. "Salad for the big boss, so make it good!"

"Duty calls," Jason said, then smiled, walking back toward the prep table. Dave watched him go as I pushed open the back door, a bit of snow blowing in.

"So Jason was a big geek deal, huh?" I asked as I pulled on my gloves.

"More like a rock star," he replied. "He went to Kiffney-Brown and took U classes, just like me and Gervais, but he was a couple of years ahead. He went off to Harvard when I was a sophomore."

"Harvard?" I glanced back at Jason, who was pulling a pan out of the walk-in. "It's a long way from there to prep cook. What happened?"

He shrugged, walking out the door and pulling his hood

up. "Don't know. I thought he was still there until I saw him upstairs the other day."

Strange, I thought as we passed by the half-open door to my dad's office. I could see him inside, leaning back in his chair, one foot on the desk.

". . . been pretty busy, with the new menu and some corporate meetings," he was saying. I heard his chair creak. "No, no. I'm not, Lindsay. I promise. And lunch . . . would be good. Let's do it."

I looked out at the snow. Dave had his head tipped back, looking up, the outside light hitting the flakes as they fell down on him.

"Your office, city hall, eleven thirty," my dad continued. "No, you pick. I'm sure you know the best places . . . yeah. All right. I'll see you then."

The door at the other end of the hallway, which led to the restaurant, suddenly opened. Opal was standing there, her wineglass in one hand. "Hey," she said, "is your dad still on the phone?" she asked.

I nodded. "Think so."

"Well, when he's done, remind him we're waiting for him to join us. Tell him Chuckles is insisting on it." She smiled. "And, um, so am I."

"Okay," I said.

"Thanks!" She lifted her glass to me, then disappeared back through the doorway, letting it swing shut behind her.

For a moment, I just stood there, right in the middle of the hallway, alone. In the kitchen, some bouncy dance music was playing, and over it I could hear the clanging of utensils, the squeaking of shoes on the damp floor, and the grill sizzling, the soundtrack to the beginning of a rush. All things I knew well. Almost as well as the tone in my dad's voice just now, finally accepting the councilwoman's offer. It was as familiar as the set of his jaw as he sat next to Opal earlier, even as she celebrated unknowingly beside him. Something had shifted, changed. Or, actually, not changed at all.

"Hey, Mclean," Dave called out through the screen door. I looked over to see him surrounded by white: on the ground at his feet, blown onto the wall behind him, and flakes still falling. "You ready to go?"

I looked back at my dad's door, now all quiet behind it. *No,* I thought. *I'm not.*

Ten

"Do you hear that?"

I looked up from the fire station I was trying to get straight on the model base. "What?"

Dave, who was across the room, cocked his head to the side. "That," he said, holding up a finger as the sound of voices, loud, in the restaurant below rose up the stairs behind him. "It's been going on for a while now."

"It's probably just everyone setting up," I said, moving the station again. It was just a small square that needed to go neatly into another small square, but for some reason, it would not cooperate. "Isn't it close to five?"

"Four forty-six," he said, still listening. "But that's not setting up. It's someone yelling."

I put down the building, then walked over to where he was standing, peering down the stairs. I couldn't see anything but the deserted side dining room, but now, I could hear the sound loud and clear.

"Oh," I said. "That's just my dad."

Dave raised his eyebrows. "Your dad?"

I nodded, listening again. This time, I was reasonably sure

I made out a *bullshit*, the word *inept*, and a mention of a road, and a suggestion that whoever he was speaking to consider hitting it. "Sounds like he's firing someone."

"Yeah?" Dave squinted as if this would help him decipher better. "How can you tell?"

"The volume," I replied. "He never really gets that loud unless he knows the person isn't going to be around much longer." Just then, equally loud, there was a stream of expletives.

Dave raised his eyebrows.

"That's whoever just got the hook."

"And you know that because . . ."

"My dad doesn't use those words. Even when he's firing someone." There was a crash. "I would wager that's whoever it is throwing something. Sounds like a bus bin." A bang. "And that's the back door. It was probably a dishwasher."

"Why?"

"Girls usually don't bang out or throw stuff. And kitchen guys yell more."

Dave was just looking at me as if I was insane. "What *are* you? The restaurant whisperer?"

I shook my head. It was quiet downstairs now, that heavy silence that falls after someone gets axed and everyone else is tiptoeing around, extra careful to keep their distance from the boss in case unemployment is catching. "I grew up in a place like this. After a while, you start to recognize things."

I walked back over to my sector, picking up the fire station. As I knelt back down, focusing on the square again, Dave said, "Must have been pretty cool, your parents having their own place. Did you, like, have the run of the joint?"

"I guess." I centered the piece, then realized it was crooked again. Damn. "It was either be there or never see them. Or my dad anyway."

"Busy job, huh?"

"Full-time and more." I sat back again. "My mom was around in the evenings, at least, and she was always on him to come home for dinner or take a weekend off to hang out with us. 'That's what we pay managers for,' she'd tell him. But my dad always said even the best-paid employee is still that: an employee. They'll never be as willing to Clorox the walk-in, mop the bathrooms, or empty the fryer when it's all clogged."

Dave didn't say anything. When I looked up, he was again studying me as if I was speaking another language.

"They'll never be dedicated the way you are when it's your restaurant," I explained. "As the owner, every job, from chef to bar back, is your job. That's why it's so hard."

"And it was hard on you," he said.

"I didn't know any different. I think my mom had trouble with it at times. I mean, she loved our place. But she did call herself a 'restaurant widow.'"

"You think that's why she ended up with Peter?"

I blinked. I was still looking at the fire station, but suddenly everything seemed askew, not just that. "I . . ."

"Sorry," Dave said quickly. I swallowed. "I just . . . That was stupid. I don't know what I'm talking about. I'm just talking."

I nodded slowly. "I know."

We were both quiet for a while, the only sound the voices of the waits, now talking downstairs. I'd learned, over the last few weeks of putting in time on the model, that the rhythm was different depending on who was working alongside me. When it was Deb, or Deb and Dave even, we kept up a pretty constant chatter, talking about music and school and whatever else. But when it was just me and him, there was a different ebb and flow: some conversation, some silence, always something to think about. It was like another language I was learning, how to be with someone and remain there, even when the conversation—and I—got uncomfortable.

From the restaurant below, there was the final touch before opening as the music came on. As a rule, my dad believed in keeping whatever played similar to the food: simple and good. He also wanted a low volume (so as not to blast out the early birds), instrumentals only (so words didn't compete with conversation), and up-tempo (to keep the staff from moving too slowly). "Fast beat, fast service," he'd say, something he claimed to have learned during a disastrous stint at a folkie organic place where he worked in college.

In a good restaurant, you'd never notice these things, which was exactly how it should be. Eating out is about just that: eating. The meal is what matters. As a customer, you shouldn't have to think about details like this. And if someone like my dad is doing their job right, you don't.

Dave and I had been working in silence for a while before he finally said, "What is that they're playing down there?"

"Cuban jazz," I told him. "My dad swears it makes people enjoy the food more."

"That is so weird," he replied. "Because I hate jazz. But I'm suddenly starving."

I smiled, adjusting the fire station one last time before

pulling off the sticky backing. Then I pressed it down and felt it click into place. Done.

"You want to grab something to eat?" I asked Dave as he wiped some dust off the main road with the tail of his shirt.

"Only if you tell me what's the best thing to order right after opening," he replied. Then he looked up at me. "Because I *know* you know."

I smiled. "Maybe."

"Cool. Let's go." He got to his feet, starting over to the stairs, and I followed him. "I'm thinking fish."

"No."

"Ravioli?"

"Getting warmer."

He glanced back at me, grinning, as I reached over to turn off the overhead light. From this distance, in the dimness, the model looked surreal, made up of parts filled with buildings, bordered by long stretches of empty space. It reminded me of the way cities and towns look when you are flying at night. You can't make out much. But the places where people have come together, and stayed, are collections of tiny lights, breaking up the darkness.

×　×　×

The next day, I came home from school and my dad was at home. Which was strange enough: with an hour or so until opening, he was always needed to oversee prep in the kitchen. Then, though, I realized he wasn't just there, but sitting at the kitchen table—not on his phone, in constant motion, or on his way out the door—just waiting for me.

"Hey," he said as I stepped inside, the side door easing shut with a click behind me. "Got a minute?"

Only one thing came to mind: AHBL. I was in big trouble or someone was dead. Maybe both.

"Sure," I said, my mouth going dry as I pulled out the opposite chair and slid into it. "What's going on?"

He cleared his throat, smoothing one palm across the tabletop as if checking for stray crumbs. Finally, after what felt an excruciatingly long time, he said, "So . . . I need you to fill me in on what's going on right now between you and your mom."

Hearing this, I felt two things simultaneously. Relief that everyone was still breathing, replaced immediately by a flare of anger so familiar it was like an old friend. "Why? What happened?"

"Did you have an argument recently?" he said. "Some sort of incident?"

"We always have arguments and incidents," I replied. "That's nothing new."

"I thought you were seeing her the other weekend."

"I did." Now my voice was rising, unsteady. "What's happening? Did she call you or something?"

"No." Another throat clearing. "But I did hear from her lawyer today."

Oh, no, I thought. "Her lawyer?" I repeated, although I already knew where this was going. "Why?"

"Well," he said, running his palm over the table again, "apparently, she would like to revisit the custody agreement."

"Again," I added. He didn't say anything. "Why? Because I finally told her the truth?"

"Ah." He sat back, leveling his gaze at me. "So there was an incident."

"I told her the divorce was her fault, and, therefore, so was the fact that I'm upset with her about it. That's not exactly breaking news."

My dad just looked at me for another moment. Finally he said, "Your mother is prepared to tell the court that we are not upholding our part of the visitation arrangement right now."

"Meaning what?"

"Well," he said, "you've only seen her twice in the last six months. And you didn't come for the full summer last year."

"I was there for three weeks. And I just saw her!" I shook my head, looking out the window. "This is crazy. Just because I won't go visit her this weekend, or go on a stupid beach trip, she's ready to drag us all back to court?"

"Mclean."

"Don't I have a say in this at all? She can't *force* me to see her against my will. Can she?"

He sat back, rubbing a hand over his face. "I don't think she wants to force you to do anything. In a perfect world, you'd want to do it all on your own."

"This world isn't perfect."

"Yes, I'm aware of that." He sighed. "Look, Mclean, you turn eighteen in eight months. You go off to college even before that. Maybe it's worth just considering making a few trips—"

"No," I said flatly. He raised his eyebrows, surprised by my tone, and I checked myself. Fast. "Sorry. Look, we just got here. I'm in school, I have friends. I don't want to just pick up and start leaving every single weekend."

"I understand that." I watched him take in a breath, then let it out. "But I also don't think you want to spend your last senior semester enmeshed in a court battle."

"Why can't she just leave me alone?" My voice was breaking now, the tears audible if not visible yet. "Jesus. Hasn't she gotten enough?"

"She's your mother," he said. "She loves you."

"If she loved me, she'd let me stay here and live my life." I pushed back my chair, the legs scraping hard against the linoleum. "Why don't I get to decide what I need? How come it's always up to Mom? Or you? Or the freaking courts?"

"Hey. Mclean." He was quiet, just looking at me. My dad was not one for outbursts, and this kind of conversation between us, rife with emotion, was rare if not a first. "You don't have to make a decision right this second. I'm just asking you to think about it. Okay?"

I knew this was not an unreasonable request. I forced myself to nod. "Okay," I managed.

He stood, then came over, wrapping his arms around me. I hugged him back, all the while looking over his shoulder to the flat green of the yard beyond. Then when he let go and went down the hallway to his room, I pushed out the door and went there. I wanted to break something, or scream, but none of these was really an option in this neighborhood at four on a Wednesday. Then I looked over to the empty building behind mine.

I walked across my yard, stepping over the low brick wall

so I was standing over the doors that led down to the storm cellar. They were shut, but there was no lock. I bent down, pulling up on both handles, which opened with a creak, revealing that narrow set of stairs. A flashlight sat on the top step.

I took another look around me. Just another afternoon, the traffic picking up as rush hour approached. Nearby, a dog was barking. My partying neighbors had the TV on too loud. And somewhere, four hours north, my mom was reaching out for me, extending her grasp further, further, to pull me to her. I'd run and dodged, zigged and zagged, and none of it had worked. I knew this wasn't a real solution either. But for the moment, all I could think to do was pick up that flashlight, turning it on. Then I pointed the beam at the stairs and followed it down, into the dark.

x x x

I probably should have been creeped out, sitting in a cellar beneath an empty house, alone. But after a moment or two to adjust my eyes and my nerves, I realized Dave was on to something. Sitting on the bottom step, the flashlight in my lap, I got the same sense I had that first night, when he'd pulled me down there with him. Like I'd literally ducked below the world, out of harm's way, at least for a little while.

What a mess, I thought, looking up at the sky, now darkening above me. And all because I'd done the one thing I hadn't been able to for all this time: speak the truth. If my mother loved me enough to fight for me, even against my will, why couldn't she accept that I was angry at her?

Up above, I heard a whirring noise, followed by an engine

starting, running briefly, and then cutting off again. I pushed myself to my feet, then climbed the stairs to see what was going on. I was just about to poke my head out when Dave stuck his in.

"Holy crap," he said, jumping back, one hand to his chest. "You scared the bejesus out of me!"

I was equally startled, and for a moment we both stayed where we were, catching our collective breath. Then I said, "Bejesus?"

He gave me a flat look. "You startled me."

"Sorry, I didn't mean to. I just needed to escape for a little while." I stood up, stepping out onto the snowy ground, and waved my hand at the stairs. "It's all yours."

He nodded at the flashlight, still in my hand. "I actually just came for that. We're about to bond and need some illumination."

"What?"

Before he could answer, I heard a scraping noise from the garage behind him. The Volvo was parked outside, and looking in, I saw Mr. Wade, moving some metal bookshelves that lined one wall.

"Garage cleanup," he explained as his dad picked up a cardboard box. "It's a chore and a father-son activity, all rolled into one."

"Sounds like fun."

"Oh, it is. You have no idea."

"Dave?" Mr. Wade said, peering out at us. "How's that light coming?"

"Got it. Be right there," he replied. His dad nodded, waving at me, and I waved back, watching as he carried the box out of the garage, placing it beneath the basketball goal, then doubled back. Dave said, "To my dad, heaven is a big mess and an endless supply of Rubbermaid bins."

I smiled, then looked up at the building in front of us. "Hey, did you ever go in here? You know, beyond the cellar?"

"A couple of times, when I was a kid," he replied. "Before they boarded up the windows."

"Is it a house?"

"If it was, it was a big one. It's huge inside. Why?"

I shrugged. "Just wondered. It seems so out of place here, with everything else grown up around it."

"Yeah?" He looked back at the building. "Never really thought about it like that. It's been here for as long as I can remember, though. I guess I'm just used to it."

We started walking across the yard, toward our driveways, where Mr. Wade had piled a few more boxes under the basketball goal, along with several Rubbermaid plastic bins. "See?" Dave said. "Welcome to paradise."

I scanned the boxes. Some were open, some taped shut, and hardly any were labeled. "What is all this stuff anyway?"

"You name it." He clicked the flashlight on, moving it across them. "Old chemistry-set parts, rat cages—"

"Rat cages?"

"My mother is allergic to all dander," he explained. "Except rat."

"Ah."

"And then, of course, my model trains." He leaned over,

lifting the flaps on a box and pulling out something. When he held it out to me, I saw it was a toy soldier, small and green, holding a gun. Bang.

"Wow," I said. "How much of this stuff do you have?"

"More than you would believe. If you and your dad are minimalists, then we're . . . maximumalists. Or something." I looked at the soldier again. "We don't throw much away. You never know what you might need."

"That's what stores are for."

"Says the girl with no thyme," he replied. There was a loud scraping noise from the garage, and we both looked over to see Mr. Wade, red-faced, his skinny arms straining as he tried to push the shelves out from the wall. "I think I'm being paged."

"Right," I said. "Have fun."

"You know it," he said, then walked over to the garage, sliding the flashlight into his back pocket, taking his place on the other side of the shelves.

As they started pushing again, I walked over to the boxes, peering into the one Dave had taken the soldier from. Inside, there were more figures, as well as horses and wagons. The box beside it, identical in size and shape, held yet another collection, this time of weapons: miniature cannons, rifles, muskets, plus more modern things—revolvers, machine guns—clearly from other soldier sets. As I dropped my single soldier back in, I looked at Dave and his dad again and thought of all of those battles he must have created, each detail perfect and accurate. The most controlled kind of conflict, all within your doing, the outcome and every consequence carefully manipulated. Maybe it was geeky, or even embarrassing. But now, especially, I understood the appeal.

× × ×

The next morning, I got up early, slipping out the front door before it was even fully light. My dad had gotten home later than usual the night before, which I knew because I was up, and remained so, listening to his familiar late-night noises: the radio on low as he had a beer in the kitchen, his routine after-work shower, and finally the sound of him snoring about two seconds after he turned off his light.

The entire evening I'd been avoiding thinking about my mother as I made myself dinner, checked e-mail, folded laundry, and ran the dishwasher. I focused on normal things, routines, as if by doing so I could keep the strangeness that was this whole custody issue at bay. Once I was in bed, though, I could think of nothing else.

Now, out in the semidarkness, my jacket wrapped tight around me, I started walking toward downtown, my breath puffing out in front of me. No one was out, save for a few bundled-up runners and some policemen, driving slowly, the entire roads to themselves. I walked down block after block, retracing my steps to that bright neon OPEN sign.

"Welcome to Frazier Bakery!"

I nodded, walking over to the counter, where this time an older guy with curly hair and glasses was standing behind the register. "Hi," he said. He looked kind of sleepy. "What can I get you to make you feel at home today?"

"Procrastinator's Special," I said.

He didn't even blink. "Coming right up."

Five minutes later, I was back in that same squishy leather chair, facing the fake fireplace. The only other people in the entire place were a group of senior citizens, having a spirited conversation about politics at a round table by the front door. I thought of my dad, asleep back at the house, not even knowing where I was or what I was about to do.

Once I'd calmed down the night before—and it took a while—I could understand why he'd said what he did about just giving in to my mom's demands. We'd been fighting for so long, and now, with only half a year left that any of this mattered, I didn't know if I wanted to be the one to put us through it all again. What was six months, in the scheme of things, when I knew I'd be leaving here by the end of the summer anyway?

But really, it wasn't about six months, or a summer. It wasn't about the divorce, or all these moves, and all the girls I'd chosen to be. This time, more than any before, it was about me. About a life I'd built in not much more than a month, a town where I felt finally somewhat at home, and the friends I'd made there. It was just my luck that at the precise moment I most needed to be able to cut and run, I'd finally found a place—and maybe even some people—worth holding on to.

"Welcome to Frazier Bakery!" the guy behind the counter yelled. He sounded more awake: I wondered if he'd had a few shots of coffee himself.

"Good morning!" a woman's voice, cheerful, called back. I glanced over, and there was Lindsay Baker, wearing yoga pants and a fleece jacket, her hair pulled back in a ponytail. When she saw me, she smiled and came right over. "Mclean! Hello! I didn't know you liked this place!"

"I don't," I said. She looked taken aback, so I added, "I mean, I've only been here a couple of times. Just found it the other day."

"Oh, I love the Frazier Bakery," she said, plopping down in the chair beside mine and crossing one leg over the other. "I come in every morning. I could not get through the seven thirty Spin Extreme without my skim caramel espresso."

"Oh," I said. "Right."

"I mean, how can you not love this place?" she asked, sitting back. "It's so cozy, and it just feels good when you walk in, with the fireplace and the little sayings on the walls. And the best thing is when I travel, there's always one on some corner. So it's like having a bit of home with me no matter where I go."

I looked around the room again, thinking of my dad. If there was one thing he hated in a restaurant, it was fakeness. He always said that eating food as an experience should be real, unique and messy, and to pretend otherwise was cheating yourself. "Well," I said. "That is convenient, I guess."

"And the food is great, too," she said, pulling off her gloves. "I eat just about every meal here, to be honest. It's halfway between my condo and my office. See what I mean? Perfect!"

I nodded. "I'll have to try that skim caramel thing."

"Do it. You won't regret it." She glanced at her watch. "Oops, gotta go. If I'm late I might not get a bike and that is *not* a good thing. Hey, it was great bumping into you! Your dad says you're really liking it here."

"He said that?"

"Oh, yeah. I think he likes it, too, especially lately. Just a hunch." She smiled, flashing those white teeth. I raised my eyebrows, but she was already turning around, flipping me a popular-girl wave over one shoulder. "See you soon, Mclean!"

Oh, God, I thought as I watched her stride up to the counter, although I had to admit I felt a little relieved. My dad could never really be with a woman who loved this place, even in the short term. We cut and runners might be sketchy, but we had our standards.

I waited until she'd gotten her drink and left, the bell sounding cheerily behind her, before I pulled out my phone and glanced at the clock. It was 7:00 a.m. sharp as I dialed, then listened to one, two, then three rings. Finally, she picked up.

"Mom?"

"Mclean? Is that you?"

I cleared my throat, looking into that fire in front of me. The logs were perfectly shaped, the fake flames flickering. Pretty yes, but no real warmth there. Just an illusion, but you didn't realize that until you were up close and still felt cold.

"Yeah," I said. "It's me. We need to talk."

× × ×

"Hey! Think fast!"

I just looked at Dave as he chucked the basketball at me with possibly the worst overhand throw I'd ever seen. It landed far to my right, then bounced past me, banging against my dad's truck.

"Do you have a vision problem or something?" I asked him.

"Just keeping you on your toes," he replied, cheerful as

ever as he ran over, picking it up again. He bounced it, then said, "Up for a game?"

I shook my head. "Too early for me."

"It's eight thirty, Mclean. Get with the program."

"I've been up since five."

"Really?" He bounced the ball again. "Doing what?"

"Compromising." I yawned, then turned toward my house. "I'll explain later."

I started up the steps, rummaging in my pocket for my keys. Inside, all the lights were still off, my dad sleeping in for once.

"Want to know what I think?" Dave called out from behind me.

"No."

"I think," he continued, ignoring this, "that you're scared."

I just looked at him. "Scared."

"Of my game," he explained. "My skills. My—"

I walked closer to him, then reached out, easily knocking the ball from his hands. It hit the driveway, then rolled onto the grass.

"Well, see, I wasn't in defensive mode just then." He reached around me, picking up the ball and giving it an authoritative bounce. "Now I am. Bring it on."

"I told you," I said, folding my arms over my chest. "I'm not interested."

He sighed. "Mclean, come on. You live in a basketball town. Your dad played for DB, your mom is married to the current DB coach, and I happen to have personal experience with your overhand shot."

"Yes, but basketball doesn't have the best associations for me right now," I pointed out.

"You can't blame the game for any of that," he said, bouncing the ball again. "Basketball is a good thing. Basketball only wants you to be happy."

I just looked at him as he dribbled sloppily around me toward the basket. "Now," I said, "you sound like a crazy person."

"Think fast!" he said, whirling around and throwing the ball at me. I caught it easily, and he looked surprised. "Okay, fine. Now shoot it."

"Dave."

"Mclean. Humor me. Just one shot."

"You've seen me shoot," I pointed out.

"Yes, but the blunt force knocked my memory out. I need a replay."

I sighed, then bounced the ball once, squaring my shoulders. Other than that random Boomerang a few weeks ago, I hadn't had my hands on a basketball in years. But that morning had been all about doing things I had never planned to do again, so I guess I shouldn't have been surprised.

At first, on the phone, my mom was wary. She knew I'd heard about her lawyer's call, and thought I was calling to tell her exactly what I thought of her latest move. It was tempting to do just that. But instead, I took a breath and did what I had to do instead.

"Are you still thinking you'll be going to the beach a lot this spring?" I asked.

"The beach?"

"Yes." I looked into the fireplace again. "You did say once

the house and the season was done you'd be going there a lot. Right?"

"I did," she said slowly. "Why?"

"I'll come for my spring break, next month," I replied. "If you call off your lawyer, I'll come that full week and four other weekends as well."

"I didn't want to have to get the courts involved," she said quickly. "But—"

"And I don't want to spend the rest of high school worrying about court dates," I replied. She got quiet, fast. "So this is what I'm offering. Spring break plus four weekends before graduation, but my choice of when they happen. Do we have a deal?"

Silence. This was not the way she wanted it, I knew. Too bad. She could have my company and my time, my certain number of weekends and my senior spring break. But she could not have my heart.

"I'll call Jeffrey and tell him we've worked something out," she said. "If you'll send me those break dates and the other ones you have in mind."

"I'll do it today," I replied. "And we'll just follow up as it gets closer. All right?"

A pause. It was like a business deal, cold and methodical. So far from those spur-of-the-moment trips to the Poseidon, all those years ago. But nobody went to North Reddemane anymore. Apparently.

"All right," she said finally. "And thank you."

Now, I stood there with Dave, holding the ball. He was

grinning, in defensive stance—or what counted as such for him—bent over slightly, jumping from side to side waving his hands in my face. "Just try to get past me," he said, doing a weird wiggle move. "I dare you."

I rolled my eyes, then bounced the ball once to the left before cutting right around him. He scrambled to catch up, doing several illegal reach-ins as I moved closer to the basket. "You've basically fouled out in the last five seconds," I told him as he batted at the ball, me, the air around both of us. "You know that, right?"

"This is street ball!" he said. "No fouls!"

"Oh, okay. In that case . . ." I elbowed him in the gut, making him gasp, and moved under the basket. In those few seconds, the net clear above, I remembered all the things my dad had taught me as if they'd been imprinted: watch the hoop, elbows tight, touch light, light, light. I shot, the ball arcing up perfectly.

"Denied!" Dave said, leaping up and batting the ball away.

"Interference," I called out, grabbing it back.

"Street ball!" he replied. And then, as if to prove this, he tackled me and we both went down onto the grass beside my deck, as the ball left my hands, rolling under the house.

For a moment we just lay there, his arms loosely around me, both of us breathing heavy. Finally, I said, "Okay, so with that, you left the realm of basketball entirely."

"Full contact," he said, his voice muffled by my hair. "No guts, no glory."

"I'd hardly call this glory."

"You didn't make the shot, did you?"

I rolled over, so I was on my back, him panting beside me. "You are, like, the weirdest basketball player I have ever seen."

"Thank you," he said.

I laughed out loud.

"What? Was that supposed to be an insult?"

"How could it be anything else?"

He shrugged, brushing his hair out of his face. "I don't know. I think my game is unique, if that's what you're saying."

"That's one word for it."

We lay there for another moment. His arm was still next to mine, elbow to elbow, fingertips to fingertips. After a moment, he rolled over, and I did the same, so we were facing each other. "Want to make it best of two?" he asked.

"You didn't score," I pointed out.

"Details," he said. His mouth was just inches from mine. "We big thinkers choose not to dwell on them."

Suddenly, I was just sure he was going to kiss me. He was there, I could feel his breath, the ground solid beneath us. But then something crossed his face, a thought, a hesitation, and he shifted slightly. Not now. Not yet. It was something I'd done so often—weighing what I could afford to risk, right at that moment—that I recognized it instantly. It was like looking in a mirror.

"I think a rematch is in order," he said after a moment.

"The ball is under the house."

"I can get it. It's not the first time."

"No?"

He sat up, choosing to ignore this. "You know, you talk this tough game and everything. But I know the truth about you."

"And what's that again?" I said, getting to my feet.

"Secretly," he said, "you want to play with me. In fact, you *need* to play with me. Because deep down, you love basketball as much as I do."

"Loved," I said. "Past tense."

"Not true." He walked around my deck, grabbing a broom there and using the handle to fish around beneath. "I saw how you squared up. There was love there."

"You saw love in my shot," I said, clarifying.

"Yeah." He banged the broomstick again, and the ball came rolling out slowly, toward me. "I mean, it's not surprising, really. Once you love something, you always love it in some way. You have to. It's, like, part of you for good."

I wondered what he meant by this, and in the next beat, found myself surprised by the image that suddenly popped into my head: me and my mom, on a windy beach in winter, searching for shells as the waves crashed in front of us. I picked up the ball and threw it to him.

"You ready to play?" Dave asked, bouncing it.

"I don't know," I said. "Are you going to cheat?"

"It's street ball!" he said, checking it to me. "Show me that love."

So cheesy, I thought. But as I felt it, solid against my hands, I did feel something. I wasn't sure it was love. Maybe what remained of it, though, whatever that might be. "All right," I said. "Let's play."

Eleven

✳ ❁ ✳

"Hi," the librarian said, smiling up at me. She was young, with straight blonde hair, wearing a bright pink turtleneck, black skirt, and cool red-framed eyeglasses. "Can I help you?"

"I hope so," I replied. "I'm interested in looking up some town history. But I'm not sure where to start."

"Well, no worries. You have come to the right place." She slid back in her rolling chair, then got to her feet, coming around the desk. "We just happen to have the most extensive collection of newspapers and town-related documents in town. Although don't tell the historical society I said that. They tend to be a little competitive."

"Oh," I said. "Right."

"Are you looking for anything in particular?" she asked, motioning for me to follow her through the main reading room. It was full of couches and chairs, most of them occupied by people absorbed in books, laptops, or magazines.

"I'm trying to find a map that might detail downtown, like, twenty years ago," I said.

"We've definitely got that," she replied, leading me into a smaller room with shelves on all four walls, a row of tables in between them. It was empty except for someone in a parka, the hood up, sitting facing the wall. "This is from the seventy-five-year anniversary of the town's incorporation," she said, easing a large book out. "They put together a commemorative record of the town, with maps and all the history. Another option is looking at the tax and land records for, say, ten years back to see who owned them, and when they were bought or sold. Usually they're searchable by address."

I looked at the stack of books as she put them on the table beside me. "This should be a good start," I said.

"Great," she replied. "Good luck. Oh, and just FYI, you might want to keep your coat on. The heat barely works in this room. It's like a meat locker."

I nodded. "Will do."

She left, and for a moment I just sat there, watching her as she wound her way through the reading room, picking up discarded books from a few tables along the way. There was a fireplace—a real one—crackling in the next room, and it was only as I looked at it that I realized, suddenly, how chilly it was where I was sitting. I pulled my coat closer around me, zipping it up again, and bent over the town history, beginning to turn pages.

In the two weeks since Deb's first day of involvement on the model, it was more on track to actually being finished than I'd ever imagined possible. And that was despite the fact that, even though she'd made several phone calls, Opal couldn't rally any more delinquents to help us. Luckily, Deb had a plan. Or several plans.

First, she had incorporated multiple systems to increase

our overall working efficiency. Besides CAA, there was STOW (Same Time Owed Weekly, a written schedule that insured one of us was at the model every afternoon), PROM (Progress Recap Overview Meeting, held every Friday), and my personal favorite, SORTA (Schedule of Remaining Time and Actual). This last one was a large piece of poster board detailing all the work we still had to do alongside the days that were left before May 1, the councilwoman's deadline.

Deb had also created a Listserv for the model project, as well as a blog that documented the progress as we put it together. Her e-mails were just like Deb herself: cheerful, concise, and sort of relentless, landing in my inbox on an almost daily basis. There was one thing about the model, though, that I wanted to do on my own.

"Mclean?"

I blinked, then looked over at the table beside me. Sitting there, in his parka with a book in his hands, was Jason, the prep cook from Luna Blu. "Hey," I said, surprised. "When did you get here?"

"Actually, I've been here." He smiled. "I was just being antisocial. I didn't realize that was you who was talking to Lauren until I turned around a minute ago."

"Lauren?"

He nodded at the reference desk, where the librarian who'd helped me was now typing away at a computer, her eyes focused on the screen. "She's the best when it comes to hunting down information. If she can't help you find what you're looking for, no one can."

I considered this as he picked up his own book—a worn paperback of something called *A Prayer for Owen Meany*—opening it again to his place. "So you hang out here a lot?"

"I guess," he replied. "I worked here for a while when I was in high school. You know, summers and after school."

"Wow," I said. "That must have been different from the kitchen at Luna Blu."

"Nothing is like working at Luna Blu," he agreed. "It's like contained chaos. Probably why I like it so much."

"Dave said you went to Harvard," I said.

"Yep." He coughed. "But it didn't really work out, so I came back here and took up cooking for a living. Natural career progression, of course."

"It sounds like it was a lot of pressure," I said. He raised his eyebrows, not sure what I meant. "The school you and Dave went to, and the college courses you took, being so driven academically."

"It wasn't all bad," he replied. "Just not what I wanted, eventually."

I nodded. Then he went back to his book, and I turned my attention to the one open in front of me. After looking through some tiny-typefaced documents and a few sketches, I turned a page and there it was: a map from twenty years earlier of the area of downtown that included Luna Blu. I leaned in closer, scanning the pages until I found my street, and my own house, identified only by a parcel number and the label SS DOM: single-story domicile. I ran my finger over it, then over Dave's next door, before moving back across the page to the square behind it. There it was, the shape familiar, and also listed with a parcel number. Above it, it said only HOTEL.

Weird. I'd been expecting something other than a house, but for some reason this was a surprise to me. I grabbed a pen and an old receipt from my purse and wrote the parcel number of the hotel on it, as well as the official address, then folded it away and stuffed it in my pocket. I was just stacking the books into a pile when my phone beeped. It was a text from Deb.

STOW REMINDER: YOU'RE SCHEDULED 4 TO 6 TODAY! ☺

I looked at my watch. It was 3:50. Right on schedule. I picked up my bag, sliding the phone into it. As I got to my feet, Jason turned around again.

"You going to the restaurant?" I nodded. "Mind if I walk with you?"

"Not at all."

We left through the reading room, passing Lauren, who was helping an older woman in a baseball cap at the computers. "Thanks for your help with the catalog system earlier," she said. "You're a genius!"

Jason shook his head, clearly embarrassed, as I followed him out the main doors and onto the street. We walked a little bit and then I said, "So it's not just Tracey and Dave who think so. You *are* brilliant."

"Three people does not make a consensus," he said, pulling his hat down over his ears. "So. Did you find what you were looking for?"

"Sort of," I told him. We kept walking, crossing the street. A few blocks ahead, I could see Luna Blu, its signature azure awning in the distance. "I'm closer than I was, at any rate."

We walked another short block. The snow was still on the ground, but gray and dirty looking now, hard and slippery beneath our feet. "Well, that's a start," he said. "That's good, right?"

I nodded. This was true. But anyone can begin. It was the part with all the promise, the potential, the things I loved. More and more, though, I was finding myself wanting to find out what happened in the end.

× × ×

"There you are!" Deb said as I came up the stairs. "We were getting worried! I thought you were coming right at four."

"It's only five after," I pointed out.

"Yes, but, Mclean," Dave, who was sitting cross-legged on the floor, said, "you know that the STOW waits for no man. Or woman."

"Sorry," I said, flicking him as I passed. "I had something to do. I'll make it up, I promise."

"Yes, you will," he said.

Deb, over at the table, began rummaging through some pieces, humming to herself as I bent down over my sector. For a long time, we worked in silence; the only sounds were distant voices from the kitchen downstairs. Hearing them, I kept thinking about Jason, what he'd said to me about Harvard and the choices he'd made. Amazing how you could get so far from where you'd planned, and yet find it was exactly where you needed to be.

About a half hour later, there was a loud knock from the

bottom of the stairs—*BANG! BANG! BANG!*—and Deb and I both jumped. Dave, though, hardly looked fazed as he called out over one shoulder, "Yo. We're up here."

A moment later, the door creaked open, the sound followed by a sudden, bustling rush of voices and footsteps. Then Ellis appeared at the top of the steps, with Riley and Heather behind him.

"Oh my God," Heather, who was in a red jacket and short skirt with thick tights beneath it, said, "what is this place?"

"It's called an attic," Ellis told her. "It's the top floor of a building."

"Shut up," she replied, smacking the back of his head.

"Enough," Riley said in a tired voice. Then she looked at Dave. "I know we're early. But being stuck in the car with both of them was about to make me insane."

"Understood," Dave replied. "I'll be done here in a sec."

"So this is where you've been spending all your time," Ellis said, sliding his hands in his pockets as he walked along one side of the model. "Reminds me of all that action-figure stuff you used to play with."

"It was war staging," Dave said loudly, "and very serious."

"Of course it was."

Dave rolled his eyes, fastening one last house onto his sector. Then he stood up, wiping his hands on his jeans. "Okay, that one's done. I'll start up the next when I come in Saturday."

Deb glanced over, checking his work. "Sounds good."

"You're leaving?" I asked.

"Previous engagement," he replied, as Heather and Ellis walked over to the windows, looking down at the street. Riley was still standing over the model, taking it all in. "We have this dinner thing we do every month. It's kind of mandatory."

"What he means is," Ellis piped up, "the food is so good you don't want to miss it for anything. Or, um, anyone."

Heather snorted, glancing at me. Riley said, "Let's just go, okay? You know how she gets if we're late."

Ellis and Heather started for the door, with Dave falling in behind them. Riley took one last look across the model, then said, "You guys are welcome to come. I mean, if you want."

"Where are you going, exactly?" I asked.

"My house," she replied. "And Ellis is right. The food is amazing."

"I don't know," I said. "It sounds great, but we've got this schedule, and owe time . . ."

". . . but it can be readjusted," Deb finished for me. I looked at her. "I mean, we can make it up. It's not a problem."

"Oh," I said, surprised she was so quick to agree to this. "Well, great. Sure, then. We'd love to."

Riley nodded, then turned to follow Dave and Heather, who were at the top of the stairs. Over her shoulder, she said, "Fair warning, though. My family's kind of . . . crazy."

"Isn't everyone's?" I replied.

"I guess," she said with a shrug. "Come on. You can ride with us."

×   ×   ×

"I know what you're thinking," Ellis said, hitting the key remote in his hand. "It's pretty much the most stunning example of vehicular perfection ever."

We all stood there, watching as the back door of the sky

blue van slid open, revealing two rows of seats, the rear of which was stacked with soccer balls and various pairs of cleats.

"Don't try to point out to him that it is just a minivan," Heather said, climbing into the backseat and pushing a ball onto the floor. "We've tried."

"It's the modern man's love machine," Ellis replied, walking around to the driver's-side door as Riley got in beside Heather, and Dave took a seat in the next row. I glanced at Deb, who was standing there clutching her purse, then slid in next to him, giving her the front seat. "How many vehicles do you know of that have an AC adapter plug-in, three feet of washable cargo space, *and* fully reclining fold-down seats?"

"It's still a minivan," Heather said. "Before you were macking around in it, it was strictly for car seats and crumbled Goldfish."

"But I am macking around in it," Ellis replied, cranking the engine as Deb shut her door. "And we'll be macking all the way to Austin in it, too. That's all that matters."

We pulled out of the lot beside Luna Blu, turning into traffic. I turned around, so I was facing Riley, who was looking out the window while Heather checked her phone beside her. "You sure this is okay? Inviting two extra people at the last minute?"

"Oh, yeah," she said. "My mom always makes too much anyway."

"You can never have too much fried chicken," Dave told her.

"She made fried chicken last time," Heather said, still studying her screen. "I remember, because Dave ate two breasts, two legs, and two wings. Which was actually . . ."

". . . an entire chicken," Dave finished for her, sighing. "A personal best for me."

"The gluttony on display is unbelievable," Riley told me. "It's almost embarrassing."

"Almost," Ellis said. Then he shot her a smile in the rearview, and she smiled back briefly, before looking out the window again.

We drove through town, past neighborhoods and subdivisions, until the road turned into a two-lane highway. The landscape began to change, with rolling hills on either side, the occasional farmhouse, and broad pastures dotted with cows. I realized suddenly that Deb hadn't said a word, so I leaned forward, around her headrest.

"You okay?" I asked, my voice low.

"Yeah." She was looking straight ahead, taking it all in. "I've just . . . never done this before."

"Been out in the country?"

She shook her head. Beside her, Ellis was messing with the radio, snatches of music and voices popping up here and there. "Been invited to dinner like this."

"What do you mean, 'like this'?"

"By, you know, a bunch of people from school. As friends." She pulled her purse a little closer to her chest. "It's really nice."

We aren't even there yet, I wanted to say, but I kept quiet as, yet again, I was reminded that as much as she'd told me about her past, there was a lot I didn't know.

"Everything cool?" Dave asked me as I sat back.

I nodded, looking at Deb again. She was sitting so still, like at any moment someone might realize their mistake and tell her to go. It made me sad, not for now but for whatever she'd been through to make this so new. "Yeah. Everything's fine."

After driving for what seemed like a long time, Ellis slowed down, turning onto a gravel road. POSTED: NO TRES-PASSING! a sign read, just past a row of mailboxes, and then we were bumping along, Dave's knee knocking into mine every now and then. I didn't move out of the way, though, and neither did he. As we came over a small hill, we saw a woman coming toward us in sweatpants, a long jacket, and sneakers, walking two big dogs. She had a beer in one hand and a cigarette in the other, and still managed a broad wave as we passed.

"That's Glenda," Dave explained. "Out for her evening power walk."

"One beer down, one beer back, cigarettes as needed," Riley added. To me she said, "My neighbor."

"Right," I said.

"And that," Heather said as we passed a short driveway, a little white house at the end of it, "is where I live. Try not to be too stunned by the size and majesty."

"I love your house," Ellis said. Over his shoulder, he added, "Her dad buys MoonPies at Park Mart in bulk. Has an entire glass jar of them on the TV. It's the *best*."

Heather looked pleased, and I realized I'd rarely seen her smile until now. "He has a bad sweet tooth. I try to make him eat healthy, but it is a thankless job."

"Let the man have his MoonPies," Dave said. "What are you, the food police or something?"

"He needs to watch his weight!" she told him. "Diabetes runs in our family. And it's not like he can keep a woman around long enough to take care of him."

I turned slightly as we passed the house. "You live alone with your dad?" She nodded. "Me, too."

"He's a mess," she said affectionately. "But he's my mess."

Ellis turned into the last driveway before the road ended, pulling up in front of a large, brown house with a bunch of cars parked in front of it. It had a silver metal roof, a wide front porch, and what looked like a barn just behind it. A thick chimney on top spouted smoke, puffing up into the sky.

"Here we are," Dave said, as Ellis cut the engine. "I hope you guys are hungry."

The van door slid open, and he and I slid out, Heather and Riley following behind. There were several lights on inside the house, casting yellow light out onto the steps as we climbed them. I turned back to check on Deb, who was bringing up the rear with Ellis.

"Something smells amazing," she said softly, as Riley moved ahead of us, pulling open the door.

She was right. I'd been brought up in restaurants, and eaten a lot of good food. But something about the smell of that house was totally unique. Like fried food, and cheese, and warmth and sugar, the best, most tasty bite you've ever taken.

"You're late," a woman's voice called out as soon as we stepped over the threshold. This was followed by the sound of an oven door banging shut.

"It was Dave's fault," Riley replied, dropping her bag by a flight of stairs.

"I was volunteering," Dave said. "Just so you know."

"Of course you were." Riley shifted out of the way, and I saw the voice belonged to a small, red-haired woman who was standing at the sink, wiping her hands on a dish towel. She had on jeans, sneakers, and a U Basketball sweatshirt, and she was smiling. "Because you are a good boy."

"Hey, what about me?" Ellis said.

"The jury is still out," she said, offering her cheek. He gave it a kiss, then moved past her, into the dining room I could see just beyond. "Heather, sweetie, your dad called. He's going to be late."

"Why doesn't he just call my phone?" she said, pulling it out of her pocket. "I have tried to explain to him that he doesn't need a cell to call a cell. But he cannot comprehend. He's such a caveman."

"Leave Jonah alone," I heard a voice say from the dining room. I looked in to see Ellis sitting next to a man with a beard, also in a U sweatshirt and a matching hat. A beer sat on the table in front of him, his hand loosely around it. "Not everyone is attached at the hip to their technology like you people."

"It's not technology," Heather said, flopping into a chair on his other side. "It's a keypad."

"Be sweet," he said to her, and she stuck out her tongue. I watched as he laughed, picking up his can and taking a sip.

"Mom, this is Mclean and Deb," Riley said. "They were hungry."

"Oh, we really weren't," Deb said quickly. "We didn't mean to impose—"

"You're not imposing," Riley's mom said. "Now come sit down. We're running late and we know how your father gets if he thinks he's going to miss the tip-off."

I glanced at Riley, who was tying on an apron patterned with red checks. "They know nothing," she assured me. "Promise."

"Tip-off?" Deb said.

"U plays Loeb College at seven sharp," Riley's dad called out, gesturing for us to come into the dining room. Once we were closer, he stuck out his hand. "Jack Benson. You know you have the same name as one of the best college basketball coaches of all time?"

"Um, yeah," I said, shaking it. Behind me, Riley and her mom were bustling around, bringing out various pans and casseroles and putting them on the table. "I've heard that."

"Can I help you with anything?" Deb asked her as she dropped the best-looking macaroni and cheese I'd seen in ages onto a trivet.

"Do you see that?" Riley's mom said, pointing at Dave and Ellis. "That's called manners. You all should take lessons. Or at least notice."

"We stopped offering because you never said yes," Ellis told her. To me he added, "She's a total control freak when it comes to cooking. Our plating skills were not up to her standards."

"Hush up," Riley's mom said, swatting at him with a stack

of napkins. To Deb and me, she said, "You two are guests. Sit down. Riley, make sure everyone has a drink, will you? We're almost ready."

"You know," Mr. Benson said as I sat down next to Dave, "I gotta say, you look kind of familiar to me. Do I know you from somewhere?"

"No," Riley called over her shoulder as she dumped ice into a pitcher.

"I think I do." He squinted at me. "You were the one at the game with Dave the other day! Talk about great seats. You must be pretty special to warrant that. He still won't tell me how he scored them."

"Because it's not your business," Mrs. Benson said. The smell of fried food, hot and mouthwatering, wafted over me as she walked behind me, depositing a huge platter of chicken on the table in front of her husband. "Now let's stop talking about basketball for ten minutes and say grace. Any volunteers?"

I looked at Deb, sort of panicking. Then Dave said, "Don't worry. That's a rhetorical question, too. You could never say grace as well as she does."

"David Wade," Mrs. Benson said, pulling out a chair and sitting down. "That is not the least bit true."

Everyone else at the table laughed, but she just shook her head, ignoring them. Then she put out both hands, one to Ellis on her left, and to me on the right. Just as her fingers closed around mine, I felt Dave take my other hand.

"Thank you, God, for this food," Mrs. Benson said, and I looked around the table, seeing that Riley and Deb both had their eyes closed. Mr. Benson, from what I could tell, was eyeing the chicken. "And for the opportunity to share it with our family and friends, old and new. We are truly blessed. Amen."

"Amen," Mr. Benson agreed, already reaching for a serving spoon. "Now, let's eat."

I'd learned from my dad that opinions about food are always biased, and to be skeptical of even the most rave review. In this case, however, what I'd been told was not an exaggeration. After a few bites, I realized that this was true southern food: crisp chicken, creamy mac and cheese, green beans cooked with pork fat, fresh-baked rolls that melted in your mouth. The iced tea was sweet and cold, the servings huge, and I never wanted it to end.

I was so immersed that it wasn't until I reached for another piece of chicken—well on my way to coming close to, if not meeting, Dave's record—that I realized how long it had been since I'd sat around a table this way, eating like a family. I'd spent the last two years eating either on the couch at home, at the end of one bar or another, or in the kitchen with my dad, picking off the same plate, as he made other people's dinners. Here at Riley's, it was so different. The talk was loud, bouncing from topic to topic, as plates were passed and cups refilled. Dave and I kept bumping elbows while Riley's mom peppered me with questions about how I liked Jackson and how it was different from my other schools. Meanwhile, Ellis and Heather talked basketball with Riley's dad, and beside them, Deb was telling Riley about the model and the plans she had for it. It was loud and hot, my face flushed. I suddenly understood again the appeal of food, how it was bigger than just having something made and then slid across a kitchen prep window. It was about family, and home, and where your heart was, like Opal had said about Luna Blu not so long ago.

"Mclean, get yourself some more of those green beans," Mrs. Benson said, gesturing for Ellis to pass them down. "And it looks like you need another roll, too. Where's the butter?"

"Right here," Heather said, picking up the dish and handing it to Mr. Benson, who passed it to Dave. As the conversation rose up again, I watched both it and the bread basket move down the table. Steadily, they went from hand to hand, person to person, like links on a chain, making their way to me.

× × ×

After dinner, Riley's mom put us all on dish duty, while Mr. Benson excused himself and went into the living room, where he eased into a big leather recliner with a fresh beer. A moment later, I heard an announcer's voice and glanced over to see two men in suits shaking hands, a referee between them.

"Look at that," Mr. Benson called out over his shoulder. "Old Dog Face is only wearing two of his championship rings tonight."

"Daddy hates Loeb College," Riley said, adding some soap to the water running in the sink. Clearly, there was a routine here, as everyone had fallen into certain places: she had the sponge, with Ellis beside her to rinse, and then me and Deb armed with dish towels. Dave and Heather were the floaters, already opening cabinets to put things away. "*Especially* the Loeb coach."

"Doesn't everybody?" Ellis said.

"No," Heather told him. "You know my dad is a Loeb fan. So stop the trash-talking."

"Jonah only pulls for Loeb to be contrary," Mr. Benson called out. "It's like rooting for Darth Vader. You just don't do it."

Riley rolled her eyes, soaping up a plate as Mrs. Benson moved behind us, putting something wrapped in Saran in the fridge. "Mom, go sit down," she said. "We've got this."

"I'm almost done," her mom replied.

"She's never done," Ellis said to me.

There was a burst of cheering from the TV, and Mr. Benson clapped his hands. "Hell, yeah! Now *that's* how you start a game!"

"Jack," Riley's mom said. "Language."

"Sorry," he replied like a reflex.

Ellis handed me a platter, which I dried and passed off to Deb. "You know," she said, taking it, "I've never really understood the whole basketball thing."

"It's pretty easy to follow, if you just watch," Heather said.

"I guess. I've never watched a game, though."

A silence fell. Even the TV went mute. "Never?" Riley asked.

Deb shook her head. "My mom and I aren't really into sports."

"Basketball," Dave said, "is not simply a sport. It's a religion."

"Watch it," Mrs. Benson warned from the pantry, where she was organizing cans.

"Let the boy speak!" her husband called out. I looked over to see him turning in his chair, lifting a finger, and pointing at Deb. "Come over here, sweetheart. I'm about to give you an education."

"Oh, God," Riley groaned. "Daddy, please. Don't."

"That would be great!" Deb said. Then she looked down at her dish towel. "Let me just—"

"It's okay," Heather said, taking it from her. "Just go. It'll be easier if you let him go ahead and start. God knows how long this might take."

"You sure?" Deb asked Riley, who nodded. "Okay. Thanks!"

We all stood there washing and drying in silence as she walked over, taking a seat on the corner of the couch closest to the recliner. The volume on the TV came on again, but we could still hear Mr. Benson begin. "Okay," he said. "Now, back in 1891, Dr. James Naismith invented—"

"Oh my God," Riley said. "He's starting with *Naismith*. College just can't come fast enough."

Beside me, Dave laughed. Heather said, "Don't say that. Next year, we'll all be eating cafeteria food and wishing we were here."

"But before that," Ellis said, "we'll be eating our way to Texas. Hey, speaking of that, our travel fund just topped a thousand bucks, thanks to Dave's FrayBake bonus."

"You got a bonus?" Riley asked him.

"Employee of the month three months running," he replied, all proud. "That's a hundred extra dollars to you and me."

"You guys have a fund?" I asked.

"We've been saving since last summer," Riley explained.

"You know, putting in what we can from our jobs and birthdays and Christmas and stuff for gas and hotels and—"

"Food," Ellis added. "I'm working on plotting a map just of diners from here to Austin. I want eggs Benedict in every state."

"Sounds like fun," I said to him.

"You guys need to stop talking about it," Heather said as she reached up, putting some glasses on a shelf. "At least while I'm here."

"You might still be able to come," Riley said to her.

"Unlikely. Unless I make employee of the month for the next, oh, twelve months or so."

"First," Ellis said, "you'd have to get a job."

Heather just looked at him. "I have applications out in several places, I'll have you know."

"FrayBake is always hiring," Dave said cheerfully.

"That place gives me the creeps," Heather replied. "It's so fake."

"The money they pay is real, though."

Heather sighed, shutting the cabinet. "I'll pay my dad back. Just probably not in time for the trip."

"It's okay," Riley said, reaching to squeeze her shoulder as she passed by. "We'll take some trips this summer. The beach and stuff."

"Yeah. I know."

"*Yesssssss!* That's how you do a layup, son!" Mr. Benson yelled. Deb, for her part, clapped politely, her eyes on the screen, while Riley's mom, who'd settled into a rocking chair by the fire, just shook her head.

"Hurry up and rinse that," Dave said to Ellis, nodding at the pitcher in his hand. "We're missing everything."

"You two are just useless. Get out of here," Riley told him. With no protest, they scrambled out of the room. She sighed. "I swear. It's like dealing with children."

"Oh, yeah!" Mr. Benson hollered as if to confirm this. "Suck on that, Loeb!"

"Woo-hoo," Deb added with a bit of a golf clap, as Dave and Ellis plopped down beside her.

"Daddy." Riley winced, covering her eyes with one hand, then said to me, "Well, you can't say I didn't warn you about the whole crazy thing."

"They're not crazy," I told her. She dropped her hand, surprised. "They're great. Seriously. You're really lucky."

"Yeah?" She smiled, then looked back over at her dad, who was pumping his fist in the air.

"Yeah. Thanks for the invite."

"No problem. Thanks for the help." She reached into the water, drawing out a soapy bowl, then handed it to me to rinse. As I did, I looked at the window in front of me, where I could see the TV reflected, motion and light as the game moved past on it, the announcer calling every play. It made me think of my mother, suddenly, and I wished in that moment she could see me here, in a real home, with a family, just like she wanted. Maybe it wasn't ours. But it was still good.

Twelve

❀ ✹ ❀

"Okay," Opal said. "Be *totally* honest. Angel Baby or Calm Waters?"

"What happened to just blue?" Jason asked.

She looked down at the two color swatches she was holding. "I don't know. It's too boring, I guess. And they're both blue."

"I like this one," Tracey said, flicking her finger at the lighter color on the right. "It looks like the ocean."

"So does the other one," Jason pointed out. "I honestly can't tell the difference."

"The other one has higher hues, more white in it. This one"—Tracey picked up the swatch on the left, flipping it over—"Angel Baby, has darker notes going to lighter, but it's more of a mix."

Opal and Jason just looked at her as she turned the swatch back over, sliding it back in place. "What?" she said. "I'm into art, okay?"

"Clearly," Jason said. "That was impressive."

"So we've got one vote for Angel Baby, and one no opinion. Maybe I should go back to the yellows." Opal sighed, picking up a stack of swatches and flipping through them, then looked up and saw me. "Hey! Mclean! Come tell me what you think."

I walked over to the bar, dropping my backpack onto a chair. "About what?"

"Colors for the new-and-improved upstairs alfresco dining area," she said.

"You're going to reopen the second floor?" I asked.

"Well, not right now. I mean, there's the model, and we still have to get the restaurant on a better footing." She laid out the two swatches. "But now that Chuckles has spared us, he might be open to some ideas for expanding and improvement. He's supposed to come in tonight, passing through town, so I'd thought I'd just plant the idea in his head."

"I do not like the idea of having to go up and down stairs to my tables," Tracey said.

"And there's the question of keeping food warm during the trip," Jason added.

"Where is your sense of adventure? Of change? This could be really, really good for the restaurant. A return to its past glory days!" Opal said. They just looked at her, and she sighed, flipping her hand, then turned her attention to me. "Okay. Mclean. Pick one."

I looked down at the colors. Two blues, different and yet so similar. I couldn't see notes of white, or various shading, and didn't know the language Tracey used to describe the most subtle of nuances. These days, though, I was sure of one thing: I knew what I liked.

"This one," I said, putting my finger on the one on the right. "It's perfect."

× × ×

It was now March, and my dad and I had been in Lakeview for almost two months. Anywhere else, those eight weeks would have followed a routine pattern. Get moved in, get settled, pick a name and a girl. Unpack our few, necessary things, arranging them in the same way as the last place, and the next place. Start school while my dad got a line on whether his restaurant had slimy lettuce or great guacamole, and plan my own moves in terms of joining clubs and making friends accordingly. Then, all that was left was following the signs so I'd know when to pull back, cut for good, and get ready to run.

Here, though, it was different. We'd come in the same way, but since then everything had changed, from me using my real name to my dad starting to date even with no next move in sight. Add in the fact that I was actually on decent terms with my mom, and this was officially an entirely new ball game.

Since I'd agreed to go to Colby for spring break, as well as committed to four other weekends between April and June, my mom and I had reached tentative peace. She'd called her lawyer and withdrawn her custody-review request, and I'd explained the plan to my dad, who was relieved, to say the least. Now, I had the third week in March circled on my calendar in Angel Baby or Calm Waters or just blue, and we had something to talk about that was not a loaded subject. Which was kind of nice, actually.

"Now, the ocean's going to be freezing, obviously," she'd said to me the night before, when she called after dinner. "But I'm hopeful that the hot tub will be working and the pool heat up and running, although it might not happen. I'll keep you posted."

"Your house has a hot tub and pool?" I'd asked her.

"Well, yes," she said, sounding kind of embarrassed. "You know Peter. He doesn't do anything halfway. But his place was a great deal, apparently, a foreclosure or something. Anyway, I can't wait for you to see it. I spent hours agonizing over the redecorating. Picking colors was a nightmare."

"Yeah, I bet," I said. "I have a friend who's doing that right now. She wanted me to help her, but all the blues looked the same."

"They do!" she said. "But at the same time, they don't. You have to look at them in the daylight, and afternoon light, and bright light. . . . Oh, it's nuts. But I'm really happy with how it turned out. I think."

It had been weird, I had to admit, to be having such a, well, pleasant conversation with my mom. Like once again, the beach had somehow become a safe place for us to be together, separate from the conflict of her house or this one. So we continued to talk and e-mail about plans for what to do on rainy days, what I wanted to have for breakfast, if I wanted an ocean or sound view. It was easier, so much easier, than what I was used to. Maybe even okay.

Meanwhile, as I was making up with my mom, my dad was busy doing something with Lindsay Baker. As far as I could tell, they'd been on several late lunches—with her giving him the tour of other local eateries—and a couple of dinners when he could get away from Luna Blu, which was rare. Normally, I could tell when my dad was laying groundwork for another escape by how committed he let himself get, as backward as that sounds. Phone calls and lunch dates meant I should proceed as I had been, that nothing was happening. But once I started finding hair elastics that weren't mine in the bathroom, or someone else's yogurt or Diet Coke in the fridge, it was time to stop buying staples like sugar and butter and use up what we had instead. So far, none of these things had materialized, at least that I knew of. I was kind of distracted myself, though, to be honest.

It had happened on the night we'd gone to Riley's, after the game, when Ellis was driving us all back home. Deb had hopped into the front seat, armed with a plate of leftovers packed up by Mrs. Benson for her mom, who Deb had said was working through dinner for overtime, which left me and Dave alone in the back. As Ellis pulled out onto the dirt road, we were all quiet, worn out by all the food and talking, not to mention a great game the U had won with a jump shot in the final seconds. When he put on his blinker at the main road, the ticktock was all you could hear.

There's something nice about the silence of a car ride in the dark, going home. It reminded me, actually, of those trips back from North Reddemane with my mom, sunburned, with sand in my shoes, my clothes damp from pulling them on over my suit, as I wanted to swim until the very last moment. When we were tired of the radio and conversation, it was okay to just be alone with our thoughts and the road ahead. If you're that comfortable with someone, you don't have to talk.

As we headed toward town, I leaned back, pulling one leg up underneath me. Beside me, Dave was looking out the window, and for a moment I studied his face, brightened now and then by the lights of oncoming cars. I thought of all the times we'd been together, how I kept coming closer, then retreating, while he stayed right where he was. A constant in a world where few, if any, really existed. And so as he sat there beside me, I moved a little closer, resting my head on his shoulder. He didn't turn away from the window. He just lifted · his hand, smoothing it over my hair, and held it there.

It was just a tiny moment. Not a kiss, not even real contact. But for all the things it wasn't, it meant so much. I'd been running for years: there was nothing scarier, to me, than to just be still with someone. And yet, there on that dark road, going home, I was.

Eventually, after dropping Deb at her car, Ellis pulled up in front of my mailbox. "Last stop," he said as I yawned and Dave rubbed his eyes. "Sorry to break up the moment."

I flushed, pushing myself out onto the curb, and Dave followed. "Thanks for driving," he said. "Next time, it's all me."

"That car is a safety hazard," Ellis told him. "We're better off in the Love Van."

"Yeah, but it needs to hold up for the road trip," Dave replied. "Gotta take care of her, right?"

Ellis looked at me, then nodded and hit a button. The back door slid closed, like the curtain at the end of a show. "That's right. Later!"

Dave and I waved, and then Ellis was driving away, bumping over the speed humps. As we started walking, he reached down, sliding fingers around mine. As he did, I had a flash of that night he'd pulled me into the storm cellar, when he'd taken my hand to lead me up to the world again. It felt like second nature then, too.

We weren't talking, the neighborhood making all its regular noises—bass thumping, car horns, someone's TV—around us. The party house had clearly watched the game as well. I could see people milling around inside, and the recycling bin on the porch was overflowing with crumpled beer cans. Then there was my dark house, and finally Dave's, which was lit up bright, his mom visible at the kitchen table, reading something, a pen in one hand.

"See you tomorrow?" Dave asked when we reached our two back doors, facing each other.

"See you tomorrow," I repeated. Then I squeezed his hand.

The first thing I did when I got inside was turn on the kitchen light. Then I moved to the table, putting my dad's iPod on the speaker dock, and a Bob Dylan song came on, the notes familiar. I went into the living room, hitting the switch there, then down the hallway to my room, where I did the same. It was amazing what a little noise and brightness could do to a house and a life, how much the smallest bit of each could change everything. After all these years of just passing through, I was beginning to finally feel at home.

× × ×

I left Opal reconsidering her yellows, then headed upstairs to the attic room, where I found Deb and Dave already hard at work. This time, though, they weren't alone. On the other side of the room, sitting in a row of chairs by the boxes of model parts, were Ellis, Riley, and Heather, each of them engrossed in reading a stapled packet of papers.

"What's going on over there?" I asked Dave, as Deb bustled by, a clipboard in her hands.

"Deb has shocked them into silence," he told me. "Which is really hard to do. Believe me."

"How'd she do it?"

"Her POW packet."

I waited. By this point, it was understood that if you said one of Deb's acronyms, you usually had to then explain it.

"Project Overview and Welcome," Dave said, popping a roof onto a house. "Required reading before you can even think about attempting a sector."

"It's not that strict!" Deb protested. I raised an eyebrow at her, doubting this. "It isn't. It's just . . . you can't come into an existing, working system and not educate yourself on its processes. That would be stupid."

"Of course it would," Dave said. "God, Mclean."

I poked him again, and this time, he grabbed my finger, wrapping his own around it and holding it for a second. I smiled, then said, "So, Deb. How'd you manage to double our workforce since yesterday? I didn't hear you doing the hard sell last night."

"I didn't have to sell anything," she replied, checking something off the top sheet on her clipboard. "The model spoke for itself. As soon as they saw it, they wanted in."

"Wow," I said.

She puttered off, clicking her pen top. Beside me, very quietly, Dave said, "Also I *might* have told them that the sooner this thing is done, the sooner I can up my hours at FrayBake for the road-trip fund. This way they can pitch in during spring break next week, and we can really knock some stuff out."

"You guys aren't doing anything for spring break?"

He shook his head. "Nah. We thought about it, but figured we'd just save the money for the real trip later. What, are you taking off or something?"

"With my mom," I said. "The beach."

"Lucky you."

"Not really," I said as I walked over to my current sector, reacquainting myself with it. "I'd rather be here."

"You know," Heather called out to him from across the room, "when you talked me into this, you didn't say anything about it being like *school*."

"It's not like school!" Deb replied from the other end of the model, where she was checking off things on another one of her lists. "Why would you say that?"

"Because you're making us study?" Ellis asked.

"If you guys just plunged in, it would totally throw off the SORTA," Deb told him. "I'm having to completely rejigger the STOW as it is!"

"What?" Heather asked. "Are you even speaking English?"

"She's speaking Deb," I said. "You'll be fluent in no time."

"I'm done," Riley said, getting to her feet, her packet in hand. "All fourteen bullet points and the acronym overview."

"Good," Heather said, getting up as well. "Then you can explain them to me."

"This *is* just like school!" Ellis said. Heather elbowed him, hard. "Hey, don't get mad at me. You're the one who can't even make it through the POW packet."

"You can take it home tonight, and really go over it then," Deb assured Heather.

"Oh, okay," Heather replied. "Because that's not like school at *all*."

"Great!" Deb clapped her hands, picking up her clipboard. "If you'll all just follow me over to our top sector here, I'll start your guided tour."

Ellis got up, then followed Riley and Heather, who was dragging her feet, as they fell in behind Deb. "Are there going to be snacks?" he asked. "I do my best work with snacks."

Dave snorted. Deb, though, either ignored this or didn't hear it. "Now, once you're confident you understand the system, you'll be assigned a sector. Until then, though, you'll share one. This one is relatively simple, perfect for beginners. . . ."

As she kept talking, I looked up at Dave, working away across from me, his hair falling into his eyes as he attached a roof to the building in his hands. "Hey," I said, and he glanced up. "You know that building, behind our houses? The abandoned one?"

"Yeah. What about it?"

"It's on here, but not identified. I realized the other day." I pulled the building out of the pile I'd assembled beside me, showing it to him. "So I went to the library, to see if I could figure out what it was."

"Did you?"

I nodded, realizing, as I did so, how much I wanted to tell him. I wasn't sure why this had been so important to me, only that it seemed fated somehow, that just as things began to feel real and settled, I'd moved onto the part of the map that represented my own neighborhood. There was my house, and Dave's. The party house, Luna Blu, the street where I caught the bus. And in the middle, this blank building, its anonymity made even more noticeable as it was surrounded by things that were clear and recognizable. I wanted to give it a face, a name. Something more than two faded letters on a rooftop, and a million guesses about what it used to be.

I put the building down in its spot, the tape catching and sticking. Then there was a click, the sure sign it was there to stay. "Yeah," I told him. "It was—"

"Oh my goodness! Would you look at *this*." I turned my head, just in time to see Lindsay Baker, dressed in black pants and a tight red sweater and smiling wide, appear on the landing. My dad, looking markedly less effervescent, was right behind her. "I assumed you all would have made a lot of progress. But this is really impressive!"

Deb, across the model, beamed. I said, "We appointed a good leader. Makes all the difference."

"Clearly," she said as she started around the model, making approving noises. After a few steps, she reached back for my dad's hand, taking hold of it. "Gus, had you seen this? I had no idea the detail was so specific!"

"It's taken from the most recent satellite-scanning information," Deb called out. "Model Community Ventures really prides itself on accuracy. And, of course, we've tried to follow their lead."

The councilwoman nodded. "It shows."

Deb flushed, beyond pleased, and I knew this was her moment, and I should be happy for her. But I was too distracted watching my father as he was led around the far corner of the model, avoiding making eye contact with anyone. Lunch dates and phone calls were one thing. But hand-holding, or any kind of PDA for that matter, was a big red flag.

"Whoa," Dave said, his voice low. "Your dad and Lindsay Baker, huh? She is a serious Friend of Frazier. Pounds lattes like they're juice."

I shook my head, although I was in no position to confirm or deny anything. "I don't think it's serious."

"Gus?" Opal yelled up the stairs. "Are you up there?"

"Yeah," he replied. "I'll be right—"

But he didn't move fast enough. Before he could even begin to extract his hand—and something told me once Lindsay took hold, she had a good grip to her—Opal was already on the landing.

"The meat supplier's on the phone," she said, slightly breathless from running up the stairs. "He says you put a change in on our standing order, so it's week to week now instead of set by the month? I told him that couldn't be right, but he's—"

She stopped suddenly, and I followed her gaze to my father's hand, still wrapped in the councilwoman's. "I'll talk to him," my dad said, letting go and starting for the stairs. Opal just stood there staring straight ahead as he walked by her.

"Opal, I'm so impressed with what I see here!" Lindsay said to her. "You should be very proud of the progress these kids have made."

Opal blinked, then looked at the model, and us. "Oh, I am," she said. "It's great."

"I have to admit, I was a little nervous after my last visit!" The councilwoman scanned the model again. "Not that I didn't have total faith in you, but at the time you seemed a bit disorganized. But Mclean says they've got a new team leader—"

"Deb," I said. I nodded at her, and she beamed again. "It's all Deb."

I could feel Opal watching me, her gaze like heat, and I realized too late it was exactly the wrong time to draw attention to myself. "Well, Deb," Lindsay said, turning her bright smile in that direction, "if that's true, we'll look forward to commending you properly at the unveiling ceremony."

"Oh, that sounds wonderful!" Deb said. She thought for a second, then said, "Actually, I have some ideas about the best way to display it. You know, to really get that optimum wow factor. If you'd like to hear them."

"Of course." Lindsay glanced at her watch. "Shoot, I've got to get back to my office. Why don't you walk down with me while I go look for Gus?"

Deb's face lit up, and she grabbed her clipboard, rushing over to join the councilwoman as she started down the stairs. We all watched them go, none of us talking. When the door at the bottom shut behind them, Opal turned to me.

"Mclean?" she said. "What's . . . What's going on here?"

I shook my head. "I don't know."

Opal swallowed, then looked around the room, as if only then realizing we had an audience. She shifted her attention to the model, scanning it from one side to the other, then back again. "I had no idea you guys had done this much," she said. "Guess I need to pay more attention all around."

"Opal," I said. "Don't—"

"I've got to go open," she said. "You guys, um, keep up the good work. It all looks great."

She turned, disappearing down the stairs. We were only down by about half, but suddenly the room felt downright empty.

"Is it just me," Heather said in the quiet, "or was that weird?"

"Not just you," Dave told her.

Riley, from across the room, said, "Is everything okay, Mclean?"

I didn't know. All that was clear was that everything, including me, suddenly felt wholly temporary. I looked down at the model again. There, the entire world was simple in miniature, clean and orderly, if only because there were none of us, no people, there to complicate things.

x x x

That night, like most nights, we only worked on the model until 6:00 p.m. This was Opal's rule, although I sensed my dad had a part in it. It made sense, though: it was one thing to have people moving around upstairs and coming and going for the first hour of service, but another to have to deal with it during the dinner rush.

Dave and I walked back to our houses together. His was lit up, as usual, and I could see his mom and dad in the kitchen, moving around. Mine was dark, except for the side porch light that we always forgot to turn off. I knew this was far from eco-friendly, and I needed to stick a Post-it or something on the door to remind me. Times like now, though, I was glad for the oversight.

"So. You got big dinner plans?" Dave asked me as we started up my driveway.

"Not really. You?"

"Tofu loaf." He made a face before I could react. "It's better than it sounds. But still . . . not so good. What's on your menu?"

I thought of our fridge, how I'd not had time to get to the store for a few days. Eggs, some bread, maybe some deli meat. "Breakfast for dinner, probably."

"Aw, really?" He sighed. "That sounds *awesome*."

"You should suggest it to your mom."

He shook his head. "She's got egg issues."

"Excuse me?"

"The short version is she doesn't eat them," he explained. "The longer one involves certain dietary intolerances combined with ethical misgivings."

"Oh."

"Exactly."

We were at the basketball goal now. I looked over his shoulder into the kitchen, where Mrs. Dobson-Wade was stirring something in a wok while Dave's dad poured a glass of wine. "It's nice that you guys eat as a family, though. Even if eggs aren't allowed."

"I guess," he said. "Although more often than not, we're all reading."

"What?"

"Reading," he repeated. "It's something you do with books?"

"You all sit together at the table and don't talk to one another?"

"Yeah. I mean, we talk some. But if we all have things we're engrossed in . . ." He trailed off, looking embarrassed. "I told you that I'm weird. Hence, my family is weird. Although honestly, you should have figured that out already."

"Weird," I said, "but together. That counts for something."

Now he looked at my house, that single outside light, the kitchen dark behind it. "I guess."

I was ready to go inside. "Enjoy your tofu loaf," I told him, turning toward my stairs.

"Eat an egg for me."

I unlocked the door, then immediately turned on the kitchen light, followed by the one in the living room. Then I put on my dad's iPod on the speaker dock—he'd been in a Zeppelin mood that morning, apparently—broke a couple of eggs into a bowl, and mixed in some milk. The bread in the fridge was a bit old, but not moldy, perfect for toasting. Five minutes later, dinner was done.

Normally, I ate on the couch, in front of the TV or my laptop. This night, however, I decided to get formal, folding a paper towel under my fork and sitting at the kitchen table. I'd just taken a bite of toast when I heard a knock at the door. When I turned around, there was Dave. And his dad.

"We need your TV," Dave explained when I opened the door. They were both standing there, plates in hand. Behind them, I could see into their dining room, where Mrs. Dobson-Wade was alone at the table. Reading.

"My TV?"

"The Defriese-U game is just starting," Mr. Wade said. "And our TV is suddenly refusing to change channels."

"Probably because it's about twenty years old," Dave added.

"It is a perfectly fine television," his dad said, adjusting his glasses with his free hand. "We hardly watch it anyway."

"Except tonight." Dave looked at me. "I know it's asking a lot. But can we—"

I stepped back, waving my hand. "Sure."

They came in, their silverware rattling on their plates, and bustled into the living room, sitting down on the couch. I turned on the TV, then flipped channels until I spotted my stepfather's face. The game was about ten minutes in, and Defriese was up by nine.

"How did *that* happen?" Mr. Wade said, shaking his head as I went and got my plate, sliding into the leather chair beside them.

"Our defense sucks," Dave replied. Then he sniffed and looked at me. "Oh my God. Those smell *amazing*."

"They're just scrambled. Nothing fancy." Now, Mr. Wade was eyeing my plate as well. "I . . . I can make you guys some. If you want."

"Oh, no, no," Dave's dad said. He gestured to his plate, where a beige square was bordered by some broccoli and what looked like brown rice. "We've got perfectly fine dinners. Your generosity with the TV is quite enough."

"Right," Dave said as on the screen, a whistle blew. Mr. Wade grimaced, reacting to the call. "We're good."

I turned my attention back to the screen. After a few minutes of fast back-and-forth, one of the U players got fouled and the clock stopped. We watched a couple of beer commercials and a news update, and then the game returned, showing Peter saying something to one of his starters. He clapped him on the back, and the guy started back out onto the court. As Peter sat down, I saw my mom behind him. No twins this time: she was alone, watching the game with a serious expression.

"Making eggs is really no trouble," I said, jumping up. "I'm done eating, and it will only take a second."

"Hey, Mclean, you really don't—" Dave began. I looked at him, then at the screen, where my mother was still in view. "Oh. Well. That would be great. Thanks."

It was easier to listen to the game than to watch, so I moved slowly as I scrambled the eggs, added milk, and preheated the pan. I wasn't sure what their position was on toast. Gluten issues? Was wheat bad ethically? I stuck some bread in the toaster oven anyway. While I cooked, the U came back, tying up the score, although they racked up some fouls in the process. Between listening to Dave and his dad reacting to the action—groans, claps, the occasional cheer—and the smell of eggs cooking, I could have been back in Tyler, in our old house, living my old life. I took my time.

There were about five minutes left in the half when I came back in, balancing two plates and the roll of paper towels, and deposited them both on the table in front of Dave and his dad. It was just eggs and toast. But by their reaction, you would have thought I'd prepared the most extravagant of feasts.

"Oh my goodness," Mr. Wade whispered, slowly pushing his half-eaten tofu loaf aside. "Is that . . . Is that *butter*?"

"I think it is," Dave said. "Wow. Look at how fluffy and yellow these are!"

"Not like Neggs," his dad agreed.

"Neggs?" I said.

"Not-eggs," Dave explained. "Egg substitute. It's what we use."

"What's in them?" I asked as Mr. Wade took a bite. He closed his eyes, chewing slowly, his reaction so full of pleasure I had to look away.

"Not eggs," Dave replied. He exhaled. "These are amazing, Mclean. Thank you so much."

"Thank you," his dad repeated, scooping up another heaping forkful.

I smiled, just at the game came back on the screen. Immediately, the players were in motion, moving down the court, the U out in front with the ball. As they passed the bench, the action slowed, and I saw Peter again, my mom behind him. As the team set up their offense, I watched as she pulled out her phone, opening it up, and pushed a few buttons, then put it to her ear.

I turned around, looking at my purse, which was on the floor by the couch. Sure enough, I could see a light flashing inside. I pulled out my phone. "Hello?"

"Hey, honey," she said over the din behind her. "I just had

a quick thought about our trip tomorrow. Have you got a second?"

Dave and his dad erupted in cheers, plates clanging in their laps as the U stole the ball and moved down the court. Where my mom was, there was noticeably less of a reaction.

"Actually," I said, "I, um, have some people over for dinner."

"You do?" She sounded so surprised. "Oh. Well, I'll just call back later, okay?"

"Great," I said, watching Dave as he took another bite of toast, then smiled at me. Real bread, real butter. All real. "Talk to you then."

Thirteen

✳ ❁ ✳

That night, I tried to wait up for my dad, so I could ask him about the councilwoman and what I'd seen between them at the model that day, although I wasn't sure I wanted to know the answer. Still, I busied myself packing and repacking my suitcase for the beach, trying not to think about all the other times I'd folded clothes this same way, in the same bag. Once that was done, I made myself a pot of coffee and sat down on the couch to study for my last big test before break, feeling confident that the task and the caffeine would keep me awake until he returned. Instead, I woke up at 6:00 the next morning, the room cold and my mother's quilt tucked over me.

I sat up, rubbing my eyes. My dad's keys were in the dish by the door, his coat thrown over our worn leather chair. Distantly, down the hallway, I could hear the water running in his bathroom. Just another morning. I hoped.

I took a shower, then got dressed before making a bowl of cereal and another pot of coffee. I was pouring a second cup when I heard a knock at the door. Glancing out the front window, I saw a black Town Car parked at the curb. Which could mean only one thing. Sure enough, when I opened it, I found myself facing a wide expanse of gray cashmere. I looked up and up, and there was Chuckles. Opal had mentioned he was back in town, but a home visit was a surprise.

"Mclean," he said, smiling at me. "Good morning. Your dad around?"

"He's in the shower," I told him, stepping back so he could come in. He had to duck under the low door frame, but something in the easy way he did it made it clear he was used to this. "He should be out in a minute. You want some coffee?"

"No thanks, I'm already covered," he said, holding up a travel mug in one of his huge hands. "This stuff has totally spoiled me. I have to take it with me when I travel now. Nothing else compares."

"Really? What is it?"

"A special blend, grown and roasted in Kona, Hawaii. I've been doing some business there lately and discovered it." He uncapped the lid, holding it out to me. "Take a whiff."

I did, although it felt a little odd to do so. It smelled amazing. "Wow," I said. "Hawaii, huh?"

"You ever been?"

I shook my head. "I'd love to, though."

"Really," he said, watching me as I folded the quilt, putting it back on the arm of the couch. "Well, that's good to know."

I glanced up, wondering at this, but then my dad was coming down the hallway, hair damp, pulling a sweatshirt over his head. "Isn't it a little early for door-to-door salesmen?" he asked.

"Trust me," Chuckles told him, capping his coffee and taking a sip, "you *want* what I'm peddling."

"You always say that." My dad picked up his keys and phone. "You on your way out of town?"

"Yep. Just wanted to stop by to bug you one more time." He smiled at me. "I was just telling your daughter about how good this Kona coffee is."

"Let's talk outside," my dad said, pulling on his jacket. "Mclean, I'll just be a sec."

"Good to see you," Chuckles called out as he ducked back through the door, onto the porch. "And aloha. That means hello *and* goodbye in Hawaii. Remember that, okay? It's useful information."

"Okay," I replied a bit uncertainly. "Aloha."

My dad shot him a look, and then the door was shutting behind them. I watched them go down the walk, their contrasting heights the oddest of pairings. Just as they got into the back of the black Town Car idling at the curb, my phone rang.

I pulled it out, then flipped it open, my eyes still on the car. "Morning, Mom," I said.

"Good morning!" she said. "Are you in a rush? Or can you talk for sec?"

"I can talk."

"Great! Today's going to be nuts, getting packed and driving down, so I wanted to just confirm our times and everything before the madness starts." She laughed. "So are we still on for four, do you think?"

"It should be fine," I told her. "I'll be back here by three forty-five at the latest, and I'm already all packed."

"Don't forget your bathing suit," she said. "Our mainte-nance guy called yesterday and it's official. The pool and hot tub are both up and running."

"Oh, God," I said, glancing down the hall at my bag, sitting by the bed. "I totally forgot about that. I'm not even sure I have a suit anymore."

"We can pick one up for you," she replied. "Actually, there's this really cute boutique on the boardwalk in Colby that my friend Heidi owns. We'll stop in there if we get in before they close." There was a loud wail in the background. "Oh, dear. Connor just dumped a bowl of Cheerios on Madison. I'd better go. I'll see you at four?"

"Yeah," I said. "See you then."

Her phone went down with a clatter—she always had to get off the phone in a hurry, it seemed—and I hung up mine, sliding it back in my pocket. I turned around just in time to see my dad coming back in, Chuckles's car pulling away in the window behind him.

"So," I said as the door swung shut, "I hope this is a good time to let you know I'm going to be needing a new bathing suit."

He stopped where he was, his face tightening. "Oh, for God's sake. He told you? I asked him *specifically* not to. I swear he's never been able to keep his mouth shut about any-thing."

I just looked at him, confused. "Who are you talking about?"

"Chuckles," he said, annoyed. Then he looked at me. "The Hawaii job? He told you. Right?"

Slowly, I shook my head. "I was talking about the trip today. Mom has a pool."

He exhaled, then ran a hand over his face. "Oh," he said softly.

We just stood there for a moment, both of us still. Coffee, Kona, aloha, not to mention Luna Blu's apparent reprieve and his date with the councilwoman: it suddenly all made sense. "We're going to Hawaii?" I asked finally. "When?"

"Nothing's official yet," he replied, moving over to the couch and sitting down. "It's a crazy offer anyway. This restaurant that's not even open yet and already a total mess . . . I'd be insane to agree to it."

"When?" I said again.

He swallowed, tilting his head back and studying the ceiling. "Five weeks. Give or take a few days."

Immediately, I thought of my mother, how I'd averted the custody issue with my promises of this trip and weekends, not to mention how things had improved between us since. Hawaii might as well have been another world.

"You wouldn't have to go," my dad said now, looking at me.

"I'd stay here?"

His brow furrowed. "Well . . . no. I was thinking you could go back home to your mom's. Finish the year and graduate there, with your friends."

Home. As he said this word, nothing came to mind. Not an image, or a place. "So those are the options?" I said. "Mom's or Hawaii?"

"Mclean." He cleared his throat. "I told you, nothing is decided yet."

It was so weird. Just then, suddenly and totally unexpectedly, I was certain I was going to cry. And not just cry, but cry those hot, mad tears that sting your throat and burn your eyes, the kind you only do in private when you know no one can see or hear you, not even the person that caused them. Especially them.

"So this is why you've been with the councilwoman," I said slowly.

"We've just been on a couple of dates. That's all."

"Does she know about Hawaii?"

He blinked, then glanced at me. "Nothing to know. I told you, no plans have been made."

"Except for the meat order going from monthly to weekly," I said. He raised his eyebrows. "Doesn't bode well for the restaurant. Means you're either running out of money, or time. Or both."

He sat back, shaking his head. "You don't miss much, do you?"

"Just repeating what you told me back in Petree," I said. "Or Montford Falls."

"Petree," he replied. "In Montford, they had time and money. That's why they made it."

"And Luna Blu won't," I said slowly.

"Probably not." He rubbed a hand over his face, then dropped it, looking at me. "I'm serious about what I said, though. You can't just pick up and move halfway across the world so close to finishing school. Your mother wouldn't stand for it."

"It's not her choice, though."

"Why don't you want to go home?" he asked.

"Because it's not home anymore," I said. "It hasn't been for three years. And yeah, Mom and I are getting along better, but that doesn't mean I want to live with her."

My dad rubbed his hand over his face, the sure sign that he was tired and frustrated. "I need to get to the restaurant," he said, starting out of the room. "Just think about this, okay? We can discuss it further tonight."

"Mom's picking me up for the beach at four," I said.

"Then when you get back. Nothing has to be decided right now."

He got to his feet, then turned to start down the hallway. I said, "I can't go back there. You don't understand. I'm not . . ."

He stopped, then looked back at me, waiting for me to finish this sentence, and I realized I couldn't. In my head, it went off in a million directions—*I'm not that girl anymore. I'm not sure who I am*—each of them only leading to more complications and explanations.

My dad's phone, sitting on the table, suddenly rang. But he didn't answer, instead kept looking at me. "Not what?" he asked.

"Nothing," I said, nodding at his phone. "Never mind."

"Stay right there. I want to keep talking about this," he said as he picked it up, flipping it open. "Gus Sweet. Yeah, hi. No, I'm on my way. . . ."

I watched him as he turned, still talking, and went down the hallway into his bedroom. As soon as he was out of sight, I grabbed my backpack and bolted.

The air was sharp, clear, and I felt it fill my lungs like water as I sucked in a breath and started around the house to my shortcut to the bus stop. The grass was wet under my feet, my cheeks stinging as I pushed myself forward through the yard and into that of the building behind us.

Dusted with frost, it looked even more bereft than usual, and when I got to its side yard, the bus stop in sight ahead, I stopped, then bent down, putting my hands on my legs, and tried to catch my breath and swallow back my tears. I could feel the cold all around me: seeping through my shoes, in the air, moving through and around this empty, abandoned place beside me. I turned, taking a breath, and looked over, seeing my reflection in one of the remaining windows. My face was wild, lost, and for a second I didn't recognize myself. Like the house was looking at me, and I was a stranger. No home, no control, and no idea where I was, only where I might be going.

× × ×

"Mclean. Wait up!"

I bit my lip at the sound of Dave's voice, calling out from behind me. Between studying and some extra credit work I needed to do before the end of this, the last day of the grading period, I'd managed to avoid just about everyone for the entire school day. Until now.

"Hey," I said as he jogged up, falling into place behind me.

"Where have you been all day?" he said. "I thought you cut or something."

"I had tests," I told him as we moved with the rest of the crowd through the main entrance. "And some other stuff."

"Oh, right. Because you're leaving."

"What?"

"For the beach. Today. With your mom." He looked at me, narrowing his eyes. "Right?"

"Oh. Yeah," I said, shaking my head. "Sorry. I'm just, you know, distracted. About the trip, and everything."

"Sure," he said, but he kept his eyes on me, even as I focused my attention steadily forward. "So . . . are you leaving right away or are you coming to the restaurant for a while?"

"Um . . ." I said as my phone buzzed in my pocket. I pulled it out, glancing at the screen. It was a text from my dad. COME BY HERE BEFORE YOU LEAVE, it read. A request, if not a demand. "I'm actually heading there right now."

"Cool. Ride with me."

Being alone, together, at right this moment, was exactly what I didn't want to do. But lacking any way of getting out of it, I followed him to the parking lot, sliding into the passenger seat of the Volvo. After three false starts, he finally managed to coax it out of the space and toward the exit.

"So," he said as we turned onto the main road, the muffler rattling, "I've been thinking."

"Yeah?"

He nodded. "You really need to go out with me."

I blinked. "I'm sorry?"

"You know. You, me. A restaurant or movie. Together." He glanced over, shifting gears. "Maybe it's a new concept for you? If so, I'll be happy to walk you through it."

"You want to take me to a movie?" I asked.

"Well, not really," he said. "What I really want is for you to be my girlfriend. But I thought saying that might scare you off."

I felt my heart jump in my chest. "Are you always so direct about this kind of thing?"

"No," he said. We turned right, starting up the hill toward downtown, the tall buildings of the hospital and U bell tower visible at the top. "But I get the feeling you're in a hurry, leaving and all, so I figured I should cut to the chase."

"I'm only going to be gone a week," I said softly.

"True," he said as the engine strained, still climbing. "But I've been wanting to do it for a while and didn't want to wait any longer."

"Really?" I asked. He nodded. "Like, since when?"

He thought for a second. "The day you hit me with that basketball."

"That was attractive to you?"

"Not exactly," he replied. "More like embarrassing and humiliating. But there was something about it as a moment. . . . It was like a clean slate. No posturing or pretending. It was, you know, real."

We were coming into town now, passing FrayBake, Luna Blu only a few blocks away. "Real," I repeated.

"Yeah. I mean, it's impossible to fake anything if you've already seen the other person in a way they'd never choose for you to. You can't go back from that."

"No," I said. "I guess you can't."

He turned into the Luna Blu lot, parking beside a VW, and we got out and started walking toward the kitchen entrance. "So," he said, "not to sound pushy or desperate, but you haven't exactly answered—"

"Yo! Wait up!" I heard a voice yell from behind us. I turned just in time to see Ellis's van sliding into the spot beside the Volvo. A moment later, he was jogging toward us, his keys jingling in one hand. "Am I glad to see you guys. I thought I was late."

Dave glanced at his watch. "Actually, we're all late."

"By two minutes," I told him. "I don't think she'll flog us or anything."

"You don't know that." He pulled open the back door. As Ellis ducked in, and I followed, he said, "This is Deb we're talking about."

"Actually," I said, stopping in front of my dad's closed office, "I need to stop in here. I'll catch up with you guys."

"Uh-oh," Ellis said. "She was our sympathy vote."

"But now we can say it was her fault," Dave said. To me he added, "Take your time!"

I made a face, and then they were gone, the door that led into the restaurant banging shut behind them. I leaned a little closer to my dad's door: I could hear him inside talking, his voice low.

"Wouldn't knock just now," someone said, and I turned to see Jason standing down the hallway, clipboard in hand, in the narrow room where they kept all the canned and dried goods. "Your dad said no interruptions until further notice."

"Really," I said, looking at the door again. "Did he tell you what was going on?"

"I didn't ask." He nodded, checking something off his list. "But they've been in there for a while."

I was about to ask him who was with my dad before deciding against it. Instead, I stepped back, thanking him, and headed upstairs.

The restaurant was empty and quiet. The only sounds were the beer cooler humming and the ticking of the fan over the hostess station, turned on too high a speed. I stopped at the end of the bar, looking down the row of tables, each neatly set and waiting for opening. Like a clean slate, I thought, remembering what Dave had said earlier. Even though each shift started the same way, on any given night, anything could happen from here.

It was surprisingly quiet as I climbed the stairs to the attic room, and I wondered if Dave and everyone else had left or something. When I got to the landing, I saw them all gathered around Deb, who was sitting with her back to me on one of the tables, her computer open in her lap. I couldn't see what was on the screen, but everyone was studying it.

". . . got to be some kind of joke," she was saying. "Either that or just a coincidence."

"I'm sorry, but they aren't just similar. I mean, look at that one and then that one." Heather reached forward, pointing at the screen. "It's the same girl."

"Different names, though," Riley murmured.

"Different *first* names," Heather said. "Like I said: same girl."

"What's going on?" I asked.

Deb jumped, startled, and shut the laptop, turning around. "Nothing. I was just—"

"—updating the Ume.com page for the model and linking our accounts to it," Heather finished for her, opening it up again. "Imagine our surprise when we put in your e-mail and five profiles popped up."

"Heather," Riley said, her voice low.

"What? It's weird, we all agreed on that ten minutes ago." She looked at me as Dave and Ellis turned their attention back to the computer. "What are you, a split personality or something?"

I felt my mouth go dry as the impact of what they'd discovered finally began to hit me. I stepped forward, my eyes narrowing to the screen on the table, and the list of names there. Five girls, five profiles, four pictures. MCLEAN SWEET. ELIZA SWEET. LIZBET SWEET. BETH SWEET. And at the bottom, just a name, nothing else for Liz Sweet. It was as far as I'd gotten.

"Mclean?" Deb said softly. I looked at her, still very aware of Dave studying the screen only a few feet from me. "What's all this about?"

I swallowed. They'd all been so honest with me, so open. Dave and his past embarrassments, Riley and her dirtbags, Ellis and the Love Van, Deb and, well, everything. Even Heather had pointed out her house and talked about her dad, the technophobe Loeb fan. With this, they had perfectly good reason to doubt everything I had told them in return. Even if, I thought, looking at Dave, it was true.

"I . . ." I began, but no words came, nothing, just a gasp of breath, and then I was turning back down the stairs, picking up speed as I went. I moved quickly back through the restaurant, past Tracey, who was stacking menus at the bar.

"Hey!" she called out, a blur in my side vision. "Where's the fire?"

I ignored this as I moved on, through the door and down the hallway to the back entrance. I was just pushing the door open, my palm flat on the flimsy screen, when I heard Opal come out of my dad's office, behind me.

"You should have told me," she said over her shoulder. Her face was flushed, angry. "You let me just go along here like an idiot, thinking things were okay."

"I didn't know for sure," my dad said.

"But you knew something!" She stopped, whirling around to face him. "And you knew how I felt about this place, and these people. You *knew*, and you said *nothing*."

"Opal," my dad said, but she was already turning, walking away, pushing open the door to the restaurant with a bang and going through it. My dad watched her go with a sigh, his shoulders sagging. Then he saw me. "Mclean. When—"

"So it's official, then," I said, cutting him off. "We're leaving?"

"We need to talk about it," he replied, coming closer. "There's a lot to consider."

"I want to go," I said. "I'll go whenever. I'll go now."

"Now?" He narrowed his eyes, concerned. "What are you talking about? What's wrong?"

I shook my head, stepping out onto the ramp that led to the door. "I have to get back to the house. Mom's . . . she's waiting for me."

"Hey, hold on a second," he said. "Just talk to me."

It was what everyone wanted. My mom, my dad, my friends upstairs, not to mention all the people in all the places I'd left behind. But talk was cheap and useless. Action was what mattered. And me, I was moving. Now, again, always.

Fourteen

❇ ✺ ❇

"Sure you're okay?" my mom asked, glancing over at me. "Not too hot? Too cold?"

I looked at the console in front of me, where there were buttons for seat heat, regular heat, fan, humidity control. Peter's SUV, one of the biggest I'd ever seen, wasn't a car as much as a living space with wheels. "I'm good."

"Okay," she said. "But if you want to adjust anything, feel free."

So far, we'd been on the road for a little under an hour, and conversation had been limited to this topic, the weather, and the beach itself. The car was on cruise control, and I honestly felt like I was, as well—just going through the motions while the chaos of the afternoon receded, mile after mile, behind us.

I'd been right: when I got back to the house, my mom was waiting, busy distributing juice boxes to the twins, who were strapped into their adjoining car seats in the vast backseat. "Hello!" she'd called out, waving a plastic straw at me. "Ready for a road trip?"

"Yeah," I'd replied. "Let me just get my stuff."

Inside the house, I splashed water on my face and tried to

calm down. All I could think of was everyone gathered around that laptop, with those versions of me up for scrutiny in front of them. The shame I felt was like a fever, hot and cold and clammy all at once, and no amount of buttons or adjusting would make a damn bit of difference.

"So what I'm thinking," my mom said now, doing a quick check in the rearview mirror of the twins, who were asleep, "is we'll go to the house and get unloaded, and then maybe take a quick trip to the boardwalk. There's a really good diner there, and we can grab dinner and then go look for a swimsuit for you. Sound good?"

"Sure."

She smiled, reaching across to squeeze my knee. "I'm so, so glad you're here, Mclean. Thank you for coming."

I nodded, not saying anything as my phone buzzed in my pocket. I'd finally turned off the ringer after logging calls from my dad, Riley, and Deb in the first twenty minutes we'd been on the road. It was either ironic, hilarious, or both to be dodging other people's calls in favor of talking to my mother. But nothing made sense anymore.

As we kept driving, the highway gave way to two-lane roads, the trees going from big oaks to scrubby coastal pines. I kept thinking of those old road trips we'd taken together, in Super Shitty, when it was newer and her car. She did the driving while I ran the radio and kept tabs on our drinks, making sure we had ample coffee or Diet Coke as needed. Sometimes we splurged on magazines, which I'd then read aloud, educating us on makeup and diet tips when the radio stations got fewer and farther between. Now, in Peter's huge car/truck/

space station, we had a built-in cooler packed with refresh-ments and satellite radio with over three hundred stations to choose from and not a single gap in signal. Not to men-tion company, in the form of two toddlers. The landscape was about the only thing that hadn't changed.

I'd been dreading the trip for any number of reasons, but especially due to the fact that I'd be stuck with my mom for four straight hours of driving with no escape from conversa-tion. She surprised me, though, by being as content as I was with long periods of silence. I started to get self-conscious about it, after a while.

"I'm sorry I'm not talking much," I told her when we were about an hour and a half away. "I think I'm just really tired."

"Oh, it's fine," she said. "To be honest, I'm exhausted my-self. And with these two, I don't get a lot of quiet. This is . . ." She glanced over at me. "It's nice."

"Yeah," I said as my phone buzzed again. I pulled it out, ig-noring the screen, and turned it fully off before sliding it back into my pocket. "It is."

It was just getting dark when we drove over the bridge to Colby, the sound spread out vast and dark beneath us. By then, the twins were up and crabby, and we'd had to put on Elmo doing covers of Beatles songs—a torture that was a first to me—in order to keep them from totally mutinying.

"Mclean," my mom said, reaching behind her to pull up the diaper bag, which was huge and overflowing with wipes, Huggies, and various other supplies, "would you mind find-ing them a snack in here? We'll be there in ten minutes or so, but food might hold off a full-on nuclear meltdown."

"Sure," I said, digging around until I found a bag packed with the familiar little fish-shaped crackers. I opened it up, then turned around in my seat to face the twins. "You guys hungry?"

"Fish!" Connor yelled, pointing at the bag.

"That's right," I said, taking out a few and handing them to him. Madison, who was sucking on a Sippy Cup, stuck out her hand, as well, and I gave her an equal portion. "Dinner of champions."

My mom put on her turn signal, taking a left onto the road that stretched down the center of the town proper. I didn't remember much about Colby itself, other than that the last time I'd been here it had seemed newer than North Reddemane, full of partially built houses, building permits everywhere. Now, years later, it looked much more established, with all the things you'd expect to find in a typical beach town: surf shops, clothing stores, hotels, and bike-rental places. As we drove past the boardwalk and kept going, the lots and houses got bigger, then bigger still, switching from duplexes and boxy weekend places to vast structures painted bright colors, swimming pools stretched out in front of them. The twins were whining in tandem, Elmo singing, "Baby, you can drive my car," in full-on pip-squeak mode, when my mom turned into a driveway, pulled up to the wide front steps of a foam-green house, and parked.

"Here we are!" she said, looking back at the twins. "See? It's the beach house."

I saw. In fact, I was pretty sure my mouth was hanging open. "Mom," I said as she pulled out her keys from the ignition, pushing the door open. "Wow."

"It's not as big as it looks," she said, getting out. Behind me, Madison let out a wail, competing with Elmo in pitch. "I swear."

I just sat there, staring up at this huge, green mansion rising in front of me. There were columns, three stories, a lower-level garage, and, visible through the high glass windows over the front door, a vast ocean view, stretching as far as you could see.

"Mama, I'm hungry," Connor whined, as my mom unbuckled his car seat. "I want mac and cheese!"

"Mac and cheese!" Madison seconded, waving her Sippy Cup.

"Okay, okay," my mom told them. "Just let us get inside."

She hitched Connor onto her hip, then came around to the other side of the car, taking out Maddie, as well, and planting her on the other side. After strapping on both the diaper bag and her purse, she started up the front steps, looking like a Sherpa scaling Everest.

"Mom," I said, getting out of the car and catching up with her. "Please. Let me get something, at least."

"Oh, honey, that would be great," she said over one shoulder. I reached out to take the diaper bag and purse, only to find myself suddenly holding Maddie, who latched her arms around my neck, her chubby legs tightening at my waist. She smelled like wipes and baby sweat, and promptly dropped a damp goldfish down my shirt. "Now, let me just find my keys . . . here. Okay! We're in."

She bumped the door open wider with her hip, then went inside, reaching to hit a light switch as I followed her. Immediately, the entryway brightened, displaying deep yellow walls lined with beach-themed framed drawings.

"So this is the kitchen and living room," my mom was saying as we headed up the nearby stairs, Connor hanging off her hip, Maddie clutching me with one hand, the other in her mouth. "The master suite is over there, and the rest of the bedrooms are on the second and third floors."

"There are four floors?"

"Um," she said, glancing back at me as she hit another switch, illuminating a wide, open kitchen. A stainless Sub-Zero fridge, bigger and much newer than the one at Luna Blu, sat at one end. "Well, actually, there are five. If you count the game-room level. But that was just unfinished attic space, really."

There was a trilling noise, a melody I recognized but couldn't place. My mom, Connor still in her arms, reached into her purse, pulling out her phone. I said, "Is that—"

"The Defriese fight song," she finished for me. "Peter put it on there for me. I used to have ABBA, but he insisted."

I didn't say anything, just stared out the row of huge windows at the ocean. My mom put the phone to her ear, then leaned down, releasing Connor, who immediately ran over to the fridge, banging his hands on it. I tried to do the same with Maddie, but she held on tighter, if that was possible.

"Hello? Oh, hi, honey. Yes, we just got here. It was fine." My mom looked at Connor, as if weighing whether to try to corral him. In seconds, it was a moot point, as he was taking off across the room at full speed. "We're about to unpack a bit and go up to the Last Chance. Did you get dinner? Good."

I walked over to the nearest window, Maddie twirling a piece of my hair, and looked out at the deck. Down below, I could see the pool, part of it exposed, the other tucked beneath an overhang.

"I'll call you as soon as we're back here," my mom continued, digging around in her purse. "I know. Me, too. It's not the same without you. Okay, love you. Goodbye."

Connor ran back past us, bumping against my hip. "Beach!" he yelled, his small, high voice echoing around the vast room.

"Peter says hello," my mom told me, dropping her phone back in her bag. "We don't usually spend nights apart, if we can help it. I keep telling him that most couples travel separately all the time, but he still worries."

"Worries? About what?"

"Oh, any- and everything," she said. "He just likes it better when we're all together. Let me just bring in a few things, and we'll go. Would you mind watching the twins for just a second? It's easier without an entourage."

"Sure," I said, as Connor ran back the other way, now spreading his palm prints across the row of glass doors that led outside. She smiled at me gratefully, then started back down to the car. A moment later, I heard a garage door cranking open, and the SUV disappeared beneath the house.

Which left me in this crazy huge living room with my half siblings, one of whom, like a one-man wave of destruction, had already smudged just about every glassy reflective surface in sight. "Connor," I called out as he banged his baby fists against a window. "Hey."

He turned, looking at me, and I realized I had no idea what I was supposed to say to him. Or do with him. Downstairs somewhere, a car door shut.

"Let's go check out the water," I said, trying to put Maddie down again. No luck. So it was with her still on my hip that I crossed the room, unlocked the back door, and put my hand out to Connor. He grabbed it, holding tight, and we went outside.

It was dark, the wind cold, but the beach was still beautiful. We had it all to ourselves, save for a couple of trucks parked way down at one end, headlights on, fishing poles stuck in the sand in front of them. As soon as we hit the sand, Connor pulled loose from me, running to a tide pool just a few feet away, and I scrambled to catch up with him. He bent down, tentatively reaching out to touch the still, shallow water there with one hand. "Cold," he told me.

"I bet," I said.

I looked up at the house, seeing my mom pass in front of that row of windows, carrying some reusable cloth grocery bags, lights on all around her. The houses on either side were dark, clearly unoccupied.

"Cold," Maddie repeated, burrowing into my shoulder. "Go inside."

"In one sec," I replied, turning to look at the water again. Even at night, you could see the foam as the waves crashed, moving forward then pulling back again. I stood there beside Connor, who was still patting the tide pool, the wind ruffling his tufts of baby hair, then looked up at the sky overhead. My mom didn't need that old telescope here, clearly. The stars seemed close enough to touch, and she'd never have to look very hard to find one. She'd never want for anything. And even though I knew that for her, and even Connor and Maddie, this was a good thing, it made me sad in a way I wasn't sure I even understood.

"Mclean?" I heard my mom call. When I turned back, I saw her framed in the open double doors, one hand on her hip. "Are you out there?"

It was so strange, but for a moment, a part of me wanted to stay quiet, for her to have to come look for me. But just as quickly, this thought passed and I cupped my hand over my mouth to be heard over the waves.

"Yeah," I yelled back. "We'll be right in."

× × ×

After doing an eat-and-run at a local diner—the twins were weary of being contained and lasted about ten seconds in their high chairs—we walked down the boardwalk in the cold to the boutique my mom had mentioned earlier, only to find it closed.

"Winter hours," she said, checking the sign. "They closed at five."

"It's no big deal," I told her. "I probably won't swim anyway."

"We'll get you a suit tomorrow, first thing," she told me. "Promise."

Back at the house, we unloaded the rest of the car, using the elevator (elevator!) to move the luggage up to the third floor. I was in a room with a coral pink bedspread, wicker furniture, and a block sign that read BEACH in big letters hanging over the mirror. It smelled like fresh paint and had a gorgeous view. "Are you sure?" I asked my mom as we stood inside, the twins scrambling up to jump on the bed. "I don't need a bed that big."

"They're all that big," she explained, looking embarrassed. "I mean, except for the twins'. I'll put them at the other end of the house, so they won't wake you up at the crack of dawn."

"I get up pretty early," I said.

"Five a.m?"

"What?" I just looked at her as she nodded. "Wow. No wonder you're tired."

"It is exhausting," she agreed, this thought punctuated by Maddie and Connor, leaping with abandon across the bed in front of us. "But they're only little once, and it goes so fast. It seems like you were just this age, I swear. Although when you were a baby I was so worried about work, and the restaurant . . . I feel like I missed a lot."

"You were always around," I told her. She looked at me, surprised. "It was Dad who was gone at Mariposa."

"I suppose. Still, though. I'd do some things differently, given the chance." She clapped her hands. "All right, Maddie and Connor! Bath time! Let's go!"

She walked over to the bed, collecting the twins despite

their protests, and hauled them off the bed, nudging them to the door. They were in the hall when Maddie looked back at me and said, "Clane corn?"

I looked at my mom. "What did she say?"

"Mclean come," she translated, ruffling Maddie's hair as Connor took off in the other direction. "Let's let Mclean get settled, okay? We'll see her before you go to bed."

Maddie looked at me. "Do you need help, though?" I asked.

"I'm fine." She smiled, and then they were gone, the sound of their footsteps padding on the carpet gradually getting more and more distant. How long was that hallway anyway? Honestly.

After checking out the view for a few minutes, I went back downstairs, where I now had the main floor all to myself. I walked to the overstuffed red couch, sinking into it, then, after a few minutes of feeling moronic, figured out how to turn on their flat-screen TV that hung over the fireplace. I channel surfed for little bit, then flicked it off again and just sat there, listening to the ocean outside.

After a moment, I slid my phone out of my pocket, turning it on. I had three messages.

"Mclean, it's your father. We need to talk. I'll have my phone with me all night in the kitchen this evening. Call me."

No question this time: it was a demand. I moved on to the next one.

"Mclean? It's Deb. Look, I'm really sorry about that whole Ume.com thing today. I wasn't trying to . . . I didn't know, I guess is what I mean to say. I'll be around if you want to talk tonight. Okay. Bye."

I swallowed, then hit SAVE. A beep, and then Riley's voice.

"Hey, Mclean. It's Riley. Just checking in. . . . That was kind of intense earlier, huh? Deb's a nervous wreck. She thinks you're mad at her. So maybe call her or something, if you get a chance. Hope you're doing okay."

Kind of intense, I thought, hitting the END button and putting my phone down beside me. That was one way to put it. I had no idea how long they'd been looking at that page on Ume, if they'd really read any of my other profiles or just looked at the pictures. I could hardly remember what was on them, now that I actually thought about it. Wondering was enough to get me off the couch and down to the garage, so I could get my laptop and find out.

I flicked on the light by the door, then walked over to the SUV and grabbed my bag from the front seat. I was just shut-ting the door when I looked over, across the empty bay beside Peter's car. There was another vehicle parked on the other end, next to a rack filled with hanging beach chairs and pool toys. It had a cover over it, but there was something familiar enough to make me come closer and lift its edge. Sure enough, it was Super Shitty.

Oh my God, I thought, pulling the cover off completely to reveal the dinged red hood, dusty windshield, and worn steering wheel. I'd thought for sure that my mom had sold it, or junked it entirely. But here it was, amazingly, pretty much how I'd left it. I reached down to the driver's-side handle, trying it, and with a creak, it swung right open. I slid behind the wheel, the familiar seat wheezing a bit beneath me, and looked up at the rearview mirror. A Gert—one of the rope and beaded bracelets we'd always bought at the surf shop in North Reddemane—was tied around it.

I reached up, touching the row of red beads dotted with shells. I couldn't remember my last trip to North Reddemane, or how long it had been. I was trying to figure it out when, in the rearview, I saw the storage rack stretched against the garage wall behind me. It was lined with rubber bins, and from where I sat, I could see at least three of them were labeled MCLEAN.

I turned, dropping my hand, and looked again. My mom had mentioned they'd been storing stuff here, because of all the extra space, but I'd had no idea she'd meant anything of mine. I started to push myself out of the seat, then reached back up to pull the Gert loose and take it with me.

Upon closer inspection, the shelf looked like Dave's dad had been at it: bin after bin, clearly marked. I squatted down, pulling out the first MCLEAN I'd seen, and pried open the top. Inside, there were clothes: old jeans, T-shirts, a couple of coats. As I quickly picked through them, I realized they were a mix of everything I'd left stashed at my mom's house when I was there for vacations and weekends, culled from all our various moves. Scuffed cheerleading shoes that belonged to Eliza Sweet, the pretty pink polo shirts Beth Sweet had favored. The farther down I dug, the older the things got, until I was down to my Mclean clothes, like layers of the earth being excavated.

The second box was heavier, and when I got it open I saw why: it was full of books. Novels from my bookshelf, notebooks scrawled with my doodlings and my signatures, some photo albums and a couple of yearbooks. I picked up the one on top, which had the words WESTCOTT HIGH SCHOOL embossed across the cover. I didn't open it, or anything else, instead just putting the lid back and moving on.

The last box was so light that when I first yanked it out, I thought it must be empty. Inside, however, I found a quilt, recognizing it after a moment as the one my mom had given me the day my dad and I had left for Montford Falls. I knew I'd taken it then, and so must have dumped it off with the clothes and books at some other point and not realized it. Unlike the one on our couch, it still felt new, stiff, unused, the squares neatly stitched, not missing any threads. I put it back, pushing the box in with the others.

It was so weird to find a part of my past here, in this place that was no part of me at all. Tucked away in a bottom floor, underground, like Dave's storm cellar. I got to my feet, sliding the Gert into my pocket, and covered Super Shitty again before picking up my bag and heading back upstairs.

My mom was still busy with the twins as I sat down at the massive kitchen island on one of about ten matching leather bar stools and booted up my computer. As it whirred through its familiar setup, I let myself, for the first time in hours, think about Dave. It had just been too hard, too entirely shameful, to think of his expression—a mix of surprise, studiousness, and disappointment—as he'd looked at that list of profiles with everyone else. A clean slate, he'd said about that moment when I knocked him down. Real. He knew better now.

I opened my browser, clicking over to Ume.com and typing my e-mail into the search box. Within ten seconds, the same list they'd seen was in front of me: Liz Sweet, the newest and most sparse, on top, all the way down to Mclean, the one I'd had back home in Tyler all those years ago. I was just clicking on it when I heard the chime of a doorbell from behind me.

I got up, walking over to the stairs. "Mom?" I called, but there was no answer, which, in a house this big, was not exactly surprising.

The doorbell sounded again, so I went down and peered out the window to see a tall, pretty, blonde woman in jeans and a cable-knit sweater standing on the welcome mat, carrying a shopping bag. A toddler around Maddie and Connor's age, with brown curly hair, was on her hip. When I opened the door, she smiled.

"You must be Mclean. I'm Heidi," she said, sticking out her free hand. Once we shook, she handed me the bag. "This is for you."

I raised my eyebrows, opening it. "Bathing suits," she explained. Sure enough, I saw a swatch of black, and another of pink. "I wasn't sure what you would like, so I just pulled a couple. If you hate them all, we have tons more at the store."

"Store?"

"Clementine's?" she said as the little girl leaned her head on her shoulder, looking at me. "It's my boutique, on the boardwalk."

"Oh," I said, "right. We were there earlier."

"So I heard." She smiled, looking down at the baby. "Thisbe here and I can't stand the idea of anyone being in the vicinity of a heated pool and hot tub with no bathing suit. It just goes against everything we believe in."

"Right," I said. "Well . . . thanks."

"Sure." She leaned a bit to the right, looking past me. "Plus . . . it was an excuse to get over here and see Katherine, and not have to wait until the party tomorrow. I mean, it's been ages! Is she around?"

Party? I thought. Out loud I said, "She's upstairs. Giving the twins a bath."

"Great. I'll just run up super-quick and say hello, okay?" I stepped back as she came in, bouncing the baby and making her laugh as she ran up the stairs. I heard her take the next flight, followed by a burst of shrieking and laughing as she and my mom were reunited.

I went back over to the computer, sliding into my seat again. Above me, I could hear my mom and Heidi chattering, their voices quick and light, and as I scanned all my alter egos I realized that my mom had one now, too. Katie Sweet was gone, but Katherine Hamilton was a queen in a palace by the sea, with new friends and new paint on the walls, a new life. The only things out of place were that car, covered up and buried deep, and me.

My phone rang, and I glanced down, seeing my dad's number. As soon as I picked up, he started talking.

"You don't walk away from me like that," he began. No hello, no niceties. "And you answer when I call you. Do you know how worried I've been?"

"I'm fine," I said, surprised at the little flame of irritation, so new, I felt hearing his voice. "You know I'm with Mom."

"I know that you and I have things to discuss, and that I wanted them discussed before you left," he said.

"What's to discuss?" I asked him. "We're moving to Hawaii, apparently."

"I may have a job opportunity in Hawaii," he corrected me. "No one is talking about you having to come as well."

"What's the alternative? Moving back to Tyler? You know I can't do that."

He was quiet for a moment. In the background, I could hear voices, Leo and Jason most likely, shouting orders to each other. "I just want us to talk about this. Without arguing. When I'm not up to my ears in the dinner rush."

"You called me," I pointed out.

"Watch it," he said, his voice a warning.

I got quiet fast.

"I'm going to call you first thing tomorrow, when we've both had a night to clear our heads. No decisions until then. Okay?"

"Okay." I looked out at the ocean. "No decisions."

We hung up, and I closed my browser, folding all those Sweet girls back away. Then I walked up the stairs, following the sound of my mom's and Heidi's voices. I passed one bedroom after another, it seemed, the new-smelling carpet plush beneath my feet, before finally coming up on them, behind a half-closed door.

". . . to be honest, I really didn't think it through," my mom was saying. "And with Peter not here, it's that much more complicated. I think it was too much to take on, even though I thought it was what I really wanted to do."

"You'll be fine," Heidi told my mom. "The house is finished, you survived the trip. Now all you have to do is just sit back and try to relax."

"Easier said than done," my mom said. Then she was quiet for a moment. All I could hear was splashing, the kids babbling. Then she said, "It was always a lot of fun in the past. But we've only been here a couple of hours and I'm already . . . I don't know. Not feeling good about the whole thing."

"Things will look better tomorrow, after you get some sleep," Heidi said.

"Probably," my mom agreed, although she hardly sounded convinced. "I just hope it wasn't a mistake."

"Why would it be a mistake?"

"Just because I didn't realize . . ." she trailed off again. "Everything's different now. I didn't think it would be. But it is."

I stepped back from the door, surprised at the sudden, stabbing hurt that rose up in my chest, flushing my face. *Oh my God,* I thought. Through all the moves, and all the distance, there had been one constant: my mom wanted me with her. For better or worse—and mostly worse—I never doubted that for a second. But what if I'd been wrong? What if this new life was just that, brand-new, like this gorgeous house, and she wanted to keep it fresh, no baggage? Katie Sweet had to deal with a moody, distant firstborn child. But Katherine Hamilton didn't.

I turned, walking down that wide hallway, toward a foreign staircase in a house I didn't know. I felt scared suddenly, like nothing was familiar, not even me. I grabbed my computer, stuffing it in my bag and taking the steps two at a time to the garage. I had a lump in my throat as I pushed open the garage door, cutting behind Peter's massive SUV, over to Super Shitty. I pulled the cover off and threw my bag in the passenger seat, then realized I no longer had a key. I sat there a second, then, on a hunch, reached down beneath the floor mat, rooting around. A moment later, I felt the ridges on my finger, and pulled out my spare. Waiting for me, all this time.

The engine cranked, amazingly, and as it warmed up, I popped the trunk and got out. It wasn't easy fitting all three bins in the small cargo space, but I managed. Then I found the garage door button, hit it, and climbed back in.

The street was dark, no cars in sight as I pulled out into the road. I had no idea where I was, but I knew how to get where I was going. I put on my blinker and turned right, toward North Reddemane.

Fifteen

✳ ❀ ✳

Twenty-five minutes later, I was unlocking the door of room 811 of the Poseidon, feeling around for a light switch. When I found it, the décor, achingly familiar, jumped into place. Faded bedspread, shell painting over the headboard, slight tinge of mildew in the air.

The entire drive, I'd been leaning forward over the wheel, peering at the road, worrying that somehow everything I remembered would just be gone, wiped clean. I had a scare when I saw that Shrimpboats restaurant was boarded up, but then, over the next slight hill, I saw Gert's, their OPEN 24 HRS sign visible. The Poseidon, same as I remembered it, was just beyond.

I thought the manager might ask questions, considering my age and the time of night, but she barely looked at me as she took my cash, sliding the room key across to me in return. "Ice machine's at the end of the building," she informed me, before turning back to her book of crossword puzzles. "Drink machine only takes bills, no change."

I thanked her, then drove down, parking in front of my room. It took only a few minutes to pull the boxes to the door, another to get inside. Now, here I was. I sat down on the bed for a few minutes, looking around me, the surf pounding loudly just outside. Then I started to cry.

It was all just such a mess. Moving, running, changing: I couldn't keep it all straight anymore, and didn't want to. I felt so, so tired, tired enough to crawl under that old bedspread and sleep for days. No one knew where I was, not a soul, and while I thought this was what I wanted, I realized, in the quiet of that room, that it was the scariest thing of all.

I reached up, wiping my eyes and taking a shuddering breath. I knew I should go back to my mom's, that she would be worried, that this would all look better tomorrow. But th at wasn't home, and neither was Tyler, or Petree, or Westcott, or Montford Falls, or even Lakeview. I had no place, no one.

I picked up my phone, shoulders shaking, and looked at the keypad, glowing beneath my fingers. A blur of faces passed across my mind: my friends in Tyler, the girls from my cheer team in Montford Falls, the tech guys I'd hung with backstage in Petree. Then Michael, my surfer, all the way up to Riley and Deb. I'd known enough people for every minute of the day, and yet still didn't have anyone as my two a.m. The one person I would have considered I wasn't even sure wanted to talk to me anymore.

But what about warts and all? I thought, thinking of that black ring on Dave's wrist. I looked down at my own wrist, the old Gert I'd tied there as I drove away from my mom's. We each had circles now on our wrists, totally different and yet equally important. I knew my faults were many, my secrets even more. But I didn't want to be alone. Not at 2:00 a.m., and not now.

I dialed the number slowly, wanting to get it right. Two rings, and he picked up.

"Yes," I said after his hello.

"Mclean?" he asked. "Is that you?"

"Yeah," I said, swallowing and looking out my open door, at the ocean. "The answer's yes."

"The answer . . ." he said slowly.

"You asked me to go out with you. I know you probably changed your mind. But you should know, the answer was yes. It's always been yes when it comes to you."

He was very quiet for a moment. "Where are you?"

I started crying again, my voice ragged. He told me to calm down. He told me it was going to be all right. And then, he told me he'd be there soon.

×　×　×

After we hung up, I went into the bathroom and washed my face, then used a nubby hand towel to dry off. I was so tired, and yet I knew I needed to stay awake, so I could be ready to explain when he showed up, whenever that might be. I sat down on the bed, kicking off my shoes, and reached for the remote. But then I looked at my boxes instead, and left it where it was.

I dragged the heavy box over, taking off the lid, and started stacking things around me on the bed. The books, the photos both framed and in albums, the yearbooks, all my notebooks and old journals, all in a circle, like numbers on a clock, with me in the middle.

I picked up a loose picture of me and my mom when I was in grade school, posing at a holiday parade. Beside it was a framed one from her and Peter's wedding, she in white and him in a dark tux, me standing in front of them, the maid of honor. A third: the twins as infants, sleeping through a professional photo shoot, their tiny fingers entwined. Pictures in brass frames and wooden ones, frames backed with magnets and decorated with seashells. I'd had no idea how many I'd once had until now, and as I laid them out on my bed, beside the quilt, I searched for my own face in each one, recognizing my different incarnations.

At the parade, it was me when things were okay: parents still together, life intact. At the wedding, I was sleepwalking, with a fake smile and tired eyes. In the early ones with the twins, taken on holidays after the move, it was hair color and makeup, the clothes I was wearing that let me know who I was as the shutter clicked. I recognized Eliza's ponytail and T-shirt with the school mascot, Lizbet's thick dark eyeliner and black turtleneck, Beth's crisp button-down shirt and plaid skirt. I looked at myself in the mirror across the room, all those things surrounding me. My hair was longer than it had been in a while, falling over my shoulders, and I had on jeans and a white T-shirt, a black sweater pulled over it. Tiny gold hoops in my ears, that single Gert on my wrist. No makeup, no persona, no costume. Just me, at least for now.

I looked over at the stack of notebooks, their covers decorated with my loopy handwriting, silly signatures, pictures I'd scribbled during boring classes. I took one out, opening it to a fresh page, taking in again the circle of pictures and history around me. Then I reached over to the bedside table, picking up the complimentary hotel pen, and started to write.

In Montford Falls, the first place I moved when I left, I called myself Eliza. The neighborhood we lived in was all these happy families, like something from an old TV show.

I stopped, read back over what I'd written, then looked outside. A single car passed by slowly, its lights brightening the empty street ahead. I turned another page.

In the next place, Petree, everyone was rich. I was Lizbet, and we lived in this high-rise apartment complex, all dark wood and metal appliances. It was like something out of a magazine: even the elevator was silent.

I yawned, then stretched my fingers. It was now 1:30.

When we moved to Westcott, we had a house right on the beach, so sunny and warm, and I could wear flip-flops all year-round. The first day, I introduced myself as Beth.

I could feel the tiredness, the heaviness of this long, long day bearing down on me. *Stay awake,* I thought. *Stay here.*

In Lakeview, the house had a basketball goal. I was going to be Liz Sweet.

The last time I remembered looking at the clock, it was 2:15. The next thing I knew, I was waking up, the room was barely light, and someone was knocking at my door.

I sat up, startled, and waited that moment until I remembered where I was. Then I pushed some pictures aside, sliding off the bed, and walked over to the door, pulling it open, so ready to see Dave's face.

But it wasn't him. It was my mom, and my dad was right beside her. They looked at me, then at the room behind me, their faces as tired as my own. "Oh, Mclean," my mom said, putting a hand to her mouth. "Thank God. There you are."

There you are. Like I'd been lost and now found. She opened her mouth to say something else, and my dad was suddenly talking, too, but for me it was just too much, in that moment, to even hear what came next. I just stepped forward, and then their arms were around me.

I was crying as my mom held me and my dad led us into the room and to the bed, easing the door shut behind us. My mom pushed aside those pictures, my dad the notebooks, as I lay down, curling myself into her lap and closing my eyes. I was so, so tired, and as she stroked my hair, I could hear them still talking, voices low. A moment later, there was another sound, too, distant but as recognizable as the waves outside. That of pages turning, one after another, a story finally being told.

Sixteen

❋ ✾ ❋

"Wow," I said. "You weren't kidding. You didn't need me."

Deb turned around. When she saw me, her face broke into a wide smile. "Mclean! Hi! You're back!"

I nodded, biting back a laugh as she ran toward me, her sock-feet padding across the floor. Partially, this was for her exuberant reaction, but also for the words, newly posted in my absence, on a poster on the wall behind her. NO SHOES! it read. NO SWEARING! NO, REALLY.

"I like your sign," I told her as she gave me a hug.

"Honestly, I tried to do without the visual," she said, glancing at it. "But there were scuff marks all over the streets! And the closer we get to the deadline, the more tempers are flaring. I mean, this is a civic activity. We need to keep it clean, both literally and figuratively."

"It looks great." It was true. There were still a few blank spots along the edge of the model, and I could tell the landscaping and smaller details hadn't been put on yet, but for the first time, it looked complete, with buildings spread across the entire surface and no huge gaps left unfilled. "You guys must have been here every day, all day."

"Pretty much." She put her hands on her hips, surveying it along with me. "We kind of had to be, since the deadline changed and everything."

"Changed?" I said.

"Well, because of the restaurant closing," she replied, bending down to flick a piece of dust off a rooftop. A second later, she glanced up at me. "Oh, God, you did know, right? About the restaurant? Because I totally thought, because of your dad—"

"I knew," I told her. "It's okay."

She exhaled, clearly relieved, and bent back down, adjusting a building a bit. "I mean, May first was always ambitious, if I'm to be totally honest. I tried to act all positive, but secretly, I had my doubts. And then Opal comes up here last weekend and says we have to be all done and out, somehow, by the second week of *April*, because the building's being sold. I about passed out I was so unnerved. I had to go count."

I blinked, not sure I'd heard her right as she moved down the model, carefully wiping her finger along an intersection. "Count?"

"To ten," she explained, standing back up. "It's what I do instead of panicking. Ideally. Although sometimes I have to go to twenty or even fifty to really get calmed down."

"Oh. Right."

"And *then*," she said, taking another step before crouching to adjust a church steeple, "we lost Dave, which was a huge deal, especially since you were already gone. I had to go count *and* breathe for that one."

"What?" I said.

"Breathe," she explained. "You know, big inhales, big exhales, visualizing stress going with it—"

"No," I said, cutting her off. "Dave. What do you mean, you lost him?"

"Because of the whole grounding thing," she said. When I just stood there, confused, she looked up at me. "With his parents. You knew about that, right?"

I shook my head. The truth was, I'd felt so embarrassed about calling him, especially since he never showed up, that I'd not ever tried to contact him, even though I knew I should. "What . . . what happened?"

"Well, I haven't heard all the gory details," she replied, standing back up and stretching out her back. "All I know is they caught him sneaking out one night last week with the car, there was some big blowup, and he's basically under house arrest indefinitely."

"Whoa," I said.

"Oh, and the Austin trip is off. At least, for him."

I felt myself blink. "Oh my God. That's awful."

She nodded sadly. "I know. I'm telling you, it's been non-stop drama here. I'm just hoping we can get this done without any more disasters."

I took a step backward, leaning against a nearby table as she made her way around the opposite side of the model. So that was what had happened to Dave. All this time I'd thought he'd changed his mind about coming down, but in the end, it hadn't even been up to him. "So . . . he hasn't been here at all?"

Deb glanced at me over her shoulder. "No, he has. But just in the last couple of days, and only for an hour here and there. They're keeping him pretty close, I think."

Poor Dave. After all that time spent toeing the line, doing the time. And now, all because of me, he was right back where he started. I felt sick.

"His parents can't really take that trip away," I said after a moment. "I mean, maybe they'll reconsider, or—"

"I said that, too. But according to Riley, it's unlikely." She crouched down, sitting back on her heels, and pressed a loose house down, making it click. "They already decided to use some of the fund to pay off Heather's car debt, so she can go. There was a meeting about it and everything."

"A meeting," I repeated.

"Here, while they were all working. It was serious multi-tasking." She smiled proudly. "I felt honored to get to witness it."

As she bent back down over the model, peering closely at a row of town houses, I just stood there. It was unbelievable to me that for the past week that I'd been in Colby piecing together what came next for me, all of Dave's plans, which had always been so clear, were falling apart. I'd thought he let me down. But clearly, it was the other way around.

× × ×

When I woke up later that morning at the Poseidon, I was alone. I sat up, looking around me: the notebook I'd written in was now closed, set aside on the bedside table, all the pictures and yearbooks stacked neatly on a nearby chair. The front door was slightly ajar, the wind whistling through the screen just beyond it. I got to my feet, rubbing my eyes, and walked over. There, outside on the steps, were my mom and dad, sitting together.

"I feel like the worst parent ever," she was saying. "All this stuff, the different girls . . . I had no idea."

"At least you can claim you were at a distance. It was right in front of my face," he replied.

My mom was quiet for a moment. "You did your best. That's all you can do. That's all any of us can do. You know?"

My dad nodded, looking up at the road. It had been so long since I'd seen them like this, just the two of them, that for a moment I just stood there, taking it in. He was rubbing a hand over his face, while she held a coffee cup with both hands, her head cocked to the side as she said something. From a distance, you couldn't guess all the history and changes. You would have just thought they were friends.

My mom turned then, seeing me. "Honey," she said. "You're up."

"What are you guys doing here?" I asked.

I watched as my dad got to his feet. "You left your mother's house in the middle of the night, Mclean. Did you really think we wouldn't be worrying?"

"I just needed some time," I said quietly, as he came closer, pulling open the door. Once inside, he put his arms around me, squeezing tight, and kissed the top of my head.

"Don't scare me like that ever again," he said, before moving on so my mom could join us. "I mean it."

I nodded, silent, as the door banged shut behind her. And then it was just us three, alone in the room. I sat down on the bed. My mom, taking another sip of her coffee, took the chair by the air-conditioner unit. My dad, by the window, stayed where he was.

"So," he said after a moment. "I think we all need to talk."

"You read my notebook," I said.

"Yes." My mom sighed, brushing her hair back from her face. "I know it was probably supposed to be private . . . but we had a lot of questions. And you weren't exactly up for answering them."

I looked down at my hands, knotting my fingers together.

"I didn't realize . . ." My dad stopped, cleared this throat. Then he glanced at my mom before saying, "The different names. I thought they were just . . . names."

God, this was hard. I swallowed. "That's how it started," I said. "But then, it got bigger."

"You couldn't have been happy," he said. "If you felt like you needed to do that."

"It wasn't about being happy or unhappy. I just didn't want to be me anymore."

Again, they exchanged a look. My mom said slowly, "I don't think either of us really realized how hard the divorce was on you. We're . . ."

She looked at my dad. "We're sorry about that," he finished for her.

It was so quiet, I could hear my own breathing, loud in my ears. Outside, the ocean was crashing, waves hitting sand, then pulling back to sea. I thought of everything being washed away, again and again. We make such messes in this life, both accidentally and on purpose. But wiping the surface clean doesn't really make anything any neater. It just masks what is below. It's only when you really dig down deep, go underground, that you can see who you really are.

Thinking this, I looked at my mom. "How did you know I was here?"

"Your friend told us," my dad said.

"My friend?"

"The boy . . ." He glanced at my mom.

"Dave," she said.

"Dave?"

She put her coffee on the floor by her feet. "When I realized you were gone, that you'd taken the car . . . I just panicked. I called Gus, and he left the restaurant to head down here, to help me look for you."

"I stopped by the house first, to pack up," my dad said. "And, just as I was leaving, Dave came over. He told me where to find you."

"He was worried about you, too." My mom slid a hand over my shoulder. "He said you were upset when you left there, and when you called you were crying. . . ."

She stopped, clearing her throat. My dad said, "I wish you'd felt like you could have called one of us. Whatever was going on, you know we love you, Mclean. No matter what."

Warts and all, I thought as I glanced at the notebook, the pictures and yearbooks piled near it. I swallowed, then said, "When I found out about Hawaii, and then came down here and everything was so different, the house . . ." My mom winced, looking down at her hands. "I heard you talking to Heidi. About how having me here wasn't what you expected."

"What?"

I swallowed. "You said you thought you'd wanted me to come, but—"

She was just looking at me, clearly confused. Then, suddenly, she exhaled, putting a hand to her chest. "Oh, God! Honey, I wasn't talking about you when I said that. I was talking about the party."

"Party?"

"To watch the ECC tournament," she said. That was an acronym I knew well: Eastern College Conference, the one to which Defriese and the U belonged. "I've had it here the last few years, when I didn't go with Peter. It was planned way in advance for this week, but once we got here, I realized I didn't want to have to deal with it. I wanted it to be . . . just us. *That's* what I meant."

So that was the party Heidi had mentioned. "I just assumed . . ." I stopped. "I just felt lost all of a sudden. This was the only place that was familiar."

"This place?" my dad said, glancing around the room.

"We had a lot of good times here," my mom told him. "It was where we always stayed when we took road trips to the beach."

"You remember," I said.

"Of course; how could I forget?" She shook her head. "Don't get me wrong, I love Colby. And Peter's right, there isn't much here anymore. But I still drive down here now and then. I like the view."

I looked at her. "Me, too."

"Although I have to say," she added, "I don't remember it smelling quite so mildewy."

"It did," I told her, and she smiled, squeezing my shoulder.

For a moment, we all just sat there, no one talking. Then my dad looked at my mom before saying, "Your mom and I think we all need to sit down and talk. About what happens next."

"I know," I said.

"Maybe, though," he said, "we can talk and eat. I don't know about you but I'm starving."

"Agreed," my mom replied. She tipped her wrist up, glancing at her watch. "Last Chance opens at seven a.m. That's only ten minutes."

"Last Chance?"

"Best diner on the beach," she told him, standing up. "The bacon will blow your mind."

"You had me at bacon," my dad said. "Let's go."

Before we left, though, they helped me pack up my boxes, each of us adding books and pictures. It seemed like a ritual, something sacred, putting all of these pieces back away again, and when I slid the tops on, pressing them shut, the sound was not so different from the one made when you pushed a piece onto the model. *Click.*

When we stepped out to the parking lot, the wind was stiff and cold, the sky a flat gray, the sun, barely visible, rising in the distance. As my mom pulled out her keys, I said, "What about the twins? Don't you need to get back to them?"

"Don't worry," she said. "Heidi called in two of her sitters,

Amanda and Erika. They're covered. We have all the time in the world."

All the time in the world, I thought as we pulled out onto the main road, my dad following close behind in his truck. If only there was such a thing, really. In truth, though, there were deadlines and jobs, school years ending and beginning, time running out with every breath. As we drove past Gert's, though, the OPEN 24 HRS sign still on, I looked down at the bracelet I was wearing, twisting it across my wrist. Maybe I didn't need all the time anyway. Just a couple of hours, a good breakfast, and a chance to talk with the two people who knew me best, no matter who I was.

We were the first ones at the Last Chance, there when a blonde woman in an apron, looking sleepy, unlocked the door. "You're up early," she said to my mom. "Kids have a bad night?"

My mom nodded, and I felt her eyes on me before she said, "Yeah. Something like that."

We took our menus, flipping over our coffee cups as the waitress approached with the pot. In the kitchen, past the counter, I could hear a grill sizzling, someone playing a radio, the notes punctuated by the register bell ringing as another waitress opened the drawer, then shut it. It was all so familiar, like a place I knew well, even though I'd never been there before. I looked at my mom beside me, and my dad across the table, both of them reading their menus, here with just me, just us, for once. I'd thought that I didn't have a home anymore. But right there, right then, I realized I'd been wrong. Home wasn't a set house, or a single town on a map. It was wherever the people who loved you were, whenever you were together. Not a place but a moment, and then another, building on each other like bricks to create a solid shelter that you take with you for your entire life, wherever you may go.

We talked a lot that morning, over breakfast and the many refilled cups of coffee that followed. And we kept talking once we went back to the house, where my dad took a walk on the beach with me while my mom hung out with the twins. We didn't make any huge decisions, not yet, other than I'd stay the week in Colby, as planned, and we'd take that time to figure out what would happen next.

After more conversations, both in person with my mom and on the phone with my dad, it was decided that Hawaii wasn't an option, at least for me: they were a united front on that. Which meant, in the end, I'd be finishing out my high school career in the same school where I'd started it, back in Tyler. I wasn't exactly happy about this, to say the least, but I finally understood it was really my only option. I tried to see it as bringing things full circle. I'd left and, in doing so, fractured myself. By returning, I'd be able to be whole again. Then, in the fall, I would start over again somewhere new. Although this time, I'd be one of many in a freshman class doing the same thing.

I spent a lot of that week at the beach thinking about the last two years, picking through my yearbooks and pictures. I also hung out a lot with my mom, and as I did so, I realized I'd been wrong about assuming that she, too, had fully reinvented herself when she left Katie Sweet behind for Katherine Hamilton. Sure, she had the new family and look, as well as a huge beach house and the entire different world of being a coach's wife. But I still caught glimpses here and there of the person I'd known before.

There was the comforting familiarity I felt, this strange sense of déjà vu, when I watched her with Connor and Madison, sitting on the floor building block towers or reading *Goodnight Moon*, both of them snuggled into her lap. Or how, when I found her iPod on the fancy portable stereo, I'd turn it on to find some of the same music that was on my dad's: Steve Earle and Led Zeppelin mixed in with the Elmo and lullabies.

Then there was the fact that every night, when the twins were asleep, the first thing she'd do was take a glass of wine out to the deck, where I'd find her looking up at the stars. And despite the high-tech kitchen created to make gourmet meals, I was surprised and pleased to see that she stuck to her old basics, fixing dinner casseroles and chicken dishes that began, always, with a single can of Cream Of soup. The biggest proof, though, was the quilt.

I'd brought it to my room with the rest of the stuff in the bins when we came back from the Poseidon. A couple of nights later, when the temperature suddenly dropped, I pulled it out and used it, wrapping it around me. The next morning, I was brushing my teeth when I stuck my head out of the bathroom to see my mom standing by my bed, where I'd folded it over the foot, holding one corner in her hand.

"I thought this was packed away downstairs," she said when she saw me.

"It was," I said. "But I found it when I found the pictures and yearbooks."

"Oh." She smoothed her hand over one square. "Well, I'm glad it's getting some use."

"It is," I replied. "It was a godsend last night. The twins clearly had lots of warm clothes when they were babies."

She looked at me. "The twins?"

"The squares are made of their baby clothes. Right?"

"No," she said. "I . . . I thought you knew. They're yours."

"Mine?"

She nodded, holding up the corner that was between her thumb and forefinger. "This cotton bit here? It was from the blanket you came home from the hospital in. And this embroidered piece, the red one, was a part of your first Christmas dress."

I moved closer, looking at the quilt closely. "I had no idea."

She lifted up another square, running her fingers over it. "Oh, I loved this little denim piece! It was from the cutest overalls. You took your first steps when you were wearing them."

"I can't believe you saved all that stuff for so long," I said.

"Oh, I couldn't let it go." She smiled, sighing. "But then *you* were going, and it seemed like a way to send some of me along with you."

I thought of her sitting with all those squares, carefully quilting them together. The time it must have taken, especially with twin babies. "I'm sorry, Mom," I said.

She looked up at me, surprised. "Sorry? For what?"

"I don't know," I said. "Just . . . not thanking you for it, I guess."

"Oh goodness, Mclean," she replied, shaking her head. "I'm

sure that you did. I was a total emotional wreck that day you left. I barely remember anything about it, other than you were leaving and I didn't want you to."

"Can you tell me about the rest?" I asked, picking up my own corner, where there was a pink cotton square.

"Really?" she said. I nodded. "Oh, well. Let's see. That one there was from the leotard you wore for your first dance recital. I think you were five? You had fairy wings, and . . ."

We stood there for a long time, with her moving from square to square, explaining the significance of each. All these little pieces of who I'd been once, with her to remember for me, stitched together into something real I could hold in my hands. There was a reason I'd found it, too, that night I'd run away. It was waiting for me. Your past is always your past. Even if you forget it, it remembers you.

Now, in Lakeview, I looked back at the model, where Deb was busy adjusting a couple of buildings on the far corner, and realized that, like my mother with the quilt, I could see a history within it that someone else would miss. The sectors just left of center, a bit sloppy and uneven, that Jason, Tracey, Dave, and I had started on the day the councilwoman arrived all those weeks ago. The thickly settled neighborhoods I'd labored over endlessly, sticking one tiny house on at a time. Tracy's old bank, next to the grocery store she'd been banned from, and that empty building, unmarked and unremarkable to anyone but me. And then, all around, the dragons, the parts not mapped, yet to be discovered.

If the quilt was my past, this model was my present. And looking at it, I saw not just myself in bits and pieces, but everyone and everything I'd come to know in the last few months. Mostly, though, I saw Dave.

He was in the rows of houses, so meticulous, in much straighter lines than the ones I'd done. In the buildings downtown he knew by heart, naming them easily without even having to look at the map. All over the complicated intersections he'd taken charge of, maintaining that only he, as a former maker of models, could handle such responsibility. He was on every piece he or I had added during our long afternoons together up here, talking and not talking, as we carefully assembled the world around us.

"So," I said now to Deb, who'd moved over to the table, where she was sorting plastic bags of landscaping pieces, "the new deadline's the second week of April. That's, what? Four weeks or so?"

"Twenty-six days," she replied. "Twenty-five and a half, if you count it to the minute."

"But look how much you have done," I said. "It's almost finished."

"I wish!" She sighed. "I mean, yes, most of the buildings are done, and we just have a couple of final sectors to do. But then there's all the environmental and civic detail. Not to mention repair. Heather took out an entire apartment complex the other day with one of her boots." She snapped her fingers. "It went down just like *that*."

"So she really worked on this over break?" I said.

"Well, working is a broad term," Deb replied. She thought for a second, then said, "Actually, I take that back. She's very good with detail. She put in that entire forest line over there on the upper right-hand corner. It's the bigger stuff she tends to mess up. Or, um, destroy."

"I can relate," I said, more to myself than to her. Still, though, I felt her glance over, so I added, "Sorry. It's been kind of a long week."

"I know." She picked up a bag of tiny plastic pieces, walking over to me. "Look, Mclean. About that whole Ume.com thing . . ."

"Forget it," I told her.

"I can't," she said softly. She looked up at me. "I just . . . I want you to know I understand. I mean, why you might have done that. All the moves . . . It couldn't have been easy."

"There were better ways I could have dealt with it," I replied. "I get that now."

She nodded, then tore open the bag. Looking closer, I saw that it was filled with tiny figures of people: walking, standing, running, sitting. Hundreds and hundreds of them, all jumbled up together. "So what's the deal with those? Are we going to just put them anywhere, or is there a set system of arrangement?"

"Well, actually," she said, taking out a handful and spreading them in her palm, "that's been a big topic of discussion."

"Really."

"Yeah," she said. "See, the manual doesn't specify, I guess because the people are optional, really. Some towns chose to leave them off entirely and just have the buildings. Less cluttery."

I looked back at the model. "I can see that. It would seem kind of empty, though."

"Agreed. A town needs a population," she said. "So I thought we should devise a sector system, like we did with the buildings, with a certain number of figures per area, and make sure they are diverse in their activities so there's not repetition."

"Activities?"

"Well, you wouldn't want all the bicyclists to be on one side, and all the people walking dogs on the other," she told me. "I mean, that would be wrong."

"Of course," I agreed.

"Other people, however," she continued, clearing her throat, "feel that by organizing the people, we are removing the life force from the entire endeavor. Instead, they think that we should just arrange the figures in a more random way, as that mirrors the way the world actually is, which is what the model is supposed to be all about."

I raised my eyebrows. "So this is Riley saying this?"

"What?" she asked. "Oh, no. Riley was totally down with the people-sector thing. It's Dave. He's, like, adamant."

"Really."

"Oh, God, yes," she replied. "To be honest, it's been a bit of a conflict between us. But I have to respect his opinion, because this is a collaborative effort. So we're working on a compromise."

I bent down by the model, studying a cul-de-sac, until I felt her move away, turning her attention to something else. *Compromise,* I thought, remembering the one Dave had been working on with his parents, and mine with my mom. It was that give-and-take he'd talked about, the rules that were always changing. But what happened when you followed all the rules and still couldn't get what you wanted? It didn't seem right.

"So," Deb said now, bending down by the far left edge of the model, "about the restaurant closing. Does that mean . . . you're moving to Australia? That's the rumor, according to the grapevine. That your dad got a job there."

Typical restaurant gossip, distorted as always. "It's Hawaii," I told her. "And I'm not going with him."

"Are you staying here?"

"No," I said. "I can't."

She turned, padding back over to the other end, by the tree line Heather had done. She bit her lip as she bent down over it, adjusting a couple of trunks. Finally she said, "Well, honestly . . . I think that sucks."

"Whoa," I said. For Deb, these were strong words. "I'm sorry."

"So am I!" She looked up, her face flushed. "I mean, it's bad enough that you're going to go. But you didn't even tell us it was in the works! Were you just going to take off and disappear, just like that?"

"No," I said, although I wasn't sure this was entirely true. "I just . . . I didn't know where I was going, and when. And then the whole Ume.com thing . . ."

"I understand, it was crazy." She took a step closer to me. "But seriously, Mclean. You have to promise me you won't just leave. I'm not like you, okay? I don't have a lot of friends. So you need to say goodbye, and you need to stay in touch, wherever you go. Okay?"

I nodded. She was so emotional, on the verge of tears. This was what I'd wanted to prevent with all those quick disappearances, the tangledness of farewells and all the baggage they brought with them. But now, looking at Deb, I realized what else I'd given up: knowing for sure that someone was going to miss me. *What happened to goodbye,* Michael in Westcott had written on my Ume.com page. I was pretty sure I knew, now. It had been packed away in a box of its own, trying to be forgotten, until I really needed it. Until now.

"Okay then," Deb said, her voice tight. She drew in a breath, then let it out, letting her hands drop to her sides. "Now, if you don't mind, I really think we should tackle these last two sectors before we go tonight."

"Absolutely," I replied, relieved to have something concrete to do. I followed her over to the other table, where the last group of assembled houses and other buildings were lined up, labeled and ready to be put on. Deb collected one set, I took the other, and we walked over to the far right top corner, the very end of the pinwheel. As I bent down, taking the adhesive off the bottom of a gas station, I said, "I'm glad there was something left to do. I was worried all this would be finished by the time I got back here."

"Well, actually, it would have been," she said, pushing a house onto her sector. "But I saved these for you."

I stopped what I was doing. "You did?"

"Yeah." She put a house on, pressing it until it clicked, then looked at me. "I mean, you were here at the very beginning, when this all started, before I even was. It's only right that you get to be a part of the ending, as well."

I looked down at my sector again. "Thank you," I said to Deb as I pulled the backing off a small building. There were only a few more left to go.

"You're welcome," she replied. And then, side by side, and without saying another word, we finished the job together.

× × ×

When I left the restaurant, it was a half hour into opening and my dad still hadn't appeared. Neither had Opal.

"It's just like a sinking ship," Tracey, who was behind the bar, told me when I asked if she'd seen them. "The rats abandon first."

"Opal's not a rat," I said, realizing a beat too late that by saying that I was basically admitting that my dad was. "She didn't know anything about all this."

"She didn't fight for us either," she replied, drying a glass with a towel. "She's basically been AWOL since they announced the closing and the building sale. Polishing her résumé, most likely."

"What's that supposed to mean?"

"Well, I can't say for sure," she said, putting the glass down. "But the word on the street is she's been having a lot of closed-door phone conversations that may or may not have included the words *relocation* and *upper management*."

"You really think Opal would just leave like that? She loves this town."

"Money talks," she replied with a shrug. A couple of customers passed me, pulling out stools at the bar, and she put down menus in front of them, then said, "Welcome to Luna Blu. Would you like to hear our Death Throes Specials?"

I waved goodbye to her, distracted, then headed toward the kitchen and the back door. As I passed the office, I glanced in: the desk was neatly organized, the chair tucked under it, none of my dad's signature clutter scattered around the many surfaces. By the looks of it, he, at least, was already gone.

Outside, I walked down the alley, turning onto my street. When my mom had dropped me off earlier, the house had been empty, but now as it came into view I saw some lights were on and the truck was in the driveway.

I was just stepping up onto the curb when I heard a *bang*. I looked over and there was Dave, coming out of his kitchen door, a cardboard box under one arm. He pulled a black knit hat over his head and started down the stairs, not seeing me. My first impulse was to just get inside, avoiding him and whatever confrontation or conversation would follow. But then I looked up at the sky and immediately spotted a bright triangle of stars, and thought of my mom, standing on the deck of that huge beach house. So much had changed, and yet she still knew those stars, had taken that part of her past, our past, with her. I couldn't run anymore. I'd learned that. So even though it wasn't easy, I stayed where I was.

"Dave."

He turned, startled, and I saw the surprise on his face when he realized it was me. "Hey," he said. He didn't come closer, and neither did I: there was a good fifteen or twenty feet between us. "I didn't know you were back."

"I just got in a little while ago."

"Oh." He shifted the box to his other arm. "I was just, um, heading over to the model for a few minutes."

I took a couple of steps toward him, hesitant. "So you got a furlough."

"Yeah. Something like that."

I looked down at my hands, taking a breath. "Look, about that night I called you . . . I had no idea you got in trouble. God, I feel awful about that."

"You shouldn't," he said.

I just looked at him. "If it wasn't for me, you wouldn't have been trying to sneak out."

"Trying to—" he said.

"And you wouldn't have been *caught* sneaking out," I continued, "and then grounded, and your trip taken away, and basically your whole life wrecked."

He was quiet for a moment. "You didn't wreck my life. All you did was call a friend."

"Maybe I can talk to your parents. Explain what was going on, and—"

"Mclean," he said, stopping me. "No. It's okay, really. I'm all right with it. There will be other road trips, and other summers."

"Maybe. But it's still not fair."

He shrugged. "Life's not fair. If it was, you wouldn't be having to move again."

"You heard about that, huh?"

"I heard Tasmania," he said. "Which I have a feeling might be bad information."

I smiled. "It's Hawaii. But I'm not going. I'm moving back in with my mom, to finish out the year."

"Oh," he said. "Right. I guess that does make more sense."

"As much as any of this does." Another silence fell. He didn't have much time, and I knew I should let him go. Instead, I said, "The model looks great. You guys have really been working hard."

"Deb has," he replied. "She's like a madwoman. I'm just trying to stay out of her way."

I smiled. "She told me about your debate over the people."

"The people." He groaned. "She *cannot* trust me to handle this myself. That's why I'm sneaking over there with my supplies when I know she's gone. Otherwise, she'll stand over me, freaking out."

"Supplies?" I said.

He stepped a little closer, holding out the open box so I could see it. "No cracks about model trains," he said. "This is serious business."

I peered inside. The box was lined with small jars of paint, all different colors, a stack of brushes standing in one side. There were also cotton balls, some swabs, turpentine, and several small tools, including a large set of tweezers, some scissors, and a magnifying glass.

"Whoa," I said. "What are you planning to do, exactly?"

"Just add a little life to it," he replied. I looked up at him, biting my lip. "Don't worry, she approved it. Most of it anyway."

I smiled. "I can't believe the model's actually almost finished. It feels like we just put down that first house, like, yesterday."

"Time flies." He looked at me. "So when do you leave?"

"I start moving stuff next weekend."

"That soon?" I nodded. "Wow. You don't mess around."

"I just feel like if I have to go to another school . . ." I sighed. "I might as well do it now."

He nodded, not saying anything. Another car drove by.

"But I have to say," I continued, "that it stinks that when it came down to it, there were only two choices. Go forward, to Hawaii, and start all over again, or backward, back to my old life, which doesn't even really exist anymore."

"You need a third option," he said.

"Yeah. I guess I do."

He nodded, absorbing this. "Well," he said, "for what it's worth, it's been my experience that they don't appear at first. You kind of have to look a little more closely."

"And when does that happen?"

He shrugged. "When you're ready to see them, I guess."

I had a flash of those Rubbermaid bins, lined up in my mom's garage at the beach behind Super Shitty. "That is frustratingly vague," I told him.

"You're welcome."

I smiled then, and he smiled back. "You should go," I said. "Before Deb decides to make an evening visit because she can't sleep due to obsessing over the model."

"You joke," he said. "But it could happen. I'll see you, Mclean."

"Yeah," I replied. "See you."

He started to turn away, toward the road again. But just as he did, I moved forward, closing the space between us, and kissed him on the cheek. I could tell I surprised him, but he didn't pull away. When I stepped back, I said, "Thank you."

"For what?"

"For being here," I said.

He nodded, then walked past me, using his free hand to squeeze my shoulder as he passed. I turned, watching him as he crossed the street and headed up the alley to the bright lights of Luna Blu. Then I turned back to my own house, took a breath, and went up to the door.

I was just reaching for the knob when two things became clear: my dad was definitely home, and he wasn't alone. I could hear his voice, muffled, from inside, then a higher voice responding. But the lights that were on were dim, and as I stood there, I noticed that their conversation began to have short lags in it, little silences that became gradually longer and longer, peppered with only a few words or laughter in between.

Oh, God, I thought, slumping against the door and losing all momentum as I pictured him lip-locked with Lindsay and her big white teeth. *Ugh.*

I stood up straighter, then knocked on the door, hard, before pushing it open. What I saw before me literally stopped me in my tracks: my dad and Opal on the couch, his arm around her shoulders, her feet draped across his lap. They were both flushed pink, and the top button of her shirt was undone.

"Oh my God," I said, my voice sounding incredibly loud in the small room.

Opal jumped up, reaching to do her button as she stumbled backward, bumping the wall behind her. On the couch, my dad cleared his throat and adjusted a throw pillow, like decorating was the most important thing at that moment. "Mclean," he said. "When did you get back?"

"I thought . . . I thought you were dating the council-woman," I said to him. Then I looked at Opal, who was tucking a piece of hair behind her ear, crazy flustered. "I thought you hated him."

"Well," my dad said.

"Hate is an *awfully* strong word," Opal replied.

I looked at him, then at her, then at him again. "You can't do this. It's insane."

"Well," Opal said, clearing her throat. "That's also a strong word."

"You don't want to do this," I told her. "He's leaving. You know that, right? For Hawaii."

"Mclean," my dad said.

"No," I told him. "It was one thing when it was Lindsay, or Sherry in Petree, or Lisa in Montford Falls, or Emily in Westcott." Opal raised her eyebrows, looking at my dad, who moved the pillow again. "But I like you, Opal. You've been nice to me. And you should know what's going to happen. He's just going to disappear, and you'll be here, calling and wondering why he doesn't call back, and—"

"Mclean," my dad repeated. "Stop."

"No," I said. "*You* stop. Don't do this."

"I'm not," he replied.

I just stood there, not sure what to say. I could see Opal out of the corner of my eye, watching me carefully, but I kept my eyes on my dad. At least, for a moment. Then, I shifted my gaze, suddenly noticing the kitchen behind him. There were grocery bags piled on the countertops, and a couple of cabinets were open, revealing cans and a few boxes of food inside. Some noodles and a couple of tomatoes sat piled by a cutting board, and there was a new glass pan, sitting rinsed on the dish rack, waiting to be used.

"What's going on here?" I asked, turning my gaze back to him.

He smiled at me, then looked at Opal. "Come sit down," he said. "We'll fill you in."

Seventeen

✳ ❂ ✳

"Oh, no," Deb said. "What happened to my STOW sheet? Has anyone seen it?"

"Nope," Heather, who was bent over a corner of the model, sticking on bushes in a local arboretum, replied. "Maybe you lost it."

"Heather, stop," Riley told her. "Deb, it's got to be around here someplace. Where was the last place you had it?"

"If I knew that, it wouldn't be lost," Deb said, walking to the table and pushing some papers around. "This is crazy! I can't finish this tonight without the STOW!"

"Uh-oh," Ellis, on the other side of the model, said. "Get ready for a FODF."

I looked up from where I was adding some sidewalk tiles. "FODF?"

"Full-On Deb Freak-out," Heather explained.

"I heard that!" Deb called out. "And FYI, that is not even a good acronym. It's supposed to be a real word, not a made-up one."

"FODF isn't a real word?" Ellis asked. "Since when?"

"Time?" Deb asked, bustling past. "Anyone?"

"You have a watch on," Heather told her.

"It's nine thirty-two," Riley said. "Which means—"

"Twenty-eight minutes!" Deb shrieked. "*Twenty-eight* minutes before we absolutely have to be out of here. Opal's orders."

"I thought Opal didn't even work at Luna Blu anymore," Riley said.

"She doesn't," Deb said. "But she owns the building. So she makes the rules."

I picked up another bush, carefully adding it on. "She doesn't own it yet," I said. "And even when she does, it'll just be a percentage. The Melmans and some other partners will own the rest."

"The Melmans?" Riley asked.

"Previous owners," I told her. "They started this place, way back when."

I looked around the room, remembering when Opal had told me about the restaurant's history, that day I'd first been up here. In the last two weeks, a lot had happened as far as Luna Blu was concerned. First, my dad had officially been re-assigned to the next project, in Hawaii, while Opal had submitted her resignation, leaving her free and clear to work on purchasing the building once Chuckles put it on the market. Which he was doing at a very reasonable price, in exchange for two things: a hefty percentage, and a return of rolls to the menu. This agreement was hashed out over a very long meal at our house, punctuated by Hawaiian Kobe beef and two bottles of very good red wine. As for the Melmans, Opal's old bosses, they'd come on shortly afterward, after she flew down to Florida with a business plan and an offer they didn't want to refuse. Turned out retirement life was a bit dull for their taste: they missed the excitement of having a piece of a daily business. Between their money, a start-up loan from the bank, and Chuckles's bargain price, Opal was getting her own restaurant. But first, Luna Blu had to close.

No one was happy about it. For the last week, as we'd been upstairs working away, the restaurant had been crazy busy, packed with locals who'd heard the news and wanted to have one last meal. I'd personally expected the entire place to implode with my dad and Opal gone, but surprisingly, under the dual leadership of Jason and Tracey, things had actually been running pretty smoothly. My dad had marveled more than once that he'd always pegged Tracey as the type to jump ship first. But as it turned out, she'd probably bailed herself into a manager position at Opal's new place, if she wanted it.

"Here it is!" Deb said, grabbing a pad of paper from the floor by the landing and holding it up. "Thank God. Okay, let me see what else we have to do. . . . Final landscaping is in progress, traffic signs are—oh, crap, where are the traffic signs?"

"I'm doing them right now," Ellis told her. "Take a breath, would you?"

"Then that just leaves the final population details," Deb said, not breathing at all. She looked around. "There was one final bag I saw here yesterday that hadn't been put on yet. What happened to it?"

"I cannot deal with these trees and questions at the same time," Heather said.

"Oh, for God's sake," Ellis said. "Learn to multitask."

"Where are those people?" Deb demanded. "I swear they were right—"

"Dave probably put them on," Riley told her. "He was here last night again."

Deb turned, looking at her. "He was?"

Riley nodded. "When I left at six, he was just getting here. Said he had a few last touches to add."

"I texted him at seven and he was still here," Ellis added.

I watched as Deb walked over to the model, scanning it slowly from side to side. "I don't see any huge differences, though," she said. "Not anything that would take a few hours, at any rate."

"Maybe he just works very slowly," Heather said.

"No, that's you," Ellis told her.

"Eighteen minutes!" Deb said, clapping her hands. "People, this is serious. If you have more than you can do in eighteen minutes, speak your piece now. Because this is crunch time. Anyone? Anyone?"

I shook my head: I only had a handful of bushes left to add on. Everyone got quiet, though, as we worked away, the minutes ticking by. Downstairs, we knew they were counting down, as well: as of ten o'clock, they'd be finished, too. It seemed like that was all these last weeks had been about, change and endings. The beginnings were yet to come.

Once again, my dad and I had been packing up the house and our things into boxes. This time, though, they'd be going to storage, not in the U-Haul. As for Hawaii, all my dad needed was a suitcase. The plan was for him to stay the summer,

helping Chuckles's restaurant get its footing, before returning in time to help my mom get me settled at whatever school
I ended up deciding to attend. Then he'd come to Lakeview,
where he'd fill in as chef at Opal's place until he decided what
he wanted to do next. Their relationship—which, apparently,
had begun the night he'd told her about the restaurant closing,
and ended up following her back to her house to talk about
it—was new. They'd already had to deal with the awkward-
ness of my dad breaking up with Lindsay Baker (Opal had giv-
en up spinning, for now) and were about to face a separation.
Neither one of them was naïve enough to think they would
absolutely make it. But just knowing he had someone to come
back to besides me was a comfort to me. I, for one, was pulling
for them.

As for me, I was packed up as well, my stuff folded away
into my same boxes, ready to make the trip back to Tyler. It
wasn't easy leaving, especially with so little left of the year
to go. Everyone was talking about final plans: the end of the
model, graduation, the Austin road trip, even though Ellis,
Riley, and Heather were less excited than they had been since
Dave was staying behind. As for Dave, he'd been pulling back
as well, mostly because he had to. He went to work, school,
his U classes, and home. His car was off-limits, parked in the
driveway under the basketball goal, so any free time he was
allowed was spent working on the model. Now though, for his
own reasons, he preferred to do that alone, coming for an hour
here and there when the rest of us were already gone.

He might have been absent, but his work was evident, as

over the last week people had slowly begun to appear on the model, here and there. He didn't put them on using the sector system, or pinwheel, or anything else. Instead, their numbers just seemed to grow, day by day, as if they were populating all by themselves. Each figure—men, women, children, people walking dogs, cyclists, policemen—was added meticulously, and clearly with great care. More than once, I'd stood at my front window, looking at the back windows of Luna Blu, and wondered if he was up there, bent over the little world, adding to it, one person at a time. I'd often thought about going to join him, but it was like something sacred he was doing, that he had to do alone. And so I let him.

"Five minutes!" Deb called out, moving quickly behind me, the STOW checklist in her hand. I looked across the model at Riley, who was adjusting an intersection, her brow furrowed, then at Heather, who was sitting back on her heels, admiring her trees. Ellis, off to my left, was clicking a stop sign into place.

"One minute!" I heard Deb say, and I pushed myself back, taking a breath as I looked over the entire model and the faces of my friends gathered around it. As the time ticked away, we all sat there, silent, and then we heard the staff counting down below us. A chorus of voices, marking the end of one thing, the beginning of another.

"Five!" I looked at the last bush I'd put on, touching my finger to it.

"Four!" I looked at Riley, who smiled at me.

"Three!" Deb came and stood beside me, biting her lip.

"Two!" Already, downstairs, someone was applauding.

And in that second, right before the very end, I looked around the model again, wanting to see one final thing. When I spotted it, I noticed something else. But by then, everyone was already cheering, in motion. One.

× × ×

"Where are you going?" my dad called after me as I turned the corner. "You'll miss the party."

"I'll be back in a second," I told him.

He nodded, then turned back to the bar, where all the employees and some devout regulars of Luna Blu, as well as Deb, Riley, Heather, and Ellis were gathered, eating up all the leftover stock of fried pickles. Opal was there as well, serving up beers, her face flushed and happy.

As I climbed up the steps to the attic, I could still hear everyone talking and laughing, their voices rising up behind me. Once on the landing, though, it was quiet, almost peaceful, the model stretched out before me. In all the excitement earlier, I hadn't been able to look as closely as I wanted to. I wanted to be alone, like now, when I had all the time in the world.

I bent down over my neighborhood, taking in the people there. At first, they'd just seemed arranged the same way they were everywhere else: in random formations, some in groups, some alone. Then, though, I saw the single figure at the back of my house, walking away from the back door. And another person, a girl, running through the side yard, where the hedge would have been, while someone else, with a badge and flashlight, followed. There were three people under the basketball goal, one lying prone on the ground.

I took a breath, then moved in closer. Two people were seated on the curb between Dave's and my houses: a few inches away, two more walked up the narrow alley to Luna Blu's back door. A couple stood in the driveway, facing each other. And in that empty building, the old hotel, a tiny set of cellar doors had been added, flung open, a figure standing before them. Whether they were about to go down, or just coming up, was unclear, and the cellar itself was a dark square. But I knew what was down below.

He'd put me everywhere. Every single place I'd been, with him or without, from the first time we'd met to the last conversation. It was all there, laid out as carefully, as real as the buildings and streets around it. I swallowed, hard, then reached forward, touching the girl running through the hedge. Not Liz Sweet. Not anyone, at that moment, not yet. But on her way to someone. To me.

I stood up, then turned and went back down the stairs, into the bar area. Everyone was talking, the noise deafening, the smell of fried pickles hanging in the air as I cut through toward the back door. I heard Riley call my name, but I didn't turn around. Outside, I pulled my sweater more tightly around me and started to jog down the alley to my street.

The lights were on in Dave's house as I came up the driveway, his Volvo parked where it had been for the full week, right under the basketball goal. I stood looking at it for a moment, remembering my dad and me pulling into the adjacent spot that first day. I looked up at the basket, its shadow an elongated circle, stretched across the windshield and driver's seat.

A Frazier Bakery cup, empty, sat in the holder, a couple of CD cases stacked on the seat. And on the center console, there was a Gert.

What? Impossible, I thought, moving closer and peering into the window. Same weird braiding, same dangling shells. Just to be sure, though, I opened the door, reaching in to grab it, and turned it over. A tiny *GS*, in Sharpie marker, was on the back.

"Freeze!"

A flashlight popped on, brightness filling my field of vision. I put up my hand, seeing stars as I heard footsteps, coming closer. A moment later, the light clicked off, and there was Dave. He looked at me, then at the Gert.

"You know," he said, "if you're looking for cars to break into, I *think* you can do better."

"You came," I said softly, looking at the Gert again. I turned, facing him. "You *were* there, at the Poseidon, that night. All this time I thought . . ."

He slid the flashlight into his back pocket, not saying anything.

"Why didn't you let me know?" I asked him. "I don't understand."

He sighed, glancing at his house, and then started walking down the driveway, toward the street. I fell in beside him, the Gert still in my hand. "I saw your dad when I was leaving. He was panicked . . . so I told him what I knew. Then I went back inside. But I kept thinking about how you'd called me, how it was so unlike you, or the you I'd seen on the Ume.com page that day."

I winced in the dark. We were coming up to the alley now.

"So I went anyway, to make sure you were okay. Drove down, found the hotel, parked. But when I went up to knock on the door, I saw you through the window. You were lying on the bed, with your mom and your dad, and it just . . . You were with who you needed right then. Your family."

My family. What a concept. "So you left," I said.

"Only after I stopped for a souvenir at the only place open," he said, nodding at my closed hand. "I couldn't resist. I can't believe you recognized it, though."

I smiled. "It's a Gert. My mom and I used to get them every time we were down there."

"A Gert. I like that." We turned the corner, to Luna Blu. "Anyway, so I drove back. And my parents were waiting for me. You know the rest of the story."

I swallowed, feeling my throat get tight. As we walked down the hallway, I could hear the noise and laughter getting louder, the air warm as Dave pushed the door open and we went inside the restaurant proper.

"There he is!" Ellis called out. "How'd you get sprung?"

"Good behavior," Dave told him. "What'd I miss?"

"Only the end of everything," Tracey said, from the other side of the bar. I was surprised to see her, cynical as she was, dabbing at her red eyes with a bar towel, while Leo, true to form, chewed a mouthful of pickles beside her.

"It's not just an end," Opal told her. "It's a beginning, too."

"I hate beginnings," Tracey replied, sniffling. "They're too new."

I looked at Dave, sitting beside Ellis at the end of the bar.

Riley was next to him, then Heather and Deb, their chairs forming a triangle, heads together as they talked over the noise, while Opal hugged Tracey on the opposite side of the taps. I looked at all of them, then down at my dad, who was at the very end of the bar, taking it all in as well. When he saw me, he smiled, and I thought of all the places we'd been, how he was my only constant, my guiding star. I didn't want to leave him, or here. But I had no other options.

I stepped away from the bar, quickly turning the corner and heading back upstairs to the model. I walked over and stood there, looking down at it, trying to center myself. After a moment, I heard footsteps behind me, and even before I turned I knew it was Dave. He was standing at the top of the stairs, looking at me, as the noise from the party downstairs drifted up behind him.

"This is amazing," I said to him. "I can't believe you did it."

"We all did it," he said.

"Not the model." I swallowed. "The people."

He smiled. "Well, model trains really teach you a lot of good skills."

I shook my head. "I know you're joking . . . but this, it's like the nicest thing anyone's ever done for me. Seriously."

Dave walked closer, sliding his hands in his pockets. In the bright light, he looked clean, clear. Real. "You did all of these things," he said after a moment. "All I did was document it."

I felt tears prick my eyes as I looked down at the model again, looking at that girl and boy on the curb. Forever in that place, together.

"You should get back downstairs," he said. "Your dad sent me up here for you. They're about to do a toast or something."

I nodded, then turned to follow him. "So I guess this is what you meant, huh?"

"About what?"

"Looking more closely," I replied as he started down the stairs.

"Pretty much," he said. "Hey, hit the lights on your way out, okay?"

I stopped, taking one last look at the model, stretched out and complete, before I reached for the switch, turning it off. At first, in the darkness, I could see only a bit of streetlight coming in the far window, illuminating the floor. Then, though, I spotted something else. Something small and glowing, in the exact spot I'd been studying before. I walked over, my eyes scanning Luna Blu, my house, and Dave's. But it was the building behind them, that empty hotel, that had the tiniest light, provided by one word, written in fluorescent paint. Maybe it wasn't what was once there, in real life. But in this one, it said it all: STAY.

I turned, looking at the stairway, the light at the bottom. I had no idea if Dave was already downstairs with everyone else, as I ran across the room, grabbing the banister to go after him. But after only one step, suddenly we were face-to-face. He'd been there all along.

"Is that really what it said, on the roof of the building?" I asked.

I could feel his breath, the warmth of his skin. We were

that close. "No idea," he replied. "But anything's possible."

I smiled. Downstairs, they were laughing, cheering, seeing out this last night in this sacred place. Soon, I knew we'd join them, and shut it down together. But for now, I leaned closer to Dave, putting my lips on his. He slid his arms up around me, and as he kissed me back, I felt something inside me open, like a new life beginning. I didn't know yet what girl she'd be, or where this life would take her. But I'd keep my eyes open, and when the time came, I would know.

Eighteen

✤ ❁ ✤

"Oh, crap," Opal said, dropping a bunch of empty plates with a clang. "AHBL!"

"Already?" I asked. "We've only been open fifteen minutes."

"Yes, but we only have one wait, and that wait is Tracey," she said, stabbing two orders onto the spindle in the window between us. "We're already in the weeds."

She bustled off, cursing under her breath, while I pulled the tickets off, glancing at them. "Orders," I told Jason, who was sitting on the prep table behind me, reading the *Wall Street Journal*.

"Call 'em," he said, hopping down.

"You sure? We're behind already."

"If you're going to be in the hole, you have to learn to call out orders," he said, walking over to the grill station behind me. "Go ahead."

I looked down at the top ticket. "Mediterranean chicken sandwich," I said. "Order fries. Side salad."

"Good," he said. "Now hit that salad. I'll do filet and drop those fries."

I nodded, turning to the back table and grabbing a small plate from the shelf above. For all my time growing up in restaurants, working in one still felt brand-new. But there was nowhere else I'd rather be.

At graduation a week earlier, I'd sat with the rest of my class, fanning my face with a damp program as the speakers droned on and assembled family and friends shifted in their seats. When we all stood up, grabbing our caps to throw them in the air, a breeze suddenly blew over, lifting the air and all those black squares and tassels up overhead to take flight like birds. Then I'd turned, searching for the faces of my friends. I saw Heather first, and she smiled.

I was supposed to go back to Tyler, yes. But things change. And sometimes, people do as well, and it's not necessarily a bad thing. At least, that's what I was hoping the Saturday after Luna Blu closed, when my mom showed up to help me pack my stuff. My dad was there, too, and Opal, all of us making trips from my room to Peter's huge SUV, chatting as we did so. Opal and my mom hit it off immediately, which I had to admit surprised me. But as soon as she found out my mom had handled all the financial stuff at Mariposa, she started picking her brain about how best to do things at her new place. The next thing I knew, they were at the kitchen table, a notepad between them, while my dad and I finished the job.

"Does that make you nervous?" I asked him as we took out my pillow and my laptop, passing by them. My mom was saying something about payroll, while Opal jotted on the page, nodding.

"Nah," he said. "Truth is, your mom kept that restaurant afloat for two years longer than it should have been. Without her, we would have closed a lot sooner."

I looked at him over the hood of the SUV. "Really?"

"Yeah. Your mom knows her stuff."

I was thinking about this later, when I was finally packed up and we were getting ready to leave. I'd said my goodbyes to Deb, Riley, Ellis, and Heather the night before, at a farewell dinner—fried chicken, naturally—that Riley's mom cooked for me at her house. My goodbye with Dave had been more private, in the hour he was allotted after I got home. We'd sat together on the steps to the storm cellar, hands intertwined, and made plans. For the next weekend, for a beach trip if he could ever get away, for all the calls and texts and e-mails that we hoped would hold us together. Like my dad and Opal, we weren't kidding ourselves. I knew what distance could do. But there was a part of me here now, and not just in the model. I planned to come back to it.

As I shut the car door, everything finally in, I looked over and saw Mrs. Dobson-Wade, standing in her kitchen. Dave was at work, their other car gone, and she was alone, flipping through a cookbook. Watching her, I thought of my mom, and all the problems we'd had over the last two years. Trust and deceit, distance and control. It had seemed unique to us, but I knew it really wasn't. I also knew that just because we'd found a peace didn't mean everyone could. But Dave had done something for me. The least I could do was try to return the favor.

When I knocked on her door a few minutes later, my mom

and dad behind me, she looked surprised. Then, as we came inside and I explained why I was there, a bit suspicious. Once we sat down at the table, though, and I told her the story of what had happened that night, how Dave had come for me, and told my dad where I was, I saw her face soften a bit. She made us no promises, only said she'd think about what we'd told her. But then, something did happen. To me.

It was when we were getting into the car to leave. Opal and my dad were in the driveway to see us off, the house mostly empty behind them. It was so weird, like the reverse of when I'd left Tyler with him all those years ago. With all my departures, he'd never been the one watching me go, and suddenly I wasn't sure I could do it.

"It's not goodbye," he said as I hugged him tight, Opal sniffling beside him. "I'll see you very, very soon."

"I know." I swallowed, then stepped back. "I just . . . I hate to leave you."

"I'll be fine." He smiled at me. "Go."

I managed to hold it together until I got into the car and we drove away. As the house, and them beside it, receded in my side mirror, though, I just started bawling.

"Oh, God," my mom said, her hands shaking as she hit her turn signal. "Don't cry. You're going to make me totally lose it."

"I'm sorry," I said, rubbing my nose with the back of my hand. "I'm okay. I am."

She nodded, turning onto the main road. But after driving about a block, she hit the signal again, turning into a bank parking lot. Then she cut the engine and looked at me. "I can't do this to you."

I wiped my eyes. "What?"

"Uproot you, make you leave, whatever." She sighed, sniffling again, waving one hand as she added, "Not after I've railed against it for the last two years. It's just too hypocritical. I can't do it."

"But," I said as she dug a tissue out of her massive middle console, blowing her nose, "I don't have any other option. Unless you want me to go to Hawaii. Right?"

"I'm not so sure about that," she said, starting the engine again. "Let's just see."

In the end, we compromised. My mom let me stay, in exchange for a promise that I'd visit her regularly, either in Tyler or Colby. As for my dad, he had to be convinced that Opal, who'd offered me her spare room in exchange for doing some setup work for the new restaurant, was not getting in over her head. It was my job to keep in close touch with both of my parents, returning phone calls and e-mails, and being honest about what was going on with me. So far, it had been easy to hold up my end of the bargain.

I loved being able to finish out the year at Jackson. For once, I was really part of a class, able to partake in rituals like senior skip day and yearbook distribution, my time at a school ending when everyone else's did. I studied for finals with Dave on his living room couch, him reading up on advanced physics, while I struggled with trigonometry. Then, while he worked, I pulled cram sessions at FrayBake with Heather, Riley, and Ellis, powered all around by Procrastinator's Specials he made personally. Dropping my napkin on the floor one day, I bent down to get it, only to catch a glimpse of Riley's foot, idly wound around Ellis's. They were keeping it quiet, but it seemed maybe she was changing her dirtbag ways, as well.

Come fall, when I started at the U, I'd move out of Opal's and into a dorm, taking my simple living skills with me. In the end, I'd gotten into Defriese, too, but there was never any question that I'd continue to follow that third option, and stay. As for Dave, he'd gotten in everywhere he applied, naturally, but had decided on MIT. I was trying not to think about the distance too much, but it was my hope that no matter what happened, at least we'd always be able to find each other. I had a feeling I'd continue to put my packing skills to good use after all.

"How's that salad coming?" Jason called out as I sprinkled a handful of carrots.

"Ready," I replied, turning back and putting it in the window.

"Great. Get the bun and sauce ready for this sandwich and we'll be golden."

As I pulled out a bun, tossing it on the grill to brown, I glanced through the window, just in time to see Deb bustling past, tying an apron around her waist. "I thought you weren't working today," I called out to her.

"I just stopped by to pick up my tips from last night," she said, grabbing two water glasses and filling them with ice. "But Opal was melting down, so I'm on now."

I smiled. With the model done, Deb had found herself with entirely too much time on her hands. As it turned out, though, the same skills that made her such a good organizer also made her a great waitress. She'd only just started, but already she'd improved Opal's working system by leaps and bounds. And acronyms.

"Where's that sandwich?" Tracey said, poking her head in the window. "Anyone?"

"It's coming," Jason told her. "Keep your pants on."

She made a face, then grabbed the salad, adding a ramekin of dressing and sliding it onto a tray. Behind her, Deb pulled off another ticket, stabbing it on the spindle.

"Order," I said.

"Call it."

I looked down. "Margherita pizza, extra sauce, add garlic."

"Good. Plate this and I'll get started."

He slid the sandwich down with a spatula, and I picked it up, placing it in the basket I'd prepared. Behind me, the radio was playing, and I could hear the customers just beyond the wait station, and Opal chattering. I thought of my dad, somewhere in Hawaii, maybe doing this same thing, and missed him, the way I always did. But then, I did what I knew he'd want me to, and got back to work.

It was a busy rush, keeping up for about an hour and a half. Even though I botched a quesadilla, letting it cook too long, and forgot to call a burger that we then had to comp, it all went reasonably well. Finally, around one thirty, Jason told me to take a break. I picked up my phone, grabbed a water, and headed outside to the back steps.

It was sunny and hot, another summer scorcher, as I started scrolling through my messages. I had a voice mail from my mom, checking in about going to Colby that weekend. An e-mail from the U about orientation. And one text message, from Dave.

There were no words, just a picture. I clicked it, watching as it filled up the screen. The shot was four hands, two with circle tattoos, all wearing Gerts. Behind them, blue sky and a sign: WELCOME TO TEXAS.

"Hey, Mclean," Jason called out. "Order up."

I slid my phone back into my pocket, then drained my drink. As I came back into the kitchen, stepping past him, I crumpled the cup in my hand, then turned to take aim at the garbage can behind me. I shot, sending it arcing toward perfect center. So pretty. Nothing but net.

Acknowledgments

Many thanks are due, again, to my agent, Leigh Feldman, and editor, Regina Hayes, for their support, wisdom, and willingness to be aboard the crazy train that is my writing process. I'm also indebted to my readers, whose encouragement makes me want to keep writing, even on the hard days, and my babysitters—Krysta Lindley, Erika Alvarado, and Amanda Weatherly—who give me the time I need to do just that.

Lastly, forever and always, I am grateful beyond words for Jay and Sasha. You are my world, filling this life with joy, chaos, humor, and endless material. Thank you.